Sticky Notes

Sherri Schoenborn Murray

www.christianromances.com

This is a work of fiction, all characters, places and
incidents are used fictitiously. Any resemblance to
actual persons, either living or dead is completely
coincidental.

The cover photos are by Clari Noel Photography and
Canola Road by Alison Meyer Photography.

Copy edit by Pamela Shea Waddell
Final edit by Carolyn Rose Editing

To my dear college friends—
Shelley, Kris, Taryl, Julie and Lia—
and our great memories of the Palouse.

Do everything without finding fault or arguing.
Then you will be pure and without blame.
PHILIPPIANS 2:14.

Chapter One

Moscow, Idaho, 2002

Alone in the dimly lit hallway, Katherine King tried to corral her nerves. She tightened her blonde ponytail and wiped her sweaty palms on the sides of her extra-long jeans. There was nothing to feel anxious about—she'd been a straight-A student throughout high school and her undergraduate years. Most likely this grade was a clerical error.

She recalled her adviser's counsel: *Be confident, diplomatic, and keep it short.*

The door creaked open. Her classmate, Angel LeFave, fanned her flushed face, like time alone with Dr. Dreamy had been too much. Upon seeing Katherine, she wrinkled her nose and shrugged.

Not very encouraging.

Katherine's grip tightened on the strap of her backpack. Maybe she should head home and have lunch with Grandma. Forget her pride.

Professor Benton appeared in the doorway. He was in his mid-thirties with coffee-brown hair, average build, and an above-average face. As the article in the *Argonaut*—the U of I student paper—had so notably put it, "a bachelor, and reason enough for a girl to change majors."

"Oh, there's someone still here?" He gripped both sides of the doorframe and leaned toward her for an awkward, heart-pounding moment.

Harp and string music to the tune of "Somewhere My Love" began to play. Katherine resisted the temptation to melt like a chocolate bar left on the dash.

"I'm the last one." It was not a time to be coy and rely on her femininity, as Angel had undoubtedly done. She was facing a mental giant—a new professor intent on getting a gold plaque on his door, instead of the yellow paper that presently bore his name.

His desk sat against the wall, his back to the closet-sized room. To his left, numerous sticky notes plastered the side of an upright filing cabinet. She handed him her essay before sitting down in the metal folding chair.

He glanced at her name printed on the front of the light blue booklet before leafing to the final page of her essay, where he'd penned the offensive grade.

There was a hint of dust and peanut butter in the room.

"And the reason for your visit, Miss King?" His Zhivago eyes narrowed. Three of the four female students in the class agreed that his dark granite eyes resembled the famed actor Omar Sharif's. The reason the girls were gathering for the movie Friday night was because Angel had voted no, which simply meant she'd never seen *Doctor Zhivago*.

"I'm hoping there's a chance that the grade you wrote is an error of some type." Beneath her chin, the pads of her fingertips tapped together in a silent clap. She gripped them tightly in front of her.

He flipped open his grade book and scanned the page. "It's a B in my book and a B on your paper."

"Oh, wow . . . um . . ." What he'd written on the last page did apply to her exam. How to proceed? "Uh, in your comments, Dr . . ." For a moment, she simply stared into his deep-set eyes. His surname had completely escaped her. "Benton!" She sat on her hands. "You wrote that you'd like more analysis rather than a *neurotic* summary of facts."

"Neurotic?" He chuckled briefly. "I wouldn't write that."

"You did . . . it's in your comments on the last page."

As he flipped through the booklet again, she recalled Joe's, her ex-boyfriend's, sentiments: to change a fellow's mind, all she had to do with her large baby blues was meet his gaze and blink.

Now was not a time to be coy.

"Hmm . . . I did write—" he cleared his throat— "neurotic."

Before Professor Benton, she'd always received A's for her *neurotic* summary of facts.

"Your closing paragraph is weak. In the future, Miss King, I'd like to see more analysis."

"Pardon me?"

"I'd like to see more analysis instead of a simple summary of facts. And I'd like you to up the size of your cursive." He turned to regard her. "I have very good eyesight, and I had a difficult time with it."

He was an excellent lecturer, but speaking to him one-on-one was a Bonnie and Clyde experience. She felt robbed.

The first day of class, when he'd written "Antebellum" on the board and said, "In Latin it means *before war*," she'd held so much hope for him. And, if she had to confess or walk the plank, perhaps it had been the start of a slight crush.

"I'm sorry to prove confrontational, sir, but there are four pages of analysis." Maybe his grading system was the reason his nameplate wasn't on the door. "The last thing I want to think about during an exam is writing big."

"Writing *legibly*." His chest inflated. "B is above average, Miss King."

Her mind wandered to her ex-boyfriend's ace serves. They often whizzed past her, out of reach. The same adrenaline coursed through her veins now. "How can I go about raising my grade?" It was a question she'd never asked before.

"Include more analysis on the next exam."

She'd graduated with a bachelor of arts in US history with a 4.0, taught at a high school level for four years, and, with a desire for a pay raise, made the difficult decision to return to the U of I for her MA. Now, some newbie professor trying to make his mark and create a reputation was going to make her final semester a nightmare.

She rose to her feet and slung her backpack over one shoulder. *If he so much as says another word—*

"Miss King . . ." Looking up, he held out her exam.

"I don't think you're aware, Professor, of how your grading system affected the class. Your D-day made even top students question if they're in the right field." The words tumbled like ice out of a machine. "I stepped over carcasses on my way out. I was nearly one of them."

Instead of lifting his gaze, he watched her hands. Below her chin, her fingertips did the little tapping thing again. She crossed her arms in front of her, locking them.

"Are you through?" His dark brows gathered.

"Yes."

"Good day, Miss King."

The B was permanent.

Chapter Two

"Where is that girl?" Ethel King mumbled as she placed two slices of sourdough bread buttered side down in a preheated skillet. Toasted cheese sandwiches were best straight out of the pan. They were never as good once the cheese firmed back up.

The little wood bird in the clock in the living room cuckooed one time. Katherine was officially forty minutes late. Ethel peered out the picture window above her kitchen table. Her gaze included the freshly mown backyard, the white picket fence that ran the perimeter of her corner lot, and Katherine, strolling into view. Hallelujah. With her long legs, blonde hair pulled into a high ponytail, and sporty blue backpack, her granddaughter, a twenty-eight-year-old grad student, looked like a model.

Katherine entered the back room, set her bag in the padded chrome chair at the table, and, without a word of greeting, washed her hands in the kitchen sink.

Hopefully, everything was okay. It wasn't like Katherine to be late or quiet.

"Fritz got into my baby radishes again." Ethel sighed and turned over a sandwich. Cheddar cheese oozed out the sides—just the way she liked. "I know it was him because I found a tunnel beneath the fence."

"Did you speak to Sally about it?" At the table,

Katherine flipped through the Scrabble dictionary that they kept wedged in the napkin holder.

"Yes." Ethel sighed. "Supposedly, Hannah is saving up for a puppy, but they assure me they won't get another Scottish terrier." Her dear granddaughter, who was usually so good about showing empathy, flipped deeper into the book. Something was indeed wrong.

"For your sake, Grandma, I hope they don't get another digger."

"What are you looking up, honey?"

Katherine paused at a page, a quarter of the way through. "Did you know *clemency* is a synonym for *mercy*?"

"Yes, let's hope Sally forgives me for complaining."

"She will." Katherine resumed reading. That's why her granddaughter was an A student. She couldn't leave the books alone.

Ethel told herself to wait until after they said prayer to ask who'd died. Sometimes when she heard bad news, she'd feel so appalled she'd forget to pray. She slid the golden sandwiches onto two plates and sat down. Holding hands, they bowed their heads for prayer.

"Dear Heavenly Father, thank You for Your many blessings. Help us to see the good in the bad. Thank You for the sandwiches. Amen." Ethel unfolded a yellow paper napkin. "Who died, honey?"

"Why'd you ask that?" Katherine sounded a tad breathless.

"You look like you lost your best friend." Ethel patted her nearest hand. "And you were late."

"I received a B today on an exam." Katherine shrugged and bit her lower lip.

Oh, dear, a B. Since she was knee-high spouting the Pledge of Allegiance, Katherine had always been their brilliant wonder.

"Maybe the Lord wanted you to know how everybody else feels. Maybe that's why your professor gave you a B."

She shook her head. "This professor has no empathy."

"Well, then . . ." Ethel nudged her glasses higher up the bridge of her nose. "Maybe he made an honest mistake. When I reconciled my checkbook yesterday, I'd transposed several numbers in my registry. I was so disgusted with myself."

"It was also a B in his grade book. He checked." Red crept up from Katherine's neck into her cheeks. "When I was in Professor B.'s office, I felt all keyed up. I was not diplomatic."

"Professor B.?"

"Yes, Professor Benton has been renamed."

"Wow." Here it was Katherine's final semester, and she'd never had a B before in her life. "You need to show him the old King fortitude. Get back on your horse and . . ."

"Grandma, he gave me a B." Katherine's voice reminded Ethel of her own mother's when President Truman had won office. Their fate had felt so final.

"Maybe the B was for *beauty*." Ethel patted her nearest hand.

"I knew the material. My essay flowed. I felt so good about it." Her large blue eyes searched Ethel's. "He wants me to be more analytical. The next paper, I'll be so analytical he won't know what hit him. The dummy."

Even though Katherine said *dummy* under her breath, Ethel had heard it loud and clear. "Now, honey…"

"I was not diplomatic." Tears moistened her long lashes.

"Well . . . the words *I'm sorry* are seven letters, and seven is the Lord's number. I don't think it's purely coincidence, do you?"

"I need to figure out a strategy. He's not a normal individual. He's—"

"Just like you did today, you march into his office, and instead of complaining you apologize. It's that easy." Ethel took a bite of sandwich. *Shoot!* The cheese was already rubbery.

"You don't understand, Grandma. I was a poor sport."

Why was she being so vague? Ethel adjusted her glasses. She sure hoped Katherine wasn't dating Joe, the tennis player, again.

"Did you play tennis with Professor B.?"

"No, Grandma." Finally, a smile tugged at the corners of Katherine's mouth.

"I know . . . we can make him cinnamon rolls." Ethel clapped her hands together. Cinnamon rolls were the family cure-all. The smell of them baking made everyone feel better.

Katherine shook her head. "That's called brownnosing! Absolutely not."

"Hmmph . . ." She'd start a batch when Katherine went upstairs to study. Ethel glanced over her shoulder at the coffee maker. Later this afternoon, she'd make a fresh pot of decaf to go with the rolls. Good thing she'd saved that shoebox. She could put half a dozen rolls in it for Katherine to take to—

"Grandma, why did you just glance at the coffeepot?"

"No reason." Ethel swallowed.

"Your mind is not hard to read. Never in a million years would I deliver Professor B. cinnamon rolls. Grandma . . ." Katherine waited for her to look directly into her eyes. Pursing her lips, Ethel eventually did. "Don't get the idea into your head. It's called brownnosing, and very frowned upon by my generation."

"What is it with you kids?" Ethel brushed toasted crumbs off her fingers and onto her plate. "When I was growing up, we used to have teachers over for dinner all the time. Once when your Uncle Stan was having problems in math, my daddy, your great-grandfather, invited the—"

"Grandma! I know the story. And times have changed."

Ethel took a bite of sandwich and chewed on the fact that her granddaughter was one of the most stubborn people she'd ever known. Hmmm... to make the frosting, she'd need powdered sugar, vanilla... was she out of powdered sugar? She looked toward the cupboard above Katherine's head.

"Grandma!"

Ж

Ethel opened the door downstairs. "Katherine?" Her voice cracked a little as she called up the steep stairwell. "I'm making the sweet dough. Can you help me knead it?"

"Grandma, I'm not giving rolls to Professor Benton."

"I need your help. You know what kneading does to my arthritis." Ethel suppressed a giggle. Whenever she wanted something done, the old arthritis excuse worked like a charm.

She heard footsteps overhead before Katherine marched down the stairs.

"Oh, good," Ethel said as she entered the kitchen. "We'll be able to enjoy a roll after supper."

"Who are the rest for?" Katherine washed her hands at the sink.

"I lined a shoebox with foil." She nodded to a bright pink-and-white Naturalizer shoebox on the counter. "Remember the tan church shoes I bought last week? I couldn't bring myself to throw out the box. I knew it would come in handy for something."

"Who are you going to give the cinnamon rolls to?"

Ethel set her hands on her hips and lifted her chin. "You're giving them to Professor B."

"I'll only give the rolls to Professor B. if you douse them with cayenne pepper instead of cinnamon."

"They'd be awful. You're awful!"

"I won't give him the rolls." Katherine pulled the wood cutting board a foot and a half out of the cabinetry and sprinkled flour over it. She muscled the palms of her hands into the yeast-scented dough.

"I'll put a couple of gooey, frosting-loaded cinnamon rolls in the box for you to take to him tomorrow. Maybe you won't even have to apologize— he'll know what you're trying to say. You messed up, and this is a sweet way to say you're sorry."

Ethel set the timer for ten minutes—the duration of Katherine's dough-kneading workout.

"It's useless to argue with you, Grandma. But, I want you to know that I've learned something from this lesson."

"Oh, what have you learned?" Ethel pushed her

glasses higher up the bridge of her nose.

"The next time I get a B and complain to a professor about it, I'm not going to tell you."

She didn't know why Katherine had to be so spiteful. "Just wait, honey, the cinnamon rolls are going to work like a charm."

Ж

Ethel knew her granddaughter's morning routine. While Katherine brushed her teeth, she hurried to the kitchen and waited, holding the box of cinnamon rolls, ready for the hand-off. Katherine strolled through the doorway from the living room and, kissed her on the cheek, and it was then that the exchange was made.

Her granddaughter promptly set the box down on the table and opened the fridge.

"What's something I can take for a healthy snack?" She peered inside.

"Raisins. I just bought some of those snack-sized boxes." Ethel turned, opened the snack drawer, wrestled a box free from the packaging, and tossed it to her.

"Love you, Grandma. Thanks for breakfast." Katherine waved.

"Love you, honey." Ethel glanced at the corner of the table. The box was gone. Good, she'd taken it. From the picture window, which overlooked the backyard, Ethel watched her granddaughter close the picket gate and then head west toward campus. With her right elbow propped against her side, she definitely carried the shoebox.

Ethel giggled and sat down to enjoy her remaining cup of coffee. She reached for the crossword puzzle book that she kept in the napkin holder next to the Scrabble dictionary. Crossword calisthenics were good for the aging brain. She slid a pencil behind one ear and glanced toward her gardening hats in the backroom. She'd work in the yard a little this morning while the sky was blue. That is after she filled in, at least, three words.

"What's a five-letter word for a common pantry item? Hmmm…" Her gaze traveled about the small, white, boxy kitchen. "Salt… no, that's four letters." Something pink caught her eye. Backtracking, she scanned the top of the fridge. There sat the box of cinnamon rolls. Katherine! She'd tucked it there, and had only pretended to be carrying the box. That girl!

I'll show her.

Ethel changed into her lime-green T-shirt, the one that her good friend Sharon had puff painted a row of pansies on right above the chest area, and her comfy elastic-waistband denim. As soon as she returned home, she planned to garden before it rained. May weather on the Palouse was unpredictable; blue skies were a gift.

She dialed the university and waited with her pencil ready. "Can you tell me where Professor Benton's office is? B… as in Benton," she told the receptionist.

"His office is located on the third floor of the Administration Building. The hall secretary will direct you."

"Thank you." Ethel smiled. She was partial to the Admin, a lovely old brick building with a clock tower.

In the back room, she donned her wide-brimmed straw hat—the one with the checkered yellow-and-white ribbon and a cluster of plastic strawberries pinned to the side. Halfway between the house and her red Chevy Nova, Ethel paused to pray. "Dear Lord, please don't let her see me. If Katherine was as awful as she says, a little sweetness is not going to hurt, amen."

Ethel headed west out of her gravel drive. A half mile later, the vast lawns and towering elm trees of the U of I campus came into view. With both hands on the wheel, she concentrated on finding a parking spot near the century-old brick building. Six minutes elapsed as she drove her car around and around the five-lane lot. How frustrating. As always, there were plenty of handicapped parking spaces available. Latah County should change at least half of their handicapped spaces to also accommodate senior citizens. The signs could have a turtle with a cane for the emblem. Being elderly was often a handicap.

Ethel finally gave up the search and parked in a handicapped space. She'd heard once that the U of I made so much money from their parking fees that they were able to pay off their new four-story library. It sounded a little far-fetched to her. Maybe they didn't have enough parking on purpose. She tucked the box of cinnamon rolls beneath her arm and ambled toward the side entrance. Inside the building, an expansive granite stairwell greeted her. Three flights! What the old place needed was an escalator, like at the big, fancy department stores in Spokane.

Ethel made it to the third floor only slightly out of breath. She walked to the end of the wide corridor. A middle-aged woman with tight, curly hair and good posture sat at a desk. "How may I help you?"

"I'm looking for Professor Benton's office." Ethel patted the shoebox beneath her arm.

"It's at the end of the hallway." The secretary peered over her bifocals at Ethel as she pointed to her left. "Professor Benton's door is the one with the yellow paper in the window."

"Is he in?" Maybe she should take off her hat.

"Yes, his office hours this morning are from eight thirty to nine thirty."

She thought he'd be busy professing. Ethel rummaged through her purse and found her late husband's old cigarillo tin, in which she stored a pad of neon-pink sticky notes and a mini blue ink pen. She wrote a simple note, stuck it to the box, and set it down on the corner of the desk. Taking a step back, she pondered the package. The bright pink-and-white box appeared so innocent. It was the message that read: *From, Katherine King* that Professor B. might find threatening.

He'd think it was a bomb.

What had Katherine said? *I was not a good loser. I was not diplomatic.* Ethel crumpled the note, thanked the secretary for her time, and started down the hallway toward his office. Up close the yellow paper read: "Quinn Benton, Ph.D. Professor of History." Despite what Katherine had said about him, his title sounded smart enough. She rapped twice on the wooden door.

"Come in."

She paused. What in the world was she going to say? She glanced over her shoulder. The secretary was watching her over the top of her bifocals—shoot! There was no going back. Katherine would hear about it, and she'd be livid.

Seated with his back to her, the dark-haired professor busily penned something.

Ethel closed the door behind her. The small room was more like a walk-in closet than an office. Similar to Katherine's style of decorating, books were squished into shelves and, piled on top of the desk, the filing cabinet, and even the tiny windowsill.

The professor glanced over his shoulder at her. He was much younger than she'd expected. His hair wasn't a toupee, but a natural, deep brown. He smiled—the easy, effortless smile of a kindred spirit. *How could Katherine not like the man?*

Chapter Three

Quinn Benton spun his chair a quarter turn. A lean, elderly woman wearing a wide-brimmed gardening hat closed his office door behind her. She cradled a pink shoebox under one arm.

"Hello." He smiled. "What can I do for you today?"

"I'm here because of my granddaughter." She patted the shoebox and ambled toward him. "We made you cinnamon rolls." She set the box on top of a pile of nearby textbooks and, removing her hat, sat down in the chair kitty-corner to his desk. Her permanent tight curls were a mix of mousy brown and gray.

He hoped her granddaughter wasn't Angel LeFave. She'd already visited his office thrice this semester.

"I'm Quinn Benton." Leaning forward, he extended his right hand.

"I'm Ethel." She gave his hand a firm shake. Her round, pale blue eyes were oddly familiar. "To be honest, I expected some grouchy old miser with white hair and a pop belly."

"Do you mean *potbelly*?" He suppressed a chuckle.

Her skimpy brows gathered. "Oh, pooh, I've been saying it wrong for years."

"Is that how your granddaughter described me?"

"No. Um, she didn't describe your outward appearance. She's more into describing people's brains and… intelligence."

"Who is your granddaughter?" He rested his elbows on the arms of his chair.

"She's one of your brightest students." She nudged her glasses higher up the bridge of her nose.

Definitely not Angel, though grandmothers were usually biased.

"She came home yesterday in tears."

Yesterday, three out of the four female students in his Civil War class had visited his office to complain about their grade, and Angel had been one of them.

"Stubbornness is a strong *King* trait," Ethel said, dropping the bomb.

The pen he'd been holding catapulted out of his grip and bounced across his desk. Otherwise, he tried to appear natural. "King, as in Katherine King?" After she'd made her D-day comment, Katherine's round blue eyes had nearly popped out of her head.

"While stubbornness is a strong King trait, so are brilliance and fortitude." There was a soft cadence to the elderly woman's voice. "Kings are also known for their compassion. Though Katherine's strong competitive spirit sometimes gets in the way."

"Did you say Katherine helped make the cinnamon rolls?" His gaze shifted to the box. Did it contain anthrax?

"She kneaded the dough for ten minutes yesterday during a study break."

"And she knows you're delivering them to me?"

"Not exactly." Ethel's mouth bunched. "I thought she'd taken the cinnamon rolls with her this morning, but when I was enjoying my cup of coffee, I saw the box sitting on top of the fridge. Of all places."

"Oh." He nodded. "So she intentionally forgot it."

"I suppose there is a slight possibility that she forgot, though our Katherine rarely forgets a thing." She nudged her glasses higher up her nose. "She's always had an enormous memory."

Dennis Evans, a good friend, and fellow professor, referred to Katherine's academic ability as *sagacious* and, as her adviser was encouraging her to pursue her doctorate.

"The rolls are from you, Mrs. King, not your granddaughter."

"Yes, Katherine thought the cinnamon rolls would be brownnosing." Ethel's chin lifted. "But I told her they could be a sweet way to say she's sorry."

"Is she?"

"She cried. She said—"

"Mrs. King"—he suppressed a chuckle—"your granddaughter is very fixated on her grades. If she cried, it was solely on account of the B, not because of the way she handled herself in my office."

Mrs. King's gaze traveled from his slightly wrinkled polo collar to his bare left hand. He'd been in a hurry this morning and grabbed the shirt from the to-iron pile.

"Please call me Ethel. And, you're right, Katherine didn't cry-cry. She's a King. In case she hasn't told you, the name's derived from nobility, not apples. Kings rarely cry."

Wait till he told Evans about this visitor.

"She intends to apologize . . . when the time is right, for her, um…" Ethel tipped back her head and studied the antique-white ceiling. "Her lack of diplomacy."

"Is that how she worded it?"

"Yes. Katherine's passion is history and being excellent at it, Mr. ..." Ethel's gaze scanned his desk. "She's brilliant, not fixated. *Stuck* is a better word for her. Katherine gets *stuck* on her opinion of things..."

"I agree with you." He nodded. "Your granddaughter is brilliant and stuck on her own opinion of things."

Ethel's wide smile exposed a dimple, one on each side of her face. She set her hat back on and tied the bow beneath her chin.

"It was her closing statement that was weak."

"I thought I'd just be a minute, so I parked in a handicapped spot."

"Oooh, that's too bad. They recently raised parking fines to twenty-five dollars."

"Twenty-five dollars!" Ethel grabbed her purse and started for the door.

"It was a pleasure to meet you, Mrs. King." He chuckled and retrieved his pen.

"You, too, Professor B."

"Huh?" Had he heard her correctly? "Mrs. King..." The base of his chair squeaked as he swiveled.

With her hand on the doorknob, Ethel's slightly hunched back appeared frozen. She slowly turned to face him.

"Is Professor B. what Katherine calls me?" He set his elbows on the arms of his chair and tapped the steeple area of his index fingers softly against his chin. Ethel's wide-eyed look of alarm told him it was a genuine slip.

Katherine King had a nickname for him as well.

Chapter Four

Friday morning, Katherine made sure she didn't arrive early to Professor Benton's U.S history class. One minute before the bell, she took her usual seat in the second row. She arranged her notebook at a forty-five-degree angle on the T-bone-shaped melamine desk and avoided looking toward the front of the room.

"Are we still on for the movie tonight at your grandma's?" Angel whispered.

"Yes. Seven o'clock." Katherine glanced toward Professor Benton. Good, he wasn't watching.

"Last night, Greg and I celebrated our three-month anniversary," Angel whispered. "He's been building me up for weeks about taking me someplace nice. I thought we were going to go to Alex's in Pullman or that fancy restaurant on the hill." She rolled her eyes. "I got all dolled up for Big Bob's Burgers."

"Wow. I'm sorry."

Professor Benton cleared his throat. "Good morning, class. We left off on Wednesday with the First Battle of Bull Run."

Katherine wrote on the edge of her notebook: "Maybe you should plan your four-month anniversary," and angled the paper so Angel could read.

Angel nodded.

"Lincoln originally called for seventy-five thousand men to serve for three months. The day after the Union's defeat at Bull Run, he signed another bill for the enlistment of half a million men for the next three years. As I mentioned earlier, the American Civil War was often a war of firsts. America's first military draft being one of them."

Angel leaned toward her. "I wonder if Big Bob's Burgers is his idea of a romantic dinner?" she whispered.

Maybe they shouldn't encourage Angel to see *Doctor Zhivago.*

"With those eyes, even Big Bob's Burgers would be romantic."

How could Angel even think about the man? He'd given her a D.

After two pages of notes, Katherine lifted her gaze. She had immediate eye contact with Professor B. Her stomach twisted like a wrung-out sponge. Only half the class hour had passed. *Lord, help me to take my last semester one lecture at a time.*

"In 1861, in the First Battle of Bull Run, there were close to five thousand casualties." Professor Benton paused mid-sentence. Seated on the front of his desk, he appeared to be chewing something. How odd, right in the middle of his lecture, he was eating right in front of everyone. On top of his trousered knee, something white and blockish sat on a yellow paper napkin. Upon closer examination, it was a frosted cinnamon roll.

The hair on the back of Katherine's neck stood up. *It couldn't possibly be...* She leaned slightly toward Angel. Behind Professor Benton sat a bright pink Naturalizer shoebox. Grandma! She hadn't... Her heart knotted in her chest. Crud, she had!

Ever so self-indulgently, Quinn Benton tucked the coveted section, the cinnamon roll heart, into his mouth and wiped his fingers on the napkin. He was having a field day, pretending they were delicious. They weren't. Grandma had forgotten an important ingredient in the sweet dough, salt. And then she'd rolled it too thick and topped it with a skimpy coating of cinnamon. But the gooey cream cheese frosting had turned out all right.

She must have delivered the rolls yesterday. That's why she'd acted so strangely at dinner. Giggly and then silent. Probably wearing one of her goofy gardening hats, Grandma had pleaded for her, tried to pardon her. That's why he toyed with her now— because he was God and he knew it.

Ж

Professor Evans ended his Lewis and Clark lecture with: "Katherine, I'd like to speak with you after class." There were only nine students in the four- and five-hundred level course; everyone was on a first-name basis.

Ever since she'd taken History of England her freshman year, Dennis Evans had been her favorite professor. A gifted lecturer, Evans played on his English accent and often leaned toward theatrical tendencies.

Katherine moved from the second row to the first and watched as he shoved transparencies into a file two inches thick. He was six feet tall, nearing sixty, with an Uncle Sam—white, well-groomed beard.

Perhaps, he wanted to discuss the most recent exam. *Please, not another B.* Perhaps, she was slipping. Her final semester in the master's program, she was losing her brain.

"Have you had a chance to review the exams?" She managed to sound matter of fact.

"As always, you received an A in my book." He glanced up at her. "Was your exam indeed a B in Professor Benton's?"

"Yes-sss." She sighed. Before her visit to Professor Benton's office, she'd confided in Evans. That was when he'd nicknamed him Professor B.

"Your first B." Evans shook his head. Though papers squished out the sides of his bulky leather briefcase, he managed to latch it.

"In the past year, there's been so much female traffic to Professor Benton's office that our department chair is considering installing surveillance cameras in the hallway. Tell me, Katherine, does it have more to do with his Ph.D. being from Duke, or the fact that he's a young, good-looking, local boy?"

Wow . . . Duke! He must be more intelligent than met the eye.

"What do you mean local?"

"Kellogg, Idaho." Evans peered at her over the top of his glasses.

Kellogg, a small ski resort town, was a good hundred miles from Moscow.

"As your adviser, I think it best to remind you that faculty-student romances are very frowned upon."

Of course, he was only kidding her. "I have no intentions of ever seeing the man outside of class." Were he and Professor Benton friends? Their offices were only two doors apart in the same dimly lit hallway.

"Good. How's your thesis coming along?"

"You know, last-minute footnotes, endnotes."

He grinned. "Now, the reason I asked you to stay after class is, I'm hosting a small get-together at my home tonight. Cindy Fancy will be there."

"Oh, bummer." She glanced toward the half-open door and the expansive granite hallway beyond. "I have a get-together at my grandma's tonight."

"We won't be meeting until eleven."

"You're kidding. Why so late?"

"We meet to discuss one sorry chap's love life. He blind dates every Friday night and gives a recap at my place afterward. It's late, but very entertaining."

Hmm . . . The girls planned to meet at Grandma's at seven and only watch the first half of *Doctor Zhivago.* With popcorn and a little social time, they'd definitely be done by nine thirty, ten o'clock at the latest.

"Being it's so late, it does work for me."

"Splendid." He glanced at his wristwatch. "Tonight is blind date number three… or four. I'll have Cindy pick you up." Evans lifted his briefcase and started for the door.

"Tell her thanks." What an honor. Cindy co-taught Lewis and Clark with Evans and was one of her favorite professors. Tonight had *fun* written all over it.

Ж

"Grandma!" Katherine closed the back door with a thud. The kitchen table was set for two. Brown and white Currier and Ives plates hosted egg salad sandwiches and raw baby carrots. In the center of the table stood a slim glass vase with two fresh-cut yellow tulips.

Looking as innocent as ever, Grandma ambled into the kitchen. For the second day in a row, she wore her lime-green T-shirt with puff-painted pansies. No one wore puff-painted clothing anymore, not even Sharon, Grandma's girlfriend who'd painted it.

"I can't believe you went to see him." Shoulders squared, Katherine faced her.

"I had to. You forgot the rolls." Grandma glanced to the top of the fridge. "Tea water's ready. It's been simmering on the stove."

Katherine washed her hands and, with a huff, sat down in her usual chair. "Grandma, you can't give any of my professors cinnamon rolls ever again. It's very unprofessional. Please promise me you'll never visit one of my professors on my behalf again."

"So he told you. What did he say? Did he tell you after class? Or did you go to his office?" As she poured boiling water into mugs, Grandma hummed. "We'll have tea with our sandwiches." She giggled like they were about to share exciting news.

Katherine inhaled slowly, deeply, and, feeling her eyes water a bit, exhaled. *Lord, I love her. On the day I was born, You gave her to me as a gift. She's always been a gift. Help me to not be offensive. She loves me. She did what she thought was best. Help her actions to not be a detriment to my future, amen.*

"What hat did you wear, Grandma?" Katherine looked toward the back room. A wooden mug rack on the narrow wall hosted three happy gardener hats.

"The one with the strawberries."

Grandma was never to wear the strawberry hat outside of the yard! And she knew it. Katherine inhaled and closed her eyes. The picture of Grandma on campus was no longer fuzzy—it was crystal clear.

Please, Lord, let Professor B. have a sense of humor.

She doubted the possibility.

"I thought I was going to just leave the cinnamon rolls with a sticky note on the box, but his secretary said he was in his office."

"Mrs. Dougal is the history department secretary; she's not Professor B.'s personal secretary."

"You didn't tell me he was young and looks like a movie star."

For the last twenty-four hours, Grandma had kept her little secret to herself. "It doesn't matter what he looks like, Grandma—he gave me a B."

"He looked just like the actor in *Lawrence of Arabia.*"

Katherine swallowed. "Do you mean Omar Sharif?"

"Yes, all day I've been trying to remember his name." A wide smile stretched across Grandma's softly wrinkled face. "You know how sometimes you just hit it off with a person?"

Oh no. What was she saying? "As long as I'm living here, Grandma, you're not allowed to *hit it off* with Professor B. He was my enemy first."

"I wish I had my little handheld recorder." Grandma nudged her glasses higher up the bridge of her nose. "I'd play back what you just said to Pastor Ken."

Katherine took a sip of tea and tried to focus on the positive side of the situation. *I'm alive. I'm still breathing.*

"I also wish I'd had my handheld recorder when I was in Professor B.'s office yesterday." Grandma's eyes warmed. "He said you're brilliant."

"In what context?" Katherine resisted the urge to melt a little.

"What do you mean?"

"I'm sure he didn't just come out and say *Katherine King is brilliant.*"

Grandma pursed her thin lips. "He agreed with me; he said, 'Your granddaughter is brilliant.'"

"And . . .? There had to be a *but* in there, or an *although.*"

Grandma's sparse brows grew closer. "Right before I left, he said something about your closing statement being weak—whatever that has to do with being brilliant. He said it, Katherine. I wouldn't lie to you. Professor B. said you are brilliant." Grandma smiled like she'd won a blue ribbon at the fair for her baked goods; which had never happened, nor in this lifetime ever would.

A little animosity melted. Grandma wouldn't lie to her. The man had actually said the *B* word about her in front of her grandmother. All hope was not lost. Out of the dark abyss of gloom, she could still pull a solid A out yet.

"You know how God sometimes gives you a heart tug for a person?" Grandma's voice took on an airy quality.

Katherine shrugged. On occasion, she'd experienced it—more with the five-year-olds in her Sunday school class than with adults. Grandma couldn't possibly be saying . . .

"I don't understand it, but meeting the man tugged at my heart. Maybe your B... was God's way of bringing the two of us together."

Please, Lord, have it merely be a passing tug. Katherine glanced to the top of the fridge. If only she'd delivered the rolls herself, none of this ever would have happened.

Chapter Five

Despite the $25.00 parking ticket in her purse, Friday evening Ethel found herself giggling. Her granddaughter was out from behind her books and actually socializing. She'd invited three of her friends over for a little movie get-together. Katherine popped popcorn and poured glasses of lemonade for the young women—a shorter girl named Angel, a tall brunette named Brenda, and a talkative redhead. Ethel had already forgotten her name.

Orchestra music played on the TV, and the word "Overture" was spelled across the screen. "The introduction's long, girls," Katherine said. "I didn't want to fast forward; it gives us a little time to talk." Walking about the room, she turned off the overhead light, and the floor lamp above the recliner.

"What history class are you girls in together?" Ethel asked.

"Civil War," Angel, the short brunette, said.

"The American Civil War," added the hoity-toity redhead. Out of Katherine's friends, she already liked Angel the most.

"The movie's four hours long," Katherine said. "If you're game, we'll watch the second half next week, or the week after, depending on our studies."

Four hours! *Gone with the Wind* was a long Civil War movie, but she didn't remember it starting with orchestra music. Since they hadn't invited her to join their little party, she'd finish up her Bible study reading for the week. Ethel yawned and strolled into her sewing room. Why Sharon had to pick Galatians for the summer focus was beyond her. Ethel was a fan of Psalms. There was a psalm for every circumstance.

A chapter later, Ethel stretched. She'd take a break from Galatians to get some lemonade. She puttered through the living room on her way to the kitchen.

"He's so gorgeous." Angel sounded awestruck.

Captivated by the tension in the room, Ethel paused near the curio cabinet where she stored her collection of salt-and-pepper shakers. On-screen was the same actor fellow who'd been in *Lawrence of Arabia*. Her memory served her well—the actor bore a striking resemblance to the girls' Civil War professor, Professor Benton.

Had they noticed?

Katherine sat on the couch, hugging her knees to her chest. She glanced over at Ethel.

"Is everything okay, Grandma?"

"Yes, what war is the movie about?" Ethel asked. The stark buildings didn't remind her of the Old South, and the men's tall hats and long wool coats looked more Russian than Confederate.

"It's about the Bolsheviks and the Democratic Party of Russia during the country's revolution. The movie is so controversial, Grandma, that for almost thirty years Russia didn't allow it to be aired."

"Oh. I thought you girls were studying the American Civil War." Whenever Katherine tried to detour her away from something, she added a lot of mumbo jumbo. It happened occasionally when they were clothes shopping together or discussing Katherine's marital status.

"We're studying both, Mrs. King," Angel said, adding a sigh.

The movie looked better than the ones Katherine usually brought home, and unfortunately, all the seating was taken. Ethel waited in the back of the room, near the phone, hoping they'd invite her to pull up one of the dining chairs and sit down. But no one did. It was best to just be quiet, as it was obviously an important part; the girls were riveted to the screen.

The man who looked like Quinn Benton walked through a low-ceilinged room that shook from the force of a train passing overhead. Harp music and maybe a ukulele played softly to one of her favorite songs, "Somewhere My Love." The movie's cinematography made it feel more like a love story, and very mesmerizing.

On-screen, a young woman, with hair the same pale blonde color as Katherine's, quite passionately kissed the arm of an older man, perhaps her father, while the actor, Quinn Benton's look-alike, watched with tears in his eyes.

And so did Ethel.

Ж

Cindy Fancy's white Camry pulled up in front of Grandma's house at eleven o'clock sharp. Katherine was under the impression that Professor Evans's get-together started at eleven, but not everyone was as zealous about being on time as she was.

"Lock it behind me, Grandma, and don't stay up late worrying."

"It's already late. What's Cindy's last name again? And where are you going?"

"Cindy Fancy. We're going to Professor Evans's home. Get a good night's sleep. I love you." Katherine kissed her forehead as Grandma paused beside the door.

"Zip up your coat; it's supposed to drop to the low fifties tonight."

Moscow's winters could linger well into late spring. On her way out the door, she zipped up her Adidas jacket. Cindy's car felt toasty warm. Under a light coat, Cindy wore a black dinner dress with high heels. Her red hair was bobbed at the ear and teased at the crown for height. Katherine guessed her to be in her early fifties. Her dangly silver earrings glittered in the light from the overhead street lamps.

"I feel underdressed." Beneath her jacket, Katherine wore a cranberry-red T-shirt and jeans, and her long hair was loose about her shoulders.

"I just finished hosting a cooking party. I still have an hour's worth of clean up, but it will have to wait until morning. You're dressed perfect. The guys dress casual."

"Guys?" Katherine's stomach lurched.

"Yes. There will be two other men besides Evans at his home. It's our largest get-together yet. Usually, it's just the three of us."

"Who's the third?"

"A professor friend of Evans. So you live with your grandmother. How does that work out with your social life?"

"What social life?"

Cindy giggled.

"I don't have time for one. What about you? Are you married?" Katherine asked as Cindy drove east on

Sixth Street.

"Divorced. It was an unfortunate case of putting my husband through vet school, and then discovering he was unfaithful. I've been single for the last twelve years."

"I'm sorry."

"We didn't have children. Praise God."

Whenever anyone said *Praise God,* Katherine felt it was an opening. "Are you a Christian?"

"I read *Daily Guideposts* every Saturday and Sunday morning. What about you?"

"My grandmother and I attend the Nazarene church here in town. You'll have to go with us sometime."

Cindy smiled.

For the next couple of blocks, well-cared-for historic homes graced perfectly manicured lawns. She turned into the driveway of a brick Tudor-style and parked next to a black convertible. "Evans is a clean-car fanatic. He always parks his car in the garage. Sometimes it's hard to tell if he's home or not. Good, he's left the front light on this time." Cindy adjusted her rearview mirror and dabbed lipstick on her lower lip.

"I usually host cooking parties on Friday nights. I hate being stuck at home alone. That's why being a Demarle cooking rep works perfectly for me."

"How in the world do you ever find the time?"

"I look forward to it all week." Cindy swung open her door.

A privet hedge bordered the curved walkway. A front light flickered, and a curtain moved in the window to the left of the arched solid oak door. Evans opened it. Wearing gray sweatpants and an untucked sage-green polo, he appeared casual for company. In the crook of one arm, he toted a Chihuahua. In between barks, the perky-eared dog licked his cheek.

"Shh! Goliath," he crooned. "Come in. You both look lovely."

A crystal chandelier lit the front entry. Near the door, an ivy plant wrapped itself around the legs of a dusty antique side table. They followed Evans down a narrow, dimly lit hallway into a bright kitchen with cherry cabinetry, chrome appliances, and a dark-haired man. He appeared staged, as he leaned back against the granite counter. His olive coloring echoed Mediterranean, possibly Greek. He appeared to be in his mid-thirties and was flagrantly good looking.

"Katherine King, meet Carl Angelos." Evans waved his hand. Mr. Flagrantly Good Looking rounded the side of the expansive granite island to shake her hand. "It's nice to meet you, Katherine."

"You too." Her cheeks warmed. Was it a setup?

"Carl's a history professor at Lewis-Clark State College in Lewiston," Cindy said. "He and Evans play golf on Saturdays."

Katherine nodded. Carl was the sorry chap.

"Carl played for the U of I golf team years ago," Evans said. "What was your handicap?"

"My putting." He grinned at Katherine.

Hmm . . . a local boy. Why did Evans invite her tonight? As her adviser, he knew the heavy load she was taking. He couldn't possibly be matchmaking.

"It's ten minutes past eleven." Cindy glanced at the clock on the microwave above the stove. "And he's not here. Does that mean the date went well?"

"He called to say he's running late, and, like always, he didn't provide any clues," Evans said. "Katherine, would you prefer tea or hot cocoa? Carl, I don't need to tell you to make yourself at home."

Katherine shook the powdery contents of a packet of cocoa into a pottery mug from the tray on the island. Evans wouldn't set her up. As her adviser, he knew her summer load wasn't leisurely.

"There's instant hot water at the sink," Carl said.

The Chihuahua's ears perked up as the front door clicked open and then closed. "Looks like everyone's here." A deep male voice echoed down the hallway.

The voice sounded familiar. It almost sounded like—

"We're in the kitchen." Rocking back and forth in his corduroy slippers, Evans glanced at Katherine.

A dark-haired figure entered the room and set his keys on top of the island.

Heaven forbid—Katherine glanced toward the patio door and every other plausible exit in the room—*Professor Benton is the "sorry chap."*

Chapter Six

With her back to the room, Katherine filled the pottery mug with instant hot water. Why had Evans invited her tonight? Was it on account of Mr. Flagrantly Good Looking? Did Quinn Benton know she'd be here? How upset would he be?

"Are you here for the weekend, Carl?" Quinn asked.

"Evans and I are playing golf tomorrow at the U of I course, and then we're heading to The Breakfast Club. Are you game?"

"Only for breakfast. I donated my clubs to Goodwill last year after we played. Don't you remember? I dropped them off on our way to eat."

"How could anyone forget?" Carl chuckled.

Maybe Quinn hadn't recognized her—her back was to him and her hair was down. She usually wore it in a ponytail to class. Katherine forced herself to turn from the sink. Slowly, she forced herself to lift her gaze from the granite island to Benton's wide-eyed, frozen expression. His lungs were the first feature to thaw as his chest expanded.

Evans hadn't informed him either.

"Hello, Professor Benton." She dropped her gaze, and her hand trembled for half a stir as she mixed the cocoa with a spoon.

"Katherine . . . Katherine King."

Flat. His reaction to her was as flat as a liter of root beer that had been left on the counter uncapped for a week. Not that she blamed him.

"The vote was unanimous for Benton to donate his clubs." Evans chuckled. "None of us wanted to golf with him again. Not after he grenaded on seventeen."

"Evans, I'd like to speak with you in your mudroom," Quinn said.

Evans clamped a hand on his shoulder as they walked toward a small room adjacent to the kitchen. Quinn closed the door behind them.

Cindy frowned. "Anything new, Carl?"

"No." Gaze averted, Carl walked halfway between the mudroom and the island. The man was an eavesdropper.

Quinn was more upset by her visit to his office than she'd foreseen.

"Cindy, would you mind taking me home?" Katherine asked. "Professor Benton's obviously uncomfortable with my presence."

"Let's go to the living room." Cindy smiled.

They left Carl in the kitchen. "Quinn always sits there." Cindy motioned to a burgundy Queen Anne chair. A gold loveseat sat beneath a heavily framed oil painting of a lake surrounded by spring foliage. On the right side of the boxy room sat a matching gold couch. "Dennis prefers the couch; which leaves the loveseat for Carl and you."

"Uh . . . Cindy, is there any chance you could bring me home? I…"

"Carl . . ." Cindy smiled as he entered the room. "I was just telling Katherine that Quinn usually sits in that chair, and Dennis here." She patted the cushion beside her.

Cindy and Evans were teaming up against her.

"Do you and Benton have a history?" Carl asked, sitting down on the right side of the loveseat.

How could he think such a thing?

Evans entered, carrying a large tray with a teapot, mugs, and a package of Mother's Taffy Cookies into the room, and set them on the chunky square coffee table.

"Absolutely not," Quinn said, sitting in his usual chair. "She's one of my students."

"You missed her wide-eyed look of alarm." Carl chuckled.

Why in the world had Evans invited her?

"So Evans was telling me that you're from Vancouver?" Carl asked.

"Yes, Washington." The University of Idaho was just close enough to the Canadian border that her answer commonly required a clarifier.

"She lives with her grandmother here in town," Evans said.

"A few blocks off the Troy highway," Cindy added.

"What street?" Quinn's Adam's apple bobbed.

Should she tell him? "Logan."

He exhaled, apparently relieved. "I believe you're one, maybe two blocks west of me."

If Grandma found out, she'd consider them neighbors and bake him something to welcome him to the neighborhood. Just like with the judges at the fair, Grandma's baking wouldn't win his affection. Or had it already? The heart tug wasn't mutual. Was it?

"You're neighbors." Evans chuckled and slapped his knee.

"Did I miss something?" Carl asked.

"Unfortunately, our dear friends started off on the

wrong foot," Evans said. "Benton gave Katherine her first college B, and she's in the final semester of her master's."

"She recently visited my office—" Quinn cleared his throat—"and so has her grandmother."

"I see." Carl smiled Katherine's direction.

"I don't think you do." Quinn took a sip from his mug; a tea label hung over the side. "Ethel delivered cinnamon rolls to me the next day to soften Katherine's…"

"Lack of diplomacy," Katherine said it for him. "I want you to know that I had no idea she'd made the delivery."

"I could tell." He smiled.

He meant yesterday in class.

"What do you mean, Benton?" Evans asked. "You can't bring this up in front of everyone and not expect us to be curious."

"He ate one of my grandmother's cinnamon rolls in front of the class. Right in the middle of his lecture." She glanced from Evans to Quinn.

"I was under the impression Katherine didn't know, and I was informing her." His cheeks bunched.

"Interesting use of your lecture time," Evans said.

"And I must say, Katherine . . ." Quinn said.

Oh, he'd actually called her by her first name. So that's how it was—outside of class she was Katherine?

"So far this semester, your grandmother's visit has been the highlight."

"Just remember it wasn't my idea."

He chuckled.

How to stop a giant boulder from rolling downhill? Katherine stared at the coffee table. Heaven forbid the heart tug between Grandma and Quinn had been mutual. She would never tell Grandma.

"You'll have to tell me later how undiplomatic you were," Carl whispered, leaning her direction.

Later . . . ? Katherine's stomach knotted. He was very good looking and well educated, but there was just something rather snake oil-ish about him. Was she wrong?

"I'll tell you later, Carl." Quinn leaned toward the coffee table and refilled his teacup.

Yes, she was sure he would.

"Before it gets too late, I'm ready to tell you about my date from..." Quinn paused and looked at Cindy. "Colfax."

Evans shook his head. "I had such high hopes for you. I must say Julia, or whatever her name is, sounded perfect."

"How many blind dates have there been?" Carl asked, toying with his left eyebrow.

"This is the fourth, maybe fifth. I want to vent, not count."

If Katherine didn't look to her left at Mr. Snake Oil or straight ahead at Professor Benton, she'd feel perfectly at home in Evans and Cindy's company.

"Get comfortable. On Friday nights, Benton is unusually longwinded." Evans tucked a pillow behind his back and crossed one leg over the other.

Katherine nestled deeper into the corner of the loveseat and held her warm mug of cocoa beneath her chin.

"I'll call her Alberta. I feel a tad uncomfortable talking bad about a woman in front of women," Quinn began. "Julia, I mean Alberta, is from Colfax. I wanted to meet in Pullman—which is almost a halfway mark—nine miles for me, sixteen miles for her—but she wasn't game. At first, I saw this as a bad sign, and I was right."

Carl chuckled under his breath.

"Yes, what you're seeing is the norm," Evans said.

After the university town of Pullman, Washington, Colfax was the next town Katherine drove through on her way home to Vancouver. The small farming town was nestled in the middle of rolling wheat fields, twenty-five miles west of Moscow.

"Alberta's married to her business—Colfax Antiques, on Main Street. It's on the right- hand side as you drive through town."

"I could swear Charlene Strauss told me Alberta's a masseuse," Cindy said, muffling a yawn.

"Charlene is the department chair," Evans informed the group. "She's this week's matchmaker."

"Tonight confirmed that Charlene does not like me." Quinn sighed. "Which surprised me; I helped her once with the plumbing in one of her rentals, which probably accounts for why Alberta thought I was a plumber. My father was a plumber, so I know more than I care to admit." Quinn set his mug down on a round marble-topped side table.

"She likes you, Quinn," Cindy said. "She's just not a good matchmaker."

How did the son of a plumber from Kellogg, Idaho, end up attending Duke?

"Never let people know you have a trade." Evans shook his head. "By the way, the sink in my laundry room has a small leak."

"Could be the drain, the faucet, or one of the water line fittings," Quinn said.

Maybe he did know what he was talking about.

"Wait, is or isn't Alberta a masseuse?" Cindy asked.

"No, Charlene Strauss met Alberta at a one-hour community ed. massage class. If I had to guess, Alberta was the one getting a massage."

Evans chuckled. "Did she make you dinner?"

"No. We dined on takeout from Taco Time on old china over candlelight in the upstairs loft of her antique shop."

"What type of china?" Cindy asked.

"I turned a plate over just for you. Blue and white Currier and Ives."

"We often frequent the antique stores," Evans informed Katherine and Carl as if they were a couple because they were seated together on the loveseat.

"The tablecloth was white. She played some seventy-eight records on an upright Victrola."

"Sounds romantic. Does she rent out the shop after hours?" Evans asked.

Was he thinking of asking Cindy out? They were both seated in the middle of their own couch cushion.

"I'll never call the woman again, but I can give you her number. The shop definitely held the potential for romance. If there'd been a home-cooked meal, and we'd talked about things other than plumbing, and she'd worn her hair differently." Quinn frowned. "She did insist on paying for our meal, most likely due to her ulterior motive—three hours spent plumbing her public bathroom."

"No!" Evans moaned.

"One bite into my crispy taco, she informs me that there's a drip, and she was told it was probably the wax ring. Usually small-town hardware stores close by seven, but as my luck goes, she'd already purchased the ring. Taking a toilet apart is not my idea of a great date."

At Quinn's expense, Katherine along with

everyone else had a good laugh. Were all his Friday night recaps this entertaining? This was a side of Quinn Benton she didn't know: the funny side, the side that could laugh at himself. Or was he laughing? It was difficult to tell. Red crept up his thick neck into his broad cheekbones.

"Charlene set you up?" Cindy asked, setting her teacup on the coffee table.

"Charlene Strauss." He nodded. "I think I'll buy her a gift certificate to the Chinese restaurant where I'm quite certain I got food poisoning last week."

"You wouldn't?" Katherine asked, staring.

"No, but you have to admit, she deserves it."

"What did Alberta look like?" Carl asked.

Katherine found herself curious too.

"I was told she was twenty-nine, but due to her weight, she looked much older. She's not someone I would see in town and think *she's attractive*. People often become more or less attractive when you spend time with them. After four-plus hours in her company, her personality did not warm in my eyes."

"Very well put, Quinn," Cindy said. "I'm proud of you."

Katherine also found herself agreeing with his philosophy. At first, she'd thought Joe was very attractive, and as she spent more time with him, she realized he was more brawn than brains.

"Looks and body weight are difficult questions to address when you're speaking on the phone to a woman you've never met. You have to trust that the friend—who's arranged for the two of you to meet—has some iota of common sense." Quinn frowned. "In summary, tonight was very disappointing."

As the evening drew to a close, Katherine carried the mugs to the sink and rinsed them. Cindy nudged her and motioned for her to follow her.

Katherine grabbed a dishtowel. What was going on?

In the dining nook area, Cindy glanced toward the doorway to the living room. "Evans wants me to stay another hour or so," she whispered. "We're planning out next week's lectures for Lewis and Clark."

The two were night owls.

"It's more work than he anticipated for summer. Carl wants to drive you home. Quinn lives in your neighborhood. I thought I'd warn you of your options."

"Oh." Wide-eyed, Katherine weighed driving home with Carl and possibly having to tell him no versus driving home with Quinn. She tossed the towel on the counter and started for the entry. She'd much rather have Quinn take her home than ward off a possible suitor.

Quinn stood near the front door, putting on his jacket. In the living room, Carl rose from the loveseat. She had to be quick.

"Mr. Benton, could you give me a ride home? Cindy plans to stay an hour longer than I anticipated."

Head bent, he zipped up his jacket. "No, I think Carl plans to drive you home."

"Yes, but you and I are practically neighbors." She didn't mask the urgency in her voice.

Reaching the entry, Carl ran a hand through his hair and grinned. "I was wondering if I could drive you home, Katherine."

It was one fifteen in the morning, and a man she'd just met wanted to drive her home.

"Thank you . . . but Mr. Benton lives a block from me." Her cheeks warmed as Carl's gaze settled on her.

"It's more like two or three blocks." Quinn wrestled on the final shoe.

"When's your next date, Benton?" Carl asked.

"Next Friday, a gal in Troy who works for the school district. Cindy set it up."

"Will you be here, Katherine?" Carl slid his hands into the front pockets of his jeans and nodded toward the living room. "Tonight was fun."

Joe often used the word *fun*. It was one of the most overused words in his vocabulary. Though she loved Joe—as a friend, of course—similar characteristics were now a red flag.

"I enjoyed tonight, but . . ." She glanced at Quinn. He looked tired, perhaps a bit agitated. "Whether or not I'll be invited again is the real question."

"Of course, you'll be," Evans bellowed from the living room. "Don't listen to Benton."

"I'll be here, then." She smiled, glad.

Despite Carl's fervent gaze, she didn't feel bad about her decision to ride home with Quinn, provided he'd take her.

"Well, it was a pleasure to meet you, Katherine."

She politely met his jade-green eyes. "Thank you; you also."

As soon as Quinn stepped away from the door, Katherine slipped past him, turned the knob, and stepped out into the brisk, early morning air.

"I'll meet you guys at The Breakfast Club at ten, and I'm not taking her home." He pulled the door closed behind him.

The front porch light lit the curved brick walkway. She walked ahead of him to where the sidewalk met the aggregate driveway. What did he mean—not taking her home? A dark, older Volvo sat parked near Evans's brick-enclosed mailbox.

"Why did you decline Carl's offer?" His voice dampened the fog-ridden night.

"I don't have time for a relationship . . . Professor Benton."

"Then why'd you come tonight?"

"Evans referred to it as a get-together. He didn't tell me he was matchmaking—when he knows perfectly well I have nine credits in the master's program." She tended to ramble when she was extremely tired.

Quinn huffed. "You just declined a decent human being."

She continued toward the Volvo.

"I am not taking you home, and Carl *wants* to take you home." He walked with both hands stuffed in the front pockets of his warm-up jacket. "I'm your professor. He isn't."

"I don't even know him." Had both Evans and Quinn teamed up for her to go out with Carl? "I don't want to stay another two hours, or however long Cindy will be."

"I can't take you home. You're one of my students."

"I'll sit down in the seat. No one will see me." A lantern-lamp post, encased in brick and a rambling of ivy, lit the edge of the drive.

"No." His jaw muscle twitched.

"I'll walk, then."

"You're not walking. It's dark, and—"

"I walk all the time after dark." She wouldn't tell him it was always a half walk, half jog, because of her over-active imagination.

"Well, you shouldn't. Moscow's a sweet little town, but it's not perfect." He spun a wad of keys around his pointer finger.

"It's Carl, or you can always wait for Cindy. You're not walking home this late at night." He opened the driver's side of his car.

"I guess I'll wait for Cindy, then." She strode back toward Evans's front door and the porch light that attracted a thousand moths. She slid her shoes off in the entry and hoped she wouldn't run into Carl.

Chapter Seven

Quinn found himself with an hour to kill before he'd meet the guys at The Breakfast Club. Despite the windy elements, Harold, his elderly tenant, was outside doing working on his side of the duplex. Over the past year, Saturday mornings had become their time to work together in the yard. Afterward, they'd share a cup of coffee.

"You're late," Harold grumbled.

"I was out late last night."

"Another blind date?"

"Yes, my date ended early, but the professors' group recap went late. They kept me out till almost two."

"How was the date?" Harold hoed the pesky red clover that had invaded the front bed.

"No chemistry. I believe all we have in common is our marital status."

"That bad?"

Quinn nodded and pulled his vibrating phone out of his back pocket.

"Hello."

"Quinn, it's Cindy. Dennis wanted me to get the scoop from you before the guys meet at The Breakfast Club this morning."

"What do you mean?" He nodded and took a few steps away from Harold.

"He wants to know why you wouldn't take Katherine home last night."

"She's one of my students."

"One mile, Quinn. Get real."

"I don't want to be seen driving one of my students around town. Ever. Especially at one thirty in the morning."

"Do you know she fell asleep on Dennis's couch? We had no idea she was there until I went to go home. It was past two thirty. And then she somewhat sleepwalked to the car. What's the real reason you didn't take her home?"

Didn't Cindy remember this was the woman he referred to as Miss A-nnoying?

"She's not interested in Carl. Evans's matchmaking backfired," Quinn said. Nearby Harold leaned on the wooden handle of his hoe. He lived alone, had little company, and in his own way enjoyed ribbing Quinn about anything he could.

"I agree, Dennis is a terrible matchmaker." Cindy sighed. "Katherine's a Christian, and you and I know that Carl is not a saint. I hope she doesn't fall for his charm."

Was Katherine saved? He would never have guessed it from her visit to his office. Yet there'd been such a sweetness about Ethel. He felt raindrops. He peered overhead at the dark, threatening sky.

"I'll call Evans and tell him no more matchmaking."

After closing his phone, Quinn grabbed a bucket and picked up the weeds that Harold had uprooted. The bending down part was tough on the elderly man's knees.

"That was one of the professors. Evans invited a master's student last night and is trying to matchmake her with Carl. Carl's a professor at Lewis-Clark State College in Clarkston."

"Save some news to talk about over coffee." Harold pointed the hoe to a weed Quinn had missed.

After a leisurely cup of coffee with Harold, Quinn grabbed his umbrella and walked the quiet, residential, tree-lined streets toward Main Street. The Breakfast Club was located on the southwest side of the historic downtown strip, in the same brick building that had once been the Nobby Inn Restaurant. He met the guys at ten o'clock in a booth near the back. Their faces were ruddy-colored from golfing for two hours in the stormy weather. He sat down on the same side as Carl, across from Evans.

"How'd you guys do?"

"Carl won." Evans shrugged and held the menu high enough to cover his face.

"Of course, he won." He used to be in the top five on the U of I golf team. "How'd *you* do, Evans?"

Carl chuckled. "He grenaded on sixteen. Threw a club."

"It slipped out of my hand. It's tough to keep your grip in the rain. I need to get a golf glove. Goliath chewed up my nice leather one."

"After tossing the club twice, he had to wrap his hankie around the shaft."

"I didn't toss it; it slipped."

Quinn smiled. He was glad he hadn't gone. He definitely would have tossed a club or two.

"Carl's going to ask Katherine out," Evans said from behind the menu.

Quinn nodded, turned the nearest mug coffee side up, and set his elbow on the closed menu. He wanted the farmer's omelet.

"So you don't get along?" Carl crossed his arms on the tabletop.

"No, but there is hope for her. According to Ethel, her grandmother, Katherine admitted she wasn't diplomatic when she visited my office."

"Has she admitted the same to you yet?" Evans closed his menu.

"No. I doubt she will." Quinn rubbed the back of his neck. "I approved it with Strauss, and on Monday, I'm going to give the class the option of turning in their essays for a second review. I'll explain the situation—that I had food poisoning, and my thinking may have been a bit skewed when I graded their exams."

"Giving Katherine King a B is proof that you were out of your mind," Evans said.

"B is above average. Everyone appears to have forgotten that."

"Katherine is not merely above average," Evans said. "I'd like to read the essay."

"I would, too." Carl grinned.

"Following her breakup with Joe, the two-time Big Sky tennis champion I was telling you about," Evans addressed Carl, "there was a period when she wasn't quite herself. I gave her an A-minus on an essay. I've had her in four classes over the years, and that's the lowest grade I've ever given her on any assignment. Her writing shows exceptional discernment. She's sagacious."

"What's *sagacious* mean again?" Carl's brows gathered.

"Perspicacious." Evans's eyes twinkled.

The waitress took their orders, poured three coffees, and left creamer.

The day Quinn had graded the essays, he'd been

dizzy, dehydrated, and on the couch. Never again would he be so determined when he was so under the weather. He hoped Katherine King's paper wasn't an A. She needed a little jewel taken out of her King pride.

Ж

Ethel set her white Sunday purse in her lap and watched Pastor Ken walk from the podium to sit in the front pew. During the last song of the service, she planned her course of action. Pastor Ken usually exited through the doors on the west side of the sanctuary. From there, he'd make his way down the hallway to the foyer, where he'd shake hands with congregants on their way out. Therein lay Ethel's plan: to detain him in the hallway.

After the second stanza of "How Great Thou Art," she rose and scooted past her older sister Gladys's wide girth and Katherine's narrow girth into the main aisle. Burt, one of the elderly ushers, pushed an exit door open for her. He probably assumed she was having an elderly moment and heading for the restrooms. Instead, she headed for the west hallway. Sharon, one of her girlfriends, was out of her Sunday school class early and waved at her.

Sharon was wearing a dress from her summer wardrobe—light blue polyester with large hibiscus flowers. Either the dress needed a vacation or Sharon needed a tan.

"Ethel, have you heard?" Sharon bellowed. "The senior potluck is—"

"Not now, Sharon, I'm on a mission."

Their church was heavy into missions. Missions were of eternal importance. Ethel turned the corner, and hallelujah, she was the first in line for Pastor Ken. Sliding her glasses higher up the bridge of her nose, Ethel peered up at their senior pastor. "I'm so glad I nabbed you before the crowd."

"Hello, Ethel." He glanced past her down the hallway.

For now, at least, the coast was clear. She had to get straight to the point. "Do you know a verse that deals with arguing? It's not for me, but for someone very dear to me."

He smiled. "There are several verses regarding the subject. Off the top of my head, I can only come up with one. It's in Philippians chapter two. *Do everything without finding fault or arguing.* I used to have the whole verse memorized, but then I hit sixty, and whoosh." He swished a hand above his thinning gray hair.

"Wait until you hit seventy," Ethel said. "My advice is to buy sticky notes to write little reminders on, and start doing crossword puzzles while you're young. They're wonderful calisthenics for the brain." Ethel rummaged through her purse, found her cigarillo tin, and, keeping the label of her deceased husband's favorite cigar somewhat hidden from her pastor's gaze, wrote *Philippians two* on the top sticky note.

Pastor Ken probably knew the exact verse, but wanted her to read the whole chapter to find the nugget, which was wise on his part.

"Is everything okay, Ethel?"

"Yes and no. Katherine's been arguing with a professor about her grade."

Pastor Ken's thick salt-and-pepper brows rose an inch. "I see this quite a bit, Ethel, in our little university town. A student's grade becomes their identity, and a low score can often feel like a personal affront. Try and remind her that she is a daughter of the King, and her identity and value lie in Him."

"Oh . . ." Ethel patted at her heart. "I wish I had my little handheld recorder." She sighed. "Unfortunately, pride runs deep in the King family. From the minute they're born and hear their surname, they think they have something to be proud about."

"Do you have e-mail yet?" he asked.

A few congregants began to gather at the end of the hall, but Ethel had been the first in line.

"No, but I have a telephone, and I'm in the church directory." She smiled. "While I have you here, how's our church's single group?"

A dimple appeared in his right cheek. "Most folks are in their twenties, but there are some adults in their thirties and early forties."

He thought she was asking for herself. How embarrassing.

The sanctuary side doors flew open. Folks appeared to be reenacting the Israelites' exodus from Egypt. The stampede had begun.

Ж

On Monday, Katherine grabbed her backpack and kissed Grandma on the cheek. It was when she reached the back door that things felt out of routine. A yellow sticky note was attached at eye level to the door's upper glass. In her slanted cursive, Grandma had written: *Do everything without finding fault or arguing. Then you will be pure and without blame. Philippians 2:14.*

"What's this?" Katherine glanced over her shoulder at Grandma, seated at the kitchen table.

"It's a little note to you from God." Grandma peered over the top of her glasses at her.

"Oh." Katherine nodded. "His handwriting's very similar to yours."

"You might want to think about it while you're walking to school."

"Oh, okay." Katherine detached the note and pulled the door closed behind her. No one except Grandma referred to it as a walk to school. Most everyone else referred to it as campus, college, or class, but never school. She made it sound so primary.

After she walked the straight stretch on Sweet Avenue, she reread Grandma's note. *Do everything without finding fault or arguing.* Her cousin Jim had warned her that the time would come when Grandma would post her little verses and claim they were from God. She'd now lived with Grandma for two years, and this was her first official "Sticky Note from God." Maybe she wasn't doing so badly.

Perhaps, Grandma and God were right; she'd argued and found fault in Quinn Benton.

Ж

Professor Benton paced the front of the room before addressing their Civil War class. "I would like the opportunity to review your exams, and re-evaluate, if I may." He inhaled and cleared his throat. "For those of you who have your essays with you, you may hand them in now. If you don't have them, you may hand them in no later than Wednesday. I'll review them with the promise that I will not lower anyone's grade."

What? Katherine's elbow slipped off the desk. Did she miss something? Was he going to review *everybody's* essays? The decibels in the room dropped to a zero. Several students flipped open their notebooks or unzipped their backpacks.

"You can do that?" Angel LeFave was the first to speak.

"Yes." Professor Benton nodded. "I spoke to our department chair on Friday about it. She said due to the extenuating circumstances, I could." Benton cleared his throat. "I had a horrible case of food poisoning the weekend I graded your exams."

Katherine flipped to the back of her binder, where she'd hidden the light blue booklet.

"To avoid slander, I won't tell you what Chinese restaurant here in town is responsible for my near emergency room admittance. My blind date was also violently sick during the same forty-eight-hour period. We agreed it was the fried rice, or possibly the shrimp appetizers. With that aside, I tried to work through my illness by grading all the exams. In retrospect, I shouldn't have."

Chuckles of disbelief surfaced about the room. Carcasses that had littered the battlefield a week ago now sat bright-eyed and upright in the saddle. Quinn Benton had at least temporarily won back all his countrymen, except, that is, for one.

Katherine didn't completely trust him.

Chapter Eight

Friday night, Katherine studied at the library for a few hours and reached home before nine thirty. She set her book bag on the couch in the living room.

"How was your Scrabble party?" she asked Grandma.

"Betty and Sharon won," Grandma said from the recliner. "Their little potty breaks are continuing. I think they have a mini-dictionary tucked in their socks or girdles. Out of the blue tonight, Sharon came up with *onyx*. I went to high school with Sharon, and she is not bright."

"Maybe she's been studying."

"Yes, in our bathroom. Cindy called a few minutes ago and said she'd pick you up at nine forty-ish."

Katherine glanced at the clock. Benton's date must have ended early; not a good sign. She had five minutes to brush her teeth and hair, change into her jade-green V-neck sweater, and calm her nerves. As she hurried about the house with her toothbrush, she pondered Benton's evening. His blind date had been with a gal from Troy, a small logging community east of Moscow. The town was even smaller than Colfax. Benton was dating small-town girls.

"There are lights out front," Grandma said, loudly.

"Remember I'll be home late. I'll lock the front door behind me." Katherine kissed her softly wrinkled cheek. She jogged down the front steps and paused at the gate while she unlatched it. A pink carpet of petals from the weeping cherry tree covered the walkway.

"When I called earlier, your grandmother had party guests," Cindy said as Katherine clicked the seat belt buckle into place. Cindy's silver teardrop earrings glimmered in the moonlight. She wore a purple velour jogging suit, which rippled with her midsection rolls.

"She often has a foursome of ladies on Friday nights for Scrabble. I usually head to the library when they're here. They're surprisingly loud."

"Sounds like fun. Evans doesn't think Miss Troy went well. Quinn was short with him when he called."

"That's too bad."

Carl's sports car sat in the front parking space. Quinn's Volvo was parallel parked along the street. Katherine walked ahead of Cindy to the door and waited for her to catch up before ringing the bell. Her stomach fluttered. Another awkward evening lay before her. She could be studying. Why was she here? Because it's fun. She giggled to herself.

Evans swung open the door with Goliath tucked in the crook of his arm. "The party has arrived," he announced.

"Has anyone told you yet that Evans has a double doctorate? English history and psychology," Cindy asked.

Katherine nodded. "Ambitious."

"Isn't he impressive?"

"Do I hear flattering adjectives? You, women, must be talking about me." Evans passed Goliath to Cindy and placed his arms around both of their shoulders.

"We were." Cindy's eyes sparkled as she gazed up at him.

Were they becoming a couple?

In the dimly lit living room, everyone sat in the same seating arrangement as last Friday. Evans and Cindy on the couch, Carl and Katherine on the loveseat, and Quinn in the burgundy wingback chair. Evans poured tea and passed around a plate of madeleines. Katherine took one of the small scallop-shaped cakes. The heavenly hint of vanilla greeted her as she took a bite.

"These are delicious, Evans," Katherine said.

"Old family recipe." He grinned. "Let's start with your evening, Katherine. Since we last saw you, have there been any updates on your love life?"

"No, of course not." As her adviser, he knew her heavy load.

"Uh-huh." Evans cleared his throat. "Well then, I guess we're all dying to hear about Miss Troy."

"I am most definitely." Cindy rose from the couch and proceeded into the kitchen.

"You were included in the 'we,' darling," Evans said.

Benton cleared his throat. In the kitchen, a flash of movements caught Katherine's eye. In a corner of the island, where hopefully, only she could see, Cindy waved a cake box back and forth. An empty cake box.

Katherine suppressed a smile and returned her attention to the conversation at hand. "Remember, everyone, Quinn is longwinded on Friday nights." Evans refilled his teacup as Cindy returned to her spot beside him.

For the occasion of meeting Miss Troy, Benton had worn a U of I gold colored polo and khaki-colored Dockers pants. If he put on a baseball cap, he'd look like a golfer; but that's right, he'd donated his clubs to Goodwill.

"I arrived in Troy right on time, and then it took ten minutes longer than I expected to find her place." He smirked. "She'd given me directions over the phone, but I hadn't written down every twist and turn. I know everyone's been there, but—"

"I love Troy," Cindy interrupted. "A girlfriend and I went to a harvest festival there once. It was like reliving the early 1900s."

"Don't get us off track, love, we're trying to find out what Benton loves about Troy," Evans said.

"You're right, Evans, it's like watching an interactive movie." Carl nabbed a madeleine. Hopefully, tonight wasn't the season finale. Despite Carl and Benton's presence, the professors' group recaps had quickly become the highlight of Katherine's week.

"Like I told you, Benton's blind dates are very entertaining," Evans said.

"I haven't said a thing." Benton held his tea saucer in both hands. "Her place is on a flag lot. A little manufactured home with a woodstove and a large dog kennel. If she didn't have a grove of pine trees in her front yard, she'd have a view of town. I remember sitting in the front room thinking: Here's a woman in her early thirties who's well established and probably getting set in her ways, and we have little in common, except she did say she was a Christian." Quinn glanced in Katherine's direction for some reason. "There were no books anywhere, just a TV guide."

"Oh, the evening was a dud"—Evans nodded—"an absolute letdown."

"You have to remember, Quinn, that when I met her, it was at a Pampered Chef party, and I wasn't able to learn a lot about her," Cindy said. "You'd just told us about your date with the Genesee woman—blind date number three—and how you didn't find her the least bit attractive. I thought you might find this woman attractive. She enjoys cooking, and has only been married once."

"It's not your fault, Cindy." He eyed her over the top of his teacup. "I'll call her Samantha."

Evans leaned toward Cindy. "I still find it odd that Benton gives the women fictitious names now that Katherine and Carl are in on our get-togethers."

Katherine's cheeks warmed. The lighting was low; maybe no one could tell.

"Why is that, Quinn?" Cindy asked.

"Now that my audience is larger, the odds of someone meeting Samantha have increased."

"If he were ever to talk bad about me," Katherine said, "he has my permission to change my name also."

"I'm so glad you're here tonight, Katherine," Evans said. "You've already brightened the boring evening that we're about to relive."

"I second that." Carl grinned.

Katherine suppressed a giggle.

"It gets a bit better." Benton cleared his throat. "Samantha made dinner."

"How romantic. Yes, Cindy, I am hinting." Evans patted her nearest hand.

"She baked frozen lasagna. She's into freezing what she refers to as her own TV dinners. The noodles were crunchy, the sauce skimpy, and there was no meat." He directed his attention to Cindy. "During dinner, she showed me a part of her body that I'm sure she didn't show you."

Cindy's eyes grew enormous.

"She has tattoos on her biceps, which were quite

ripped for a woman."

"Your date was a total dud"—Evans slapped his knee—"and you're embellishing for our benefit."

"What kind of tattoos?" Cindy nudged Evans. "If I remember right, she put on a leather jacket before she left the party that night."

"On her right arm was a rose, and tattooed on her left arm was her ex-husband's name in the middle of a heart."

"What's her ex-husband's name?" Evans asked.

Benton peered at the ceiling. "Chuck."

"Heebie-jeebies." Evans scratched the side of his neck.

"What'd she serve for dessert?" Katherine asked.

"Sponge cake, the freezer kind—and it wasn't entirely thawed—with fresh strawberries, but I'm getting to that. There I was sitting on her deck, overlooking the pines and listening to nature, when I hear a Harley motorcycle rev up her gravel driveway."

"No!" Evans said. "I entirely misread you tonight. I thought you'd had the most mind-numbing evening, but it's the opposite—you're in the midst of post-traumatic stress."

"She brings out three dishes of strawberry shortcake. Did you catch that? Three. And informs me that her ex-husband and she are still very close. Her father passed away a few years ago, and her ex-husband's taken it upon himself to interview her dates."

Cindy leaned forward. "Has Charles remarried?"

"No."

"I hope he didn't follow you here." Evans peered toward the front windows.

"Of course not." Benton continued, "Out the patio door walks this 250-pound-plus dude, black leather coat, chains, boots, and he sits down at this little round table with us and proceeds to drill me."

"Go on," Carl said.

"He threw questions at me: Why did my fiancée and I split? Have I ever been into drugs? Have I ever been convicted of homicide? Nothing about my education."

He'd been engaged. Perhaps that's where his bitterness stemmed from.

"How's Samantha during this time?" Cindy asked.

"Smiling. I think she gets a kick out of his jealous behavior. He was still there when I left."

"Did you want to ask her out again?" Evans asked.

Benton's brows furrowed. "You're kidding, right?"

"You should start journaling," Cindy said. "It would be healing."

"Healing?" Evans repeated.

"Yes, that's how my therapist used to refer to it, years ago."

"Benton is quite healed. Now he only needs counseling due to his blind dates. Who's next? I've forgotten."

"Miss Palouse."

"Oh, the woman you've been waiting months to meet." Evans eyes narrowed "Now, she's canceled on you once before if I remember correctly."

"Unexpected company dropped in from out of town."

"Yes, well, next Friday will be a recap that none of us will want to miss." Evans nodded toward Carl and Katherine.

"Katherine, I thought I'd take you home tonight,"

Benton said, with no warning. "Supposedly, I live a few blocks from you."

Wasn't he against taking her home? Was it a treaty or a dare?

"Benton, you know . . . I wanted to drive Katherine home." Carl nodded toward her like they'd discussed this earlier over a game of pool.

"Thank you both, but Cindy is taking me." Katherine gripped her hands tightly in her lap.

"I'm sorry." Cindy waved a hand. "Evans and I need to work on lesson plans, again."

Cindy had stayed so late last week.

"After golf tomorrow morning, we're going to The Breakfast Club," Evans said, looking at Benton.

"I'll just meet you there again. I didn't find clubs this week," Benton said. "I went to Goodwill twice. And I've decided it's a sign: I don't ever need to play again."

"You can rent clubs at the clubhouse," Evans said.

"No, I find golf to be a very frustrating way to spend good money."

Carl chuckled. "The only reason Evans wants you to come is so he has someone to beat."

"I'm well aware of the reason I'm invited."

"Katherine, do you have plans tomorrow?" Evans asked. "The breakfast invitation extends to you ladies as well."

"Joe and I are playing tennis in the morning."

"Not the Joe Hillis?" Evans asked.

"Yes, we play every Saturday. I go from the courts to the library."

"Isn't he your old flame?" Evans asked.

He only pretended not to remember. Five years ago in his class, she'd written her infamous Joe List.

All the reasons she'd never fall in love with Joe Hillis again. After writing it, she'd slid it in her backpack, and somehow, God forbid, it had ended up inside the typed essay she'd handed in to Evans. He'd read it and promptly lost it. For weeks, she'd fretted it would turn up in the *Argonaut*, the U of I student paper.

"Joe and I are good friends now."

"Well, Katherine, that's nice to hear, but between you and me, friendship rarely works between old flames," Evans said. "Take my first ex-wife, for example, one always likes one more than the other."

"Then Joe and I are the exceptions."

"That's a very nice quality, Katherine," Carl said.

"It hasn't happened very often in your case, has it, Carl?" Benton picked his mug up from the side table.

Was he trying to warn her about Carl? Why else would Benton offer to take her? He didn't take students home.

"Benton, be nice," Evans said. "How about whoever wins golf tomorrow gets to take Katherine home next Friday?"

"Sounds fair to me," Carl said.

"Evans!" Cindy giggled. "I'm sure Katherine won't agree to being a golf trophy."

It was almost one thirty in the morning. The whole conversation was a bit ridiculous, really, but entertaining. Katherine stretched and yawned.

"It's time to go, Katherine. Get your things."

Wow. . . Benton was indeed taking her home tonight.

Chapter Nine

Katherine slipped her shoes on at the door and waved her goodbyes. Cindy, Evans and Carl were still seated in the front room. She slid past Benton as he held open the door. The air was brisk. When she reached the aggregate driveway, she waited for his stride to fall in line with hers.

"Why the dramatic change?" she asked.

"Carl doesn't need to be taking you home this late at night." He swiveled his keys around one finger before clutching them in his hand.

"You don't trust him, do you?" The house and street were blanketed in dark shadows.

"Not entirely. I wouldn't want my granddaughter going home with him."

"Oh, I didn't know you had grandchildren."

"I don't. I was thinking of your grandmother." He paused near her door and unlocked her side first before he walked around to his.

How long had it been since she'd been on a one-mile date with a guy? *Put the thought away. He's your professor.* "Why are you driving me home tonight? I mean, you were so opposed to it last week."

"It was Carl or me. Now, Miss King, I think we should play the silent game for the rest of the way home."

Good thing she didn't like the man at all. Not one

bit. "Thank you for being neighborly." She sat stiffly, her hands in her lap.

He turned on the radio to "Unchained Melody," one of the most romantic songs of all time. Thankfully, he spun the dial to another station.

"Why would Evans try and set me up with Carl?" She shook her head. "Let me reword that. If Carl is indeed a snake-oil womanizer, why would my dear Professor Evans, of all people, try and set me up with him?"

"Evans thinks solely on an academic level." Leaning toward the dash, Benton adjusted the dial to another station. "You Are So Beaut—" He spun the dial. "Carl usually likes women with low IQs. Evans *hoped* you'd be a breath of fresh air."

"Oh, I see . . . and you don't think I've been."

"You were smart enough to decline him." He shrugged. "From now on, not another word."

"Okay, but . . . I don't understand. Last week you referred to Carl as a decent human being."

"He is." Benton tuned the station to KMOK out of Lewiston, and "To All The Girls I've Loved Before . . ." He turned off the radio. "But Carl's not a Christian. Now, please be quiet."

"That is very important to me." How did Benton know she was a Christian? It probably wasn't something he'd figured out on his own. Maybe Cindy had told him.

"What religion are you?" she whispered. A number of possibilities came to mind.

"I'm also a Christian."

"Oh." She held up a pointer finger. "Are all the women you've been blind dating Christians, or is it—"

"Dating is about marriage. I do not want to be yoked with an unbeliever. So, yes, to answer your question, quite a few prospects have been eliminated for want of a better word, with the *Are you a Christian* question."

"Eliminated?" She tried to think of a softer synonym, but only eradicate and exterminate came to mind.

"Most people date with the intention of marriage, and I'd prefer to date someone who shares my beliefs."

"I agree." She nodded. "Uh, I have one more question."

"Miss King, self-control is not one of your gifts."

"I beg to differ." Now that they were alone, he sounded like he knew his Bible. "If there are any cars on the road, should I duck down in the seat?" He'd been so worried last week.

"Yes, but be quiet about it. Now shh!" In front of Evans's mailbox, he did a U-turn and headed south.

The man was serious.

"If you had duct tape, it would be easier." She peered out her side window at the dark shadows of East City Park.

He laughed—a solid, hearty laugh like he genuinely couldn't contain it.

Despite the hour, she found herself almost smiling in Quinn Benton's company.

He took a right on Sixth Street.

"Grandma's exact address is—"

He held up his hand. "I'm almost certain I know where it is."

"Did you look us up in the phone directory?" Maybe he was the one she needed to worry about, not Carl.

"No, but Cindy said it was a few blocks off the Troy highway."

"Well, you've obviously never taken a class from Cindy. She's great with facts, but not with observations."

"That's insightful of you, but I'm pretty sure I can get us there based on what I remember her saying. Now be quiet and let me drive."

"Okay, Mr. Benton." She bit her tongue.

On Sixth Street, they headed west. In the other lane off in the distance, the headlights of one car headed east. Katherine leaned forward in the seat. The seatbelt restricted her. She undid her seat belt and leaned forward chest to knees until the headlights passed. She sat back up in the seat and rebuckled.

He chuckled. "I find this amusing enough that I'm almost tempted to drive to WinCo."

Driving to WinCo Foods meant driving west across town to the Palouse Empire Mall. Miles away, with a lot of stoplights. "I thought you liked being employed by the U of I. I suppose you could still get a job there as a janitor."

"Shh!" he said, reminding her of the quiet game. He took a left on Lynn, a right on Mabelle, and then a quick left on Logan. He knew his little side streets almost as well as he knew his pocket-sized towns.

Slowing the vehicle to a stop, two blocks too early, he pulled up in front of a white bungalow, shifted into park, and grinned across the console at her. She shook her head. He had no idea where she lived.

He eased the sedan slowly forward to the next house, shifted into park, looked at her, and waited. She rolled her eyes. For some reason, he was leaning toward the west side of the street, which was correct, but he was one block and four houses shy.

He turned sharply into a driveway across the street and turned off the engine. It was an older ranch-style home with nice landscaping.

She suppressed a smile and batted her lashes. This could go on all night.

He reached toward her and pretended to shake her by the neck, without touching her, of course. She almost laughed out loud. In the dimly lit cab, their eyes met. The knot in her chest cinched tight. *He's your professor and entirely off limits.*

Benton pulled out of the driveway and headed north, the wrong direction. He pulled up alongside a single-level brick home and pointed toward the well-lit front door. Palm up, hand held shoulder high, he waited for her response.

Brows raised, and trying to appear apologetic, she shook her head. In a strange way without words, they were getting along.

They crossed Lewis Street and headed up a small hill to a white farmhouse that sat back in the trees. He put his right blinker on as he simultaneously took a right into the long gravel driveway. She touched the shoulder of his navy-blue jacket and shook her head.

His arm reached around the back of her headrest, as he shifted into reverse. They were going to grow old together in his Volvo.

House by house, Benton drove north. Pausing at Sixth Street, his headlights shone on a small sign across the two-lane road: Logan Street. He glanced at her.

Katherine shook her head. He turned around in the next driveway and headed back toward the Troy highway. The streets were deserted. Most likely all their neighbors were asleep—as they should be—in the quiet university town. One by one, he pulled up alongside the houses on the west side of the street. Home by home, she shook her head. He quietly became more dramatic, shaking his hands in the air, grimacing.

She covered her mouth, stifling a laugh. They were having fun. Too much fun.

Her future began to unfold before her, making her feel uneasy. If he knew where she lived, then he might stop by and see Grandma. The heart tug sounded mutual. If he ever did see Grandma, she'd invite him in for coffee. And someday, heaven forbid, Katherine would come home, and Quinn Benton and Grandma would be playing Scrabble at their kitchen table. The next house, whichever one it was, she was going to pretend it was hers and get out.

He crossed over Lewis Street onto Logan. At the end of the next two blocks, Grandma's white picket fence came into view. There were only two houses left on the west side of Logan, Grandma's and then her neighbor's across Hunter Street between her and the Troy highway.

He pulled up beneath the large weeping cherry tree in front of Grandma's house. Katherine looked out the passenger window. The street lamps outlined the white picket fence and the yellow bungalow home. Shoulders heavy, Katherine shook her head.

Lines creased his forehead as he shifted back into drive.

"Do you give up?" She broke the silence.

"Yes, I've nearly depleted the neighborhood, unless, of course, it's that home." He pointed across Logan to the Wootens' home. They weren't Grandma's favorite neighbors, and their front door was very visible from the street. The neighbors Grandma had the best rapport with were the Hamiltons right next door, whose home they'd already passed. If he backed up and dropped her off at their front door, he'd be able to see her walk up. The best route was the gravel easement that ran along the west side of Grandma's detached garage. She'd have him drop her off back there, and she'd pretend to walk to the Hamiltons' back door.

"Take a right here on Hunter."

"Huh?"

"You take a right here on Hunter Street, and then there's a gravel easement past this garage." She narrated while he drove. "Right here before the maple tree, you take a right."

"I never would have known this street was here."

"It's not really a street; it's an easement. We use the back door, not the front."

"It's exactly one block off the Troy highway. Cindy was wrong."

"I tried to tell you that."

"That's why you were so quiet." He drove up alongside the Hamiltons' back gate and shifted into park.

"Good night, Miss King." He turned and rested a hand along the top of her bucket seat.

"Good night." She glanced toward the dark bungalow. A laurel hedge blocked most of the view into their backyard, and unlike Grandma's house, they hadn't left the light on.

She gripped the door handle. "Thank you, Mr. Benton."

"Thank you for keeping the title in tack."

At the Hamiltons' back gate, she glanced over her shoulder and waved. Benton sat motionless behind the wheel. She lifted the latch and then entered the dark confines of their shadowy yard. His car still had not moved. The Hamiltons only had Fritz, an eleven-year-old Scottish terrier, which Grandma claimed was deaf.

No Great Dane or Rottweiler to worry about. She took the brick walkway halfway to the neighbors' back door before hiding behind their apple tree. Benton's car slowly rolled up the long easement. The glowing red tail-lights eventually disappeared.

She smiled at her brilliance.

Ж

Fences and detached garages lined the long, gravel, pothole-ridden alley. By the time Quinn cleared the narrow easement, Katherine was undoubtedly inside brushing her teeth. He pulled into his driveway, parked, and, curiosity getting the best of him, dialed Evans's number.

"What is it, Benton?" Evans's voice came on the line.

"May I speak with Cindy, please?"

"She has a cell phone." There was a heavy sigh as Evans handed her the phone.

"Yes, Quinn."

"Katherine's grandma's house . . . I though you said it's on the corner of Hunter and Logan Street? A yellow bungalow with a large, umbrella-like pink tree overhanging the road."

"Yes, there's a flowering pink tree. Right on the corner. Why?"

"Did you *actually* see her come out of the house?"

"Yes, Quinn. What are you getting at?"

"You saw her come out of the yellow bungalow on the corner of Hunter and Logan? Out the front door? There's a white picket fence in front, and a porch with a bush on each side with lavender-colored flowers."

"Yes, Quinn—they're called rhododendrons. Twice now I've seen Katherine come out the front door, down the porch steps, out the little white picket gate, and to my car. Why?" She was doing a good job of narrating their conversation for Evans as well.

"Ask him if she's still alive. Or is he just dropping off the body?" Evans said in the background.

"Quinn, why are you calling?" Cindy sounded concerned.

"No reason. Thanks." He flipped his phone closed. He wasn't about to tell them that Katherine had no intentions of telling him where she lived. She'd out-and-out lied.

That woman!

Before his front door closed behind him, his phone vibrated. He set his keys on the coffee table, sat down, and leaned his head back against the top of the couch.

"What, Evans?"

"What are you implying, Benton? Did she have you drop her off at a different house?"

"She led me to believe she lives at the neighbor's home, right next door. She had me drive around back, up an easement alley area. She went in through the back gate."

"And, you watched her go in the back door of the neighboring home?" Evans now narrated for Cindy.

"Not exactly. I tried to watch her. It wasn't well lit, and then she disappeared into the side of the hedge."

"She disappeared into the side of the hedge?"

"Yes, that's *exactly* what I said."

"How did the two of you get along prior to her telling you the wrong house?"

"Surprisingly well. We played the quiet game for the latter part of the drive. I sometimes play it with my niece, Hailey. When she chatters too much, the game works like a charm."

"You played the quiet game because you felt Katherine was chattering too much?" Evans said.

"No, I wanted to see if it were possible for us to get along without arguing."

"So you played the quiet game to avoid arguing, and then Katherine led you to believe she lives at the neighbors'. I know there's a conclusion here."

Quinn studied the textured ceiling. "Yes, I came to the same conclusion."

"I don't know why you were so insistent on driving her home. Carl *wanted* to drive her home."

"You know very well why." Quinn rolled a kink out of his neck. "You were getting ready to invite her next Friday, and I'd already told you tonight's her last time with the group."

"I didn't invite her here for you; I invited her for Carl."

"She doesn't like Carl, plus she's not comfortable with him taking her home. So I get stuck taking her home."

"Shouldn't we take a vote?"

"No, I'm the featured speaker."

"That you are, Benton, that you are."

Chapter Ten

On his way home from work Monday afternoon, Quinn took a left off the Troy highway. Usually, he drove home on Logan Street, but today he'd taken Hunter, the short gravel side street so that he could drive past the south side of the Kings' home instead of the front. Hoping he wouldn't run into Katherine, he watched the yellow bungalow and yard for Ethel.

He grinned at the sweet memory of her visit to his office.

A wide-brimmed straw hat bobbed near the side picket fence, and then he glimpsed her lean, slightly stooped figure beneath it. Carrying a long weed, Ethel ambled toward a debris can. Quinn rolled his car to a stop beside the gate and powered down the automatic window. Would she recognize him?

"Is there something I can help you with?" Ethel ambled closer, set one hand on top of the gate, and adjusted her amber-framed glasses.

"Hello, Mrs. King, I'm not sure if you remember me."

"Professor B.!" She lifted the latch and nudged the gate open.

"I don't know if you've heard that we're almost neighbors. I live around the corner on Lynn Street." He shifted into park as she approached.

"Well, I'll be. How in the world did you ever figure it out?" Using her forearm, she brushed her hair away from her face and then set both of her pink-gardening-gloved hands on her narrow hips. "Does Katherine know?"

He nodded. Her granddaughter hadn't told her a thing.

"Shame on her. I was afraid I'd never see you again."

"I agree with you." *Shame on Katherine.*

"I told Katherine about how we'd hit it off, and of course, she wasn't very happy on account of the B. Did she ever apologize?"

"She hasn't." He frowned.

"I see." He could tell by the furrowed wrinkles on her brow that her granddaughter's hard-heartedness concerned her. "I've been praying about it. I never told you how embarrassed she was for the way she behaved. Maybe given time, you'll see that she rarely behaves that way." Ethel glanced toward the house. "She's home now. Otherwise, I'd invite you to have dinner with us. It's just horrible leftovers." She waved a hand. "A ramen noodle salad that I made from my girlfriend Sharon's recipe, and it tastes nothing like the one she brought to my Scrabble party last month. I swear she left out something important when she wrote the recipe. The ingredients cost me ten dollars, and I just can't bring myself to throw the rest away. In the old days, we would have just given it to the chickens, but they're too much work for me now."

Quinn smiled and nodded. Ethel had no idea he'd seen Katherine the last two Fridays and even brought her home once.

"Why don't you come over for dinner tomorrow?" She smiled. "About five o'clock. We'll have meatloaf. I'm in the phone book, the only listing under King."

"What about your granddaughter?" He suppressed a chuckle.

Ethel's brows lifted. "She has the same number too, but she didn't want her name listed."

"What I meant is . . . won't Katherine mind that you've invited me to dinner?"

"We won't tell her." Ethel pretended to zip her lip as she glanced toward the house. "If she finds out about our secret meeting—she finds out. In the meantime, I'm not telling her."

"Why's that?"

"She'll be so happy we're not having Top Ramen noodle salad again that she may not even notice you."

"I find that hard to believe." Like Ethel, he watched the west-facing windows in case Katherine happened to look out for some reason.

"I'll make meatloaf. Katherine loves my meatloaf. If you ever want to buy me flowers, I'm fond of yellow. Red is far too serious, and should be reserved for very special occasions."

"I'll try and remember that, Ethel." He grinned.

Now was as good a time as any to make a run to Tidyman's. He'd get a few groceries and some yellow flowers for Ethel.

Ж

Keyed up about seeing Professor B. again, Ethel told herself to get a grip, or Katherine would know she was up to something. She took the leftovers out of the fridge, set the Tupperware containers on the counter, and announced, "Dinner's ready."

After three days of having Top Ramen noodle salad for dinner, maybe Katherine would be so hungry tomorrow she'd be too weak to complain about Quinn Benton. Ethel giggled.

"Why are you in such a good mood?" Katherine noticed immediately.

"Oh." Ethel waved a hand. "It's just that tonight's our last night having these terrible leftovers."

"Again." Katherine pulled a plate down from the cupboard. "The noodles are so soggy, Grandma. I don't mean to complain."

"They're awful. Let's make toast to help fill us up."

Katherine took the yellow quilted cover off the toaster that resided on the counter next to the boxed cereal. Next, she plugged it in and slid two pieces of Roman Meal bread between the rungs.

Tomorrow night was going to be so much fun. Ethel couldn't wait to see the look on Katherine's face when she saw Professor B. sitting at their kitchen table.

"What are you so giggly about, Grandma?"

Wide-eyed, Ethel bit the insides of her mouth. "I'm on a new medicine," she fibbed. "It's to control gas."

"I'm sure your doctor referred to it as flatulence, not gas."

"You're right, it's to control flatulence." Just saying the word made Ethel giggle. "He warned me that there might be silly side effects."

"I've never heard of uncontrollable giggling being a side effect."

"Haven't you ever heard of laughing gas?"

A smile escaped Katherine's otherwise serious demeanor.

"Are there any other silly side effects mentioned on the label?"

"Yes, the desire to make meatloaf. I'm craving it. I'm going to make it tomorrow."

"Grandma, before I forget, Joe invited me to lunch on campus tomorrow."

"But . . . you'll be home for dinner?"

"Yes." Katherine dribbled ranch dressing over the noodle salad.

The green onions had shriveled, and the ramen noodles were saturated in soy sauce. Ethel had always been a firm believer in not throwing good food away—even when it wasn't good. No wonder Katherine wanted to eat on campus.

"Part of Joe's coaching package is a food plan. He lives off campus now, and the only thing in his refrigerator is Cherry Coke."

"Oh, when did you see inside his refrigerator?" Ethel set down her fork. Were Katherine and Joe seeing each other again?

"He told me, Grandma."

Ethel let out a relieved sigh. "So, you'll still be home in time for meatloaf tomorrow night?" Half the fun of having Professor B. over would be seeing Katherine's reaction.

Katherine nodded. "I'll come home *after* lunch."

"Not on Joe's motorbike, I hope."

"Grandma, you were married and had three boys by my age. Twenty-eight," Katherine reminded her. "Joe can drive me home on his motorbike if I want."

"Honor your parents in the Lord, and you'll live a long life," Ethel said, adding a sigh. She didn't like the idea of Katherine sitting so close to Joe again. Usually, women wrapped their arms around a fellow when they were together on a bike. It would be best if Katherine just walked home, or . . . was there any possible way Professor B. could pick her up?

"You've got that look you get when you're scheming something."

"What look?" Ethel lifted her brows.

"Your, uh . . . wrinkles gather right here." Katherine pointed to the bridge of Ethel's nose. "And you get this faraway look. Whatever you're scheming, Grandma, know that I love you."

Ethel sighed. When Katherine got all sweet like this, she just wanted to tell her everything, even her news about Professor B. coming to dinner. She mentally zipped her lips together and for the moment, at least, was able to resist the temptation.

Chapter Eleven

"Would a Miss Katherine King please stay after class?" Professor Evans asked with a wave of his hand from the front of the classroom. There were only nine students in the class, and they all knew each other by name.

"Yes, I will." After the others had left, Katherine remained seated in the second row while Evans filed lecture notes into his briefcase. "You wanted to speak with me, Professor Evans?" she asked.

"Yes." Setting his hands on his hips, he scanned the thirty desk classroom. Wood paned windows lined the north wall of the century-old building, which overlooked the elm-lined walkway below.

"Prepare yourself, Katherine." Evans inhaled deeply.

She nodded and did the same.

"While Carl, Cindy, and I are especially fond of your presence on Friday nights . . . Benton is not."

The truth—though not a huge surprise—stung only a millisecond.

"I'm not to inform you of this, but Benton's intent on my not inviting you again."

"I see." The truth stung for several seconds this time. And they'd gotten along so well last Friday, early Saturday morning, when he'd taken her home. Or, at least, she'd thought so.

"Cindy and I have reached the conclusion that maybe this all stems from your visit to his office."

Really? Lately, it had felt like they were almost past their rocky start. Maybe there were other reasons behind Benton's dislike of her.

"Do you enjoy our Friday night get-togethers?" Evans peered over his spectacles at her.

"Yes, very much."

"The majority loves having you there. We'd overrule him if we could, but without Benton, we'd be wanting for entertainment."

In his own way, Benton was very entertaining.

Evans pointed to the front-row seats. "Outline, if you will, a persuasive apology for Benton. We love having you there on Fridays. Do your winsome best. Show him the Katherine we so dearly love. I'll sort through my briefcase for however long it takes."

With dutiful posture, Katherine remained seated and stared at the blank piece of paper. *Pride* was the first word that came to mind. The B had been such a blow. But it all came down to pride. She began writing. Hmm . . . what else did he dislike about her? Maybe it was merely her presence.

Evans chuckled. "That's where that bill disappeared to."

"A little spring cleaning?" She glanced his direction.

"Yes, what was that?" Brows furrowed, he read something.

"I said, 'A little spring cleaning?'"

"Yes, I should every spring," he mumbled. Folding the paper, he looked over the top of his briefcase at her. "Already I've unearthed a few things I've been searching for—for eons."

She nodded and penned her last thought. Rising, she tucked the outline for her *sorry* speech into her front pocket and returned her pen to her backpack.

"I'll escort you halfway." Evans clicked his briefcase closed.

Katherine laughed. "You *do* want me at your get-togethers."

"Yes, this visit is to apologize, nothing more. Short and sweet, like Carl's last girlfriend."

Katherine's pulse raced. "I feel like a third grader going to the principal for the first time. I mean second," she confessed as they walked up the stairs to the third floor.

"Good, remember to have that kind of respect and regret when you're in Benton's office. Show him the Katherine that Cindy, Carl, and I so dearly love."

"You know how to make a girl feel convicted. I'm sorry, Professor Evans, that it's—"

"Save that for Benton; it's a very good first line, except insert his name where you put mine. Cindy and I will be next door in my office."

"You make it sound prearranged."

"Yes, to be honest, it was a mutual idea."

Tapping her on the shoulder, Evans paused. "I'll have to walk ahead now, Katherine. I don't want Benton to see the two of us together. Pause a moment, but try not to pause so long that you change your mind. Stick to the plan. Short and sweet." Evans continued down the wide corridor ahead of her.

In between classrooms, Katherine leaned against the wall, took the paper out of her pocket, and reviewed her *sorry* speech. Maybe it was a little too longwinded. Maybe she should keep it simple, something like . . . "I'm sorry I behaved so . . . abominably." Hmmm . . . Dear Lord, help me to be humble, not proud. Help me to appear broken, even though I'm not completely broken. Help me to say a nice, meaningful apology. I would like to go to the professors' group in the future. I suppose I am willing to brownnose Benton if that's what it comes to. Not for a grade, mind You, but for the group. Help my heart to be right, amen."

The light was on in Benton's office. She paused outside his door and knocked.

"Come in."

Be brave and get it over with. She inhaled deeply and closed his door behind her. Benton turned slightly in his chair, his eyes widening before turning to face his desk. "Hello, Miss King. I was expecting Evans."

"Hello, Professor Benton. It's just me."

"Why are you here?" He did not sound pleased.

"Well, um . . ." Her shoulders dropped. "I'm not here to hound you if that's what you're worried about. Evans informed me that I need to apologize for my first visit."

"Evans!" He shook his head.

"Yes, he said you don't want me at the professors' group on Friday because of my lack of apology. And I'll be honest with you . . ." Without his bidding, she sat down in the chair kitty-corner to his desk. "Despite Carl's presence, I enjoy the get-togethers." She glanced at the industrial-style clock on the wall. It was already noon, and she'd forgotten to remind Grandma that she'd be having lunch with Joe. If Grandma forgot, she'd undoubtedly worry.

"Is it all right if I use your phone?"

"Yes." Instead of handing her the base, he simply stretched the long black cord in front of him and handed her the receiver.

"What's the number?" he asked.

"Eight, eight, two." If she said their number in its entirety, would he remember it? She cruised around the back of his chair and, blocking his view of the phone, pressed the remaining four digits.

"You're too much, Katherine King." He sighed as Grandma's voice came on the line.

"Grandma, it's Katherine." Phone cord wound around the back and front of Professor Benton. Maybe Cindy and Evans were watching on a mini hidden camera. She glanced up at the corners of his ceiling and didn't see any signs of one. A pot of yellow gerbera daisies sat atop his desk. Hmm . . . the man finally had an admirer. The poor woman had no idea.

"I wanted to remind you, Grandma, that I'm having lunch with Joe."

"You're not seeing Joe again, are you, Katherine?"

"I'll be seeing him when I eat lunch." Grandma had always voiced her aversion to Joe. She simply didn't understand how a male and a female could be good friends. It was probably a generational thing.

Behind her, Benton loudly cleared his throat. "Tell Ethel hello for me."

She wasn't about to tell Grandma hello.

"Did I hear someone in the background, Katherine?"

"No, no one of importance, Grandma."

"Ethel, it's Quinn Benton," he said loudly.

Katherine covered the mouthpiece and closed her eyes. Now Grandma would bombard her with a gazillion questions.

"Oh, tell Quinn hello."

She wasn't about to tell Quinn hello. Grandma would then ask her to hand him the phone, and when

Katherine refused, she'd give her the little "honor thy grandparents" lecture.

"I'm in his office to apologize"—she lowered her voice—"for my first visit."

"And I'd had such a fine morning." Benton was probably addressing the plant.

He had an admirer, possibly one of his past blind dates. Maybe no one had told him that yellow meant friendship. In romance, yellow flowers were the kiss of doom.

"Oh, I'm so proud of you, honey. I need to go, as I'm already running late for the senior luncheon. I'll get off right now, and say a wee prayer for the two of you." Grandma hung up on her.

"Uh, my grandmother says hello." She returned to the folding chair and sat down. The thick, black curlicue phone cord encased three sides of Benton.

Instead of untangling himself, he rested his chin on his hand, looking at her. He appeared bored by her charades. She bit the insides of her cheeks to keep from smiling. If he didn't do something about the cord soon, she'd flub her apology.

"Miss King, I'm at the point that an apology is no longer necessary. And yes, I am sorry to say that I do not desire your presence at Evans's get-togethers. He knows full well it has nothing to do with the apology or lack thereof. It has more to do with . . ."

Was he implying that he didn't care about her as a person or a student, not that it mattered? Well, yes, it did matter! After last Friday when he'd taken her home, and the silent camaraderie they'd shared in the car, his renewed aversion to her company surprised her.

She bit her lower lip. It was time for a stellar apology. Evans said something about respect. She needed to show Benton the same respect and regret that she would have shown Evans or Cindy given the same situation.

"Miss King . . . are you listening?"

She fished her apology outline out of her front pocket.

"Charlene Strauss, the department chair, occasionally stops by, randomly, unannounced. I value being employed by the university, and this situation could be misconstrued." His chest expanded beneath the cord.

"It's not like I wrapped it multiple times and knotted in the back and slapped a swath of duct tape across your mouth." She bit the insides of her cheeks at the picture she'd painted. "Unwind yourself if you're so inclined."

"*Unwind yourself*, what kind of term is that?" He sighed deeply and glanced toward the door.

"Professor Benton, I'm sorry that it's taken me so long to tell you that I am indeed sorry for my behavior in your office."

"I think now is a good time to interrupt, Miss King, as I already see the need for an ongoing apology. I think it best that you simply consider the job done."

She hadn't even reached the heart of her sorry speech. "After several days of contemplation, I now understand why I was so abrupt, abrasive"—she glanced up at him—"rude, disrespectful, and alarming."

"I forgive you."

"I'm sorry, Professor Benton. I've been convicted several times now to tell you how poorly I feel for my behavior in your office. And, it comes down to this: I was a poor loser.

"During my undergraduate years, I played tennis for the U of I."

"Evans already informed me. Apology accepted."

His tone was pleasant enough that she did not find him altogether convincing. "Though I was usually ranked fifth *and* finished fifth in the conference, I somewhat got numb to losing in important matches. I had a solid serve, good endurance, but not quite enough speed to be great. Not like Joe—he has fantastic speed and natural explosiveness."

"Yes, that's why they call him Mr. Dynamite." Benton rolled his eyes. "Now unwind me."

She glanced up from her paper. He knew Joe's nickname. Hmm . . .

"But in the classroom, I've always been able to shine. And, the B was a new emotion for me. It felt like a slam. Bottom line, Benton . . . Professor Benton." She looked directly into his eyes. "I should have been a graceful loser. I'm sorry that I wasn't."

"Apology accepted. Please untie me."

"*Untie* is the wrong verb, Mr. Benton." She walked behind him. "It's simply a matter of lifting it up, which you've been reluctant to do." Holding the receiver to the base, she lifted the cord up from around him. Was he kidding about the department chair?

"Sit down, Miss King."

She didn't like his tone and dutifully returned to the cold metal chair. He was going to threaten her with a minor lawsuit.

"Now that I no longer fear dismissal, I can focus on your first loss at Wimbledon."

She shook her head. "I am not going to repeat my apology."

"My attention was divided between Charlene Strauss popping in, and focusing on your little speech."

"I've officially apologized. Here, you can put it in your scrapbook." She placed the speech on his desk. "Who's the admirer?" She nodded toward the potted daisies. "Or are you going to make us wait until Friday to find out?"

His mouth twitched. "They're a gift for a very special lady who I'll be seeing tonight. I didn't want the flowers to wilt in the car."

"I didn't know you dated during the middle of the week."

"There's six days you don't know about." His dark brows lifted. "Or need to know about, for that matter."

"You're right. It's just that you're such an open book on Friday nights that, well, I don't think the group knows you're also a mid-weeker."

He glanced over his shoulder at the door. Of course, he was hinting. He was ready for her to leave.

"What town is she from?"

"Moscow."

"Oh, Miss Moscow. I'm surprised, Mr. Benton, you're finally dating someone closer to home. And who's the gal in the photo?" Her gaze halted on a brass-framed beauty—an auburn-haired young woman who smiled fondly at the camera.

"My sister, but don't tell anyone else that. There have been a couple of young women who like to visit my office on occasion, for tutoring, odd bits of advice, apologies." He met her gaze.

"How can you even suggest such a thing?" Maybe Angel was one of his regular visitors. She didn't doubt it.

"If you do come Friday night, I will not drive you home again. Evans knows that's the main reason I'm opposed to your company. Driving students home alone is not good protocol."

The shrill of the phone reminded her that she'd overstayed her welcome.

"Hello. Hi, Evans." He glanced at Katherine. "Miss King, consider the apology complete. Finished." He covered the mouthpiece. "Do not ever feel compelled to return to my office ever again. Do you understand?"

For a moment, there was solid eye contact between them. Awkward, yet if she were honest with herself, mesmerizing. Had he always been so appealingly attractive, or was it the angle? He had one of those fine English noses, straight and smooth.

She should leave now before he read into the, uh… stare.

"Yes, Professor Benton." She nodded. "I will never, ever, ever, ever again visit your office." She didn't want him to think she were interested. Or even put her in the same category as Angel and whoever else was visiting him.

A half smile lit his lips, but not his eyes, before he uncovered the receiver.

"Yes, Evans, Katherine's leaving. She's picking up her backpack and starting for the door."

Did he really mean what he'd said? *Do not ever feel compelled to return to my office ever again.* She set her hand on the knob.

"Yes, she's alive. I'm alive too. Yes, she apologized. Yes, it was definitely a valid apology, the finale. Yes, it's finally the end."

He sounded relieved.

Katherine scanned the dimly lit hallway for surveillance cameras. None appeared to be installed yet. From there, she strolled toward the Wallace Cafeteria, where she'd meet Joe.

Benton was her professor, and she'd just wrapped the phone cord about him, and she should never have mentioned duct tape. Would he consider her behavior flirty? What an awful thought! *He has a score of blind dates lined up, including a Miss Moscow tonight.* She couldn't possibly think about the man—he was unpredictable and flighty.

She needed to talk to Joe. Definitely not Grandma. Despite his flaws, Joe often gave good advice.

Ж

Quinn had twenty minutes before his next class. He drummed his fingertips on top of his desk and waited a few minutes in the hope that when he went to Evans's office, he'd find him there alone. What had just happened was a lot to discuss in front of Cindy and Evans at the same time. They'd often collaborate and gang up on him, but one on one, they were, for the most part, excellent listeners.

One more minute passed. He couldn't wait any longer. He knocked on Evans's office door and stepped inside. Good, he was alone. Head bent, Evans flipped through a textbook.

"We never heard any yelling. Was her admission of guilt convincing?"

"Remind me again, so we're on the same page, and I wish you wouldn't have encouraged her. Now that she's apologized, she thinks she can continue coming to the professors' group."

Evans grinned. "Sounds like you finally saw the side of Katherine we've been telling you about."

"I suppose." Quinn sat down in the solid wood chair.

Over the top of his wire spectacles, Evans peered at him. "Not only is she a very sagacious and attractive young woman, she's also amiable . . . gifted—"

"Would you say she's good with duct tape?"

Evans leaned back in his chair and folded his hands in front of his projected tummy. "What are you implying?"

Quinn waved a hand toward the door. "Your Katherine wound the phone cord around me once, and even mentioned duct tape."

Evans chuckled. "You expect me to believe that?"

"It's the truth. I was so worried about Charlene Strauss popping in to say hello and being fired on the spot, that I can only recall snippets of her lengthy Wimbledon speech."

Evans peered at him for a moment and then, picking up the phone, dialed a four digit extension, probably Cindy's. "Hi, Cindy, Benton's here. I wanted your female opinion regarding Katherine's apology when she was in his office. Yes, uh-huh. Benton said she wound the phone cord around him and mentioned duct tape." Evans glanced at him. "Yes, I'm absolutely serious. Well, you and I both know the two don't get along. Uh-huh . . ." He nodded and added a couple more *uh-huhs* before hanging up.

"What'd she say?"

"Cindy's opinion is . . . Katherine's either afraid of you or very attracted to you. Which I highly doubt. She thinks the phone cord might be her way of

---

channeling energy. I could do further research if you're so inclined?"

"Very attracted to me?" Quinn scratched the side of his neck.

"Cindy thinks it may be possible that Katherine's not even aware of it. I think it's highly unlikely myself given your history. She wouldn't even tell you where she lived. That is not the typical sign of an infatuated female."

"So your interpretation is she's afraid of me?"

"If she's afraid of anything, it's your grading system, but you're right: wrapping you in phone cord is not a logical way to improve her grade." Evans's stroked his beard.

Quinn rose to pace the small room. "So you're saying . . . Katherine is quite possibly interested in me?"

"Highly unlikely. The two of you don't get along."

How she'd gone about unwrapping the cord from around him had almost been like being at the barbershop. There'd been an indifference, not intimacy. No, he couldn't possibly think Katherine was interested in him. Like Evans had said, it didn't make one iota of sense. There was only one other theory remaining: Katherine King was afraid of him.

But that didn't make sense either. Hmm . . . his memory returned to Friday night when he'd driven her home. In an odd sort of way, they'd gotten along.

Chapter Twelve

Blond, blue-eyed, and tan, Joe grinned across the small melamine table at her. He was the best-looking older guy in the cafeteria, and many a female eye measured up Katherine—the girl with Joe Hillis. The food hadn't improved much since her freshman year when she'd lived on the tenth floor of Theophilus Tower.

"What have you been up to, Joe?" Katherine asked, hoping his update would be short so that she could share her latest.

"Christy's in love with a fellow who goes to Montana State. She may transfer there and sit out a year."

"Bummer." Christy was his best singles player. She'd been seated second in the Big Sky Conference earlier in the year before rolling her ankle.

"She's only a sophomore, right?"

Joe's nod was followed by a heavy sigh. "Did I tell you I saw Tabitha the other day?"

Tabitha was one of his old girlfriends. Joe's narrative went from Tabitha to Sarah, another old flame, who he'd seen from a distance when he'd been running stairs in the Kibbie Dome.

Katherine eyed the clock. They had fifteen minutes before Joe's next class, and if she was going to get a word in, it had to be now.

"I'm having trouble with a particular professor."

The vertical line deepened in the middle of Joe's forehead. She used to call it his thinking line. He wrapped his serving arm around the back of his chair.

"Is he hitting on you?" Joe's eyes widened.

"No."

"Then why are you so red?"

Joe saw right through her.

"He's the one who gave me a B."

Joe nodded.

"About a half hour ago, after my last class, I went to his office to apologize for how I complained last week about the B." Katherine gripped her hands beneath the table.

"Are you hitting on him?" Joe's eyes sparkled.

"No." She rubbed her eyes with both hands. "Both times that I've been to his office, I've behaved oddly, Joe." There, she'd said it.

"What do you mean, oddly?"

She shrugged. "Not myself. It's almost how I used to feel before a match."

"Adrenaline." Wide-eyed, he nodded.

"I . . . I . . . uh . . ." Flashes of the phone cord around Benton teased her memory. She should have spun his chair, for a final effect, but no, that would probably have unplugged the phone. "Um . . . I wrapped his phone cord around him . . . once. I'd just called Grandma, and the cord encased him, and then I sat down and apologized for the way I behaved my first visit."

She sighed deeply and then, slouching her shoulders, waited for Joe's opinion.

He tipped his chair back, crossed his arms, and looked around the semi-crowded cafeteria. "How many times have you gone to his office?"

"This is only the second." Katherine shook her head. "It's always because of Evans. Evans inspires me. I get up there, and then I botch it."

"Who's Evans again?"

"My favorite professor. He and Benton are best friends."

"Do you like Benton?"

Katherine peered down at her salad. "He's such a dummy."

"That's what you used to say about me." Joe chuckled. "Is he an older professor?"

"Younger."

"Do you think he's interested in you?"

"No. He wouldn't drive me home the other night when I asked." She explained how they'd been at Evans's home for the professors' group.

"It doesn't sound good, Kate."

Joe knew she didn't care for the nickname, but he still called her by it.

"But then he did take me home last week, and we had a surprisingly good couple of minutes alone in the car. And then I made the mistake of calling him Benton, without the title, and he asked me to keep it intact when I refer to him in the future."

"It doesn't sound good, Kate."

"It's a waste of mental energy. Isn't it?" She pinched the bridge of her nose. "I'm taking a heavy load, Joe. I don't have time to think about men."

"You never do." He nodded to his right. "I need to get back to work." They set their food trays on the conveyor belt and headed out the double doors into the bright sunshine.

"Do you remember your sophomore year, when we first met?" Joe jogged ahead of her on the sidewalk and walked backward so he could see her face.

"Yes." She knew exactly where the conversation was heading.

"You avoided me to the point that on my own, I never would have figured out you were interested in me."

Katherine remembered well her desire to run each time she saw Joe Hillis.

"Then our junior year, Rikki flagged me down and told me." Rikki was her old roommate. Joe would never have pursued her on his own without Rikki's insider information. "Do you like this guy, Kate?"

"Not like that." She grimaced. "He's an intelligent dummy."

"He sounds perfect for you."

"Except he doesn't like me."

"He'd be a fool not to."

"He doesn't. He abhors professor-student relationships. So do I. What am I thinking, Joe? I can't go wasting mental energy on a professor. Not to mention, I'm taking nine credits in the master's program, and . . ."

"What are you always telling me, Kate?" Joe grinned. "Maybe you should pray about it."

He grinned, jogging backward. "Gotta run. I have a one-thirty appointment." He jogged off in the direction of the Kibbie Dome—the indoor sports stadium, which looked like a giant soda can turned on its side.

Joe was right; she needed to pray about it.

"Dear Lord, be with Joe. Open his heart up to You. Help me with my studies. And about Benton, and what happened today in his office, I keep making messes. Can You somehow wipe the slate clean? And take the attraction away. It's not within my mental jurisdiction. Amen."

Chapter Thirteen

"Katherine, dinner's ready," Grandma called up the stairwell. The door clicked closed.

It was the perfect time for a study break—three times in a row she'd lost her place in the middle of the Battle of Fredericksburg. Katherine yawned and swung her legs off the bed. From Grandma's opening and closing of the door, the delicious, earthy aroma of meatloaf had climbed its way up the stairwell.

Barefoot, Katherine jogged down to the main floor. Curious if Hannah still had her little lemonade stand set up next door, she peeked through the front lace curtains. Sure enough, Hannah sat, knees swinging beneath the folding card table as she read a book.

"I'll just be a second, Grandma." Katherine grabbed two quarters from her stash on the windowsill and pulled the front door closed behind her. The little girl sat in the dappled shade and held a hand over her eyes as Katherine approached.

"What do you think of a Norwich terrier?" Hannah asked. She held out her hand palm up, keeping her cute little freckled nose behind the paperback.

"I know very little about dogs. The only one we had growing up was a lab."

"I don't want another Scottie." Hannah rolled her eyes. "After Fritz, Mom says we can't have a dog with a nose for trouble. He's always digging."

The Kings knew well Fritz's love for digging. Katherine set the quarters in Hannah's open palm. "Grandma has dinner on the table, so I better get back. Thanks, Hannah." She picked up two Dixie cups of lemonade and hip bumped the open gate. Closing Grandma's front door behind her, she giggled.

"Sounds like Mrs. Hamilton doesn't want another Scottish terrier, Grandma," she said loudly as she crossed the shag carpeting into the kitchen. "Hannah said their next dog can't have a nose for trouble. She is just the cutest little—" Quinn Benton, of all people, was seated at Grandma's Formica-and-chrome table. She set the cups down near Grandma's elbow and, making an abrupt 180-degree turn, strode out of the kitchen and back to the stairwell door.

"Katherine . . ." Grandma's voice trailed after her. "Kath . . . rine."

With her heart in her throat, Katherine set her hand on the knob. Quinn Benton was sitting at their table. Why in the world? Grandma! Her hair was down. She was wearing cut-off plaid pajama pants and an oversized gray T-shirt with a coffee spot near her belly button. She was in her relaxed study attire for when no one, especially a professor, was expected to see her.

Grandma had been giggly all afternoon, but other than that she'd provided no clues or warning.

"Katherine, Professor B. stopped by for dinner," Grandma said.

Katherine leaned her forehead against the white-painted door and closed her eyes. This was not happening.

"I made meatloaf," Grandma said.

Yellow. She'd seen yellow. There had been

something yellow on the kitchen counter. When she'd been in his office, he'd known. They'd conspired against her, formed an alliance. He knew she lived here in this house.

She inhaled and headed back into the kitchen. The yellow gerbera daisies were indeed on the counter.

Grandma was Miss Moscow!

Katherine sat down and clasped the traitor's outstretched hand. Across the length of the table, Professor Benton did the same. They bowed their heads for prayer.

"Our dear Heavenly Father, thank You for this meal, for our new friend and neighbor, for second chances, for little Hannah, and for Moscow, our wonderful little town, population eighteen and some thousand, can You believe it? And, for Your Son Jesus, who died on the cross for us and rose again on the third day. Thank You. Amen."

Katherine unfolded a yellow paper napkin over her lap and glanced in Benton's direction. "You knew you were coming here. The flowers are for Grandma." When she visited his office, did he think she was flirting? Was that why he was here now? No, he already knew he'd be here for meatloaf; that's why he'd bought the daisies.

"I kept the flowers in my office today," he informed Grandma. "I was afraid they'd wilt in my car. When Katherine visited my office to apologize, she saw them. She's under the impression they're for a Miss Moscow."

"Am I Miss Moscow?" Grandma's eyes and voice sparkled.

"Yes," Katherine said. Avoiding the gleam in Benton's eyes, she studied the white cook stove to the left of the doorway. "I should have asked who was coming to dinner, Grandma. You only make meatloaf when we're having company."

Grandma had just taken a bite and pointed to her mouth.

"Your grandmother flagged me down yesterday," Benton said.

"No." Grandma shook her head and finished chewing. "Don't you remember, Quinn? You saw me first, and rolled your Buick to a stop beside the gate."

"Volvo, Grandma. The paperboy has a Buick. It's dark blue," she informed Benton.

Grandma nodded.

"You're right, Ethel, I saw your straw hat."

"I was deadheading flowers," Grandma said.

During his drive home, he'd seen Grandma. As of yesterday, he knew that Katherine had lied. He officially knew that she didn't live at the neighbors', which also meant he was aware that she was capable of lying to keep Grandma and him apart.

"I just read in the newspaper this morning that our little old Moscow is not so little." Grandma patted Benton's arm.

"In a recent men's magazine, it was ranked as one of America's top ten college towns to live in," Benton said.

"Probably because there are so many beautiful female grad students," Grandma said, suppressing a smile.

"I'm sure the magazine was referring to the locale—fishing, boating, skiing, plus the Snake River is only thirty miles away." Katherine wanted to take her plate into Grandma's sewing room, wrap herself in quilts, and never come out.

"It sounds like Katherine's also read the article," Benton studied her.

For Grandma's sake, he was, at least, trying to be civil.

"I hope that magazine doesn't have a very wide circulation. Katherine and I like our towns small." Grandma patted his arm. The two were getting along like two elderly coots on a park bench.

"How was your senior luncheon today, Grandma?" Katherine interrupted their festivities.

"Good. Carol brought her raspberry Jell-O salad recipe that I've been after for weeks. I made one and have it setting in the fridge for dessert. I made it when I was on the phone to your mother. She called to check in, and see how your classes are going and—" Grandma adjusted her glasses—"if any men were calling here for you yet."

Katherine had just taken a swig of milk, and of course, it went down the wrong pipe. She darted to the sink and hoped to die.

Why in the world did Grandma bring it up now? Couldn't she have waited?

"I told her that there have been several men calling."

"You didn't!" While Katherine rinsed her face and hands, Benton's chuckle was steady behind her.

"Didn't you see the sticky note on the mirror? The one from Carl is only a few hours old." Grandma sounded delighted. "Carl had such a nice-sounding voice that at first, I thought he was a solicitor."

"He's from the professors' group, Grandma." Katherine strode to the curio cabinet. There on the mirror were two separate sticky notes, and of course, Joe's message was in much smaller print than her new admirer's.

"A professor?" Grandma's voice rose octaves.

"Yes, Grandma, but no one to call home about.

Did Joe say why he'd called?"

"No, not that I remember."

Why had Carl called? The man was most definitely a time monster.

She glanced at her reflection in the curio cabinet's square-framed mirror. Her cheeks were pink, her eyes bright, her hair loose about her shoulders; from the spot on her T-shirt up, she looked pleasant enough.

Why was Benton here? Was it purely on account of Grandma? It must be. For one, he was not going to date students, his or anyone else's—God forbid—and two, she and Benton couldn't stand each other.

She returned to the table and quietly finished the remainder of her meatloaf, mashed potatoes, and green beans. A large glass pan of raspberry-studded Jell-O now graced the table.

"I couldn't wait." Grandma cut the Jell-O into squares. "There's a secret ingredient in it, but you have to guess what it is before you taste it."

"I won't know without tasting." Holding the dessert plate at eye level, Katherine studied the multi-textured concoction. "Looks like there's crushed pineapple."

"There is." Grandma nodded.

"Red Jell-O," Benton said.

"Yes, that too." She giggled.

"Cool Whip," he said, referring to the middle layer of white.

"Noooo. Give up?"

"And you read the recipe through twice?" Katherine asked. For some reason, Grandma liked to wing things in the kitchen, a seat-of-the-pants type of cook.

Grandma rolled her eyes. "Carol walked me through her recipe, step-by-step. Her handwriting nowadays leaves a lot to be desired. The white stuff is sour cream. I couldn't believe it."

"It's delicious, Ethel." Benton studied his second spoonful.

The Jell-O was fruity and delicious.

"Katherine, do you think you sleepwalk?" he asked out of nowhere.

"What do you mean?" She frowned.

"Do you think you sleepwalk?" He lifted his brows. "It's not a crime. I've recently read that four percent of adults sleepwalk. It often has to do with stress."

What was he getting at? He hadn't seen her sleepwalk, had he?

"The other night when I dropped you off, I could've sworn you opened the neighbor's gate and walked through their backyard."

Her shoulders relaxed.

"Katherine does sleepwalk," Grandma said, wide-eyed. "There have been several occasions when I've been up in the middle of the night for something and had several conversations with you that you do not remember in the morning."

"That's called talking in your sleep," Katherine corrected her.

"Sleepwalking, sleep talking, they go together." Grandma was more feisty with Benton here. "You also sleep eat." Her forehead wrinkles deepened. "Remember that time I told you that you mumbled something about being a cheese whiz."

"Grandma!" She wished she'd explain something right for once.

Benton's face reddened and his cheek muscles bunched.

There had been a fund-raiser for the McConnell

Mansion in Moscow, and she'd done surprisingly well at naming samples of cheese. Much of it had been luck.

"Don't you remember?" Grandma covered her mouth with a yellow napkin while she spoke. "You'd gone to that cheese-tasting party and amazed everyone."

"You know very well I wasn't sleepwalking." Katherine addressed Benton. "I purposefully *wanted* you to believe I live at the neighbors'."

Grandma's jaw dropped. "Why in the world?"

"I don't understand either." Above a spoonful of red Jell-O, Benton's dark brows gathered.

"Because . . ." Several reasons came to mind. He was her professor, and a bachelor, at that. They already saw each other at Evans's on Fridays. "I knew there was a mutual heart tug between you and Grandma, and you're still the only professor who's ever given me a B."

Chapter Fourteen

Friday evening, while Katherine's history girls watched the second half of the *Doctor Zhivago* movie, Ethel sat at the kitchen table, working on a crossword puzzle.

The girls appeared to be having such a good time in the living room that Ethel couldn't help feeling a bit left out. Didn't Katherine trust her? She'd sworn she wouldn't say a thing about the time Quinn Benton had dined at their home, or that the yellow daisies on the living room side table were from him.

Ethel sighed and focused on the crossword. *What's a four-letter word for food for the computer?* She tapped her forehead with her pencil. How was an elderly woman without a computer supposed to know what they ate? She glanced toward the living room. Would the girls mind if she interrupted their Zhivago staring for one little word?

The phone rang. She set the puzzle aside and hoped it was Pattie; often her daughter-in-law could just rattle off the word.

"Hello." The movie was just loud enough that she covered her free ear with one hand.

"Hello, Ethel, it's Quinn Benton." He had such a deep, masculine voice. She giggled and, stepping into the kitchen, pulled the pocket door closed behind her.

"Hello." She looked out the window above the

kitchen sink toward the empty, lamp-lit street.

"How are you?" he asked.

"I'm great." His timing was perfect. "I'm in the middle of doing a crossword puzzle and . . ."

"Would you like me to let you go?"

"No, hold on a second . . ." She set the receiver on the counter and hurried to the table for her book. "You don't happen to know a four-letter word for *food for the computer*? Katherine usually helps me when I'm stumped, but she's . . . busy."

"Hmm . . ."

"I'm very computer illiterate," she confessed.

"Data."

"Data," she repeated, scanning the little boxes. "There is a *T* in the row. You may be right. Thank you, Quinn." She giggled at her good fortune, pulled the pocket door open, and returned the receiver. At the table, she filled in two more words. Why had he called? He'd asked her if she had time to talk, but then he hadn't said a word. How peculiar. Tonight was Friday; wasn't he on his blind date with . . . Ethel peered at the Latah County Credit Union calendar that she'd thumb-tacked near Katherine's side of the table. Tonight was Miss Pullman. She was so glad she'd written it in. The man's social life was like a crossword puzzle—tricky to keep track of.

Halfway through a new puzzle, the phone rang again. The poor girls. Ethel hurried to answer it.

"Hello." Orchestra music blared behind her.

"Hi, Ethel, it's Quinn Benton again."

Entering the kitchen, she pulled the pocket door closed. "Hello." He'd just called no more than thirty minutes ago; maybe he had early Alzheimer's. "Aren't you on your blind date now?"

"I was wondering if you'd mind if I dropped by? I

have a whole nacho from Alex's Restaurant in Pullman, and they're never as good the next day."

No wonder Katherine had gotten a B; the man was hard to follow.

"Drop by?"

"Yes, I thought we could share the nacho."

"Oh . . ." She giggled. "I already had dinner."

"So have I."

Was he simply saying that he just wanted to get together? She hated being alone, too.

"Come over, then, and park in back."

Ethel hung up the phone and recalled the spot on her lime-green T-shirt. A red Gatorade dribble stained the front. Trying to be as quiet as a mouse, she scurried to her room. She changed into the coral-colored T-shirt, the one on which Sharon had puff painted a row of sunflowers across the chest area. Headlights spanned the windows on the west side of her home as Quinn's car pulled into the gravel drive. He was quick. He must have been at the light at the Troy highway when he'd called.

"Is everything okay, Grandma?" Katherine asked as Ethel ambled through the living room toward the kitchen.

She gulped. If the girls found Quinn in their kitchen, Katherine would never forgive her. "Yes, honey. Make sure the girls use the front door when they leave." Ethel waited for Katherine's nod before she pulled the pocket door closed.

She patted at her short hair on her way toward the back door. Professor B. stood on the middle step, wearing a royal-blue polo and holding a white Styrofoam container.

"My blind date in Pullman didn't go very well." The lack of light in his dark eyes meant he was disappointed, tired, or maybe both. "By tomorrow, the chips will be soft. They're never as good the next day."

"What a wonderful man you are. I've been so bored." She waved him inside. Quinn brushed past her into the kitchen and set the container on the table.

"Looks like you're cooped up in the kitchen." He nodded toward the pocket door.

"Yes, Katherine and some of her girlfriends are watching a movie." Ethel took a glass down from the cupboard. "Would you like some pink lemonade?" She opened the refrigerator.

"That sounds great." He sat down in the chair nearest the back door, the one that neither Katherine nor Ethel usually occupied.

"So your blind date didn't go very well." She set a glass of yellow lemonade in front of him. Would he notice it wasn't pink?

"No. If we'd both been blind, it still wouldn't have gone well." His near smile didn't begin to reach his eyes. "Our personalities clashed, I'm afraid."

"Sometimes that happens." Ethel sat down in her usual chair, kitty-corner to him. "I've been a widow for almost ten years, and I was married for forty-two. We were both young when we married, but I still remember dating and clashing."

Quinn nodded. "I was engaged two years ago—a year and ten months, to be exact." He flipped back the lid on the container, exposing a beautiful layered nacho. Melted cheddar cheese covered beans and chips, garnished with olives, tomatoes, green onions, and a dollop of sour cream. "I started dating again a few months ago; it's been difficult."

"In what way?" She wasn't going to be shy, and took a cheese-covered chip and popped it into her mouth. Even on a full tummy, it was delicious.

"Well . . ." He frowned. "So far it's been disappointing. Instead of chemistry or friendship at the end of the evening, there's usually this . . . apathy. Tonight, the woman was simply rude."

"That's too bad." Why would any young woman be rude to a nice young man like Quinn? Ethel shook her head. "If I were in your shoes, I'd find a good home church and then start your search for a bride. Do you attend church?"

"I used to with Sylvia. We attended a small Baptist church within walking distance of here."

"But you haven't been back?"

He shook his head. "It was Sylvia's church first, her friends and family. She moved to Spokane. Moscow's too far from Nordstrom and Costco for her."

"That's funny. Katherine feels her hometown of Vancouver is too big compared to Moscow, and mind you, Vancouver, Washington, is not big. Even when she was a little girl, she liked knowing where everything was. Everything had its special place." Ethel knew she was rambling, but she was on a roll. "My girlfriend Sharon says that Katherine must have some deep-rooted psychosis when it comes to men, maybe relationships. And my other girlfriend, Betty, agrees. They're both from my Scrabble group. They think Katherine's excuse for not dating because of her master's is just an excuse."

"What do you think?" Quinn loaded a chip into his mouth.

"Ever since Joe, she's buried her heart in the books. He cheated on her, you know, with a boxed Malibu blonde. Katherine's hair is the real thing, in case you didn't know." Ethel waved a hand. The little gesture sent the round of jalapeno rolling off her chip and onto the floor. Quinn didn't appear to notice. "They're just friends. He's the head tennis coach at the university now."

"I've heard." He nodded. "In the time I've wasted on blind dating, I could have completed this new course I've been working on for the fall."

"Don't fret. When you find your girl, she'll be worth all the time you've wasted." Though he smiled, there was heartbreak in his deep-set *Doctor Zhivago* eyes.

"Thank you, Ethel; I've needed a woman friend."

She patted his hand. Quinn's big-city girl had broken his heart. He was working all week, cooking and cleaning for himself, and trying to find a bride on Fridays. Despite Katherine's personal history with him, Ethel liked Professor B. very much.

"It sounds like a war scene." He nodded toward the closed pocket door. "Not the typical girly movie."

The volume from the living room had risen again. But Ethel couldn't tell if it was orchestra or cannons.

"After the movie, Katherine's going to witness to them."

"Really?" He cocked his head to one side.

"Yes," Ethel whispered. "She remembered after she'd invited them that there's an affair in the movie."

"Oh." His eyes widened. "Sounds like she's seen it before."

"There's no nudity, thank heaven. But, because she's not super close with these girls, she wants them to know her faith and values. She does not condone extramarital affairs."

"She's using it as an opportunity to share her faith." Quinn nodded. "That's good."

"We should pray that despite this actor's good

looks, these young women see that his actions are not God-honoring."

"Well put, Ethel."

She reached for his hand above the table before they bowed their heads in prayer. "Oh, Lord, You know the evening that is at hand. We lift Quinn up to You and pray that in the midst of his dating, he finds the sweet young woman You've intended him to share his life with." Ethel paused to collect her thoughts.

"And about these young women in the next room, Lord, I pray they're able to discern that a relationship outside of the bonds of holy matrimony is sin. Sin used to be so black and white on our little TV sets, and now it's in Technicolor. Help them to see sin for what it is, in black and white. Be with Katherine as she gives her testimony. Help the girls to see past her smart stuff to her sweet spirit, and the love she has for You."

After their prayer wound down, Quinn patted her hand. "Ethel, you are such a breath of fresh air." Tender emotion shimmered in his eyes. "I know where to come now when I need some cheering up."

"If I'm not home, God always is," she said, touched by his words.

Ethel couldn't help but marvel that while the girls were in the living room watching their professor look-alike on-screen, she was enjoying his company in the kitchen.

Ж

"Ladies . . ." Katherine said. It was time for the little speech she'd rehearsed. "I haven't done anything outside of the class with you girls before, and to have you over and watch a movie in which the main conflict is an affair, well, I feel that I need to follow it up by sharing my faith."

"Please not a sermon," Ronnie said.

Katherine's tongue clicked against the roof of her mouth before her jaw dropped. *Ronnie.*

"No, I think she's doing more of a little footnote by . . ." Angel rolled her wrist, "following it up."

"You mean a conclusion." Ronnie rolled her eyes. "A footnote goes at the end of your paper to show your references."

"Oh, I thought that was an endnote," Angel said.

"Endnotes go at the end of the document. Footnotes are at the end of each page." Ronnie flipped her red hair over her shoulder. "If you put your footnote for a conclusion, no wonder you got a D."

"Okay, my turn." Katherine breathed in deeply. "I'm a Christian, and I believe that when you marry and say *I do*, you're making a covenant with God." She paused, waiting for Ronnie to make another landfill remark. "So when Yuri was unfaithful to his wife, he'd also broken his vows with God."

"Don't forget Laura was married, too," Ronnie said.

"Absolutely." Katherine nodded.

"Thank you for pointing it out, Katherine. My folks are always saying 'we've moved away from morals and into entertainment,'" Brenda said, sitting up nice and tall.

Thank you, Jesus.

"I hated the way it ended. He was there. She was there." Angel swayed from side-to-side. "And, oh . . ."

"You know there are more Zhivago movies," Brenda said.

"Omar Sharif movies," Ronnie corrected Brenda.

"There are?" Angel's face lit up.

Katherine's gaze traveled to the pot of yellow daisies on the side table to the right of the TV. There wasn't any chance Benton would drop by for dinner again, was there? Wednesday night's dinner with Grandma had been a one-time thing. Hadn't it?

The little carved wood bird on Grandma's clock cuckooed ten times.

"If we do, you'll need to leave by ten," Katherine said.

"Or you turn into a pumpkin?" Brenda asked.

"Maybe she has late dates?" Ronnie's mouth bunched as she studied her.

"No, it's because of her grandma, she probably goes to bed early," Angel said.

Katherine smiled. She'd leave it at that.

Chapter Fifteen

"I'll refer to tonight's date as Paula," Benton began. "I still feel a tad uncomfortable talking badly about a woman to women."

"Don't feel bad; we do it all the time." Cindy waved a hand.

For his blind date with Miss Pullman, Benton had worn a Wazzu-red polo. Maybe it was due to the low lighting in the room, but his resemblance to Zhivago was uncanny. He even had a little bit of a cleft chin. Katherine melted a bit into the loveseat, her tea sloshing onto her saucer. Had anyone noticed?

She glanced at Carl.

Their eyes met. He did a double take, followed by a double lift of his brows.

Her stomach double knotted.

"Did you say *badly*, Benton?" Evans sighed. "We'd held such high hopes for Miss Pullman. And I must say, from the moment you stepped through the door tonight, there was an extra spring in your step; I could have sworn your evening had gone well."

"Paula and I met at Alex's Restaurant in Pullman. Has everyone been there?"

The response was unanimous. Alex's was a landmark, famous for nachos, enchiladas, candle-lit tables, and ambiance. Katherine sighed; she loved Alex's.

"Paula met me downstairs, right before the steep carpeted stairwell—right on time, six o'clock sharp. Punctuality is important to me."

"Too important." Evans rolled his eyes.

Cindy giggled.

Katherine carefully returned her teacup to her saucer. Did Evans recall that line of her Joe List? In a laundry-list style, she'd written: *Doesn't understand the term "punctuality."* Out of the corner of her eye, she ever so briefly glanced at Evans—there was no sign of recollection on his slightly flushed, bearded face. What had happened to her Joe List? Had he truly lost it, or had he only pretended to?

"The evening started off promising." Benton crossed one knee over the other. "There was solid eye contact. She had a pleasing manner, and—" he looked at Evans—"there were several seven-plus-letter words."

Without moving his head, Evans glanced at her. *Why?* In her Joe List, she'd written something about Joe's *limited vocabulary.*

"Seven-plus-letter words are a significant improvement," Evans said. "Carl, this is only your third blind date recap, correct?"

"Yes." Carl set his cup and saucer on the coffee table. "Unless Quinn's counting the woman he'd met at the Polish Sausage Feed."

"Uniontown." Evans chuckled. "I was there, as well. I witnessed the entire ignominy."

Carl smiled at Katherine. "I felt embarrassed for Miss Uniontown."

"I felt embarrassed for me," Benton said.

Perhaps, Evans invited her here more for Benton than Carl? Because of her Joe List and Benton's similar traits, it wasn't a far-fetched presumption. No,

Evans knew she had a huge credit load, and Benton didn't date students. And she, for that matter, didn't date anyone.

"Her mobile phone rang shortly after we ordered." Benton smirked. "The evening went downhill from there. For the next fifteen minutes, Trish, I mean Paula, talked on the phone to a friend."

"About what? It may have been some type of girl code," Evans asked.

"It was a woman from work. Paula asked about the caller's daughter, and off the top of her head gave the woman some kind of a recipe."

"What kind of recipe?" Cindy leaned forward and nabbed a madeleine.

Carl had ever so inadvertently nudged himself an inch closer.

"Some of the ingredients were balsamic vinegar and Kalamata olives; that's all I remember."

"You fool, the woman cooks gourmet!" Evans sighed and set down his teacup. "It was girl code. They'd rehearsed their conversation so you'd discern that she is both caring and a gourmet cook."

"You give our gender far too much credit," Cindy said.

"Paula went onto say something about needing to buy a new can opener before next Friday."

"They're going camping. She's an outdoor girl. If you'd been listening, you would have heard what a great catch Trish . . . er . . . Paula is, but all you could focus on was the fact that she wasn't paying attention to you."

Was Evans serious? Except for Benton, they all had a good chuckle.

"Did she say manual or electric?" Katherine asked.

"She said *can opener*." Benton set his mug down on a coaster on the nearby end table and looked at Cindy. "Evans always does this. He becomes more interested in my blind dates than I was able to be."

"I hope you run out of friends soon, Benton," Evans said. "Your blind dates are creating baggage."

"The problem is people who I thought know me well, I'm finding . . . don't know me at all. Paula is a prime example." Benton studied the brocade ceiling. "Paula continued talking on her phone. She even set an elbow on the table. After ten more minutes, it was like I was no longer seated across from her. That's when I thought of calling Ethel, Katherine's grandmother."

He'd called Grandma.

"Now, Ethel is the woman you wish was forty years younger?" Evans asked.

"Thirty would also be fine. My conversation with Ethel strangely appeared to bring Paula to her senses. She ended her call and, for a moment or two, eavesdropped on mine." His gaze veered to Katherine. "Your grandmother needed help with a crossword puzzle."

Katherine nodded. One or two words usually stumped her.

"After I hung up, Paula drilled *me* about who *I* was chatting with. I proceeded to tell her that I thought her conversing on the phone for sixteen minutes in the middle of our dinner date was rude."

"You didn't?" Evans said. "But of course, you did. That is the pattern. Sometime in the course of the evening, Benton *always* muddles it. What did you tell Paula about Ethel?"

"I simply told her that Ethel is an elderly neighbor woman who I've recently befriended."

"I'm surprised you didn't tell her that she's also

the grandmother of your loveliest grad student. That would have broken the ice."

Wide-eyed, Katherine stared at the bowl of walnuts on the coffee table.

"Evans!" Cindy nudged him.

Carl cleared his throat.

"I'd like to clear the air." Benton glanced from Evans to Carl. "My friendship with Ethel has nothing to do with her granddaughter."

"In my day, I found nothing regarding faculty-student relationships in the university handbook." Evans sounded matter of fact. "Thus, I dated and married my second wife, who was finishing her master's, and was only three years younger than me. I too frown on those professors who take advantage of the power a professor can wield over their awe-gripped victims."

"You married your student?" Katherine couldn't believe her ears.

"He did." Cindy nodded.

"Just to warn you, Carl, when the jowls start to droop—grow a beard." Evans stroked his well-groomed chin. "Otherwise, the young female students no longer gaze starry-eyed. But don't worry; you both have several good years left."

Evans's gaze narrowed. "Benton, where did you go after you called me? It was only eight o'clock."

"Uh, I killed time and felt sorry for myself."

"I'm surprised you didn't just come here. We could have been done by ten."

"I had a lot of ironing." Quinn inhaled. "I still do."

"You don't iron when you're depressed." Evans glanced back and forth between Benton and her.

"It probably gave him something to do." Cindy

patted his arm.

Eyes downcast, Benton peered at the Persian rug. Even though he was holding out for Miss Palouse, in the meantime, he'd surprisingly held high hopes for Miss Pullman.

"Get back to Paula." Evans wrapped his arm around the back of Cindy's section of the couch. "We are all going mad in anticipation."

"After I told her that I thought she was rude for talking for sixteen minutes straight, she told me I had initiated my call and that *she* was simply responding politely to hers." Benton shook his head. "Our conversation went downhill from there. My response was: she failed to inform the caller that she was seated across the table from an intelligent and quite good-looking man who'd looked forward to meeting her for two weeks."

"You didn't!" Evans groaned.

"I most certainly did!"

"You have a doctorate, so *intelligent* is probable, but please tell me you didn't refer to yourself as quite good looking."

"I did." Benton nodded. "Sylvia made the mistake of convincing me that I am."

"But her love was blind . . . for a while."

Ouch. How long would it take for Benton to recover?

He appeared fine.

"About a minute after my blatantly honest remarks about myself, Paula excused herself from the table to use the senoritas' room. Ten minutes passed. Our dinners arrived—my chimichanga with sour cream and her beautiful cheesy nacho. In her absence, I nibbled on one of my olives and then I started looking at my wristwatch. Another ten minutes rolled by. Finally, I got up and asked the cashier if she'd seen a slim blonde woman with a black-and-white fur-looking purse."

Evans sighed.

"The cashier said, 'Yes, she left twenty minutes ago.' Paula told the cashier to give me this." Benton pulled a blue sticky note out of his front pant pocket.

"You're kidding, right?" Carl asked.

"No." Unfolding the note, Benton cleared his throat. "Quinn, I'm sorry. We obviously are not meant for one another. Good luck finding someone.—Paula."

"I'm sorry, old friend. At least, you found this out before either of you wasted too much time on one another," Evans said.

"Don't be. I am getting tired of people who matchmake based on marital status and age. 'They're both over thirty and unmarried—they're perfect for each other.'"

"Are you running out of friends yet?" Carl asked.

"Next week is Miss Palouse. I've looked forward to meeting her for months."

"Since the Jazz Festival." Evans nodded.

"That's right. Evans's good friend Guttenheimer is responsible for this pairing. And just so this group knows, my next three Fridays are mapped out. Miss Palouse. Miss Harvard—"

"Harvard as in university or small, minuscule town north of here?" Evans asked.

"Miniscule town." Benton yawned.

"The saga continues." Goliath appeared from beneath the coffee table, jumped up on the couch, and cuddled in the crook of Evans's arm. "Miss Palouse has mastered prolonging the inevitable. One cannot fall in love on the phone."

"She has a very attractive phone voice, plus she's

intelligent, candid, a great listener." Benton begged to differ.

"Doesn't she work for 9-1-1?" Cindy asked, hugging a maroon pillow.

"Yes, she often works nights."

Benton's social life was mapped out, and in a way, so was Katherine's: going to the library, pacifying Joe, avoiding Carl.

"The mysterious Palouse woman . . ." Evans yawned. "She's canceled once before, or is it twice?"

"Once." Benton nodded. "A perfectly legitimate excuse."

During their day trips to Spokane, Washington, Grandma and Katherine had often driven through Palouse, a small, picturesque back roads town.

"I shouldn't have scheduled anyone past Miss Palouse."

"Because you think she's the one." Cindy smiled.

"Definitely the most intriguing."

If he did think Miss Palouse was the one, wasn't dating in the interim just a waste of emotional energy? Why did he allow friends to set him up on a continual basis for what appeared to be a continual disappointment? Didn't the man have a brain?

Chapter Sixteen

Cindy opened her briefcase on Evans's kitchen table. She'd informed Katherine on the way here that she'd be staying late again. Benton had already told her he wouldn't be her chauffeur again. So, when Carl walked her to the door, the time had come to accept his offer.

"I'd like to drive you home tonight, Katherine. That is if it's all right with you?" He rubbed the back of his neck with one hand.

"Thank you, Carl." Katherine swallowed.

"But . . ." He rolled a kink out of his neck.

"She said thank you. What didn't you hear?" Benton slid on his leather loafers.

"Oh, sure, here . . . let me grab my keys."

"And coat," Katherine added, as the man was only wearing a heather-gray T-shirt. Carl took the curved stairwell two steps at a time.

Carl was probably a decoy. Most likely Evans, her beloved adviser, was not trying to matchmake her with Mr. Snake Oil. Unbeknownst to anyone, he was secretly trying to matchmake her and Benton. In the meanwhile, Carl was merely pretending to be interested. At the last second, he'd probably find an excuse not to take her home, and Benton or Cindy would have to.

Her heart pounded in her ears. There was always

the chance he wasn't a decoy.

"Good night, Katherine." Benton started to pull the door closed.

"Mr. Benton," she whispered, glancing over her shoulder toward the empty stairwell, "I'll make you cinnamon rolls tomorrow if you'll take me home."

"No, thank you."

"Mine are better than Grandma's. She usually forgets something because she doesn't proofread the recipe or follow it, for that matter."

"I don't feel bad." He pulled the door firmly closed behind him.

Behind her, Carl jogged down the stairs. Katherine turned to face her fate. Wearing a hooded gray sweatshirt, he reached the bottom and slid his feet into sheepskin-lined slippers. "Ready?" He opened the door for her and waved her through.

How to determine if a man was truly interested? Katherine paused a bit in the doorway. Carl set his hand to her lower back and nudged her along. Unlike last Friday, when she'd walked ahead of Benton to the car, Carl made it a point to walk beside her.

"It's a beautiful evening. Look at the stars." Tucking his hands into the pocket of his sweatshirt, he tipped back his head.

There was indeed a bounty overhead. Men who were interested often noticed stars.

"To be honest, Katherine, I've done quite a bit of dating in the last year. And in doing so, I'm trying to come up with better and better dating questions. Is there one you've always wanted to be asked?" They were having a mini-date in Evans's driveway.

She shrugged. "The most important question that I ask before accepting a date is . . . are you a Christian?"

"What's the one question you've always wanted to be asked?" He tilted his head toward her.

"'Are you a Christian?' would be a great start."

"Yes, but by saying *most important,* you implied there's one that you might enjoy being asked."

Funny how Carl was the first guy she'd share this with. "Well . . . if you were a journalist and could cover any American war, Carl, what war would you choose and why?"

He chuckled. "It's a great question if you're dating a journalist, historian, or someone zealous about war . . ." His voice trailed off.

"You're a historian, Carl. Not that we're dating..."

"Yes, but I try to keep work and my personal life separate."

His lack of passion for his profession surprised her. Standing near the passenger side of Carl's sports car, she waited for him to ask her the same question.

"Katherine, what are you doing tomorrow night?"

"Studying. I have a nine-credit load in the master's program."

"Evans said it's more like six credits. That before the start of your research class, your thesis was ready to turn in."

Evans! For years, she'd researched her thesis topic: the Hudson's Bay Company's impact on the Northwest, specifically Fort Vancouver.

"Evans used it as an example of your work ethic. Not to contradict your desire to not date." Carl attempted apology on Evans's behalf. "How about dinner and a movie tomorrow night?"

Was Benton right about Joe being her best excuse?

"Joe . . . and I often get-together on Saturday

nights." It wasn't a lie except for the *often* part. They occasionally did for a Mountain Dew in between books.

"You're the one who's still in love, aren't you?"

Could she lie? What if it got back to Joe? She'd have to warn him.

"Does he know?"

"Yes." She smiled. She told Joe she loved him all the time, and he told her the same. But of course, it wasn't in the same context that Carl was thinking. Tonight Joe was her alibi.

Carl hummed the melody to "I Only Have Eyes For You," under his breath. "I know a great little sushi place in Pullman."

Perhaps Benton was right; her nine-credit excuse didn't fly.

"I'm sorry, Carl, I'd only think about Joe the entire time."

Headlights were visible up the street. A dark sedan proceeded closer and parked behind Cindy's Camry. It was Benton's Volvo. Had he forgotten something?

Benton powered down his side window. "Katherine, get in. I'm taking you home."

Huh? Hallelujah! Her hero had returned to save her.

"What?" Carl's arms flew up horizontal with his shoulders. "Benton, I am!"

She suppressed a giggle as she hurried around the front of Benton's car.

"Katherine, wait!"

"Thanks for the offer, Carl, but he only lives a block from me." She closed the passenger door and pulled the seat belt across her. "I do not feel guilty." She buckled it into place as Benton backed out of

Evans's driveway.

"I do not feel guilty." She sighed, closing her eyes.

"I take it you do not feel guilty," Benton said, driving south.

"Thank you SO much!" She threw her head back and laughed.

"The poor guy. I thought for sure I'd have to follow you home and chaperone from the street."

"Was he okay? I couldn't bring myself to look." She turned in her seat, but they were too far away to detect shapes.

"He just stood in the driveway watching us until I reached the park." Benton glanced in his rearview mirror.

"I'm SO grateful that you arrived when you did. He'd already asked me out twice."

"I got all the way to Mabelle Street before I thought of Ethel, and what I'd have to tell her if you and Carl ended up a couple, and he broke your heart six weeks later. That's his longest relationship to date, in case Evans hadn't told you."

"You're kidding?" Six weeks—even she and Joe had made it eight.

"No." Benton glanced in her direction. "And of course, the cinnamon rolls were in the back of my mind, too. I'm meeting the guys at The Breakfast Club, and I probably won't be home until after noon or so."

"They won't be ready until after two o'clock tomorrow. After tennis with Joe, I usually go to the library for a few hours. Knowing Grandma, she'll want to deliver them. She hasn't visited you yet for your official welcome to the neighborhood."

"That's great. I'll be home. Tell her my place is

740 Lynn Street—a brown ranch-style duplex with a maple tree in front."

Katherine stared out the windshield and was surprised when he drove past Logan, which was the quickest route. For some reason, he was taking the long way home. They crested Sixth Street hill. The lights of the downtown area of Moscow were lovely at 1:48 in the morning. Quinn slowed to a stop at the red light on Main Street, waiting to turn left. Thankfully, no one else was on the road, except for an old lime-green Volkswagen bug which pulled up beside them in the right-hand lane.

Crud! The car looked just like Angel's. Katherine sank down in her seat until the top of her head was beneath the window, the seat belt stopping her below the chest.

"What are you doing?" Quinn murmured.

"Is there a plastic Hawaiian lei hanging from the rearview mirror in the car beside us?"

Leaning forward, Quinn's gaze shifted from left to right. "Yes." He half smiled and did a small wave. He sat back in the seat and stared wide-eyed at the road in front of them.

Katherine didn't dare speak, breathe, move.

The light finally changed.

From her lowered position, she viewed the second floor of the brick fire station on their right, and the lights of Gritman Hospital on their left.

Quinn chuckled. "Angel LeFave. Just my luck. She's one of the girls who like to visit my office on a regular basis. Her head swiveled just like a Barbie doll. Completely stared. Stay down in case she takes a left at the next light and tries to follow me home."

"She wouldn't."

"Carl had it happen."

"Angel has a boyfriend."

"Then why has she visited my office three, maybe four times this semester?"

"Probably because of your grading system. I don't think she saw me, do you?"

"She didn't, but stay down."

"If she did see me, I'm not going to lie." *Please, Lord, don't have Angel ask.*

"Was Angel one of the girls you had over tonight? You two look fairly close." He glanced in the rearview mirror.

"Can I sit up yet?"

"I wouldn't. What movie did you watch tonight?"

She couldn't begin to explain the movie, and the girls, or the get-togethers. He'd think that she was just another one of his starry-eyed admirers.

"A girly-flick drama." Katherine ignored his advice, sat up in the seat, and watched her side-view mirror for any signs of Angel's bug.

"Oh, what was the storyline?"

"You know . . ." Katherine peered out the passenger window. "The typical girl-meets-guy movie. She already has a boyfriend. He already has a girlfriend. They end up working together. You know, the usual."

"What was the name of it? I think I've seen it."

"You'd know if you had. It's such a relief that Carl didn't drive me home." Now she only had Angel to worry about, and Benton possibly losing his job.

"Yes, I tried to tell Carl to hold off on doing anything about the attraction until he got to know you better. But, he'd set sail. You know how people get that faraway look in their eyes."

"Yes, and there's no talking reason into them. Take you and Miss Palouse, for example, you haven't even met the woman, and, well, you've set sail."

"Exactly." He smiled. "The phone is a great way to get to know someone. There are no physical attributes or attractions to get in the way. One soul to another."

"You're an idealist, just like Woodrow Wilson."

He chuckled. "The man made a positive impact." After taking a left on their little side street, he slowed near the picket gate that aligned with the side entrance to the back door.

"Grandma prefers that people park near the detached garage. She worries about her purple gladiolas, which are planted on both sides of the fence. To be honest, Angel parked a little too close to one of her beds this evening. I hope they survive."

"Oh, so she was one of the girls. I'm glad you told me about Ethel's flowers." He parked to the left of Grandma's car and turned off the headlights. Grandma had left the porch light on. It brightened the narrow concrete walk and set a halo of light around the back door.

"Thank you for the ride home." She lifted the door handle.

"Here, I almost forgot." Turning toward her, he fumbled in the backseat for something. "You don't have to read it immediately, maybe over the summer. I'm structuring a new course, and I'd value your opinion." He handed her a cream-colored hardback book.

"Oh, this is the real reason you drove me home tonight—*American Scripture*." She read the subtitle: *Making the Declaration of Independence* by Pauline Maier.

"You know the last thing I need right now is another history book. I'm taking nine credits, and there's my thesis, a huge load for summer. Plus there's Grandma and . . ."

"Evans informed Carl, in front of me, that you're really only taking six credits. That you're pretty much done with your thesis, but he had you take the research class for credit fulfillment."

Who needed a matchmaker with an adviser like Evans?

"And you were also in the room?" She nodded.

"Yes, it's probably why Carl hasn't taken your excuse too seriously. And good job, by the way, getting your thesis done early. Should I walk you up?"

"No, of course not." She giggled. Why in the world would he ask that? "Though I'm flattered, I'm sorry, I can't commit to another book." She set it on the console between them.

"You don't have to read it all at once. Small snippets. Over a bowl of cereal."

"All my small snippets go to Grandma, but thank you. I am flattered." She stepped out of the car.

As she monkeyed with the gate, Benton's door closed behind him. What was he thinking following her? In the moonlight-dappled walkway, she strode toward the back steps. Benton mumbled under his breath before the gate creaked open and closed. She was on the top step, sliding the key into the lock when he stopped on the concrete walk below her.

"Despite what happened tonight, Carl will most likely call tomorrow."

Over her shoulder, she frowned at him.

He held out the book like it was a box of chocolates. The book had to be the real impetus behind not letting Carl drive her home.

"You could have warned me about Carl in the car."

"Carl's taken with you. God knows why. Probably because Evans speaks *too* highly of you."

"You speak unkindly of me, yet you walk me to the door. Why is that, Professor B.?"

"Believe it or not, I value your opinion and insight. I'm designing a lower-level class on the history of the Constitution."

"Have you reread my essay yet?" She turned to face him, gripping the metal railing with her left hand. "Is that why you value my insight? It's an A, isn't it?"

"No, I haven't reviewed them yet. I need to."

"You were so quick about grading them the first time, and now you're taking your time."

"I plan to buckle down tomorrow afternoon and reread the lot."

She turned toward the door.

"I'm pleased that I no longer loathe you," he said. "I'm always disappointed with myself when I loathe."

Loathe . . . was he serious? She glanced back at him, which was when he handed her the book.

"Your third apology was eloquent and moving enough that I believed it. Even though you'd wrapped three sides of me in phone cord." His brows gathered. "Why did you do that?"

"It wasn't what I'd call wrapping. I simply hung up the phone. You make it sound like a misdemeanor."

At the base of the steps, he stood one hand gripping his other wrist, as she'd often seen groomsmen stand at weddings. For some quirky reason, she felt drawn to him. Maybe because he was intelligent and attractive. Maybe he had her number. Reverse psychology. Loathe? If they didn't fight, there might be tidal wave type chemistry between them that could pummel her well-laid plans.

"Why did you do the phone cord?"

"I was nervous. And it was kind of funny. It won't happen again."

"If it was solely because of nerves, I'm afraid it might happen again."

"It won't. Because I won't visit your office ever again. Thank you for walking me to the door. Good night." Her house key spun out of her fingers to clatter down the concrete steps. Chin lifted, she waited for him to step aside before she bent to retrieve it. While she picked up the solo brass key, she grappled for something harsh, something destructive to say. She had to think quick before one of them stepped closer.

"Can you hold the book for me?" She passed it to him as she started up the steps. "Though I'm often what you call brilliant, I can't seem to do two things at once."

He chuckled under his breath. "You think too highly of yourself. I said *I no longer loathe you,* and you misconstrue it to imply I'm now coming on to you. One of the stipulations of my contract is we are not to become involved with students. No matter how intelligent or attractive we may think they are."

Was he saying that he thought her both intelligent and attractive? Wow, it was quite a contrast to loathe.

Wide-eyed, he stared at her. "Becoming involved with students is a serious breach of professional ethics and proper standards of professional behavior."

"Sounds like you've memorized it."

Why had he really walked her to the door? He was almost complimenting her while he quoted the bylaws of his contract. Could he possibly be trying to give her hope?

"Don't worry, Professor B., your grading system long ago obliterated any attraction I may have felt for you given your, um . . . looks." Turning, she faced the door. She probably didn't need to admit that she'd ever thought about his good looks. She wrestled the key in the lock, but it didn't seem to catch. Had he taken a step closer on the stairs?

"Evans refers to you as Miss A. And as you may already know, I've *often* referred to you as Miss A-nnoying."

Her jaw dropped. They were serious fighting words, and he was winning.

"Uh . . . Maybe you didn't know but, well, now you do. You, uh, turn the key to the right. Unlocks it every time."

She pushed the door open, stepped inside, and glanced back at him. With one hand on the metal railing, he leaned forward, an intent look on his face.

"Next Friday, Carl or Cindy will be driving me home. Good night, Professor B." It was then she noted the book was still in his possession. She smiled and locked the door behind her.

What she'd viewed as contempt between them might possibly be the Big *C* . . . chemistry. Enough dynamite to blow up the Grand Coulee Dam.

How had this ever happened?

She sat down in her chair at the table and leaned her head against the wall beneath the calendar. Headlights shone on the picture window in the kitchen as Benton's Volvo reversed out of the back gravel drive and then headed east.

Moonlight streamed through the window; a half-empty glass salt shaker stood alone in its path. Katherine pulled the half-empty pepper shaker over to join its mate. Like ice skaters skimming the surface, the shakers waltzed in the moonlight.

Did Benton know it was chemistry, not contempt, between them? Maybe on his side, it was still contempt; maybe because of her two visits to his office, it always would be. Why had he walked her to the door? It made their one-mile drive home together almost feel like a date.

Learn from this, she told herself: Never bribe your good-looking professor with cinnamon rolls in exchange for driving you home. If he accepts, your overactive mind may read into everything that happens. Everything.

Chapter Seventeen

Wrist-deep in sweet dough, the phone rang. "If it's for me, take a message?" Katherine said over her shoulder.

Grandma was in the middle of cutting out her "welcome to the neighborhood" letters. "The phone has never rang as much as it has this summer." She set the scissors aside. "Hello, Katherine King's answering service.—She's making cinnamon rolls for a male friend of hers, and her hands are all sticky. May I take a message?"

Katherine rolled her eyes. Grandma didn't need to tell whoever it was ALL that. How embarrassing.

"Oh, I'm sorry, Carl, I thought you were a solicitor again. You have such a professional-sounding voice. I know you're a professor. That must be where you get it. I'm writing your number on a sticky note, and yes, I'll tell Katherine that you called."

"Carl, the professor, called." Grandma paused in the kitchen doorway.

Wow! After last night, she'd felt certain he was going to leave her alone.

"Even though he's flagrantly good looking, I'm not interested." Using her forearm, Katherine brushed her hair away from her face.

"Flagrantly good looking?" Grandma giggled. "Is that the way you and Rikki used to talk?"

"Sometimes." Her freshman and sophomore year,

her older cousin, Tim, had boarded with Grandma, while Katherine stayed in the dorms; Rikki had been her roommate. Rikki, a Moscow native, lived on campus to get away from her parents, and then went to grad school at the University of Texas to get even farther away.

"Once you've washed up, call him back?" Grandma swished her hand.

"This is not the type of guy you call back. It would be too encouraging for him."

"Too encouraging. Listen to you."

Fifteen minutes later, the phone rang. It was Katherine's turn. She set aside her handwritten rough draft of an essay for Quinn's Civil War class and rose from the couch. "Hello," she said into the receiver.

Grandma sat in the recliner, her back to her as she pretended interest in a crossword. But Katherine could tell that she'd tilted her good ear up.

"Hi, Katherine, it's Carl. Did your grandmother give you my message?"

"Yes, she did, Carl."

"I was hoping you'd return my call."

She wrapped the long, black phone cord around her left hand. "Yes, she did."

"We're at The Breakfast Club on Main, and we were hoping you'd join us. I thought I'd take you to Bucer's for coffee afterward."

"You forget, Carl, I have nine reasons to decline."

"Don't you mean ten?" He chuckled. "Nine credits plus Joe equals ten."

"Are you seated with the guys?"

"We're waiting for the tab."

"Evans and Benton?"

"Yes, Evans and Benton are with me." The background noise dimmed.

Benton knew now that she'd resorted to the Joe excuse. Carl was asking her out with an audience! It was no longer about dating her; it was about his ego.

"Carl, put me on speaker, please."

"Certainly."

"Am I on?"

"Yes, Katherine. I hear you clearly, love," Evans said quite loudly in the background.

She cleared her throat. "Carl, I now have eleven reasons why I won't meet you for coffee. Any man who would call with his buddies as an audience is not someone I'd consider future dating material."

"Joe's at the top of your list, Katherine, isn't he?" Carl said.

"Katherine is fond of lists, Carl," Evans said. "Katherine, I recently stumbled upon your Joe List. All these years, it's been buried in my briefcase. According to Carl, you need a refresher of all the reasons you weren't going to fall in love with him again . . . Joe, I mean, not Carl. Give me a call, Katherine, and I'll remind you."

"Four years ago you told me you were going to shred it." She grabbed a scalp-full of hair and squeezed.

"How could I shred it when I'd misplaced it?"

"You found it the other day when I was writing Benton's apology!" She knew he'd found something of secretive importance.

"She wrote it in front of you?" Benton asked in the background. "You put her up to it, didn't you?"

There was a pause on the other end of the line. "Katherine, you must try The Breakfast Club's Huckleberry Zucchini Bread the next time you're here," Evans said.

"Carl, please take me off speaker."

There was the screech of a chair's legs being pushed back on hardwood. "Katherine, I've just clicked you off speaker phone. I'm now heading toward the banquet room, which is very quiet at the moment. I could pick you up in about fifteen minutes at your grandmother's, and we could pretend this conversation never happened."

With his ability to not be discouraged, he should really be in sales, not history. "I'm sorry, Carl, I prefer someone less insistent. Thank you, though, I wish you luck." She lowered the receiver.

"Katherine . . . the more we converse, the more I'm convinced—"

"You obviously like a challenge, Carl. I'm sorry, I'm sincerely not interested."

"Because of Joe?"

"Have a nice day." She hung up on Carl. With both hands finally free, she grabbed handfuls of hair near her scalp and grimaced.

"Was that Carl the professor?" Grandma asked.

"Yes, Professor Carl."

"The flagrantly good-looking one?"

"Yes." Katherine sat down on the couch and lifted the ten-pound history textbook to her lap.

"I remember, when I was younger than you, of course, when a young man showed me attention, even if I didn't like the fellow, I still felt a little flattered. I'd always try to paint a pretty picture. Not like you. You're just slapping on the paint." Grandma swished an imaginary brush in large X-like motions through the air.

"I think you need to take a little more time, honey. Would you have spoken to that young man that way if Pastor Ken was sitting at our kitchen table?"

"His nerve is a bad sign. I do not want an admirer

this semester." If she were honest with herself, Carl's voice held a little disappointment. Had she been too harsh?

Grandma looked at her crossword. "I forgot to tell you that Joe called earlier when you were in the shower."

"Oh . . ." Returning to the curio cabinet, Katherine found a sticky note that read: *Joe called* in minuscule print. Grandma had printed Carl's sticky note three times larger. She dialed Joe's number.

"Joe, it's Katherine."

"Hi, babe. Are we still on?"

"Yes." She'd hardly accomplished anything this morning, but she'd given Joe her word.

"Should I pick you up at Bruneel Tires at ten minutes till?"

"Yes." Years ago, when they'd dated, meeting at Bruneel Tires had been their way to get around Grandma and her strict no-motorcycle policy. After Joe annihilated her playing tennis, which usually took under thirty minutes, she'd get in a couple of hours of study at the library.

"Love you," Joe said.

"Love you, too," she whispered, hoping Grandma couldn't hear. Katherine hung up and returned to the couch and her textbook.

"Why were you whispering?"

Katherine shrugged.

"You said 'Love you, too.' I heard you." Grandma's eyes didn't blink.

"We're like brother and sister now. We always say it. Joe's been telling me it for years." Though she'd been honest, heat flooded her face.

Grandma's eyes narrowed.

"Don't you remember, Grandma?" Katherine's

chest ached with the memory. "Ever since Joe's dad died, he's been telling me he loves me, and I tell him, too. I do love Joe, like a brother."

"I remember." Grandma nodded. "I was just making sure you did."

Ж

Katherine waited out front of Bruneel Tires. Ready for tennis, she wore Adidas shorts, a fuchsia fitted top, and her backpack and tennis case strapped to her back. Directly across the four-lane highway, huge grain silos marked the south side of downtown Moscow.

Only ten minutes late, not bad for Joe, he pulled up on his motorcycle, grinned, and handed her his extra helmet. She pulled it on over her high ponytail. The compressed knot on the top of her head would only be a temporary headache. She sat behind Joe with her arms wrapped around his middle, and they rode north toward Sixth Street.

Traffic was unusually congested due to the farmer's market. Saturdays were always busy, and parking was at a premium. Joe stopped at the red light on Sixth and Main.

"How was the professors' group last night?" he asked over his shoulder.

"Fun." The word was growing on her. She glanced toward the corner florist across the street. She loved this little college town, a pocketed oasis nestled in the rolling hills of the Palouse. The area was the lentil capital of the world. She loved the ambiance of the downtown area, the brick courtyard, the hanging baskets on lamp posts, the eclectic shops on the main street. Pedestrians carried their farmer's market finds—plants, bouquets, baskets of strawberries . . . A man who looked very much like Benton stood on the corner holding two tomato plants.

Crud! It was Benton.

Chapter Eighteen

Quinn carried a shallow cardboard box hosting his farmer's market finds—two tomato plants and a dozen farm fresh eggs. At the four-way intersection on Main and Sixth Street, Quinn stopped beside Evans and Carl. Before meeting at The Breakfast Club, the two had lucked out by finding a parallel parking space in front of the sports store. Quinn had walked; it was a pleasant seventy-degree day.

At the intersection, a motorcyclist on a nice bike, a Yamaha 650 Seca, waited first in line. A girl's arms were wrapped around his middle. Over the fellow's shoulder, the girl stared wide-eyed at him. Quinn had no doubt whatsoever; the big, blue eyes belonged to Katherine.

He had to remind himself to breathe.

As Joe drove by, a bright blue backpack and tennis racket were strapped to Katherine's back. According to her grandmother's instructions, she was not to be motorcycling about the countryside with Joe.

Evans nudged him. "Isn't that Katherine?"

Quinn nodded.

"The girl on the bike?" Carl's voice rang with humor. Everything Katherine did seemed to grip Carl more.

"Doesn't appear that she's using her nine-credits excuse much with Joe Hillis, does it? I'm sorry, Carl.

If you needed another rebuff spelled out in brilliant color..." Evans extended a hand west. "There it is."

At the end of the next block, where Sixth Street and the Lewiston highway converged, the couple on the motorcycle waited at a red light.

"There sits our Katherine, with her arms around another man. Remember that picture, Carl, and move on with your life." Evans beefed up his English accent as a somewhat attractive middle-aged woman strode past.

"I'm moving on."

It never took Carl long to move on.

"I don't believe her." Evans looked over his shoulder at Quinn. "When you talk with her tomorrow find out what's going on with Mr. Dynamite. I would've sworn after reviewing her Joe List that she would have stuck to it."

They'd voted two out of three that Quinn should be the one to speak with Katherine about the way she'd handled Carl. He'd wait until after Ethel took her to church. Maybe after hearing the Lord's Word, she'd be penitent. In the meanwhile, he'd pray about it.

The woman was unpredictable.

Instead of walking straight home, Quinn took a right on Logan. Before the start of Ethel's fence line, a table was set up in the center of the concrete sidewalk. The little girl who manned it had her nose behind a paperback—*Charlotte's Web*. A plastic pitcher of lemonade sat on top. Her Crayola signage read: **Lemonade 25-cents.** On top of the table sat a glass fish bowl with a small sign taped to the front: Hannah's Puppy Fund. Donations Welcome.

"I'm saving money to buy a puppy," she said from behind the book.

"What kind of puppy?" Quinn's hands were full. Otherwise, he would have happily plunked down a quarter.

"Not sure. We're going to the Humane Society." Lowering the book a couple of inches, she looked up at him. Freckles were sprinkled across her nose and cheeks.

Since Tammy Morris in third grade, he'd always had a weakness for freckles. He set the dozen eggs down on the table. "One for here, and one to go," he said dropping two quarters into the fish bowl.

"Thanks, Mister."

Near Ethel's side gate, he set down his purchases, that way she wouldn't think he'd bought them for her. Holding the Dixie cup of lemonade, he knocked on the back door. His memory returned to Katherine on Joe's motorbike; her arms wrapped around him. Framed by the motorcycle helmet, her large blue eyes had appeared stunning.

Ethel opened the door. "As soon as I saw you walk by, I put on the kettle. Hopefully, you're a tea-drinking man." She wore a peach-colored T-shirt over faded jean capris and pink slippers.

"I am. I bought a lemonade for you." He handed her the Dixie cup.

"Come in." Ethel waved him inside and appeared genuinely happy to see him. "Our little neighbor girl's saving up for a puppy."

"So I've heard. Do you think she gets much business there?" He sat down at the table in his usual chair. An earthy aroma in the room triggered a childhood memory of his visits to his Aunt Alice's home.

"No. Katherine has a pile of quarters on the windowsill for Hannah's lemonade." One brow lifted as Ethel appeared deep in thought. "She's sold about four dollars worth that I know of."

"Not very much." He nodded. "The guys from the professors' group—Carl, Evans, and I, met for breakfast this morning."

"Did you know Carl called Katherine this morning?"

"Yes, I was present at the table when he made the call." He glanced around the white, boxy kitchen. "Something smells delicious."

"It's the sweet roll dough for *your* cinnamon rolls. Katherine started it this morning after breakfast." Ethel waved a hand toward the counter, where a damp tea towel covered a large bowl. "Tell me your side of the story." She carried two mugs and a chipped royal-blue teapot to the table and sat down. "Why is my granddaughter making you cinnamon rolls?"

"Katherine didn't want Carl driving her home last night. She mentioned cinnamon rolls, and well, given the circumstances, I caved. If she ever gets another B in my class, I've already told her that cinnamon rolls are the perfect answer." His face warmed, and for a moment, he was thankful that none of his superiors were friends of Ethel's.

"Your stories match." She pressed her lips together in a slight frown. "I can't believe she's such a ninny about Carl."

"Is she here?" Did Ethel know her whereabouts?

"She left a little while ago to play tennis with Joe. After tennis, she's going to study at the library."

After tennis, she was probably going to Joe's place. The girl was officially not to be trusted.

"Did she walk?"

"Yes. She'll be home for a late lunch before attacking your cinnamon rolls, as she put it."

What other things did Katherine not tell her grandmother?

"Do you have dinner plans?" Ethel patted the table between them.

"No." Except for a dozen essays to review, his Saturday evening was a blank page.

"We're just having omelets and toast if you care to join us." She poured him a mug of darkly brewed tea.

"That sounds great." Even though he'd had a farmer's omelet and toast at The Breakfast Club, he wouldn't mind the same meal again this evening with Ethel, and he supposed Katherine would be here as well. His mind returned to her on the back of the motorbike, her arms wrapped about Joe.

"Is everything okay?" Ethel patted his hand for the second time.

"Yes . . . er . . . is there anything you'd like me to bring? I planned to do my grocery shopping for the week at Tidyman's after I leave here."

"If you could pick up some of those frozen hash browns, that would be a treat. Before Katherine left, I overheard her conversation with Carl. She was so rude."

"Yes, but so was he." Quinn didn't agree with how pushy Carl had been.

"After she got off the phone with Mr. Flagrantly Good Looking, I got on my soapbox."

"Is that what she calls him?" He chuckled.

"Yes. I thought it was funny, too. She said he's not the type of fellow you call back, that it would be far too encouraging for him."

Quinn took a sip of tea. Katherine was probably

right. Carl could be fearless when it came to women.

"She was completely annoyed, not at all flattered." Ethel shook her head.

"Do you think she's interested in Joe . . . again?" Like an old slide show, the picture of Katherine on the back of Joe's bike clicked past.

"There's too many things wrong with Joe." Eyes narrowed, Ethel returned her mug to the table. "He wouldn't go to church with her. He was never on time. And . . . he didn't have a brain."

Suppressing a chuckle, Quinn carefully lowered his mug to the table.

"After Joe, a man with brains became higher on her list. Ask her. She was such a baby when he broke her heart." Ethel appeared thoughtful before glancing over her shoulder toward the doorway to the living room. "I'm surprised she was able to squeak out all A's that semester."

"What do you mean, such a baby?" Hadn't Ethel said during her first visit to his office that Kings rarely cried?

"Joe was the first fellow to ever break her heart. She was completely shocked by the experience. You know, the first time you fall, you don't have a landing net."

Quinn remembered his first crash landing all too well.

"Why do you keep asking about Joe?" She set both elbows on the table. "Don't tell me you know something I don't. Don't tell me she likes him again."

"Joe's not hearing the nine-credit excuse as often as Carl."

"Well, she and Joe *are* friends now." Ethel waved a hand. "They're close."

"It's rare, Ethel, don't you think?" He smiled

slightly. "I mean, he broke her heart, and *now* they're close friends."

Ethel clasped her vein-riddled hands above the table. "They played on the same tennis team for years. But, it was after Joe's father died that they truly became friends. The day he died . . ." Ethel's chest expanded. "Joe came here looking for Katherine. They sat together in the living room." She nodded over her shoulder. "For a couple of hours, Joe wept in her arms. She loves him in a different way now. You know . . ." Ethel dabbed at the corner of her eyes with a paper napkin. "When you go through something like that with someone, you grow closer."

Quinn remembered Katherine's large, historic-blue eyes staring at him from beneath the helmet. Her arms wrapped about Joe. Evans was wrong. Her Joe List needed to be rewritten.

Ж

Joe always gave Katherine a sizable lead. When she managed to get one point against him, she was always ecstatic. The start of their last game, he tossed the tennis ball for his serve, then caught it in one hand. Jogging toward the net, he smiled his I know I'm good looking smile.

"I'll give you a fifteen-love lead. If I win, you'll go out to dinner with me tonight. If you win, I'll . . ."

"Joe . . ." She shook her head. "I have a ton of studying, and I've been sidetracked all day. I don't bet when I know I'll lose."

"I'll play right-handed."

Joe was left-handed. He'd played her once before right-handed, and she'd scored an ace serve.

"Okay." She nodded. "If I win, you'll go to church with Grandma and me tomorrow."

"And if I win, you'll tell me over dinner *all* that's going on with the professor."

"That's easy. Nothing." Katherine jogged toward her serve line. "I get to serve."

"It's my turn to serve."

She glanced over her shoulder at him. Had she ever seen him serve right-handed? Could he?

"Shoot yourself." She tossed two balls over the net toward him.

His first attempt went right into the net. She giggled. As she rocked back and forth in her ready stance, the second serve whizzed over the net into the far right corner, out of reach. An ace serve.

Joe was ambidextrous.

His next three serves were almost as menacing as when he served left-handed. She didn't even return one. Chin held high, she approached the net.

"You're mad, Kate; I see it in your eyes."

"You failed to tell me you're as awesome with your right as you are with your left. I didn't stand a chance, and you knew it."

"I've been practicing. Learning to serve with both; works both sides of the brain. Makes you a more complete athlete."

"Why dinner?" Reaching over the top of the net, she shook his hand.

"I want you to meet my future girlfriend."

She should have known. "Wow, you made it a whole two weeks."

"It's not official yet; I want your opinion. You've been right about the last two . . ." His voice trailed off.

"Betty and Veronica."

"Hey, no name calling. I thought I'd get your

opinion this time before . . ."

"What time do you want to meet?"

"I'll pick you up at the orthodontist's at six o'clock."

The orthodontist's office was just far enough away that Grandma wouldn't hear the rev of Joe's bike. "Where are we going?"

"Five four one North Main. Great little hole-in-the-wall, family-owned restaurant. Her family."

That's all Joe was going to tell her. He wanted it to be a surprise.

Ж

The phone rang. It was probably for Katherine. They couldn't even finish a cup of tea without a fellow calling for her. "I need to get one of those go phones that go where you go." Ethel rose from her chair.

"They're called cell phones." Quinn chuckled.

"Hello," Ethel said, setting a hand on her hip.

"Hi, Grandma, I'm at the library. There's been a change in plans; Joe's taking me to dinner tonight."

"Oh, honey, I hope the two of you aren't getting back together."

"We're not. I lost to him at tennis. If he won, he wanted to take me out for dinner. If I won, I wanted him to go to church with us tomorrow. But I lost."

"Of course, you lost; he's the Big Sky champion."

"He gave me a fifteen-point lead, and he played right-handed. He's left-handed." Katherine sighed. "He's amazing."

"Just remember he doesn't have a brain. Are you going from the library to dinner, or are you coming home first?"

"I need to take a shower."

"Okay, honey. Tonight's a good night to wear your red shirt."

"Grandma!"

"Good-bye." Ethel hung up on her.

Quinn chuckled while she returned to her seat. She had big news for him. She'd watch his face closely for any telltale signs.

"If Joe won, he wanted to take her out to dinner. If Katherine won, she wanted him to go to church with us in the morning." Ethel sighed. "Of course, she's going to lose. He's the Big Sky champion."

"Yes, the odds were not in her favor."

"He gave her a fifteen-point lead, and even played right-handed. She said he's amazing. I sure hope they're not back together." Ethel sighed.

Quinn's eyes twinkled as he suppressed a smile. He didn't appear to be in the least bit concerned. He was probably relieved.

"Do they go out to dinner very often?"

"About every month or so when Joe's in between girlfriends."

"Sounds to me like you don't need to worry."

"I worry a little bit more now that Carl's shown some attention. Super-duper smart professors do not come along every day." She patted Quinn's nearest hand.

"Carl's a bit like Joe." Quinn smirked. "He doesn't go too long in between girlfriends."

"Oh, well, we won't even think about him, then." Ethel pushed her glasses up the bridge of her nose for a better view of Quinn. "We'll focus on another super-duper smart professor."

Quinn's Adam's apple bobbed. "You're not insinuating me, are you?"

"And if I were?"

"Then I'd need to remind you that for almost two months, I've looked forward to meeting a woman from the town of Palouse. We've spoken on the phone numerous times, but due to our schedules, we won't be able to meet until this coming Friday. And as you well know, Katherine and I don't—"

"Over two months? Is she a stewardess?"

"No." He smiled. "She works nights. She's a 9-1-1 operator."

"And you're really interested in this one?"

"I enjoy her personality, her voice—" he inhaled—"and she's a very good listener." He was smitten. Even his breathing was affected when he mentioned her.

"But, you've never met?"

"No."

"But . . . you've seen pictures?"

"No." He shook his head. "She doesn't have anything current."

"Voices can be deceiving. There was this radio commentator in the forties who my sister and I imagined to be extremely good looking. When we first laid eyes on him, we were shocked." Ethel shook her head as she recalled the eye-opening experience.

"At the moment, at least, I feel certain that she'll be worth the wait."

"How can you wait a week? In romance, that's a lifetime."

Quinn's downcast gaze proved he agreed with her.

"You should just hop in your car tomorrow after church and drive to Palouse. I'll go with you. There's a hamburger place on the left-hand side of town that Edwin and I used to stop at on our way to Spokane. Do you have her address?"

"I've talked about dropping by, but for some reason or other, she hasn't been receptive to the idea."

"Maybe she's trying to lose weight before she meets you. You're her incentive."

"No, she said she could afford to lose a few pounds, but she's comfortable."

"What's her name?" After church tomorrow, she and Katherine could drive to the town of Palouse, Washington. The canola fields would be in bloom, making for a beautiful Sunday drive. Katherine could study on the way. They'd have hamburgers and very casually look up this Miss Palouse.

"When I discuss my blind dates at Evans's, I give them fictional names. Her family has lived in Palouse for three generations, and Miss Palouse is running for mayor this fall."

"Wow . . . mayor." She couldn't picture Quinn with a woman of power. And she couldn't believe he was fine about being in limbo for another week, but it was his love life.

Chapter Nineteen

After finishing some errands and shopping at Tidyman's, Quinn set three bags of groceries on his kitchen counter. His phone vibrated in his back pocket. He slid a can of Folgers coffee onto the shelf above the coffee maker and flipped open his cell phone.

"Hello."

"I was wondering if you're home," Katherine said.

"Yes, I am."

"Is now a good time for Grandma to deliver the cinnamon rolls?"

"Sure."

"I'm glad; the rolls are always best while they're still warm, and Grandma wants to officially welcome you to the neighborhood."

Katherine had a surprisingly pleasant phone voice. He put away the groceries, tidied the living room, fluffed a pillow on the couch, and sat down at his dark oak desk, an estate sale find. He reread two poorly crafted student essays and then glanced at his wristwatch. Fifteen minutes had passed. The walk from Ethel's to his place should have taken the spry, elderly woman five minutes max. He yawned. Why had Katherine commented "while they're still warm" if Ethel was going to dawdle on her way here?

Holding down the six on his phone, he speed-dialed the Kings' number.

"Hello," Katherine said.

"Hi again, it's Quinn Benton. Has Ethel left yet?"

"Yessss. She should already be there. She left a good fifteen, twenty minutes ago."

"Hmm . . ." He strolled to the front window and peered out at the empty street. "Maybe she ran into neighbors that she knows."

"No, she was on a mission to deliver the rolls while they're still warm. Call me when she gets there or I'll worry."

"I will." He returned the phone to his back pocket. Where was Ethel? Quinn stepped out onto his front walkway, which overlooked Lynn Street. In the early afternoon, the brightly lit tree-lined street was void of cars or pedestrians. The first time Evans visited, he'd accidentally knocked on Quinn's tenant's door. Evans had seen the 432 on the mailbox and not paid any attention after that. Maybe Ethel had done the same.

In the year he'd owned the duplex, he hadn't had enough company to get in the habit of reminding visitors that his front door was the one on the left.

As Quinn strolled by Harold's side, he ever so casually peered in the front room window. Then he stepped back and did a double take. Seated in the kitchen nook area, with her profile to the window, Ethel sat drinking a cup of coffee.

He chuckled and dialed the Kings' residence.

"Hello."

"She's here and fine. No need to worry."

"Good . . ." Katherine sighed with relief. "What took her so long?"

"I'll let her tell you about it when she gets home." He slid his phone back in his pocket and eased Harold's front door closed behind him.

Harold's voice echoed from the kitchen—"I'm an old World War II man myself."

"Anybody home?" Quinn called out a greeting. The floor plan mirrored his side—1280 square feet, sixties ranch with popcorn ceilings, brick fireplace, and accordion-style closet doors.

"Took you long enough." Harold waited until Quinn stepped into the galley kitchen to add, "Pour yourself a cup of coffee."

"Where have you been, Quinn?" Ethel glanced over her shoulder at him. Her gardening hat hung on the back of her chair.

A square glass pan of gooey, frosting-loaded cinnamon rolls sat on the table. One large square, a quarter of the pan, was missing. Only a smear of cinnamon syrup remained on Harold's dinner-sized plate. *How to diplomatically address the situation?* Quinn pulled a striped mug down from the cupboard, poured himself a cup of dark coffee, and added cream.

"Ethel, I don't know if Harold informed you—"

"Uncle Harold," Harold interrupted.

So he'd lured Ethel in by lying to her. Would she think the worst? Leaning back against the counter, Quinn cradled the warm mug in both hands and studied the elderly man. In his early eighties, Harold didn't get much company or home cooking. Though swindled, the cinnamon roll must have been a treat for him.

"I don't know if my *neighbor* explained to you…" Quinn turned his attention to Ethel.

Her jaw slowly lowered.

"When I purchased the duplex from Harold . . . Gillespie, he wanted to continue living here as a tenant. We are *not* related."

"You lied." Wide-eyed, Ethel stared at Harold.

"Look at it from an elder's perspective . . ." Harold addressed Quinn as he set down his coffee cup and pointed his thumb over his shoulder. "I'd just taken a shower, and when I came in here, there's someone sitting at the table hidden behind my newspaper. To be frank, it gave me a heck of a start. I asked, 'How may I help you?' I didn't know if it was you"—he nodded toward Quinn—"or a thug." Harold held a hand out toward Ethel. "Instead, I find this attractive young woman sitting at my table."

"Hogwash." Ethel rolled her eyes.

Quinn supposed from Harold's point of view it was an unusual situation.

"And lo and behold, she'd brought me home-baked goodies."

"I thought it was you, Quinn, in the shower," Ethel said. "I made myself at home. Put my jar of strawberry jam in the freezer, and instead of decorating your front doorstep, I decorated the inside." She held up a roll of Scotch tape and nodded over her shoulder.

"Welcome Home" in six-inch-high letters cut out of red construction paper was taped to the front of Harold's pine cabinets.

"I usually spell out *Welcome Neighbor,* but I ran out of red paper." Ethel shook her head.

"I was telling Ethel her welcome to the neighborhood was more of a homecoming than I received from my ex-wife when I returned from World War II."

"I'm sorry to hear that, Harold." He now understood why the elderly man had been married twice.

Quinn wasn't about to forget Ethel's freezer jam. From the top freezer shelf, he retrieved the pint-sized jar from an avalanche of ice. He'd just bought a sleeve of English muffins that it would prove tasty on. He spun a dining chair around backward at the table and, straddling it, sat down.

"Ethel said that you and Katherine see quite a bit of each other," Harold said. "I thought your university frowned on professors dating students."

"I don't." Quinn shook his head. "We aren't."

"I said just the opposite." Ethel rolled her eyes. "I said, the two tolerate each other because of me."

Harold chuckled.

Quinn took a sip of the darkly brewed coffee. "Katherine is a very focused student and has no intention of dating until she's completed her master's."

"The Kings are known for their . . ." She looked at Quinn. "What's a synonym for *pigheadedness*?"

"*Stubborn, obstinate . . . Katherine King.*" He smiled.

"I worry about her." Ethel's shoulders dropped. "If she did have feelings for someone, she's so good at studying that she might. . . " Ethel's eyes narrowed. "Oh, what's the word I'm looking for?" She glanced at Quinn.

"*Smother, suppress, annihilate.*"

"Yes, she could very easily *annihilate* any feelings she might have for someone."

Using a butter knife, Harold cut a cinnamon roll in half and took the larger section for himself. Bare handed, Quinn reached in and snagged the remainder and took his first bite. A generous amount of cinnamon flavored the tender dough topped with vanilla-spiked cream cheese frosting. The rolls were a vastly different gastronomical experience from the ones Ethel had delivered to his office.

"Tell Katherine they're delicious," Quinn eyed the two nice-sized rolls remaining in the pan.

"It's the same recipe that I use," Ethel said, matter of fact.

Quinn nodded while maintaining a straight face.

"Do you think she has the makings of an old maid?" Harold asked. Using a fork, he carved his next bite.

"No." Ethel shook her head. "She loves kids way too much, and she's way too pretty. My worry is that there will be no good men left by the time she's finished reading all her textbooks."

"Way too pretty." Harold's gaze shifted to Quinn.

"She has very stunning aqua-blue-colored eyes." Quinn focused on his next bite. That's all he'd tell Harold or himself about his opinion of Katherine King. It was best not to dwell for too long on the subject.

"Way too pretty, with aqua-blue, stunning eyes..." Harold repeated.

"Joe, her ex-boyfriend, told her once that to change a fellow's mind about something . . . all she had to do was meet his gaze and slowly blink," Ethel said.

"Has she ever employed the slow blink with you?" Harold addressed Quinn.

Quinn recalled her visit to his office. She'd tapped her fingers together nervously, and at one point had even sat on them. "No." Had she employed it last night at Evans's door? He'd been in such a hurry to leave. No, she'd only employed the wide-eyed plead. No slow blink.

Quinn loaded a large cinnamon roll onto his plate.

"Did you teach your granddaughter how to make these?" Harold lifted his salt-and-pepper brows.

"No." Ethel giggled and waved a hand. "Her mother is quite the baker."

Quinn took another bite of the soft, not overly sweet dough with just the right amount of cinnamon and cream cheese frosting. Why had Katherine made the rolls for him? Did she secretly like him? No, that's right, she'd bribed him to take her home so Carl couldn't.

Chapter Twenty

Katherine wrapped up her Lewis and Clark reading and carried her empty coffee cup downstairs. When she opened the door into the living area, a fog-like smoke greeted her as it crept its way through the main floor. Burnt bacon permeated the air. The full-cycle hum of the exhaust fan above the stove informed her that Grandma was aware of the problem.

It had happened before on occasion. Grandma would become immersed in a crossword puzzle or her gardening and forget something on the stove. On Katherine's way to the sink, she passed Benton. He stood in front of the stove, wearing one of Grandma's full-bibbed, tie-in-the-back aprons. Was she seeing things? She set the mugs in the sink and peered over her shoulder. He was indeed wearing Grandma's dark blue calico apron with a scalloped bodice. Shredded hash browns filled a deep cast-iron skillet.

"I told him he looks cute." Seated at the table, Grandma whisked eggs in a green Tupperware container.

"She made me put it on."

"Bacon gets so messy." Grandma waved a hand.

Benton was playing house with her grandmother.

"We're having omelets, toast, and crispy hash browns," Grandma said. "Where's Joe taking you?"

"Some restaurant on Main." Katherine shrugged.

"Grandma, where's your camera?"

"I'm out of film."

"Good!" Benton chuckled.

On her way through the living room, Katherine was surprised the furniture hadn't been rearranged; the kitchen looked so different. She showered and then changed into jeans and her red scoop neck T-shirt. She blow-dried her hair and put on a light coat of mascara. In the medicine cabinet mirror, her eyes sparkled with nervous energy.

Boy, Benton was sure here a lot. Could there be a chance he was interested in her? She recalled the way she'd behaved in his office, the countless times they'd argued, and how he didn't want her to be included at the professor get-togethers. That had been the clincher.

The man was not fond of her. He was fond of her grandmother.

"You wore your red shirt." Grandma smiled at her. "You got a little too much sun today, dear. Red and red."

"Is it too much red?" Katherine asked.

"No, it's just Joe." As Grandma stood beside Quinn at the stove, she poured omelet batter into a Teflon pan.

"What restaurant are you going to?" Benton asked.

"Joe didn't say. Unless the name is 541 North Main."

"Is he picking you up here?" Grandma asked.

"No, I'm meeting him."

"Where are you meeting him?" Benton's brows lifted.

"I'm walking."

"Are you meeting him at the restaurant?" he asked.

She strolled to the window and, with her back to him recalled that he'd seen her earlier in the day on the back of Joe's bike. Had Benton guessed that they had a meeting place? When he was carrying his little box of tomato plants home, he'd indeed seen her. Any second, he was going to tattle on her. Grandma and Benton were perfect for each other; they were two overly protective, doting people at heart.

"I'm walking." It wasn't a lie.

"Are you walking all the way to 541 North Main?" he persisted.

"Would you like to drive her, Quinn?" Grandma asked.

"No," they both said in unison.

"Ethel said if you'd won the match, you wanted Joe to go to *church* with you in the morning."

He'd learned Grandma's roundabout code for telling her not to lie. It wasn't a lie; she was walking part of the way. She was twenty-eight—of legal age to drink, vote, and drive, but because of these two ninnies, she couldn't walk alone after dark or hitch a ride on Joe's motorbike. Well, just watch her.

"She's been asking Joe to go to church with us for years. Do you *still* want to go, Quinn?"

Katherine inhaled and closed her eyes.

"Yes, Ethel. It's been on my heart to find a home church again. Thank you."

That was the clincher. Things were getting out of hand. Should she report him to the dean, or maybe the president of the university? There had to be something about getting too close to the grandmothers of your students, allowing yourself to be brownnosed by cinnamon rolls, and coddled by sweet elderly women. Katherine glanced at the pot of yellow gerbera daisies in the living room. Unfortunately, the coddling appeared to be mutual.

Ж

Katherine unclipped Joe's extra motorcycle helmet and ran a hand through her tangled hair. The restaurant at 541 North Main was a little hole-in-the wall Chinese food place. A green, fang-toothed dragon mural was painted on the window. Joe walked ahead of her inside but remembered to hold the door open for her. One long, narrow room with low lighting made up the seating area. A red mesh bowl with a candle adorned the center of each table. A young, cute Asian woman seated them in a booth. Katherine faced the front while Joe faced the kitchen.

"Was that her?" Katherine nodded toward the hostess and opened the tall laminated menu.

"No, I think she's her older sister." Joe grinned and nodded toward a slim young woman who was taking the order for the couple seated across the aisle. "That's her." Chopsticks crisscrossed through her high, glossy bun.

A silver pot of tea was delivered, and two glasses of iced water, and then Joe's possible future girlfriend stood beside their table. "Are you ready to order?" She glanced from Joe to Katherine and, with a deep breath, back to Joe.

"Hello, Anna, this is Katherine, my good friend."

"Hello, Joe . . . Katherine." With a brief bow of her head, she greeted Katherine.

"Hello, Anna. Are you a student at the U of I?" Katherine asked.

"No. Tonight's special is Szechuan beef, very spicy."

Joe grinned.

"I'll have the number five combination dinner." It had all her favorites: almond chicken, pork chow mein, and fried rice.

"You like egg flower soup or hot and sour?"

"Egg flower, please."

Anna inhaled and turned to Joe. Her dimpled profile and heavy sigh meant she liked Joe. Most likely Anna didn't know Joe. For most girls, to not know Joe was to like Joe. He was attractive; he had a great smile. He was fun.

"I'll try your special. Szechuan. What was it again?" Smiling up at her, Joe dripped charm.

"Szechuan beef, very spicy."

"Yes, I'll have that." He closed the menu.

Szechuan beef, very spicy was all this cute little waitress had to say to get Joe down the aisle. Some men were that brainless. In a way, Benton was being brainless too—letting himself fall for Miss Palouse, a woman he hadn't even met, hadn't even seen. God made men visual, and Joe's vision was twenty-twenty.

What was Benton thinking? He was a good-looking, well-educated man. He could place a higher value on physical attraction than the norm, because like Joe, he could get away with it.

Joe leaned across the table. "What do you think?"

"She's cute. How'd you meet her?" She unfolded the paper napkin on her lap.

"Jeff and I ate here last week."

Jeff was a Moscow native, an old hall buddy of Joe's from when he'd lived in the Gault dorms.

"Anna was your waitress?"

"Yes." He grinned.

"And have you called or spoken with her since?"

"No, if you approve, I'll get her number tonight."

Frowning, Katherine closed one eye and looked at him with the other. "She probably thinks I'm your girlfriend, Joe."

"Nah, that's why I said you were a good *friend*."

Anna delivered two bowls of egg flower soup. Katherine eyed the clear broth with chunks of egg and green onion suspiciously. It probably contained some kind of Chinese poison.

"Do you play tennis, Anna?" For Joe's sake, Katherine would try to find out as much as she could.

"No."

"What do you think of motorcycles?"

Craning her neck, Anna looked directly at Katherine. "What did you say?"

"Do you like riding on motorcycles?"

She smiled and looked at Joe. "When it's not raining."

He must have driven his motorcycle here last week and parked in the front parking space. Now Anna knew it was an interview question, and that Katherine was indeed on her side.

After Anna left, Joe smiled and leaned back in his seat. "Good question, Kate."

Ten minutes later, when Anna delivered two white platters heaped high with enough food to feed a family of eight, Katherine had formulated a dating question tailored to Joe's personality.

"Are you a punctual person, Anna?"

Miss Chopsticks appeared confused.

"She's trying to see if you and I are right for each other." Joe wagged a finger back and forth between Anna and himself. Stretching her neck, Anna appeared two inches taller.

"Is it important for you to be on time?" Katherine asked. "Or is it okay to arrive a few minutes late, as the party won't really start until you're there anyway?" It was Joe's mentality to a T, but this early in the game, she wasn't about to tell Anna.

Anna giggled. "Joe, your friend . . ." She twirled her finger near her ear.

"Wait a second . . . it's a good question." He grinned up at Anna. "What's your take on being late?"

"It's very important to be on time. A courtesy."

Joe's shoulders sank. The flame was partly doused.

Confused, Anna glanced back and forth from Joe to Katherine.

"Being on time is not one of Joe's strengths." Katherine shrugged.

"Timeliness very important, Joe, but nobody perfect." Anna proceeded to another table, a group of three.

"Can you believe all this food?" By Joe's glum expression, it was apparent his fling was flung.

"I personally think being on time is a good trait—not one you should hold against her." Katherine sank her fork into the chow mein and teamed it with half a forkful of fried rice.

"Good dating questions, Kate. What other great qualities of mine are you going to pick next?"

"I don't have to inquisition her further unless you want me to."

"Of course, I do. By the end of the evening, I want to know *yes,* I'll ask her out, or *no,* she's not right for me."

Katherine smiled. He was like Benton—he wanted to eliminate her in one date.

"Speaking of love . . ." Joe grinned. "Something's going on with the professor."

"He's my new grandfather. As of last week, my

grandmother and Grandpa Benton have teamed up to ruin my life."

"What do you mean? What's going on?" Joe's captivating blues narrowed.

Chapter Twenty-One

Quinn slathered Ethel's delicious strawberry freezer jam on a piece of toast. "Is this hard to make?"

"It's easy. I know the recipe by heart. You buy some Sure-Jell, a carton of strawberries, and a bag of sugar. Too bad they don't have a freezer jam category at the fair. I'd finally win a blue ribbon."

"You would. Aren't strawberries in season right now?"

"Yes. Tidyman's has them on sale. I really should make one more batch to give away as Christmas gifts."

"I'm very happy about the jar I have in my fridge." Quinn brushed the crumbs off his hands. "Ethel, where's your phone book?" he asked, rising from the table. "I want to look up the restaurant that Katherine's at."

"Why?"

"All she knew was the address. I had the worst case of food poisoning a month or two ago. I almost went to the emergency room, except I was too sick to drive myself there."

"What an *awful* thought. It's in the top drawer of the curio cabinet."

In the living room, Quinn found the half-inch-thick Latah County phone book and flipped to Restaurants in the yellow page section. He returned to the table and scanned the Chinese food section first, searching by address, not by name.

There it was: 541 N. Main, The Green Dragon.

He closed his eyes and took a deep breath.

"Ethel, it's the same place."

Her eyes narrowed. "What do you mean?" She regarded him over her half-eaten omelet.

"Five four one North Main is The Green Dragon, the same place I got food poisoning."

"Aw . . . raunchy potatoes. You need to tell Katherine."

"I'll drive there. In the meantime, call the restaurant and try and warn her."

He wrote the number on a sticky note and handed it to Ethel. "I should have reported getting sick. Hopefully, their food-handling practices have improved."

"Hopefully, she won't get sick." Ethel scanned his legible print. "She's such a baby about pain."

Ж

Ethel dialed the number for the Chinese restaurant. The female voice that answered was muffled "Is this The Green Dragon?" Ethel asked.

"Yes. You want takeout?"

"No, we're having omelets tonight. The reason I'm calling is . . . I was wondering if you could find one of your customers for me. We need to warn her about your food."

Click. The receptionist hung up on her.

Flustered, Ethel looked at the sticky note again and redialed. She had to be smarter about her wording this time.

"The Green Dragon, this is Anna, how may I help you?"

It was a different receptionist this time. "Yes, I

was wondering if you could find a young woman for me."

Click.

The Green Dragon hung up on her again.

Ж

The digital clock on the dash read 6:45; Katherine and Joe could easily be into the middle of their meal by now. Quinn sighed. The minute he'd heard *North Main,* he should have connected the two. He found a parking space in front of a computer repair store, three buildings north of The Green Dragon.

Quinn swung open the glass door and briefly scanned the two long rows of booths that lined each side of the room.

"Seating for one?" a young hostess asked, holding a menu.

"No, I need to get an urgent message to a young woman who's here, somewhere." He scanned the booths. "But I don't see her."

The hostess frowned.

"She's wearing a red shirt. Straight blonde hair." Quinn gestured past his shoulders.

"Is she very beautiful?"

The question was loaded; admitting that Katherine King was beautiful was a giant, soul-searching step. He inhaled. "She has her moments."

"Follow me."

He followed the hostess past several booths and halted behind her as she paused to speak with a busboy clearing an unusually large mess.

"Crud!" Off to his left, a familiar voice resonated.

Quinn turned. Three booths away sat Katherine.

She probably thought he liked her, was even stalking her. He'd inform her and leave, and someday maybe she'd thank him. But, knowing Katherine, he doubted it. He stopped in front of Joe's and her table and awaited her sarcasm.

"Hello, Mr. Benton, you wouldn't happen to be"—she frowned—"stalking me?" She set down her fork.

A silver pot of tea and a bottle of soy sauce sat in the center of their table. He scanned their meals. Joe had white rice, and Katherine, poor Katherine, had half a mound of fried rice.

"We have a slight problem. Has Ethel gotten a hold of you?"

"No." The color in her face drained. "Is everything okay?"

"At the moment." With two flicks of his wrist, he motioned for her to scoot over. They were really only one-person booths, so he was asking a lot. But, he didn't want to announce to the entire restaurant that within twenty-four hours she'd wish she'd never been here.

She uncoiled one foot from beneath her and scooted over toward the half wall. "Oh, crud. My foot's asleep." She moaned.

"You shouldn't have sat on it." Joe rolled his eyes.

Katherine grimaced and shook her foot beneath the table.

"Kate has no pain tolerance—physical, emotional…"

"Mental." Quinn nodded. It made perfect sense.

"That's enough, Mr. Benton."

He was surprised she hadn't elbowed him. He could tell she wanted to. Perhaps when she'd been in the womb, some type of cushioning had gone wrong in her cells. Was there a term for her condition?

"In case you didn't know, she really prefers to be called Kate," Joe said.

"I do not. He's lying." She kicked Joe under the table. A smile followed her unladylike behavior. "That appears to have done the trick. I'll have to remember that for the future."

"When in pain, kick Joe." Quinn nodded and cleared his throat. "Remember how I got food poisoning four, maybe five Fridays ago?" He paused but didn't wait for her reply. "This is the place. My date and I determined it was the fried rice." He pointed to her remaining half pile. "It also could have been the deep-fried shrimp appetizer, but we both leaned toward the fried rice."

"I just ate here last week," Joe said. "Not a problem."

"Did you have fried rice?"

"I had white." Joe glanced down at his heaping platter of food, served with a separate bowl of white rice.

"I think you're fine, but it looks like I'm a little late for Kate." Quinn eyed her meal. "Sorry, I didn't think to look up the address in the phone book until halfway through dinner. The omelet was very good, by the way."

"How soon did your symptoms show up?" She stared at her plate.

"Let's see, I ate here on a Friday night at about seven thirty with Miss Genesee."

"Is that really her name?" Joe chuckled.

"No, Benton doesn't disclose the real names of his blind dates, so the group has resorted to fictional names based on residence."

Wide-eyed, Joe appeared to be waiting for the punch line.

"Our meal arrived at about seven thirty, seven forty," Quinn said.

"Is anything okay?" The waitress addressed the group and set a glass of iced water down in front of him.

"Anna, you mean, 'Is everything okay?'" Joe chuckled.

Narrowing her gaze, the young woman appeared confused.

"Would you like a menu?" Anna asked Quinn.

"No, thank you." He waited until she was several steps away from the table before he elaborated on his last visit. "My stomach began to gurgle a bit that night. By two o'clock, I was in utter pain and agony. Miss Genesee's symptoms didn't appear until five o'clock Saturday morning." He sighed and studied Katherine's puzzled gaze. "Don't forget there's a paper due on Monday."

"I have the rough draft done."

"I suggest you make it an early evening, and address the final draft as soon as you get home."

Joe laughed. "You like her. This is all some crazy plot because you want her home early, and you don't want me spending time with her."

Katherine shook her head. "I'm helping in child care tomorrow morning at church. Should I call in now?"

Was she mocking him? Quinn couldn't tell. "There is the possibility."

"Wait a second . . ." Joe held up a pointer finger. "If everyone got sick from their fried rice, this place would be out of business."

"Maybe it was just my luck." Quinn shrugged. "I

should have reported it. I feel bad now that I didn't."

"Why'd you refer to it as 541 North Main?" Katherine asked Joe.

"I wanted it to be a surprise. I know how you love Chinese."

It was a good note to leave on. "Sorry to be the bearer of bad news." He sighed. "And, Katherine, I finished reviewing the essays."

Wide-eyed, she swallowed. "I'm not sure if I like how you prefaced that."

"I didn't know if you wanted to wait until Monday to find out."

Her rib cage expanded. "What's your final verdict?"

"I upped your grade to a B-plus."

"Why?" She didn't blink.

What she really meant was *Why wasn't it an A?*

"I still think your conclusion could have been stronger. Your writing in many areas was brilliant, but your conclusion was wanton."

"Thank you for making my evening complete."

Hmmm . . . He'd thought she'd be pleased.

"Did you say her 'conclusion was wonton?'" Joe's gaze narrowed.

Quinn grinned. "I believe Ethel wants to get in a game of Scrabble. If you two care to join us later . . ."

"Isn't that the game you always wanted me to play with the little wood letters?" Joe appeared intrigued.

"He's not really the word-game type." Katherine avoided looking Quinn's direction. Probably because there were daggers in her eyes.

It was too bad—in Scrabble, four was a better player number than two.

"You're welcome to join us." Quinn rose to his

feet.

"We'll pass." Katherine scooped a forkful of chow mein.

Quinn strode toward the door. That's right, Evans had told him *limited vocabulary* was one of the items on Katherine's Joe List. He doubted if that was enough to keep them apart. Joe was athletic, good looking, and, if he'd read the situation correctly, very taken with Katherine.

Ж

Near the end of the Sunday school hour right after snack time, Katherine assisted the children at the sink. One by one the four-and five-year-olds climbed on the toddler step and squirted dabs of liquid soap into their chubby little hands. In the last half hour, Katherine's stomach had begun to churn. Was she simply being psychosomatic? Her symptoms were seven hours later than Benton's had been. Still, she couldn't help feeling uneasy.

Lord, please help me not to get sick. I have a paper due tomorrow, and I'm taking nine credits in the master's program, and, well, You know.

In the middle of Pastor Ken's sermon, the stomachache and other symptoms were no longer a figment of her imagination. Pastor Ken was at his best. His sermon explored Romans and loving without hypocrisy. Katherine didn't want to get sick in the middle of it.

Was she getting a fever? Any minute now she might need to hightail it to the bathroom. In between aches, she felt convicted: loving men was difficult at times. She stared at the cross. She wanted to be kind to

Carl, yet firm. She wanted to be the friend that Joe needed. Her thoughts drifted to Benton. Seated on the other side of Grandma, he'd followed through on her invitation to join them. Her prayer was the clearest for him. *Help him to find the woman he's searching for, Lord, and boy is he searching. I pray for his happiness, amen.*

She nudged Grandma. "I'm getting sick."

Grandma opened her church purse and handed her the car keys. "I'll have Quinn take me home. If you have to on your way out, throw up in your purse. You need a new one anyway."

Every Sunday Grandma made comments about her black handbag. As she strode toward the exit doors, she simultaneously felt flushed and chilled. They must have prayed along the way, as she made it to the car without an incident.

Hallelujah!

Chapter Twenty-Two

Quinn was in the middle of grading papers when Evans called. "When are you going to address Katherine for the way she spoke to Carl?" Evans asked. "He said she hasn't called. The majority nominated you."

Quinn rolled his eyes. "She's sick. Joe took her out to Chinese food last night, and it ended up being the same place that I took Miss Genesee to."

"You're kidding! The Green Dragon?" Evans remembered the name. "Did you ever report them?"

"No, I'm kicking myself now."

"Well, when she's feeling better, have her call Carl. Hold it over her head if you have to. Tell her we need everyone in the group to be amiable with one another, and we need a resolution before Friday."

"Carl's equally guilty, Evans. He didn't let up."

"If she initiates, Carl will follow suit. How often is it that your fellow colleagues truly enjoy one another's company without all the intellectual egotism? Or, as Cindy so eloquently put it, 'without all the mumbo jumbo hoity-toity.' We can't let Katherine and Carl's little romantic spats get in the way."

"You messed up on your matchmaking, Evans; she is sincerely not interested."

"I'm surprised Carl's handled it so well, you taking her home like you did. But knowing Carl, he hasn't forgotten. Maybe you both should apologize" were Evans's parting words.

Quinn made a pot of decaf coffee, graded some papers, and finally got around to calling the King residence. After two rings, Ethel picked up.

"Ethel, it's Quinn."

"She's still sick, Quinn, and the sermon was so good. He said exactly what Katherine needed to hear. I kept thinking, I wish Katherine were here."

"I enjoyed it too, Ethel. How sick is she?"

"Just horrible, and to top it off, she's always such a baby when she's sick. You wouldn't believe it."

Poor Katherine. He'd been so sick he'd wanted to die.

"Does Joe know?" Quinn asked.

"I doubt very much if she's called him. She's not very sociable right now."

"What's his number? I'll call him." He was curious if Joe had also been poisoned.

"It's somewhere on one of these notes. Wait a second, she wrote several numbers all on one sticky note. I need my magnifying glass to read it. Her print is so tiny. Hold on." A slight thud followed as Ethel set the phone down. "Oh, where is it?" she mumbled before picking up the receiver. "When she doesn't want me to read something, she writes in itty-bitty flea-sized print. I almost need Edwin's old binoculars, not a magnifier."

Ethel was unusually chatty, maybe because she didn't have Katherine to converse with.

Quinn dialed Joe's number, leaned back against the oak desk in his living room, and surveyed the front room. A heaping pile of polo shirts on the ironing board was a permanent fixture. He often had good intentions, but rarely followed through. There were always other far more exciting distractions.

"Hi, Joe. This is Quinn Benton—Katherine's US history professor slash chauffeur driver."

There was an uncomfortable silence.

"Hey," Joe finally said.

"Katherine's sick. I just spoke with Ethel, her grandma."

"How sick?"

"Ethel said she's horribly sick. Definitely food poisoning. I thought one of us should drop by some ginger ale. It helped me a lot a while back."

"Tell her I'm sorry she's sick. I have a private tennis lesson at three."

It didn't sound like Joe planned to stop by and play caregiver. Maybe Joe and Katherine's friendship *was* platonic. Maybe she was telling the truth.

"Do you have any symptoms yet?"

"No."

"Then we've narrowed it down to the fried rice."

Quinn couldn't help recalling the two of them on Joe's motorcycle as they waited for the light to turn green. Chummy, if not intimate. Hmm... they'd just been chummy.

A half hour later, Quinn stopped by Ethel's place. He carried two liters of ginger ale to the back door, one under each arm. He told himself it was the least he could do for not putting 541 North Main and The Green Dragon together earlier.

"You just can't get enough of us." Ethel giggled, opening the door wide.

The kettle was already on. Quinn set the ginger ale on the counter and returned to sit in his usual chair by the door. "How's the patient?"

"She's mad at you." Ethel set down a tray with a

jar of Folgers instant coffee, an assortment of teas, a sugar bowl, and spoons.

Quinn should have expected an unreasonable woman like Katherine to blame him, instead of The Green Dragon, for her bout of food poisoning.

"She said if you had simply reported your case of food poisoning to the proper authorities, this never would have happened."

Katherine did have a point.

"And she's mad that you didn't announce it to the whole restaurant last night. She said they deserved a little bad press."

Katherine was indeed upset.

"Do you know Joe calls her Kate?" he asked.

"Yes. He does it to irritate her." Ethel sighed. "She keeps saying 'I want to die.' When the time comes, I don't know how she'll ever get through childbearing. You should see her with the little kids at church. She just loves them. But, if she *ever* marries and has to go through labor, her poor husband."

Quinn couldn't agree more.

"Is she better?" He nodded to the living room.

"She won't come out of the bathroom."

"I'm sorry, Ethel, I won't stay long. I have papers to grade, ironing—"

"How much ironing?"

Ethel almost acted like she liked it.

"An overwhelming and expansive, mortifying amount."

"I do, too." Her eyes brightened. "A girlfriend and I once had an ironing party. We both set ironing boards up in my living room and had the babies in their playpens. We gabbed all afternoon, and then her husband's job moved to Spokane." Her shoulders sank. "That was the one time I really had a good time ironing. It's kind of like bingo, so mindless."

He nodded and recalled how Katherine had laughed at him for wearing an apron.

"Thank you for the tea, Ethel. I want to apologize to Katherine while I'm here."

Ethel nodded. "She's in the bathroom."

Feeling brave, he marched through the living room and knocked firmly on the bathroom door. "Katherine, it's Benton. I mean Mr. Benton."

"Go away."

He stared at the white-painted, solid wood door and knew he should have foreseen this. Yet, he couldn't help feeling surprised. Sylvia, his ex-fiancée, had been such a peacemaker. Maybe that's why she'd moved before she'd officially broken off their engagement. He'd deemed it so cowardly of her. He often reasoned that maybe she loved him enough that she knew she wouldn't be able to break up with him in person. But he knew better; she simply had no backbone for conflict.

"I brought you some ginger ale. When you're feeling a little better, try taking small sips."

"Thank you. Don't come in."

"Of course, I won't."

"Good."

He placed a hand on the molding. "I called Joe. He's fine. It's definitely the fried rice. You're the third person to confirm it. Joe said to tell you he's sorry."

"Will you report them, please?"

"Yes. I'll call The Green Dragon today. Tomorrow, I'll call the authorities. They aren't open on Sundays."

"Thank you. Now, go away—I don't want you to hear me."

He understood now. Katherine's earlier "'go

away'" request had not been rude; it made complete and perfect sense.

"If it's any consolation, Katherine, I wanted to die, too."

"Go away, Mr. Benton."

He took her advice.

"I'm sorry she's so rude." Ethel was still seated in her chair at the table.

"Her reaction is entirely understandable," he said on his way to the door.

"I'm glad you understand her. Do you know she didn't get her paper done?"

He paused mid-stride. "I told her to work on it last night." He paused with his hand on the knob. This was not good news for him or Katherine.

"When she got home last night, she went to bed. She's not used to staying up so late on Friday nights yet. Is it true that you'll knock her down a grade for turning it in late?"

He frowned. "Not with her extenuating circumstances."

"She has a doctor as her witness."

"Tell her I'll give her until Tuesday."

"Thank you, Quinn; you're a good friend to us both."

He stopped halfway to his car. Did he foreget something? He'd brought in the ginger ale; was there something else he intended to do while he was here?

During his short drive home, Ethel's comments bothered him. *You're a good friend to us both.* Today, for some strange reason, he'd gone to the Kings to see Katherine, and he hadn't been able to see her. The antagonism between them pumped blood a little faster through his veins. His blood felt a little sluggish at the moment.

Needing to be mindless, Quinn ironed two shirts and stared at his mobile phone on the corner of the coffee table. He'd call Claire, also known as Miss Palouse. They were both very open with each other. With Claire, Quinn had shared the ongoing saga of his blind dates, Katherine joining the professors' group, Carl's interest in her, having to drive Katherine home, Ethel's visit to his office, and later when she'd asked him over for meatloaf.

Had it been only yesterday when he'd stood on the corner of Main and Sixth Street and seen Katherine on the back of Joe's bike? For a brief second, he'd been concerned about Carl's reaction. But Carl had been fine. Carl had chuckled. In retrospect, it had strangely been Quinn who'd fought the tight constriction in his chest and shortness of breath at the sight of Katherine's arms around Joe.

He unplugged the iron and dialed Claire's number.

"Claire, it's Quinn."

"Quinn." He sensed her smile on the other end of the line.

"I need to talk."

"About Miss A-nnoying?"

How had she known? He sighed.

"It's only a twenty-five-minute drive from Moscow to Palouse. I'd like to visit this evening if it's all right."

"My brother and his wife are visiting from Coeur d'Alene. They'll be here at six, but I can talk while I'm preparing dinner."

"What are you making?"

"Cornish game hens with wild rice stuffing."

"Do you have seating for four?"

"You mean seating for eight. They have four

children. I'm making dinosaur chicken nuggets for the kids."

"You know I like children, Claire."

"Yes. But, it's not ideal. Let's wait."

He sighed. "I think it would be perfect."

"Does she still refer to me as a beauty pageant queen?" Claire giggled.

"She refers to all my blind dates as Miss and then their town name. Yes, you're still Miss Palouse."

"I've never been pageant material."

"And you know my response." Why did she continue to put off meeting him?

"Does she know I call her Miss Moscow? Or is she aware yet that she's in the running?"

"I didn't call to talk about her."

"You sound agitated, Quinn." The sound of a kettle hissing and the clatter of pots and pans briefly interrupted their conversation. "Is there a chance you're putting off your feelings for Miss Moscow on account of not meeting me?"

"I am tired of waiting." Quinn paced the length of his living room sisal rug. "I don't care if you have family there tonight. I actually think it would be a great way for us to meet." He'd never been pushy before, but he hadn't felt so impatient before.

"I'd be entertaining you instead of them. The relationship between my sister-in-law and me is already strained."

"I understand, Claire." And he did.

"We'll finally meet this Friday. Only five days."

Between her evening work at the emergency hotline in Pullman and his work at the university, little of their free time overlapped. They said their good-byes. Trying to be mindless, he ironed two more shirts.

His home phone rang.

"Quinn." Ethel sounded tired. "At what point should I worry about Katherine getting dehydrated? She can't keep anything down."

"Tell her to take sips of ginger ale. Not gulps. Just tiny sips."

"Tiny sips. I tried to call your mobile number first, but it was busy. I hope I didn't interrupt."

"I was talking with Miss Palouse."

"You sound down. I hope you're going to meet her soon."

"She has company tonight—her brother and his wife and family."

"I see. What's Miss Palouse's name? A high school friend of mine lives in Palouse. Maybe she knows her."

"Claire Westin." It would be nice to have another person's input.

"Claire Westin . . . sounds like a movie star, like she could costar with John Wayne."

He agreed—he'd always liked Claire Westin's name.

Chapter Twenty-Three

Ethel had several errands to run Monday morning. Right before she'd left home, Katherine had yelled at her from the living room not to wear her strawberry hat. So Ethel had promptly exchanged it for her other straw hat with the lime-green-and-white polka-dotted tie. It looked better anyway with the peach-colored shirt she was wearing.

The parking lot at the U of I Administration Building was a hub of activity. Looking for a parking space, Ethel drove her red Chevy Nova around and around the perimeter of the five-lane lot. Numerous handicapped spaces were vacant. How long would it take her to pay her parking ticket and turn in Katherine's paper to Quinn? Five, ten minutes. In so short a time, what were the odds that she'd get another ticket?

Parking at the Admin was more difficult than parking at the Palouse Empire Mall the day after Thanksgiving. Tired of wasting time and fuel, she gave up the search and parked beneath a handicapped sign in the fourth row, three spaces in. There was a chance no one would notice her here.

The experience had been so nerve-racking that Ethel peered in the flip-down mirror and half expected to see that all her hair had turned gray. A decent mix of mousy brown and dowdy gray remained. Thanks goodness.

In the registrar's office, she waited in line behind three young people. When it was finally her turn, Ethel plunked twenty-five dollars on the counter for her parking ticket.

"How are you today, ma'am?" The young brunette clerk behind the counter was so pleasant that Ethel felt inspired.

"Just peachy, thank you. I'd like to speak with someone about an idea I have to improve the university."

"What department?" The gal was so friendly and attentive; she wondered if Quinn had ever met her. They worked in the same building, but then she noticed a wedding ring on the young woman's hand. Quinn really needed to start dating women closer to home.

"It, um . . . has to do with . . . senior relations." Ethel tried to sound prepared.

With lifted brows, the young woman appeared baffled. As Ethel suspected, they had no Senior Relations department, staff, or chairperson. The three gals in the office debated for several minutes on where to send her. It felt like a waste of precious time that she'd hoped to spend with Quinn. She sighed and loosened the bow beneath her chin. Finally, they decided on the president of the university.

Heaven forbid, she was going straight to the top.

It was Monday morning, nine o'clock. Didn't she need an appointment? A middle-aged blonde, wearing a miniskirt that was far too mini, escorted her down the hallway to an elevator. From there, they rode to the second floor. Holding her handbag close to her, Ethel told herself to pay special attention to where the elevator was when they landed. She'd take it later to the third floor.

She glanced down at her escort's attire. The woman wore naughty fish net stockings. Though she seemed sweet enough, her attire was very immodest for office work. From the elevator, she escorted Ethel past a hallway secretary to a trio of chairs. "Wait here, Mrs. King, he's expecting you."

"Thank you." Ethel wished the middle-aged woman would remain with her so the president of the university could see how a woman in his employ was dressing. The university needed a grandmother to help run things more professionally.

A century-old-looking door, very similar to Quinn's, creaked open, and a balding gentleman, tall, with massive shoulders, stepped forth. "Ethel King," he said, and with an outstretched arm beckoned her into his office.

She felt very unprepared.

While she strolled through his open door, she read the gold plaque: President Morrison. His name sounded like one of the US presidents. There had been a President Hamilton, or was it Harrison? She'd have to ask Katherine.

President Morrison had the same view as Quinn, with wider windows in a much larger room with expansive walls lined with expensive books. There were so many books that they were probably more for decoration than education.

"What can I do for you today, Mrs. King?" He extended his hand. His hands and face were covered with freckles. When he was young, he'd most likely been nicknamed Freckles, and now he'd risen to the top. What a wonderful success story.

After firmly shaking his hand, she took a seat in a comfy padded chair. "The reason I'm here, Your

Honor . . ." She began to untie the bow beneath her chin and then decided not to take off her hat, as she'd undoubtedly have hat hair. "I visited the campus several weeks ago." Wide-eyed, she realized this meeting could easily cost her another twenty-five dollars if she weren't careful.

"Oh, are you thinking of taking classes here?" There was a definite twinkle in his eyes.

She suppressed a giggle. She was seventy-one, or was it seventy-two? Now was not a good time to begin a new career, not after thirty-plus years of being a grandmother. She was finally getting good at it.

"No, I'm not thinking of taking classes." Ethel waved a hand. "My granddaughter, Katherine King, is taking classes here. The reason I'm here is . . . this is the second time I've recently visited the university, and it's also the second time I've driven around and around your Admin parking lot and could not find one available space. There were several handicapped parking spaces available. Probably ten, if I'd taken the time to count all of them."

He nodded.

"Do you know a Professor Quinn Benton?" Ethel asked.

"Yes, of course. He's on staff in our US history department here at the university."

"He's our neighbor. We think the world of him, or at least I do."

He nodded and smiled, but that was it. Good, he didn't appear to know about the cinnamon rolls or Katherine's fuss over the B.

"I think that the University of Idaho, as well as Moscow, maybe all of Latah County should assign a number of parking spaces for senior citizens. I was fine with walking and all until I hit seventy; then things started to act up. For the sign . . ." She held up two fingers of each hand and did the little bunny-ear sign like Katherine often did. "It could read 'Senior Parking.' You could have a turtle walking on its two back legs holding a cane. I think the sign should be white with green lettering." Ethel nodded. That's how she'd always pictured it.

The president's gaze appeared a bit glazed. Of course, it was Monday morning.

"I know you may not be the right person for me to have spoken with first about this, but three very sweet ladies downstairs did not know where to send me. And one, I might add, was not dressed appropriately for public work."

Not that she, Ethel King, was dressed appropriately for speaking with the president of the university. "I have hat hair," she admitted. "Otherwise, I would have taken off my gardening hat. I came in this morning to pay my parking ticket. I had no idea I'd be so royally received."

His smile started in his sparkly brown eyes and worked its way down his facial muscles to his thin lips. His response reminded her of Quinn and the first time she'd visited his office. The poor university professionals—they were probably up to their ears in young people and their overactive hormones, and they were simply hungry for down-to-earth senior wisdom.

"The law requires that we have one handicapped space for every ten parking spaces," President Morrison said.

"I didn't realize it was so high." She sighed. "Is it a state law or federal law?"

"To be honest, Ethel, I'm not certain, but if I had to guess, I'd guess state. At the moment, our population of students who are over sixty-five is at about ten, and most are part-time students at that."

"An expensive undertaking for so small an age group." Ethel nodded.

"Yes, though I feel your idea is visionary on a broader scale."

Ethel felt herself beam. He was a person who saw the good in others' ideas and called it *visionary*. He'd been made the president for a reason. Meeting the man made her feel proud that four of her grandchildren called the University of Idaho their ala mater, or was it alma mater? She'd have to ask Katherine.

"President Morrison, do you really mean that? You like the idea?"

"Yes. My parents are aging." He nodded. "They're also over seventy and have dropped by from time to time to check in on me." He smiled. "They've also complained about parking."

"You have a law school here." Her heart pounded in her chest like she was still a teen.

"Yes, we do, Ethel."

"Can you make senior parking a senior project, or maybe a class project? Have the students learn to make a difference in their community? Have them push this wonderful idea of ours into action?"

He chuckled and tipped his head back against the top of his leather chair. "I'll see that your wonderful idea, Ethel, falls into the right hands. With a little guidance, of course."

She rose to her feet. "Four of my grandchildren have lived with me while attending the U of I and earning their degrees. I've never felt as much pride in our little town's university as I do right now. God bless you, President Morrison."

By the time Ethel reached Quinn's office, they'd only have five minutes together before he needed to be at his nine-thirty class. So Ethel didn't waste any of their precious time by sharing the news about her meeting with the president. She got right to the point by handing him Katherine's paper.

"Usually, she types her papers in some computer laboratory on campus, but last night, she used my old Brother typewriter instead." Ethel paused to smile. "Thank heaven I had half a bottle of Wite-Out. Katherine was yelling "Oh, brother" until at least two o'clock this morning. But . . . it's handed in on time. Early, even." She looked at the overhead clock. They still had four minutes before his history class started.

Now that she'd spoken her piece, she sat down in the metal folding chair and took a fresh look at Quinn. His yellow polo shirt appeared freshly pressed and was such a nice color on him, bringing out the gold highlights in his dark eyes. Sporting a summer tan, he appeared even more handsome than her first impression of him.

"Did you tell Katherine she had until Tuesday?" Quinn set the paper aside on his desk.

"Yes, but she hates to be late for anything." Ethel sighed and for a moment, reflected on where she'd parked.

"Is everything okay, Ethel?"

"I sure hope so. Lack of punctuality is one of her biggest pet peeves. Joe was fifteen minutes late to their first date, and she almost didn't go out with him. She thought his tardiness was a bad sign. I made the mistake of convincing her she should forgive him." Ethel sighed. "I was so excited that she finally had a date."

"I didn't know that about her." While he nodded, Quinn's brows remained in an elevated position.

"Yes, that's why she's such a pain to live with.

She expects everyone else to live up to her perfect expectations. She left a small sticky note for you on the last page. We're out of the other sizes." Ethel made a mental note that she needed to buy some today while she was out running around. They were down to the size that was really only big enough for one medium-sized word.

He leafed through Katherine's essay to page five.

"I need a magnifying glass. Her print is microscopic."

Ethel giggled. Now, if she'd been the one to describe it, she would have referred to it as itty-bitty or flea-sized. Quinn was just like Katherine, using highfalutin words. Before Ethel had left home, she'd used the magnifying glass she kept on the curio cabinet to peek at what Katherine had written.

"I memorized what it says if you want me to tell you."

"I'm curious." He nodded. "Your granddaughter has mastered being unpredictable."

"She wrote: I'm sorry for the crossed-out lines on page four. We ran out of Wite-Out. Oh, and thank you for the ginger ale. It helped."

"Hmmm . . ." Quinn's cheek muscles bunched, like Katherine's sticky note had genuinely touched his heart.

"Between her trips to the bathroom, Katherine worked herself into a tizzy fit trying to type it out perfect. She completely wiped herself out. Who knows if anything makes sense, Quinn, but I think she should get an A for effort under *awful* circumstances. Don't you?"

Ethel hoped he'd, at least, smile, but Quinn merely nodded like he was still dwelling on Katherine's flea-sized note. Or maybe his mind was elsewhere.

"Your granddaughter is very determined."

She didn't like the sound of it. *Determined* started with *D*. *Brilliant* started with *B*. She hoped he wouldn't hold the crossed-out lines against her. Quinn was difficult to read this morning. Something about him wasn't quite centered, but maybe it was because of her timing during his workday.

They walked together from his office down the hall and paused near the elevator. "I have some exciting news." She patted his arm. "I'll tell you tonight when you stop by." She added a wink, but she was so out of practice that it probably looked more like her eye twitched.

He chuckled none-the-less.

They held no plans for him to stop by; it was simply her way of hinting that she hoped he would. Quinn had no idea her next errand was in his honor. She was going to track down Miss Palouse. He might be patient enough to wait until Friday to meet Claire Westin, but Ethel King wasn't!

Ж

Another goldenrod parking ticket sat beneath Ethel's windshield wiper. She stewed about it for the first nine miles of her drive, and then, as she reached the summit of Moscow Mountain, the view of the rolling hills in all their patchwork grandeur took her breath away. Early summer on the Palouse was one of her favorite seasons. Beneath the glorious blue sky, the rolling hills were quilted in blocks of gold and vivid greens, stitched by the Master's hand. Following the signs to the town of Palouse, Ethel took a left off the

Coeur d'Alene highway and headed west.

She drove her Chevy Nova on the quiet, two-lane country road through the rolling hills of knee-high golden canola. Miss Palouse had one of the most splendid settings in Whitman or Latah County. If Ethel were Claire, she'd get Quinn to meet her soon while the canola was in full bloom. During the drive, he was bound to fall more in love with her.

Too bad he didn't like a local girl . . . like Katherine.

Katherine was pretty and made amazing cinnamon rolls, but how would Quinn describe her personality? Three words came to mind: Brilliant. Stubborn. Determined.

Near the cusp of town, Ethel passed the museum. Palouse had only one main street of businesses. A hillside with lovely historic homes lined the north side of the street, and the Palouse River the south side. She parked her car in front of the little hamburger place where she planned to dine sometime before she left town. Burgers and Fries. What kind of name was that? No wonder she'd had a difficult time remembering it.

Ethel carried her black everyday handbag and strolled to a public phone booth that sat in the corner of the gas station parking lot. In the thin phone book, she found Claire Westin's name listed. Next, she looked up Noralee—a girlfriend from high school. Was she still alive? What was her married name? For a moment, inside the warm telephone booth, Ethel racked her brain. It started with a *D*. Now was not the time to have a senior moment. Dobrensen. Praise the Lord! She scrolled through the *Ds* and found Noralee's number.

"Noralee, it's Ethel King. You may remember me best as Ethel Pettigrew from Moscow High School."

"Hi, Ethel, yes, I remember. I saw a brown ribbon on your baked goods at the fair last year."

It was just like Noralee to boast about other people's eighth-place finishes. Ethel's eyes narrowed. *I'll show her.*

"I was wondering if you were still alive," Noralee said. "So many of us have passed on, you know."

"Too many of us, Noralee. The reason I'm calling is, I was wondering if you're familiar with a woman who lives in the same town as you. Her name is Claire Westin." Ethel stretched the phone cord outside, so she didn't have to stand in the stuffy phone booth any longer.

"Yes. Palouse is a small town, and Claire is a big woman."

"How big?" Ethel asked.

"She's currently the county clerk, with her sights on running for mayor this fall. I was at the beauty parlor last Thursday and saw one of her posters in the window. Did you hear about Ed Burright? He was in our graduating class. Within a week of his wife Margaret's funeral, he married her first cousin."

"No, that's too bad."

"That's how so many elderly men are. Can't be alone more than a week. Did you hear—"

Ethel cleared her throat. "Noralee, are you going to vote for Claire Westin?"

"Of course. I don't know if Ronald Reagan himself could beat her, at least among the voters of Palouse. Why, Ethel? Are you working for the paper?"

"No." Noralee had never been someone to share a secret with. "I'm just doing a little research for a friend. If you go to the fair this year, I usually sit at one of the round tables near the baked goods area."

"My daughter, Jill, and I go every summer. I'll

look for you."

Ethel went inside the gas station to ask directions. An elderly man sat on a stool behind the counter, snoring. The name tag on the front of his coveralls read Burt. She tapped the smudged glass counter and hoped he was a light sleeper.

Burt blinked several times, yawned, and then scratched his balding head.

"Where's the beauty parlor in town?"

His eyes scanned Ethel's wide hat. "Somewhere in that block." He nodded across the street.

Half of working in a garage was giving people directions. He'd probably lived in this one-street town all his life and couldn't tell a person where the beauty parlor was. If she had a mind to, she'd report his sleeping on the job to his boss. Ethel read the signs in the window of the garage as she strolled past. "Burt's Garage—serving you since 1958."

It should read: "Sleeping on the job since 1958."

Shaking her head, Ethel gripped her purse closer to her. Curious about Quinn's future bride, she walked across the street and past several storefronts. A tavern, an antique store, and then Fran's Beauty Parlor. Just like Noralee had said, a colorful, fancy poster was Scotch-taped to the glass. Sunlight danced on the window reflecting the outline of her straw hat. She narrowed her gaze.

The caption read: "Vote for Claire Westin or be run out of town." From the waist up, the photo pictured a woman pert near as buxom as Dolly Parton. Hands on hips, she wore a long-sleeved cowboy shirt and a Stetson hat. Her hair was as blonde and as fake as Marilyn Monroe's. Mouth agape, Ethel stared. The woman was, at least, fifty-some-years-old, maybe even past childbearing years.

For all Quinn knew, his Claire Westin might already be a grandmother.

Ж

Quinn knocked on the Kings' back door. While he waited, he noticed Ethel's car wasn't parked in the gravel drive. Maybe Katherine hadn't heard his knock. He'd give her twenty more seconds, and if she didn't answer the door, he'd go home and start dinner. He was starving.

Dressed in a tank top and shorts, Katherine answered the door. Her hair was down, her face pale, her eyes appeared larger than he remembered, and if he wasn't mistaken, there were tears in her lashes. She'd lost ten pounds overnight.

"I'm sorry, Katherine." He nodded toward the detached garage. "I didn't see that Ethel's car wasn't here until after I knocked."

"She just called. She's at Tidyman's. Do you know she's been gone all day?" Katherine left the door open and walked ahead of him through the kitchen.

"No. She dropped your paper by early this morning before class. That is a long day for her. Is it all right if I grab something to eat?"

"Make yourself at home." She waved a hand.

While she turned off the TV in the other room, he opened a loaf of bread that was on the counter next to the boxes of breakfast cereal. From there, he knew which cupboard harbored the peanut butter.

"Looks like you're on the mend," he said loudly.

"I've even been able to keep down a piece of toast."

He folded the sandwich in half and entered the

living area. Katherine was lying down on the sofa. At first, all he saw of her was her long, lean legs. Turning, he went back to the kitchen. He'd, uh . . . pour himself a glass of milk. They were just legs, and they just happened to belong to Katherine King, also known as Miss Annoying. He gulped the milk, squared his shoulders, rolled a kink out of his neck, and returned to the living room.

A blanket now covered her legs. *Thank You, Lord.* He sat down in the La-Z-Boy recliner.

"Do you know where Grandma went today?" With her hands held prayer-like between her cheek and the scratchy green sofa pillow, she gazed up at him.

"No, but she told me she had exciting news to share." He set the glass of milk on the end table that serviced both the couch and the recliner. "I've been curious all day."

"*Exciting* could mean a number of things in Grandma's mind." Katherine's eyes took on a faint sparkle.

"Such as?" He raised his brows in between bites.

"She may have learned a new word to use up *Q's* and *X's* in Scrabble. *Exciting* to Grandma does not mean the same thing that it means to our generation."

He suppressed a smile. When he'd seen Ethel earlier in the day, there had been unusual energy in her eyes. "You underestimate her."

"Grandma didn't say anything about it to me when she called. So I dare to say that it's probably a three, maybe a four at the most on the *exciting* scale."

"I believe you're wrong, but because you're still pale, I won't argue with you."

"I'm feeling one hundred percent better than last night."

He nodded. Food poisoning was a powerful body-racking experience. He downed his last bite. "Do you think you're up for apologizing to Carl?"

"I'll take a rain check. Just the idea makes me feel a bit queasy." She rolled to her back and flung an elbow across her forehead.

Quinn leaned back and fished his phone from his pocket. Pressing firmly on the five, he speed-dialed Carl's mobile number. It immediately went to recording. He waited until after the beep. "Carl, it's Quinn. The reason Katherine hasn't apologized yet is she's been ill. Believe it or not, her old boyfriend, Joe, took her to the same Chinese food restaurant that I took Miss Genesee to several weeks back. We've determined it's the fried rice. She appears to be on the mend. So in the next day or two, you should expect to receive an apology from her. See you Friday night." He flipped the phone closed and turned off the power. Carl might call back, and then he'd have to explain that he was alone with Katherine waiting for Ethel's return. It was complicated.

"What if I don't feel apologetic in the next couple of days?" She held her hands beneath her chest, her diaphragm filling with air. "Carl's the one who owes *me* an apology—asking me out in front of an audience, and being so insistent."

Katherine King was definitely feeling better. He shimmied his shoulders into the recliner and closed his eyes. Tidyman's was a large grocery store. He wondered if Ethel were a daily, weekly, or monthly shopper.

"But then again, Carl is very good looking, and he may not have had many women decline him before."

Her soft tone surprised him. He opened one eye to

look at her.

The phone rang. "Do you want me to get that?" he asked.

"I can," she said, rising from the couch. "Carl and I could have lengthy discussions regarding how the United States rose to be a world super-power, the Cold War, US foreign policy . . ." She hurried around the far side of the coffee table. "Not that sharing history is enough to sustain a relationship, but I suppose it's a start." On the fourth ring, she picked it up. "Hello."

She'd never posted any real interest in Carl before. Was she entertaining the idea of going out with him? Was Carl right for her? Quinn's blood not only pumped faster—it coursed through his veins like Niagara Falls.

"Hi, Angel."

Crud. Angel LeFave—it was a good thing he hadn't answered the phone.

"I'm recovering from a terrible case of food poisoning. Joe and I went—yes, Joe, my ex, we went to Chinese on Saturday, and I've felt terrible ever since.—No, Joe wanted me to give him my opinion regarding the waitress. We're just friends.—The Green Dragon. Yes, never go there."

Quinn smiled. Eavesdropping on Katherine was fascinating.

"Tell him you're making him an extra-special dinner, and unveil a can of chili."

What was she going on about now?

"You're kidding. Did he see you?" Katherine's became more animated as she turned to face the room.

"You're kidding? Oh, I'm sure he was just being polite. Yeah, I'll be back Wednesday."

Katherine returned to the couch. "That was Angel LeFave. She said she saw you at a traffic light

Saturday night at one thirty in the morning and that you waved."

"So she didn't see you?" He suppressed a chuckle.

"No. Praise God."

He couldn't agree more. "I heard something about chili?"

"Angel and her boyfriend are celebrating their four-month anniversary soon, and I was giving her ideas."

"You sound like a romantic." He grinned.

"There's more to it that you don't need to know." Her chin lifted.

"You were going on about Carl before you answered the phone. And in case you didn't know, in the past year, he's dated and *liked,* at least, six women, none of them very bright. Not like you."

"Six?" Her jaw dropped. The floor lamp highlighted the freckles that were sprinkled across her upper cheeks.

Katherine King was down-to-earth gorgeous, and if he paused to reflect on it, what good would it do him?

"Yes, he's dated and liked six different women in one year's time." He stared at the white mantle above the empty fireplace to the left of the front door. His chest tightened. Being alone with Katherine when she wasn't quite her annoying self might not be such a good idea.

"Six women!"

He nodded. "Carl likes the chase better than the catch. Maybe this pattern is because he hasn't been very smart about the women he's pursued. To be fair, perhaps he's reached a point in his dating that he'll appreciate you . . ." Quinn cleared his throat. "I mean, you are a graduate student."

"Finally!" She huffed. "A little insider information. I sensed that you and Evans were not telling me the entire truth about him." She flopped back into the pillow. She'd exhausted herself and lay quiet for a moment—a rarity.

"Evans and Carl are close. I'm able to be less subjective."

He opened one eye and glanced at her. God forbid, Katherine was beautiful, especially when she wasn't talking. He powered his phone and checked to see if Carl had tried to call.

"How was your day, Mr. Benton?" she asked.

"It started off on a particularly good note with your grandma's brief visit to my office."

"Did she wear her gardening hat inside the building again?" Katherine scrunched up her nose.

"Yes." He grinned.

"I don't know why she wears it around town."

"It adds character." He smiled. "Yesterday afternoon, I called The Green Dragon and informed them that three people I know have experienced food poisoning and that I was going to have to report them. I also told them it was the fried rice."

"What'd they say?"

"The woman was very apologetic. When I reported it to the Better Business Bureau today, they said another case was reported last week."

"Thank you. I was afraid you'd forgotten."

He chuckled, surprised by her pleasantness. Maybe it was because Katherine was in a weakened state, but strangely enough, the two of them were *talking* and getting along.

The back door creaked open. Ethel was home. She probably needed help with groceries. He pulled the side lever, returning the chair to its upright position.

"I remembered to buy sticky notes," Ethel said loudly from the kitchen.

Quinn chuckled. Was that all she'd purchased at Tidyman's?

"That's probably her exciting news," Katherine whispered.

"No, definitely not."

"I bet it is." Brows lifted, she nodded.

"It's something far more substantial."

"Maybe, but I bet it isn't."

Would a freckle ever go away once it was a freckle? He liked Katherine's freckles. Why had he never noticed them before?

Chapter Twenty-Four

After much consideration about what to make for dinner, Ethel had purchased a rotisserie chicken, a loaf of crusty French bread, and a package of Caesar salad that you just tossed together in a bowl. She took the plastic lid off the rotisserie chicken so its aroma filled her little kitchen before she asked Quinn if he'd like to stay for dinner. Of course, he said yes.

"What's your exciting news, Ethel?" Using a carving knife, Quinn sliced the chicken. "Or would you prefer to tell Katherine and me while we're seated at the table?"

"Over dinner would be best." The salad was tossed; she just needed to pour three glasses of milk. "Katherine, honey, are you up for sitting with us in here?" If she wasn't, Ethel had already decided she'd plead for her to join them.

"I'll see how it goes." Her granddaughter ambled in with a blanket wrapped around her mid-section. "You got your hair done."

"Yes. I had the gal take an inch off." Ethel patted near her ear.

"It looks nice," Quinn said.

Once they were all seated, Ethel held out her hands and gripped both Quinn's and Katherine's, one on each side of her. Saying the Lord's Prayer together always proved powerful. Afterward, she buttered a slice of bread.

"Where'd you get your hair cut?" Leaning her head to one side, Katherine studied her.

"At a beauty parlor." Ethel wasn't about to tell her at Fran's Beauty Parlor in Palouse.

"You're awfully vague, Grandma. I meant what beauty parlor?"

Without looking Katherine's direction, Ethel kicked her shin beneath the table. "You know, the one with the sign out front."

Eyes narrowed, Katherine cast her a look that read, *"I don't know."*

"It looks nice." Using the tongs, Quinn transferred the salad to his plate.

"What color of sticky notes did you get, Grandma?" Katherine asked, glancing from her to Quinn.

"It was a difficult decision for me today. I spent quite a bit of time choosing between my two favorite colors: yellow and the neon pink. I finally decided that I like yellow best. The neon pink can be a tad dark, especially when one writes in pencil. None of the other colors are even in the running."

The chicken was tender and moist, with good flavor. Both Katherine and Quinn took a leg. It was nice that there were two legs on a chicken, so they didn't have to fight over them. They fought about everything else.

"You said you had some exciting news." Quinn lifted the drumstick to his mouth.

"Yes, before I forget. Is it *ala mater* or *alma mater*?"

Katherine's jaw moved, but Quinn beat her to it. "Alma mater."

"What does it mean?" Ethel asked.

"It's Latin for *fostering mother*." This time, Katherine beat Quinn.

"Or nurturing mother," Quinn added.

Ethel smiled at Katherine. "The U of I is your alma mater, and so am I."

While Katherine's head bobbed back and forth, Quinn smiled. He was always so good about smiling at the appropriate times.

"Does alma mater play into your exciting news?" Quinn asked, gently trying to remind her.

"Yes." Ethel nodded. For a moment, she caught her breath. She'd decided during her drive home from Palouse that she wouldn't tell Quinn about Miss Palouse. This coming Friday he'd finally meet her. Maybe he already knew that Claire was older. Maybe he didn't care. Maybe having his own biological children wasn't important to him. They could always adopt, or get a dog.

"Do you remember what it was, Grandma?" Katherine patted her left hand.

"Yes, of course, I do." Though Katherine's tone had been soft and rather sweet, in her own way she was implying that Ethel had forgotten. How could someone forget exciting news?

Ethel wiped her hands on her paper napkin. "I drove to the Admin Building this morning to pay my parking ticket. And just like before, but worse, this time, there were no available spaces. I drove around and around, and as you both are probably aware, there is not enough parking to begin with up there."

"It's an ongoing problem." Quinn nodded.

"After I finally found a space, I felt certain that my hair had gone completely gray; I even checked the flip-down mirror."

He smiled and appeared to only admire her eyes.

"Where were you all day?" Katherine asked. "I called Aunt Gladys. She didn't know. I called Sandra and Sharon. I was just about to call the police when you called from Tidyman's."

"I was busy getting my hair done," Ethel said and smiled at Quinn.

"It doesn't take all day to take off an inch. They didn't even curl it."

"I think it looks nice," Quinn said.

"I know you went to Benton's office, the beauty parlor, and Tidyman's. Did you visit someone? Grandma, you were gone for over seven hours."

"I was out and about. It was a beautiful day." Looking at Quinn, Ethel ever so casually used her left foot to kick Katherine in the shinbone again beneath the table.

Katherine's jaw dropped. But, of course, she had no idea where she'd been.

"Back to your exciting news, Ethel," Quinn said.

"Yes, when I paid my parking ticket, you see . . . I was inspired to tell the young woman behind the counter that I had an idea to improve the university in regards to senior relations. These three sweet gals rallied together and decided to send me straight to the top. I was escorted from the ground floor up to President Morrison's office."

For some reason, Quinn smiled first across the table at Katherine before he smiled at her.

"Believe it or not, President Morrison liked my idea so much that he said . . ." Ethel pinched the bridge of her nose, trying to recall his exact wording. "He said, and I quote"—she held up two fingers of each hand and did the little bunny ear sign—"'I feel your idea is visionary on a broader scale.' He wants me to write up my plans, and he'll submit it to the law school, maybe even Latah County."

"What was your idea, Grandma?"

"Well . . ." Ethel took a sip of milk. Out of the corner of her eye, she saw Katherine waving the new package of yellow sticky notes. Maybe Katherine's electrolytes were off. Too bad she hadn't bought her Gatorade when she'd been at Tidyman's. When Ethel turned to look fully at her, Katherine dropped the sticky notes onto the counter behind her and rubbed the back of her head like she had a sudden ache.

The bout of food poisoning had affected her brain. Hopefully, it wasn't too severe. Had Quinn read Katherine's *Oh, brother* paper yet? Maybe he was in for a good laugh.

"Yes, Ethel, I'm curious, too." Quinn leaned forward and snagged another slice of bread. "What idea did you tell President Morrison?"

"Has the US ever had a President Morrison?" Ethel wanted to get the question out of the way before she forgot about it.

"No. We've had a Hamilton and a Harris," Katherine said. "No Morrison."

Even Quinn looked impressed.

"Back to my idea." Ethel giggled. "It was parking for seniors—over age sixty-five. The sign will be a white background with a green turtle walking on her hind legs carrying a cane. I kind of like the idea of it being a female turtle wearing a straw hat with maybe a flower pinned to the side."

Quinn clapped.

Ethel turned to Katherine and waited for her response.

Mouth ajar, she set both elbows on the table. "That's wonderful, Grandma. I'm very proud of you. For your sake, I hope it gets put into action."

"Me, too. Especially at the Palouse Empire Mall and Tidyman's."

Quinn dangled his fork and smiled whole-heartedly across the table at Katherine.

And she smiled back.

The two were finally getting along.

ж

Friday morning after Katherine strolled off to school, Ethel ambled out the back gate and opened her trunk. She pulled out the rolled-up poster of Miss Palouse. Fran, one of Claire Westin's staunch supporters, had just happened to have an extra behind the counter. When Ethel returned home yesterday, she'd parked next to Quinn's car and immediately stashed the poster in her trunk. Whew! It had been a close one.

According to Fran, Claire Westin had once owned the only video rental store in Palouse and knew everyone in town by name. Just like Ronald Reagan, she was making the big step from movies to politics.

Ethel carried the poster into the house. She knew exactly where she was going to hang it. She pulled open her junk drawer in the kitchen, nabbed the roll of Scotch tape, and proceeded to her room. Years ago when she'd been trying to slim down a bit, she'd taped a poster of calories to the back of her bedroom door. The fancy molding on the door almost made the poster look framed. It was the same with Claire's. The poster gave her room a fun, Western feel. After the November elections, she might just keep it there.

During her drive home yesterday, Ethel had prayed about how to handle Miss Palouse's poster and where to hang it. That was when the Lord had reminded her of the big cupcake on the front of her old calorie poster. If for some reason, Quinn or Katherine ever went into her bedroom and saw Claire Westin, it was God's doing, not just hers.

Chapter Twenty-Five

Friday evening while Katherine did the dinner dishes, she contemplated if she should stay home or go to the library to study. She didn't have any research that she needed library resources for, but the idea of simply staying home while Benton was on his date with Miss Palouse didn't sit well for some reason. She needed to keep her mind busy.

The last time Quinn had visited, he'd left his beloved book on the kitchen table. Grandma had moved it to the coffee table. Seated in the recliner, Grandma was immersed in a crossword puzzle. Katherine picked up the books *The Last of the Mohicans* and *American Scripture* off the coffee table and strolled into the kitchen. She held the books against each other. They were exactly the same size. She smiled and switched jacket covers. She slid *American Scripture,* which was now titled *The Last of the Mohicans,* into her backpack and carried *American Scripture* into the living room.

"Grandma, Quinn left his book here last night." She set it down on the coffee table.

"I tried to get him to take it home, but right before he left, he set it on the table. I agree with you. You should focus on your studies; your studies come first."

"Thank you, Grandma." Her heart warmed.

"And I think for Quinn's sake, you should read a

chapter or two of his book and then tell him you tried."

"That's called straddling the fence."

"Can you heat me up a cup of coffee?" Grandma peered over the top of her glasses at her.

"Sure."

While a cup of coffee rotated in the microwave, Katherine began reading the lengthy introduction to *American Scripture.*

The phone rang. The clock on the stove read 6:50. Maybe it was Benton. Maybe Miss Palouse had canceled, again. She hoped not for Benton's sake.

"Hello," Katherine said into the receiver.

There was a sniffle on the other end of the line. "Is this Katherine?"

"Hi, Angel. What's wrong?" Katherine pulled a chair over from the dining table and sat down.

"Greg and I just broke up."

"What do you mean?"

"I built him up for our four-month, just like he'd built me up for our three-month." Sniffle. "He wasn't very happy about the chili."

"Oh, no! I'm so sorry." *Poor Angel.*

"I just found out that my boyfriend." Sniffle. "My ex-boyfriend has no sense of humor. I had candlelight, Billy Joel music, and one of those silver lid things covering the chili. When I lifted it up, I knew we were history."

It wasn't a very pretty picture.

"Remember how I told you about Joe and how he broke my heart?"

"Yeah."

"After he broke my heart, I wrote a list of all the reasons I'd never fall in love with him again. My Joe List helped me see that he wasn't the one God intended me to be with."

"Yeah, but you're too smart to fall for another dumb jock like Joe. But Greg, I thought we were perfect."

"When we get off the phone, I want you to write a list, and I'm going to pray for you tonight. And I'm so sorry that I ever told you to make chili."

"Greg's so stupid."

"Write that as your first line of your Greg List."

"I will right now." Sniffle. "Thanks for praying for me."

After Katherine hung up the phone, she lifted Angel up in prayer.

"Was that Angel, who was here the other night?" Grandma asked.

"Yes, her boyfriend just broke up with her. She's heartbroken, and asked for prayer."

"Awh . . . I'll do that right now for her, too."

Katherine delivered Grandma's coffee. She couldn't just sit at home for the next four hours waiting for the clock to cuckoo away four hours. What if Benton's date went well? Would tonight be the last professors' group? Would he still come to dinner occasionally at Grandma's? She had to get out of the house. She grabbed her backpack off the floor near the couch.

"Where are you going, honey?"

"I think I'll study at the library tonight." She shrugged and gave Grandma a brave smile.

"Oh, well, before you leave why don't you go in my bedroom and look at yourself in my mirror."

"Why?" Didn't Grandma like her outfit? She was still wearing the clothes she'd worn to class. The day had been overcast, and she'd chosen jeans and a short-sleeved, crisp white blouse with little black buttons and a gathering of front ruffles.

"Well, you don't have a full-length mirror in your

room."

"Okay." Katherine flicked on the overhead light in Grandma's bedroom and strolled across the shag carpet. In front of the oak framed cheval mirror, she checked her zipper, turned and swiveled. Lastly, she peered at her face, smiled like a horse, and checked to see if there was something in her teeth. Hmm . . . She looked fine.

The phone rang in the living room. There was only one phone on the main floor, and Grandma was quick to pick it up.

"I think it's the guy from that radio commercial for Werther's candies," Grandma said covering the receiver. "Maybe it's a survey."

Who in the world?

"Tell him I like butterscotch best." Grandma handed her the phone.

"Hello."

"Katherine, it's Evans. We have a social emergency."

"What's happened?" Knees weak, Katherine pulled a dining chair close to the cabinet and sat down.

"For the second time in a row, Miss Palouse has canceled on Benton. Water issues in her basement, most likely it's her water heater."

"Oh." It dawned on her that Evans had said *social* emergency. Relief flooded her. "How's he holding up?" In the kitchen, Grandma closed a cupboard.

"As we all know, Benton could have easily fixed it, but Miss Amazing Phone Voice had already called a plumber. He's in need of cheering up. Therefore, Cindy and I have decided . . ." He exhaled a heavy sigh. "To make our date at the antique store a fivesome."

"Miss Colfax's antique store?"

"Yes. I just got off the phone with her, and she is absolutely fine with our party being upped from two to five."

Five meant Carl was going. Benton wasn't with Miss Palouse. Their evening had been canceled for the second time. The poor man.

"Bring your checkbook or cash. Miss Colfax won't be on site for Visa transactions."

"Oh, I won't buy anything."

"Can you be ready in the next ten minutes?"

"Huh?" She glanced at the cuckoo clock. Usually, the group met at eleven not seven. "I have so much reading; I really shouldn't."

"Bring your books. I expect we can find a place for you to study. Dinner will be Taco Time takeout on fine china. Cindy made a Bundt cake for dessert."

Katherine had already eaten, not that it mattered. Could this possibly be just another creative way to set her up with Carl? She hoped not.

"Cindy confirmed—you can bring your books."

Katherine pictured Cindy's dangly earrings bobbing as she nodded in the background.

"It's going to take *all* four of us to bring Benton out of his quandary."

She inhaled deeply. Evans wasn't going to take no for an answer.

Hopefully, Evans wasn't kidding when he said she could study. Katherine packed a flashlight and extra AA batteries. She might have to camp out in a separate room if the group was loud. She'd always been a studier who needed peace and quiet to focus; she should have declined.

"That was Evans, Grandma; Miss Palouse canceled on Benton for the second time."

"Wow, poor Quinn. That's the second heart broken tonight. Be careful," Grandma said from the recliner.

"Grandma." Katherine bent down and kissed her cheek. "I have no idea what time I'll be home. Knowing this group, it'll be late; they're a bunch of night owls."

"Then they're a parliament, not a bunch. Are you discussing Miss Palouse tonight?"

Clasping her hand, Grandma looked up at her.

"Yes and no. She canceled, which is why the group's going to Colfax to cheer Benton up. Why I'm invited is an oxymoron." In the front windows, Evans's silver Cadillac Seville rolled up beneath the weeping cherry tree.

"I bet he's crushed." Grandma sighed. "What's an oxy . . . moron again?"

"Bittersweet. Um . . . me cheering Benton up." It was the best that she could do at the moment.

Grandma's skimpy brows gathered as she nodded.

Katherine strolled down the concrete walk and unlatched the gate. Cindy sat in the front seat; her Giorgio perfume was subtle, pleasant. Katherine placed her backpack on the floor in the back and glanced across the cab at Benton. For some reason, Carl wasn't present. Maybe they were picking him up on the way, which most likely meant she'd sit in the middle.

"Cute little place. Has your grandmother lived here long?" Evans asked, turning onto the Troy highway.

"Forty years."

"So you grew up coming here?" He glanced back at her in the rearview mirror.

"Yes, I always wanted to attend the U of I and live with Grandma, like several of my older cousins."

She forced herself to acknowledge Benton, somber in jeans and a Yale-blue polo. "I'm sorry to hear that Miss Palouse canceled."

His jaw muscle twitched. "If it happens a third time, I won't try again."

"I should hope not," Evans said.

They passed several good restaurants as they cruised north on Main Street; instead, they were driving over twenty-five miles to order fast food. The atmosphere was what Evans and Cindy were definitely after.

"Is Carl coming?" Katherine forced herself to ask.

"Yes; he'll be pleased to hear you inquired of him," Evans said. "He's meeting us there."

"I was simply curious."

Benton was quiet while Cindy and Evans conversed up front. It was going to be a long, uncomfortable drive. Katherine unzipped her backpack and pulled out her Lewis and Clark textbook.

"You won't get carsick?" Benton asked.

"No, thank goodness." In her undergraduate years, she'd spent countless hours studying in the team van while the coach drove to away matches.

Benton flipped open his phone and, looking at a piece of scratch paper, entered a number. "Hello, Marci, it's Quinn Benton. A group of friends and I are heading to Colfax tonight for a get-together at Colfax Antiques, the two-story brick building on the main drag. I don't know if you're doing anything tonight, but Colfax is, at least, ten miles closer than Pullman for you."

The man was interesting; probably another woman from a neighboring small town. He was zealously searching, she could say that for him.

"Yes, she's a regular member of the group. Uh-huh. I see. Well, in case you change your mind, we'll be there for several hours. Great group of people." Benton clicked his phone closed. "Miss Garfield is a Realtor. She had a sale fail today."

"Is the *she* that Marci referred to . . . Katherine?" Cindy asked, glancing over her shoulder.

"Yes. I informed her once that one of our graduate students attends the group."

Nothing to read into, Katherine told herself. It was odd that Marci asked about her, though. Hmm . . .

"Isn't she the one who's also actively blind dating?" Evans asked.

"Yes. I forgot she's on a blind date right now."

"Oops." Cindy giggled. "Isn't she the one who describes herself as *quite attractive*, but won't send a picture?"

"Yes, that's her."

"Do you send pictures?" Katherine asked.

Benton frowned and shook his head.

"All he has to say is 'college professor, early thirties, never been married,'" Evans said.

"Tonight, while we're there, remind me that I want to look for a chair for my office," Benton said, "something solid and a little more inviting than that old, metal one."

"Miss Colfax said there's a calculator at the front counter, and to remember to add seven percent sales tax," Evans said.

"She's very trusting," Cindy said.

"She knows Benton, and most professors are a good lot." Evans pulled his phone out of his trouser pocket and handed it to Cindy. "It's Carl. Tell him I'm driving."

She flipped it open. "Hello, Carl; it's Cindy. We're just reaching Pullman. Where are you? Oh. Uh-huh . . ."

Katherine capped her highlighter. Was he canceling?

"Yes, I'll remember." Cindy snapped the phone closed. "Carl's running twenty minutes late. But he wants us to get him two burritos and an empanada."

"Make sure he reimburses you, Benton," Evans said.

Another clue about Carl.

"And make sure that you both apologize to him tonight," Evans added. "He was a little peeved with you for your driveway getaway scene last week. Was it planned?"

"No," Benton said.

"Good." Evans glanced in the rearview mirror. "Katherine, I'd personally like you to apologize to Carl about The Breakfast Club scene. It's very difficult for most men to summon the courage to ask a woman out."

"Not Carl," Benton said.

"To be rejected on speaker phone in a public place proved difficult even for Carl. It's affected him more than you realize," Evans said.

Brows gathered, Katherine glanced at Benton.

"There were three tables of people listening," he said. "Have you ever been to The Breakfast Club?"

"No." She shook her head.

"Oh, you should," Evans said. "It's in the old Nobby Inn on Main Street."

"We were seated near the front windows. There're three to four tables in that section, and just prior to calling you, Carl made the mistake of asking customers at neighboring tables where the best place in town is to take a girl to coffee."

"He didn't?" Katherine closed her eyes.

"He did. And the majority opinion was Bucer's is best," Evans said.

"The rest is history," Benton said.

Katherine rubbed her forehead. "But I'd already told him no."

"Yes, but you were the first woman EVER to rebuff Carl three times," Evans said. "He was feeling very lucky, probably due to the eagle he had on fifteen."

"What were your excuses again?" Though Benton turned toward her, he focused on the view out her passenger window, and the pastoral landscape. Towering green hills rolled off into the brilliant blue sky. "Something about eleven reasons."

"Nine of them were in reference to my credit load."

"What were the other two?"

Her heart felt tangled. Did Benton want to know for Carl or simply the group? "Carl calling me with an audience was one of them." She cleared her throat. "And you know very well I ended up using Joe as an excuse. Carl wouldn't accept no for an answer."

"You have time every Friday night for the professors' group. Long stretches, not study breaks," Benton said. "Your excuse doesn't fly. Carl's seen it firsthand. Joe knows it, too."

Remain calm. Miss Palouse, the smart woman that she was, rejected him, and he was taking it out on her.

"After Joe, I decided I wouldn't date again until I've completed my master's. It was too much of a juggling act for me." Like they had a mind of their own, her fingertips tapped together beneath her chin. She picked up the highlighter and gripped the edge of the book with her free hand. "Men are time monsters. That's what my experience in relationships has been."

"Your conclusion is based on *one* relationship, years ago. And I just realized that you do the little silent clapping thing because you're nervous." He chuckled softly. "You do not like talking about this."

The conversation almost made her feel carsick.

"And your point?" If she'd been Miss Palouse, she would have canceled too.

"We may meet to discuss my dates, Katherine, but if you haven't noticed, I'm not the only one being discussed."

Evans was behind all this, constantly trying to set her up with Carl and hiding her Joe List. Katherine watched him in the rearview mirror.

"It's called group therapy," Evans said, without taking his eyes off the road. "You're a beautiful, intelligent young woman in the season of life in which it's only natural to begin your search for a lifelong mate."

Heat bottlenecked in her cheeks. She should be in the library right now accomplishing the mountain of work ahead of her. Katherine uncapped her highlighter and scanned the textbook. Where had she left off?

Chapter Twenty-Six

Upstairs, on the second floor of Colfax Antiques, Katherine helped Cindy move an assortment of knickknacks and a wire birdcage from a farmhouse table to a neighboring desk. Next, they draped a gold-colored tablecloth on top, and Cindy set five blue-and-white place settings in the middle of the table. From a picnic basket, she produced more fine china, candles, and long wooden matches.

"This is our first date," Evans said. He carried three plates to the far end of the table, several feet away.

"Yes, and it's a double date." Cindy returned the place settings to the center of the table.

"Except Katherine has two fellows; you only get one." Evans again picked up the place settings.

"Katherine, Carl, and I will take our food downstairs." Benton motioned for Evans to hand him the plates. "I saw a table when we first entered, and as far as we're concerned, tonight is a get-together—not a date."

"You're staying right here." Cindy struck a match and lit two tall candlesticks.

"Would you please leave?" Picking up a Jim Croce album, Evans peered at them over the top of his wire spectacles. "For two years, my objective has been to get this woman in a romantic setting alone."

"What happened to the theme of trying to cheer Benton up?" Katherine asked, uncomfortable with the atmosphere shift.

"He's not at home stewing and feeling sorry for himself. Now, everyone needs to make the most of it," Evans said.

Benton carried plates and votives while Katherine grabbed their drinks and the remaining contents of the Taco Time bag. With his back to them, Evans plugged in a 'fifties wooden stereo cabinet.

"I'm sorry, the evening's not turning out as planned," Benton said as they descended the stairs.

"I guess we'll just have to make the most of it." She tried to ignore the feeling of being framed.

"That was quite diplomatic of you, Katherine."

She followed him to a dimly lit nook area to the right of the stairs. A collection of dessert-sized plates, oil lamps, and a variety of salt-and-pepper shakers cluttered a round oak table. If she inhaled too deeply, there was the hint of dust. He lit a votive candle, illuminating a nearby baby buggy filled with patchwork quilts.

"Miss Colfax doesn't want us turning on the lights on the main floor. People start calling her home. It's a small town," Benton said.

"Hopefully, Miss Colfax alerted the police that there will be candlelight tonight inside her store."

He chuckled. "We wouldn't want that kind of press."

"No, we wouldn't." Katherine's mind drifted to the headlines: U of I Professor and his Female Student Caught After Hours in Local Candle-lit Antique Store.

Jim Croce music filtered down from the open loft. They set the oil lamps on a nearby buffet and cleared a trail through the middle of the table. Crud, it was romantic. The situation wasn't Benton's fault. It was Carl's more than anyone's. Still, she was glad he was running late.

Benton dove into his chimichanga with a plastic knife and fork, while Katherine's hard- shell ninety-nine cent taco crumbled on the first bite; a chunk of shell ended in her lap. How embarrassing, it felt like a date. No, if it were a date, one of them would be trying to fill the uncomfortable silence that had dredged on between them for the last five minutes.

"I'm sorry, Katherine." Benton glanced at her. "Cheering me up was supposed to be a group effort. I wonder what's taking Carl so long?"

"It almost feels like they're trying to set us up."

"No, Evans is trying to set you up with Carl. I've overheard him on several occasions."

His response was a solid reminder for her not to read anything into the situation. "Are you up for talking about Claire?"

"No."

She took a sip of iced tea. "Evans said this is the second time she's canceled."

"As you know, my father is a plumber; water heater issues are common in the summer months."

"She's canceled on you twice. Could Claire be stringing you along for some reason?"

Setting an elbow on the table, he dangled his plastic fork and looked at her through the cleared clutter. "She's caring, nurturing, very down-to-earth, honest. What could possibly be her motive?"

"She sounds wonderful." Katherine shrugged. "Perhaps it simply hasn't worked out."

"She is wonderful." He sank his fork into the chimichanga.

Jim Croce's music "Time in a bottle" drifted down from upstairs. A collection of old glass bottles was on display across the aisle. She and Benton didn't belong here alone.

"I hope they have more records than this one." The setting, the music, the good-looking man across the table from her were all factors that culminated toward romance, except he was thinking and talking about Claire.

"It's a great album."

She nodded and took the final bite of her taco.

"You should call Miss Palouse." She gripped her hands beneath the table. "And tell her where we are. I mean, you are. See if Claire will meet you here. It would be a very romantic first date."

He shook his head. "She hasn't had the most blissful afternoon."

"Meeting you may change her outlook on the day."

"You must be uncomfortable to be so congenial."

"I am." He'd pegged her well. "Aren't you?"

"No." He wadded his straw wrapper to the size of a spit wad, tossed it toward the open Taco Time bag, and missed. "I like you this way."

"Uncomfortable?" Avoiding his gaze, she peered about the cluttered nook.

"Maybe it's your penitent mode. I've come to the decision that I should meet Miss Palouse before I schedule any more blind dates."

"Does Miss Palouse want children?"

"We've talked about children, and she's hesitant, but some people are until they know they've met the right person." He half grinned. "Look at us, conversing like two normal people."

Her hands were clammy. She slid them under her knees and pretended interest in the dark corners of the nook, anywhere besides his eyes. Using a paper napkin, he dabbed at his mouth.

He crumpled up the Taco Time bag. "Do you have siblings?"

"Yes, I'm the middle of five, and the only one not married. That worries my parents, and Grandma, at times. What about you?"

"Oldest, with one younger, married sister. The beautician." His smile was steady. He glanced from her eyes to her mouth.

A tugboat-sized docking knot formed in her gut. Had they ever been alone before—looking at each other? Where was Carl?

"You should call Claire."

"I've already called her today."

"You called her hours ago."

He peered at his wristwatch. "It was only three hours ago that I bugged her."

"You just finished telling me how wonderful Claire is—and now you're ready to give up so easily. A girl doesn't mind being bugged twice if it's the right guy."

He sighed and flipped open his phone.

For Benton's sake, she hoped he was the right guy.

Chapter Twenty-Seven

Benton held down one digit on his phone, because, of course, he had Miss Palouse on speed dial. "Claire, it's Quinn." He pushed his chair back from the table, rose, and walked toward the front windows. "I'm at Miss Colfax's antique store. Yes. Evans rented the building for his first date with Cindy." He sounded relaxed, at ease, like they indeed held a special bond.

Katherine uncapped her highlighter and pretended interest in her boring old history book.

"I was wondering if you've recuperated enough to meet me here? There's an ambiance to the place." Benton's gaze traveled about the expansive room, toward the glass display counters that lined the main aisle. "I think it would prove a great way for us to finally meet. Yes, Katherine is here, and Carl's on his way."

Miss Palouse knew about her? He'd probably told her about the B paper, and what a fool she'd made of herself. Katherine wouldn't let her mind return to her phone cord visit to his office.

A hand settled on her shoulder. Startled, she jumped an inch in her chair. She looked up to see Carl's green eyes in the candlelight.

"Who's he talking to?" He nodded toward Benton.

"Miss Palouse," she whispered, not wanting to miss a word.

"Sorry, I'm late. I stopped to get my car washed, and then there was road construction in the valley, on the way out of town." Carl dove into the Taco Time bag and made thirty seconds of rustling noise during which she couldn't hear Benton, who'd halted in the middle of the store. Katherine began to fear the worst: the woman was telling him no.

"I understand. Maybe sometime next week."

Couldn't Claire hear the disappointment in his voice?

On his way toward them, Benton returned his phone to his back pocket. "Claire's exhausted. The plumbing company left an hour ago, and she took a bath and retired with a cup of cocoa."

The woman sounded low on iron. Now it would be just the three of them for the remainder of the evening. Miss Palouse!

"Hello, Carl. You decided to finally make it."

"Yes. I got waylaid on my way out of town. Traffic." Carl was a quarter of the way through his burrito. "Claire is Miss Palouse, right?"

Benton nodded. In one short phone call, his eyes had gone from hopeful to flat.

"I'm sorry, Mr. Benton. If Claire had seen your disappointment, I believe she would have summoned the energy." While Katherine had grown to care for him, he was venting about Katherine to small-town women. It was best not to think about him. Not give him another thought, never, ever again.

For the next half hour, Jim Croce music floated down from above.

"It sounds like Evans brought only one record," Carl said.

"Yes. It used to be a favorite of mine." Benton yawned.

Over her shoulder, Katherine studied the dimly lit, high-ceilinged room. Street lamps illuminated the outline of merchandise in the front of the store: kerosene lamps on a dresser, a kitchen queen, a few high-backed chairs—if she had to, she could study someplace else.

"I asked her out twice in one night." Benton frowned. "I'm getting as bad as you, Carl."

All he could think about was Miss Palouse.

"*Determined* is a better word for it, and I doubt it, Benton. I asked Katherine out four times in one phone call, didn't I?"

She nodded and managed a sympathetic smile in his direction.

Benton flung an arm over the back of his chair. "Katherine appears very favorable in this light. Don't you agree, Carl?"

She cast Benton a look that read, *Don't encourage him.* "I hope you're not rebounding, Mr. Benton," she said in jest.

"I'm not." He grinned.

She continued to feel uncomfortable under his gaze. "Should you suddenly find me unusually attractive and be drawn to me in a way you've never been before, please warn me."

"You sound like an expert." Carl chuckled.

"I am. I've gone through approximately twelve of Joe's breakups, and the rebound period that inevitably follows. He doesn't understand that the emptiness of being alone is an ache only God can fill." She glanced at her books. Maybe now was a good time to escape with her flashlight.

Benton scratched behind one ear. "Carl, Evans said I owe you an apology for the other night—for my getaway scene with Katherine. It wasn't planned. It's because of Ethel, Katherine's grandmother, that I found myself feeling personally—"

"Don't worry about it." Leaning back in his chair, Carl turned his attention to Katherine.

It was her turn to apologize for her abruptness on the phone: her eleven-reasons remark, her lack of sensitivity, hanging up on him.

"Katherine, I've given your dating question some thought this week." Carl glanced at Benton. "When we were standing in Evans's driveway studying the stars, I asked Katherine what question she's wanted to be asked but hasn't been."

"Oh . . ." Benton's brows rose.

"Her question was . . . 'If you could be a journalist in any American war, which would it be?' And I apologize, Katherine; my answer was a discredit to my profession. It was one thirty in the morning. I'd been grading exams all afternoon and well, why don't we try another crack at it?"

"Okay." She nodded. "If you could have been a journalist in any American war, Carl, which war would you choose and why?"

"Without a doubt, World War I. It was what I based my thesis on for my master's. It was our first international war after becoming a world super-power, and it set the precedent for. . . ." Carl's intelligent answer took up the next ten minutes.

Katherine waited for him to ask her the very same question.

He dabbed a moistened finger on the crumbs of his cherry empanada wrapper. "I also wanted to tell you something that you've probably already heard from Benton, and maybe Evans." Facing, her, Carl crossed his arms on top of the table. "I've done my share of dating in the past year. I've dated some women, who for the most part have fit Evans's label of 'Sweet and Low.'"

Right in front of Benton, Carl was making his move.

"Evans was right. The more I'm around you, the more I appreciate your wit, your intellect. Even the way you rejected me last Saturday kept me in the game." He grinned. "Do you remember what you said?"

Carl was buttering her up to slide her into a preheated pan. *Come to my rescue, Benton. Do something.* Or maybe she should employ her own brain.

"I . . . now have eleven reasons." Was he finding a roundabout way for her to preface her apology?

A faint knocking sound echoed from the hallway. They all paused to listen.

"Are we expecting anyone?" Carl asked. "The door is unlocked, whoever it is."

Katherine met Benton's gaze across the table and suppressed a smile. At least a half hour had passed since his phone call with Miss Palouse. Could she have possibly taken him up on his offer?

The knocking continued. "It could be Miss Colfax checking in on Evans," Benton said.

In the dark of an early summer evening, in an antique store, they supposedly had to themselves, who would be knocking?

"Where are you Benton, Katherine?" Holding a candlestick, Evans stood near the top of the stairs. "Someone's at the door," he bellowed. "Are you two alive?"

"Three." Benton moved to the aisle. "Carl's here now. I'll get it. It's probably Miss Colfax."

"Good. If it is her, invite her in for a piece of cake."

"She's probably here to tally our finds." Instead of staying alone at the table with Carl, Katherine followed Quinn to the door.

Wouldn't Miss Colfax have a key? Or was she simply being polite in knocking, as the building was rented for the evening?

Benton opened the solid wood door. The outside light illuminated an attractive young woman with auburn curls framing her petite features.

"Hello . . . how may I help you?"

She smiled. "Quinn, it's me, Marci. I took you up on your invitation."

Chapter Twenty-Eight

Benton had referred to Miss Garfield twice, and only briefly, at the professors' get-togethers. So of course, Katherine was as surprised as he appeared to be that Marci was exceptionally pretty and had indeed joined them at the antique store. Now they only needed Claire to arrive to make the evening complete.

Was Katherine a threat? What were Benton's sentiments? *Yes, Katherine's with the group tonight.* Maybe he'd told Marci everything about the B grade and Grandma. In a roundabout way, maybe he'd even referred to her as attractive.

Stop thinking, she told herself.

Slim and attractive, wearing perfume, with a fitted magenta blouse over black tights, black heels, and a gray Coach purse, Marci gave an entirely new impression of the term "Realtor." Marci sat down across from Carl, in the remaining chair at the round oak table. Benton made his introductions and informed Miss Garfield that Evans and Cindy were dining upstairs, and were also in charge of the music.

"My blind date with this guy named Trent ended before six thirty." Marci rolled her eyes. "We met in Pullman at the Old Post Office restaurant. He said he was in real estate also, which was odd, as I should have been able to place him. He's actually in escrow. When he was in the restroom, I called a friend of mine who's also in title, and she said this man has a poor reputation. Sloppy paperwork and a near lawsuit for sexual harassment. He's very good looking and aware of it." Her eyes rested briefly on Carl.

"You must feel very disappointed," he said.

"How did you manage to escape?" Benton asked.

"I had the same friend call me back and pretend there was an emergency with her child. It was awkward, but I left." Marci's gaze shifted from Benton to Carl and remained at the latter. "I had a sale fail today, and then the title guy was the icing on the cake who, I'm sorry to admit, sold himself very well on the phone."

"Quinn's had the same type of evening." Carl nodded to his right. "There's a particular woman, a Miss Palouse, that he's quite enamored with."

Shame on Carl. He'd purposefully made Benton's heart sound taken. Katherine kicked Carl's shin beneath the table. He didn't even blink.

"As you probably know, Marci," Katherine said, "Mr. Benton has never met Miss Palouse, so to say he's enamored with her is a tad far-fetched."

"As I told you earlier, Katherine, I am enamored with her." Benton met Katherine's gaze across the table.

He wasn't helping the situation much. "Do you blind date often, Marci?" Katherine asked.

"Yes, and no, in spurts. It was another blind date that set up tonight's. I should have known better." She frowned and puffed a whimsical curl away from her face. "Carl, what line of work are you in?"

"I'm a US history professor at Lewis-Clark State College in Lewiston."

"Ohhhh." Turning her head to the side, Marci gave him a glimpse of her sweet profile.

"Just like Mr. Benton; they both teach US history," Katherine tried to divert Marci's attention from Carl's chiseled features to Benton's handsomeness. Wide-eyed, she implored him to do something, get Marci away from the table, away from Carl—go for a walk, look at chairs, or the moon. Instead, arms crossed, he appeared slightly amused by the turn of events.

Carl rolled a kink out of his neck. "Marci, Katherine has a dating question she's always wanted to be asked. One I rather like. If you could be a journalist in any American war, which war would you choose?"

"Oh, that's easy." Marci smiled. "I'm fond of the architecture of the Old South. Especially the . . ." Her eyes darted north and then south. She cleared her throat. "The American Revolution. No . . . the . . ."

Brows gathered she stared at Carl's mouth.

Benton watched Marci while Katherine watched Carl's lower lip drop into a straight line as he mouthed "Civil."

"The American Civil War."

Everyone breathed a sigh of relief.

"Benton," Katherine said, trying to get the party going in the right direction, "maybe now would be a good time to look for a chair." She bobbed her head slightly toward Marci.

Dark brows gathered, Benton slowly stood up. "Katherine, um, I need a chair for my office. Would you bring your flashlight and assist me?"

Not me, you dummy! She didn't move an inch. What was he thinking?

He nodded toward the front of the store.

"Oh, but . . ." Marci crooned and glanced from Benton across the table to Carl. "Are you sure, Quinn? I mean, I can . . ."

"I think it's for the best. Come on, Katherine." Benton nodded toward the front of the store.

He was such a ninny. Here was finally a cute girl with a career. Not the smartest when it came to US history, but it was forgivable. After finding her flashlight in the front zipper area of her backpack, Katherine rose from the table. She paused for a moment, with her hands on the rungs of the chair, and gave Marci ten more seconds to realize she was being a poor judge of character. Then she joined Benton on the periphery of the candle's light.

Taking the flashlight from her, he took the lead toward the front of the store. As soon as they reached their destination, she'd give him a piece of her mind.

Flooded in moonlight, the floor-to-ceiling windows outlined the merchandise near the front. Benton shone the light on a kitchen queen, an antique cupboard. It was tall and broad. Maybe he was into antiques, or perhaps he liked the fact that the monstrous piece completely hid them from Carl and Marci's view.

"You just let him win." Katherine stopped beside him. "She's a cute girl with a career. You're a ninny."

"Yes, Katherine, you've been very consistent about giving me a piece of your mind."

"And Carl of all people." She sighed. Her gaze followed the path of his flashlight. It outlined a pair of salt-and-pepper shakers in Grandma's Currier and Ives pattern.

"Uhhh, shine the light there again, Benton." She guided his flashlight hand to where the shakers sat on a shelf in the kitchen queen. "Grandma's been looking for those for years." Holding the pair up to the light, she checked for nicks and found a six-dollar price tag. "I didn't bring money. Can I borrow six dollars and forty-two cents?"

He chuckled. "Yes, of course. I've eaten how many meals at your home? I should be the one to buy them for Ethel."

His soft tone made her stomach flip-flop, and why did he chuckle? Wasn't he down about his second rejection of the evening? Feeling cautious, she glanced up at him. He was studying her. The light in his eyes was aided by moonlight and the street lamps of downtown Colfax.

"You just let Carl win. Within six weeks, it'll be over. Marci will be heartbroken, and it'll all be your fault."

"Marci's a venter. Always has to talk about her work. Something goes wrong every day for her. I knew that beforehand, but I'd told her I'd meet her all the same, and I've followed through."

"So you're okay?" Despite how cute Marci was, he appeared fine.

"Absolutely. You didn't need to come to my rescue, but you were marvelous back there."

Her knees felt weak. Was this really Benton speaking?

"I always root for the underdog. Carl's so smooth. He's like Jiffy peanut butter without peanuts." Did that make sense? The sparkle in Benton's eyes combined with his nearness made her feel nervous and chatty.

"Katherine." There was a nuance to his tone. He moved slightly to face her. They were too close, inches apart. She inhaled. He probably had duct tape. He'd probably stocked up on it since the first night he'd driven her home, except his hands were free, and he lifted one to gently grip her shoulder. The simple gesture was so sudden and intimate. She inhaled and blinked. If one of them didn't say something soon, something unfortunate might happen.

"Um . . . you have a big slop of taco grease on the front of your shirt." He glanced down briefly, drawing her own gaze to a large, unsightly smudge right above her chest, and on her favorite white shirt.

How embarrassing. How could he even look at her?

"It was almost sweet how you battled for me back there. I believe it was the first time we've ever been on the same side about something."

He obviously hadn't completely recovered from her first *or* second visit to his office. Maybe he never would. Except there had been a softness to his voice. "Like allies," she whispered. *Please don't be rebounding.*

"Yes . . . Carl's used to winning. Golf, women, door prizes. That's why you choosing to go home with me over him last week provoked tonight's challenge."

"Marci being the prize?" She wanted to peer around the side of the kitchen queen. "You don't really think . . . ?"

"Evans warned me. I purposefully invited Marci hoping you wouldn't take center stage. You have your studies."

Touched by his thoughtfulness, she briefly hugged his arm.

"Now, do me the honor of helping me find a chair for my office." He shone the flashlight toward a grouping of furniture to his left.

ж

"Benton, Carl . . ." Evans yelled. "Katherine . . ." Evans's voice carried to the main level.

Katherine patted Benton's shoulder, trying to wake him. Groggy, he slid his feet over the side of the sofa and sat up. Due to sharing the same reading light, he'd fallen asleep on a couch pillow placed beside her hip.

"We're over here, Evans," Katherine said. "Near the front of the store . . . behind the wall of tall boy dressers." She lowered her voice as he approached.

Holding a dessert plate in each hand, he paused at the entry to their palace. His sweeping gaze took in Katherine's open textbook, her flashlight taped to the overhead lamp, and Benton stretching.

"Don't tell me you've been sleeping." He handed them each a piece of Cindy's homemade Bundt cake topped with a drizzle of white icing.

"How much longer do you plan to hold us captive?" Benton rolled a kink out of his neck.

"It's only eleven thirty. Take another nap if you're so tired. Where did Carl and Marci Garfield disappear to?"

Benton shrugged. "They hit it off."

"Are you okay about that?" Evans's eyes narrowed.

"Yes. It worked out perfectly."

Evans's gaze shifted to Katherine. Brows lifted and highlighter in hand, she peered up at him. He was trying to read into the situation, but there wasn't much to read into.

"We'll stay a couple more hours if you don't mind?"

Benton shook his head.

Katherine shrugged. "It's fine with me."

"Do I detect a peace treaty?" Evans asked.

"Yes." Benton nodded. "Katherine and I are now allies. I'll tell you about it later."

"That's good news." Evans grinned. "Cindy and I are having a wonderful time. Do you know she used to scuba dive?"

"No." Katherine laughed.

"Only because her ex-husband wanted her to, an anniversary present in the Florida Keys."

"You don't happen to have any coffee left?" Benton stood up and stretched.

"Yes, I'll have Cindy bring two cups down."

"Thank you," Katherine said.

Cindy's peach and blueberry-studded Bundt cake was delicious. "This is so good." Katherine pulled her feet beneath her on the couch and was surprised by how comfortable she finally felt in Quinn's presence. Perhaps the attraction was gone, that or she was just plain tired.

Carrying two cups of coffee, Cindy entered their abode. There was a keenness in her eyes as she handed Katherine the cup of coffee.

"The cake is delicious," Katherine said.

"I second that." Benton took a sip of coffee before setting his mug on the floor.

"Mark Twain said he could live on a compliment for two months. I've had enough tonight to last a year." Cindy smiled.

"Sounds like the two of you are getting along." Benton watched her closely.

"I haven't laughed so much in eons, maybe ever."

"Do you think Evans is game for us to finally join you?" he asked.

"No, as you know, he's been trying to get me alone without lesson plans for years." At that, Cindy exited their boudoir.

Had Evans been behind the evening's turn of events? No, he couldn't have planned Miss Palouse's water heater and Marci's response to Carl.

Chapter Twenty-Nine

Katherine awoke to someone fastening the seat belt near her hip. She was sitting in the backseat of Evans's Cadillac with her left cheek pressed against Benton's shoulder. A wooden chair, with its legs positioned toward the ceiling, occupied his prior space.

"I just read that four percent of adults sleepwalk," Cindy said.

"Sorry, Katherine. The trunk's full. Cindy bought three chairs, and this one wouldn't fit over the hump." He motioned to the middle of the floorboard.

They were still in Colfax. Benton must have walked her to the car. She rubbed her eyes.

"Katherine, how'd your studying go?" Evans peered in the rearview mirror.

"Good." She sat up and covered a yawn. The cab felt too quiet; hopefully, everyone hadn't discussed everything already.

"Are Evans and Cindy officially a couple now?" she whispered.

"I think so. I'm very tired of the album they were playing."

"Time in a Bottle" was also Carl and Marci's first song.

As they drove out of the valley town into the open countryside, the full moon cast a monochromatic aura of gray-blues across the knee-high fields of rolling wheat. Van Gogh would have been inspired.

"How was your first date, Evans?" Benton asked.

"What do you think, Miss Fancy?" Evans glanced at Cindy.

"I had a marvelous time."

Strangely, so had Katherine. Now Benton's nearness, his shoulder pressing into hers, his knee brushing against hers, was a raw reminder of the strong attraction between them, or at least on her side.

"So Miss Garfield was far more attractive than you anticipated?" Evans glanced in his rearview mirror at Benton.

"She and Carl are a great couple." He shrugged. "Though Marci didn't admit it, I think hearing that Katherine was with us got her here."

"Nothing like a little competition, even if it's fictitious," Evans said. "Was it love at first sight for Carl, or could you tell?"

What a bold question to ask, and at this hour.

"I'm sure we'll hear Carl's side tomorrow at breakfast." Benton yawned.

"Now, who's your blind date next week?" Cindy asked.

"I'm getting my hair cut in Princeton, Idaho, at the same time as Miss Harvard."

"How was your evening with Katherine?" Evans asked.

Katherine's breathing shallowed as she waited for his recap of their time together.

Quinn cleared his throat. "When Marci showed favoritism to Carl tonight, Katherine rallied to my aid. She was surprisingly concerned about my state of mind. Enough so that I am willing to drop all former, and perhaps incorrect, impressions I may have had regarding her."

"Please speak English, both of you," Cindy said.

"Katherine rallied to your aid?" Evans sounded pleased.

"Yes. Carl was dealt a better hand in Marci's eyes, and, Katherine, how did you put it?" Turning his head slightly, he smiled at her. "That's right, you said you always root for the underdog. Katherine tried to encourage me to stay in the fight."

"Oh, you were the underdog in Marci's eyes." Evans sighed. "It sounds like Carl was at his usual best."

Katherine gazed out her side of the car at the moonlit rolling hills. How could Evans—her dear, sweet professor—have even thought of matchmaking her with such a womanizer?

"How many dates do you presently have lined up?" Cindy asked.

"Three," Evans said.

"I believe Grandma has them written on the calendar," Katherine whispered.

"Really?" Quinn smiled at her.

"Yes, if you ever need a reminder, it's on the wall, adjacent to where I sit at the table."

He nodded slightly, gazing right into her eyes.

A cruise-ship-sized docking knot formed in her gut. There was an attraction as big as the Princess Cruise Line between them, or at least on her side, and now they were squished together in the backseat.

"Who's after Miss Harvard?" Cindy asked. "I think it's the hour; I feel confused."

"The nurse," Quinn said. "She works in Moscow at Gritman Hospital but lives in Princeton. The following Friday, Miss Palouse and I will try again."

"Three weeks," Katherine whispered.

"Third time's a charm," Evans said.

"Harvard University or Harvard, the tiny town past Princeton?" Cindy asked.

"The town. My sister cuts hair in Princeton and set this up. The gal, a sales clerk in the town of Harvard, doesn't know about the setup."

"I stopped at a pay phone in Harvard once," Cindy said. "That's all I remember of the town."

"There's also a church, a tavern, a wee little grocery store." Benton glanced over his shoulder at her, a soft sparkle in his dark eyes.

What to think? What to think? Stop thinking!

"You fell asleep," he whispered. "One minute we were talking, and the next you were asleep."

She was surprised she ever could have fallen asleep in his company.

"What time is it?"

He peered at his wristwatch. "Two minutes past two."

"That's probably why."

In between the bucket seats, he watched the road ahead for a few minutes, and then he leaned toward her. "I apologize for the situation," he whispered. "Despite my repacking, the chairs wouldn't fit in the trunk."

"Thank you for trying." Maybe it was the softness in her voice, but his shoulders turned slightly toward her. As he regarded her in the moonlit cab, his chest slowly expanded.

"I *miss* the *Palouse* when I'm away . . ." Evans cleared his throat. "Particularly this stretch of the drive. The rolling hills of the *Palouse*, and how the countryside changes abruptly from pastoral to urban, as you descend into the university town of Pullman."

Katherine stared out the passenger window as the scene Evans described unfolded. He'd cleverly reminded them both of Miss Palouse.

Had Benton been about to kiss her? For self-preservation, she couldn't let him, not when he had three more blind dates on the horizon. Not when he had questions about Miss Palouse. Not when he was her professor, lest she forget.

She sighed. It was best just to bury herself in the books and never, ever again think about her professor—Quinn Benton.

Chapter Thirty

Sunday evening, the phone rang in the living room. Katherine thought about letting it go to the recorder, but before she could say anything, Grandma answered it.

"Oh, hello, Quinn." Grandma sounded pleased to hear his voice.

Katherine chewed quietly and leaned slightly toward the living room. There were several long pauses, which meant Benton was doing his share of the talking. She got up and filled the left side of the sink with hot, sudsy water. Pulling the phone cord behind her, Grandma moved deeper into the living room.

"My girlfriend Sharon visited this afternoon. She brought a mile-high strawberry pie. I still have a couple of pieces in the fridge left for Katherine and me to enjoy tonight. Might even be three; I haven't counted."

Katherine crossed the kitchen and opened the fridge. Sure enough, Saran Wrap tented a tall quarter section of pie, seated on a clear plastic plate. Yum.

"Quinn's coming over for mile-high strawberry pie," Grandma announced, strolling into the kitchen. "He said he needed to talk to you about something."

Katherine's stomach plummeted like she'd just descended ten floors in an old elevator. Was he going to address Friday night, and how well they'd gotten along? Too well. To keep her mind busy, she started a fresh pot of decaf coffee. While it brewed, she poured half-and-half into a white ceramic creamer. Did he finally realize there was a tidal wave of chemistry between them? She sprayed the window above the sink with Windex and dried it with a paper towel while Grandma carefully divided the remaining quarter of a pie into three pieces. She should never have gone to Colfax with them. She should have stayed home and studied at the library.

Benton knocked on the back door. Katherine proceeded to pour three cups of coffee while Grandma greeted him.

"You walked." Grandma set the loaded dessert plates on the table.

"Yes, it's a perfect evening." Wearing khaki-colored trousers and a Princeton-orange polo, Benton pulled his usual chair out from the table and sat down.

"You should wear that polo when you meet Nurse Princeton," Katherine said.

"If you could live anywhere you wanted, Ethel, would you live near the ocean or the mountains?" Quinn asked, ignoring Katherine's excellent observation.

It sounded like a dating question. Katherine suppressed a chuckle.

"I'd live eight miles from Moscow Mountain," Grandma said.

Quinn nodded. "I think you're saying that you're happy where you live right now."

Grandma nodded.

Moscow Mountain wasn't a mountain; compared to Mount Hood, it was more of a molehill. But if Moscow residents wanted to make mountains out of

258 Sherri Schoenborn Murray

molehills—

"What about you, Katherine?"

"Huh?" Her eyes locked on his. *Be smart, be intelligent, be yourself.* "Neither, I'd live here in Moscow. I love this little town, even though it's a good eight hours inland."

"The Portland-Vancouver area is beautiful." His brows gathered. "Why would you prefer to live here?"

Another mini-date at Grandma's.

"I love the Palouse. Like you, Benton, I love the little pocket-sized towns. Being able to see for miles and miles. Even though the change of seasons isn't always as apparent as back home, you learn to watch for it in the rolling hills."

Grandma sat up a bit in her chair, suppressing a smile.

"Ethel said you like it here." He nodded. "I grew up in Kellogg. My folks are still there."

Hmm . . . Kellogg was a beautiful little resort town south of Coeur d'Alene. "How did a small-town fellow like you end up at Duke?"

Grandma kicked her beneath the table. "I think that this month's *picture* on the calendar is so *pretty*."

Katherine looked over her shoulder to the Latah County Credit Union calendar thumb tacked to the wall. The July picture was of a grain silo in a rolling field of deep green wheat. What Grandma wanted her to focus on was her wording *pretty picture.*

"We have family in North Carolina—my mother's youngest brother. I worked part-time at my uncle's hardware store in exchange for room and board. Otherwise, I'd be paying off student loans for the next twenty years."

"Grandma, Duke is a prestigious Ivy League school, in case you didn't know."

"Duke. Wa-luke. Idaho has ivy." Grandma waved a hand.

"Katherine, I'm sorry to correct you, but you're wrong. Duke is not an Ivy League school. Actually both Stanford and Duke aren't Ivy schools. The Ivy League is a football division, and Duke is part of the Atlantic Coast Conference."

Quinn could be quite impressive when he wanted to. "Why does it feel like a date?" she voiced out loud.

"If I were ever to write a list of all the reasons I would never fall for your granddaughter"—Quinn looked at Grandma—"the first line would be . . ." Katherine frowned at him. "That Katherine King is not old-fashioned enough for me."

Wide-eyed, Grandma giggled.

"That's sure from left field, Benton."

Had Evans shared her Joe List with him? Exposed the ramblings of her twenty-something heart? "I haven't written a Quinn List, if that's what you're hinting at."

"Why not?" His dark brows gathered.

"There's been no reason to." She laughed. Did he want her to? Her mind wanted to return to last night and their moonlit car ride home, but her pincushion heart told her not to.

"After pie, Quinn, why don't you take Katherine for a walk? She hasn't had her walk today."

"You make me sound like a dog, Grandma."

"We could walk to Bucer's for a cup of decaf." His chest inflated slightly.

He was finally going to make her apologize to Carl, or was there more to it? Something was different about him tonight, and it wasn't just his polo.

"I suppose we'll be coffee-d out." He glanced out the window, which spanned the length of the table. "It is an exceptionally nice evening for a walk, though."

Grandma stirred sugar into her coffee and smiled.

"It is." Katherine chewed on her lower lip. She and Benton had never gone on a walk before. *Taking a walk* used to be Joe's secret term for making out.

Why did Benton want to go for a walk? Harp and string music began to play in Grandma's boxy kitchen. For a full measure, she couldn't look at him. She glanced at the salt-and-pepper shakers, the stove, and over her shoulder toward the living room. When she'd been sick, she'd watched *Doctor Zhivago*. She needed to put the VHS tape away before Grandma found it.

"You'll need to change into walking shoes." He obviously didn't think her flip-flops suitable for a long walk. "The pie and coffee were great, Ethel. Thank you for inviting me."

"You invited yourself."

Katherine jogged up the narrow stairwell for her shoes. *Get a grip. He only wants to go for a walk to reprimand me for Carl. Not to make out.* The phone rang as she reached the landing. She sat down on the bed and pulled on her Adidas tennis shoes. The main level door creaked open. "Phone, Katherine," Grandma called.

Sighing, she picked up the phone from the top of her waterfall dresser. "Hello." There was the click as Grandma set the receiver down.

"Katherine, it's Cindy." Her voice was unusually monotone. "Is now a good time to talk?"

"Hi, Cindy. Um . . . Benton's here. We're just getting ready to go for a walk."

"Is he in the same room?"

"No, I'm upstairs. Why?" Katherine gripped the phone cord in one hand.

"Well . . . I was at Dennis's place this afternoon.

Quinn didn't get to talk much at The Breakfast Club this morning. He doesn't talk in front of Carl. He sometimes confides in me, but lately, he's confided more in Dennis. I don't know why, but Dennis's advice is really off this time."

"Regarding?" Katherine brushed her hair in front of her dresser mirror.

"Quinn is torn between you and Miss Palouse. I don't know if that surprises you."

Katherine stared wide-eyed in the mirror.

"And . . ." Cindy continued, "Dennis's advice is that Quinn should kiss you before he meets Claire."

"What?" Katherine held the brush midair. "Is Evans crazy? That's horrible advice."

"That's what I thought, too. Dennis thinks that because it's summer school and you're only a few weeks away from graduating, the board would be able to overlook it if it were ever brought to their attention."

She hoped Benton knew better than to take advice from a professor who'd married one of his students.

"Dennis seems to think that if Quinn kisses you, he'll be able to understand his feelings for you more. Men are different than women in that respect. For the most part, I think we know how we feel, don't you?"

"It's kind of you to warn me, Cindy." Katherine's laugh sounded hollow, shaky even to her own ears.

"If you care to call me later, I'll be home."

"Thanks. I may take you up on that."

Chapter Thirty-One

Five minutes earlier . . .

The phone rang right in the middle of a great episode of *Sixty Minutes*. Ethel monkeyed with the remote control and turned it off. Using her forearms, she pushed herself out of the recliner and strode to the phone. "Hello." She turned from the curio cabinet to face the front door.

"Hi, Mom, it's Pattie," her daughter-in-law said. "Is Katherine there?"

"No, honey, not at the moment."

"I gave Phil the update this afternoon about Professor B. and Carl. You remember that your son and I met during summer school. There's a relaxed chemistry on campus during the summer. Katherine's finally experiencing it."

"I don't think she's too tickled about it at the moment." Ethel scanned the lace-curtained windows for any sign of Katherine and Quinn.

"Why's that?"

"She went for a walk with Professor B. He told me that out of their professor group, he was chosen to speak with her regarding the way she handled Carl, the flagrantly good-looking—" Their conversation was interrupted by what sounded like a newspaper being tossed against the screen door.

"That's funny, we don't get the paper in the evening. Hold on a minute, Pattie."

Ethel set down the receiver on a pile of junk mail and crossed the shag carpeting. She'd look through the peep-hole first before she'd open the door and let in moths. Placing her hands against the door, she peeked through the itty-bitty, flea-sized window.

Katherine stood with her right profile to the door. Ethel adjusted her glasses, switched to her left eye, and squished her cheek into the wood. Quinn's left profile, and then his shoulder, covered the peephole as . . . Stepping away from the door, Ethel's hands flew to her mouth as she stifled a gasp. Quinn and Katherine were about to kiss! She'd seen it through the peep-hole with her own two eyes!

Suppressing a giggle, she ambled back to the phone.

"Pattie, are you still there?" she whispered.

"Yes, Mom, is everything okay?"

"Yesssss. Why yes, it is!" Ethel smiled.

"Was it the paperboy?" Pattie asked.

Ethel glanced toward the door. "Yes . . . Yes, it was. I should go now. I don't want to miss Andy Rooney."

"Are you sure everything's okay?"

"Yes, honey, everything's fine."

"Keep us posted."

"I will." Ethel practically hung up on Pattie as she hurried to the recliner and turned the TV back on. She glanced toward the door and pretended to be immersed in Andy Rooney's narrative about something as Katherine entered the front room alone.

Before the door closed, Ethel glanced toward the sidewalk. Quinn was nowhere in sight. How odd. For a moment, she questioned if it was indeed Quinn that she'd seen on her front porch. She nodded yes, it had been Quinn's profile, and Katherine had left with him.

"How was your walk, honey?" With a lift of her chin, Ethel watched Katherine closely as she passed through the living room on her way to the kitchen.

"Good, Grandma, it went fine." Besides being a little bit red, Katherine appeared surprisingly calm for having just been kissed for the first time in over five years. Ethel turned off Andy and followed her granddaughter. When Ethel entered the kitchen, Katherine flung open the refrigerator. The bottles of relish and mayonnaise smacked together in the door.

"There's a little Jell-O salad from the other day," Ethel said.

Katherine shook her head and continued searching. Except for the fridge, there was no other light on in the kitchen. Ethel sat down in the chair that Quinn usually occupied. As her granddaughter explored the fridge, her profile was as red as an Early Girl tomato.

"How did the apology go with Mr. Flagrant?"

"Benton told you?"

"Yes. He said that your walk would take awhile because he knew you wouldn't take kindly to calling Carl and apologizing."

"You remembered his name."

"Yes, Carl from Lewiston. It's the daily crossword puzzle that keeps me sharp. Where were we? Oh, yes, how was the apology?"

"Better than I expected." Katherine shrugged and grabbed a carrot. "He was more sensitive and understanding than I imagined."

"Oh?"

"It's definitely for the best."

"Why's that?"

Katherine peeled and washed the carrot at the sink. "I don't have time for a relationship, Grandma." She sighed. "Once you're a couple, there's the longwinded phone calls, the movies, the fights, more phone calls, the breakups. It all takes time, and with my schedule, I'd be an idiot to even entertain a relationship."

Who was she talking about Mr. Flagrant or Quinn? Ethel pushed her glasses higher up the bridge of her nose and propped both elbows heavily on the table. Her granddaughter's logic left a lot to be desired. The shrill of the phone ringing made both their heads turn.

"If it's Benton, Grandma, I'll speak to him upstairs."

"Why upstairs, honey? And, why would he call, when he just left?" Ethel followed her into the living room and picked up the phone. "Hello."

"Hello, Ethel, it's Quinn. May I speak with Katherine?"

"Yes, please hold." She waved her hand for Katherine to hurry upstairs. "For some reason, she wants to talk to you in private, so she's grabbing the phone upstairs in her room. I hope you two haven't been fighting."

"No, we haven't been." Quinn cleared his throat.

She suppressed a giggle. How long had they been kissing on her front step behind her back?

"I'm on, Grandma. You can hang up now."

Didn't Katherine trust her? Ethel put her finger down on the little button. If it made a loud enough click, would Katherine think she'd hung up?

"I still hear you breathing, Grandma."

Ethel set the receiver in the cradle with a solid click.

Ж

Katherine held the receiver against her ear. Benton had just left. That was the problem with relationships—they took time.

"Katherine, we need to talk."

"Yes, I suppose we do." He'd called to talk. Lying on the quilt-covered full-sized bed, she looped the phone cord between the fingers of her left hand and stared up at the attic room's peaked ceiling. She just needed some Hubba Bubba bubble gum, and she'd be back in her junior high days.

"I called Evans. I told him everything." He sighed. "He thinks I may have misplaced my affection for Claire on you because I haven't been able to meet her."

What? She'd never heard anything so ridiculous in all her life. He couldn't possibly believe Evans? Why had Evans inspired him to take the walk and kiss her tonight if he was only going to turn around and tell him that?

"What does Evans think you should do?" Her voice was as sweet as Laffy Taffy.

"He thinks we should wait until I meet Claire before you and I spend any more time together."

What? That meant, at least, three weeks!

"I think he's right, Benton. You could have, unknowingly, transferred feelings that you have for Claire to me." Was he really such a dummy? "Even though you've never met Claire, you've talked very highly of her, and you don't even really like me."

"Listen to yourself, Katherine. You're bright, beautiful, and, when you allow yourself to be, very diplomatic."

Hmm . . . *Lessons in Diplomacy* by Professor Quinn Benton Ph.D. Katherine sighed. Diplomacy was comparable to biting your tongue so hard you tasted blood while your words were honey.

She stared at the hairline crack in the ceiling's plaster. Had he ever said she was beautiful before? The compliment felt like a dull machete.

"Let's just move forward and pretend the kiss on Grandma's front porch never happened." Her voice was natural, bright . . . diplomatic. "Within three weeks, you'll have met Miss Palouse, and you'll have this all figured out." One traitor tear coursed down toward her ear. "In the meantime, I'm not going anywhere. You know me, I'll just have my nose in a book."

Poor, poor Angel. She'd thought she and Greg were really going somewhere; that is until the chili. At least with Benton, she'd only thought they were going for a walk. And there had only been one kiss. One amazingly wonderful kiss.

"It would be much easier for me, Katherine . . ." Did he always sound so airy when he said her name? "If you were your old argumentative self."

"Oh, okay. I still have two hours of Lewis and Clark to read, so I should get off the phone."

"Oh . . . kay." Was there pain in his voice?

"Good night, Mr. Benton."

"Good night."

Katherine stared at the ceiling. Why did Evans encourage Quinn to kiss her, and then tell him not to spend time with her for three weeks? Transferring his feelings for Claire to her—why it should be illegal!

Evans should be shot.

Chapter Thirty-Two

The phone rang right in the middle of a great episode of *Sixty Minutes*. Ethel monkeyed with the remote control and turned it off. Using her forearms, she pushed herself out of the recliner and strode to the phone. "Hello." She turned from the curio cabinet to face the front door.

"Hi, Mom, it's Pattie," her daughter-in-law said. "Is Katherine there?"

"No, honey, not at the moment."

"I gave Phil the update this afternoon about Professor B. and Carl. You remember that your son and I met during summer school. There's a relaxed chemistry on campus during the summer. Katherine's finally experiencing it."

"I don't think she's too tickled about it at the moment." Ethel scanned the lace-curtained windows for any sign of Katherine and Quinn.

"Why's that?"

"She went for a walk with Professor B. He told me that out of their professor group, he was chosen to speak with her regarding the way she handled Carl, the flagrantly good-looking—" Their conversation was interrupted by what sounded like a newspaper being tossed against the screen door.

"That's funny, we don't get the paper in the evening. Hold on a minute, Pattie."

Ethel set down the receiver on a pile of junk mail and crossed the shag carpeting. She'd look through the peep-hole first before she'd open the door and let in moths. Placing her hands against the door, she peeked through the itty-bitty, flea-sized window.

Katherine stood with her right profile to the door. Ethel adjusted her glasses, switched to her left eye, and squished her cheek into the wood. Quinn's left profile, and then his shoulder, covered the peephole as . . . Stepping away from the door, Ethel's hands flew to her mouth as she stifled a gasp. Quinn and Katherine were about to kiss! She'd seen it through the peep-hole with her own two eyes!

Suppressing a giggle, she ambled back to the phone.

"Pattie, are you still there?" she whispered.

"Yes, Mom, is everything okay?"

"Yesssss. Why yes, it is!" Ethel smiled.

"Was it the paperboy?" Pattie asked.

Ethel glanced toward the door. "Yes . . . yes, it was. I should go now. I don't want to miss Andy Rooney."

"Are you sure everything's okay?"

"Yes, honey, everything's fine."

"Keep us posted."

"I will." Ethel practically hung up on Pattie as she hurried to the recliner and turned the TV back on. She glanced toward the front door and pretended to be immersed in Andy Rooney's narrative about something as Katherine entered the front room alone.

Before the door closed, Ethel glanced toward the sidewalk. Quinn was nowhere in sight. How odd. For a moment she questioned if it was indeed Quinn that she'd seen on her front porch. She nodded yes, it had been Quinn's profile, and Katherine had left with him.

"How was your walk, honey?" With a lift of her chin, Ethel watched Katherine closely as she passed through the living room on her way to the kitchen.

"Good, Grandma, it went fine." Besides being a little bit red, Katherine appeared surprisingly calm for having just been kissed for the first time in over five years. Ethel turned off Andy and followed her granddaughter. When Ethel entered the kitchen, Katherine flung open the refrigerator. The bottles of relish and mayonnaise smacked together in the door.

"There's a little Jell-O salad from the other day," Ethel said.

Katherine shook her head and continued searching. Except for the fridge, there was no other light on in the kitchen. Ethel sat down in the chair that Quinn usually occupied. As her granddaughter explored the fridge, her profile was as red as an Early Girl tomato.

"How did the apology go with Mr. Flagrant?"

"Benton told you?"

"Yes. He told me that your walk would take a while because he knew you wouldn't take kindly to calling Carl and apologizing."

"You remembered his name."

"Yes, Carl from Lewiston. It's the daily crossword puzzle that keeps me sharp. Where were we? Oh, yes, how was the apology?"

"Better than I expected." Katherine shrugged and grabbed a carrot. "He was more sensitive and understanding than I imagined."

"Oh?"

"It's definitely for the best."

"Why's that?"

Katherine peeled and washed the carrot at the sink. "I don't have time for a relationship, Grandma." She sighed. "Once you're a couple, there's the longwinded phone calls, the movies, the fights, more phone calls, the breakups. It all takes time, and with my schedule, I'd be an idiot to even entertain a relationship."

Who was she talking about Mr. Flagrant or Quinn? Ethel pushed her glasses higher up the bridge of her nose and propped both elbows heavily on the table. Her granddaughter's logic left a lot to be

272   Sherri Schoenborn Murray

desired. The shrill of the phone ringing made both
their heads turn.

"If it's Benton, Grandma, I'll speak to him
upstairs."

"Why upstairs, honey? And, why would he call,
when he just left?" Ethel followed her into the living
room and picked up the phone. "Hello."

"Hello, Ethel, it's Quinn. May I speak with
Katherine?"

"Yes, please hold." She waved her hand for
Katherine to hurry upstairs. "For some reason she
wants to talk to you in private, so she's grabbing the
phone upstairs in her room. I hope you two haven't
been fighting."

"No, we haven't been." Quinn cleared his throat.

She suppressed a giggle. How long had they been
kissing on her front step behind her back?

"I'm on, Grandma. You can hang up now."

Didn't Katherine trust her? Ethel put her finger
down on the little button. If it made a loud enough
click, would Katherine think she'd hung up?

"I still hear you breathing, Grandma."

Ethel set the receiver in the cradle with a solid
click.

Ж

Katherine held the receiver against her ear.
Benton had just left. That was the problem with
relationships—they took time.

"Katherine, we need to talk."

"Yes, I suppose we do." He'd called to talk.
Lying on the quilt-covered full-sized bed, she looped
the phone cord between the fingers of her left hand
and stared up at the attic room's peaked ceiling. She
just needed some Hubba Bubba bubble gum, and she'd
be back in her junior high days.

"I called Evans. I told him everything." He sighed. "He thinks I may have misplaced my affection for Claire on you because I haven't been able to meet her."

What? She'd never heard anything so ridiculous in all her life. He couldn't possibly believe Evans? Why had Evans inspired him to take the walk and kiss her tonight if he was only going to turn around and tell him that?

"What does Evans think you should do?" Her voice was as sweet as Laffy Taffy.

"He thinks we should wait until I meet Claire before you and I spend any more time together."

What? That meant at least three weeks!

"I think he's right, Benton. You could have, unknowingly, transferred feelings that you have for Claire to me." Was he really such a dummy? "Even though you've never met Claire, you've talked very highly of her, and you don't even really like me."

"Listen to yourself, Katherine. You're bright, beautiful, and, when you allow yourself to be, very diplomatic."

Hmm . . . *Lessons in Diplomacy* by Professor Quinn Benton PhD. Katherine sighed. Diplomacy was comparable to biting your tongue so hard you tasted blood, while your words were honey.

She stared at the hairline crack in the ceiling's plaster. Had he ever said she was beautiful before? The compliment felt like a dull machete.

"Let's just move forward and pretend the kiss on Grandma's front porch never happened." Her voice was natural, bright . . . diplomatic. "Within three weeks, you'll have met Miss Palouse, and you'll have this all figured out." One traitor tear coursed down toward her ear. "In the meantime, I'm not going anywhere. You know me, I'll just have my nose in a book."

Poor, poor Angel. She'd really thought she and Greg were really going somewhere, that is until the chili. At least with Benton, she'd only thought they were going for a walk. And there had only been one kiss. One amazingly wonderful kiss.

"It would be much easier for me, Katherine . . ." Did he always sound so airy when he said her name? "If you were your old argumentative self."

"Oh, okay. I still have two hours of Lewis and Clark to read, so I should get off the phone."

"Oh . . . kay." Was there pain in his voice?

"Good night, Mr. Benton."

"Good night."

Katherine stared at the ceiling. Why did Evans encourage Quinn to kiss her, and then tell him to not spend time with her for three weeks? Transferring his feelings for Claire to her—why, it should be illegal!

Evans should be shot.

Chapter Thirty-Three

Katherine sat in her usual seat, second seat in from the left in the second row of Benton's Civil War class. Would he still be employed by the university next semester? Only last night he'd kissed her, one of his grad students. His favorite grad student. She smiled.

After taking two pages of notes, Katherine lifted her gaze toward the front of the room. Dressed in dark blue Dockers and a perfectly pressed Yale-blue polo, Benton appeared especially handsome as he leaned against the desk. If their eyes met, would he flub his lecture? Would it be obvious to fellow students that they'd kissed? It was best not to take a chance.

He'd pursued her, three times, to be exact. But he'd also said, *I don't think it's very good timing, do you?* He'd displayed a little common sense. Most likely their nearness during Carl's call had been too much. Benton probably hadn't stood that close to a woman in over two years. That was probably the reason he'd kissed her. He didn't even like her. His nickname for her was Miss Annoying, for goodness' sake.

The poor man must be kicking himself. She smiled. For a first kiss, it had been awfully wonderful. But it was best not to think about it. Not here. Her cheeks felt warm. Was she blushing?

At the end of class, Professor Benton returned their most recent essays, the one that Katherine had stayed up until two in the morning to finish, the day she'd had food poisoning. Did she dare peek at the grade, in case he was watching? It wasn't a gift; it was something she'd earned. Feeling hesitant, she flipped to the last page of the essay that she'd typed on Grandma's old Brother typewriter. Beneath her conclusion, he'd written: *A solid A. If you're unhappy with this grade, my office hours are 8:30 to 9:30 and 12:30 to 1:30.*

A solid A. Why would she want to go to his office to complain? She didn't usually complain about A grades. Did he want her to visit and complain? Did he miss her? She smiled. He'd given her an A.

Wow! She'd managed to pull off an A the night she'd been sick.

"Miss King." Benton voiced her name out loud.

Was he singling her out? Would anyone notice? Think it odd? Caught up in the throng of students milling to the door, she glanced ever so discreetly his direction.

"If anyone would like to discuss their grade, my office hours this afternoon are twelve thirty to one thirty." For a moment, he caught her eye.

He wanted her to stop by. What would she say? Hi, I stopped by to thank you for my A. Oh, and by the way, did you grade it before or after we kissed? She needed someone to talk to. It couldn't be Evans or Cindy, Grandma or Angel . . .

All through Cindy and Evans's Lewis and Clark lecture, Katherine contemplated and was tempted by the idea of visiting Benton's office and complaining about something. She could complain about his new wooden chair. Maybe it needed a cushion. Or she could complain about the dull cover of the light blue essay booklets they were required to write in. Or the fact that he'd written her grade in blue ink instead of black, which could be deemed far more professional. Once the one hour lecture was over, she couldn't bring herself to be anything else but happy with her A.

Instead of heading up the stairs to the third floor and Benton's office, she showed some restraint by taking the stairwell down. Why did Benton want to see her? He knew they weren't supposed to see each other. For at least three weeks, they were off limits to one another.

Ж

The last paragraph of Ethel's summer Bible study read: Bring your favorite Galatians verse next week, and we'll discuss it. Oh, no. Sandra should have mentioned that at the beginning of the study so that Ethel could have been on the lookout for it. In the first chapter, she remembered that a verse had made her think about Katherine.

Ethel scanned the first page of Galatians. Hallelujah, there it was: *Am I now trying to win the approval of men, or of God? Or am I trying to please men? If I were still trying to please men, I would not be a servant of Christ. – Galatians 1:10.*

Wow! It was a great verse for Katherine. While Ethel wrote it on a sticky note to put in the front of her Bible, the phone rang. That was odd, Katherine was at school. *Hmm . . . the call might actually be for me.* She hurried toward the living room.

"Ethel." The female voice was unusually deep on the other end of the line.

"Joyce . . . is that you?" She and Joyce Wooten, her neighbor across the street, hadn't been on speaking terms for almost a year; not since Joyce had waved her green ribbon for her baked goods under Ethel's nose at the Latah County Fair.

"Yes, it's me."

"Oh, Joyce, how I've missed you!" Ethel patted a hand against her chest. "Now that I hear your voice, I realize that you sincerely are one of my closest and dearest of friends. I'm sorry that I've held your green ribbon against you."

"I'm sorry for flaunting it. I've missed you, too." Joyce cleared her gravelly throat. "The reason I'm calling is . . . you know the pair of binoculars that I keep by my phone?"

"Of course, I do; I gave them to you after Edwin passed away. I wanted you to help me keep an eye on my grandkids." Ethel's eyes widened. Had Joyce seen something?

"That's right, I remember now. Well, there's been activity again on your front porch."

"What kind of activity?" Ethel suppressed a giggle.

"Katherine, your little studier finally has a boyfriend."

"What do you mean?" Ethel bit the insides of her cheeks.

"Well, I was on the phone with my girlfriend, MaryAnn Morrison—her husband's the president of the college, you know."

"Our college—the U of I?" Ethel pulled a chair away from the table to sit down.

"Yes. The Wootens and the Morrisons go way back."

"Oh, I remember now that you've reminded me." Ethel nodded. "What did you see exactly, Joyce?"

"Well . . . I was on the phone when I first caught a glimpse of the two. You know my long range vision is not what it used to be. So I grabbed the binoculars and, it was your Katherine and a very attractive man with dark hair. Let me tell you, Ethel, it was not a peck on the cheek, first date type of kiss." Joyce giggled. "I believe I told MaryAnn at least twice that *the two are still kissing.*"

"Did anything else happen? I mean did they appear to argue or . . ."

"My call ended abruptly. MaryAnn had finally informed me that she was on a walk. When I focused on the scene again, Katherine's fellow swung himself over your front gate, is that the right way to say that?"

"I can picture it," Ethel said.

"And I'm almost positive he ripped the cuff of his pants."

"Let me know, Joyce, if you see any more shenanigans on my front porch." Ethel giggled. Quinn and Katherine might not even notice if she strolled past. "Maybe I'll visit next time."

"I'd like that."

Ж

Grandma made bacon, lettuce, and tomato sandwiches for lunch. The perfect pick-me-up. Katherine sighed and took a bite. *Couldn't see each other for three full weeks? What a load of hooey.* This was the reason she didn't like dating: the mind games. Before Benton, she'd been so focused on her studies and getting good grades, and now her mind often wandered to thoughts of him.

Was Evans trying to use reverse psychology?

"Is something wrong?" Grandma asked.

"No, just college stuff."

Wide-eyed, Grandma stuck a piece of bacon in her mouth. "Has Quinn graded your *Oh, Brother* paper yet?"

"Yes. He gave me an A. I mean, I earned it and everything." Not that she didn't feel good about it, but she'd been sick at the time, and her perceptions of good may have been slightly abnormal given the circumstances, not that she'd ever admit it to Benton.

He should never have kissed her. Everything was working out fine until then. Now, what about Miss Palouse? He'd been looking forward to meeting her for months. Katherine sighed and looked out the window. The kiss had been amazing.

Don't think about the kiss!

"Is everything okay, honey?" Grandma patted her hand.

"Yes." Katherine nodded. "It's absolutely fine. Just fine."

Chapter Thirty-Four

Three weeks! Not seeing the King girls was a double whammy of loneliness. Quinn wasn't only cut off from Katherine; he was cut off from Ethel. He should never have kissed Katherine. He paced the worn, tan-colored carpet of his living room. He made sure the front curtains on his window were closed before he tipped his head back and petitioned God.

"I shouldn't have kissed her. You told me to wait, but I listened to Evans." He sighed. "Because I liked Evans' advice more. How can I even look Morrison in the eye now? I kissed one of my students. One of the gravest sins a professor can make. Forgive me."

He waited on the Lord, waited for peace; but instead, he was tortured by the memory of Katherine's engaging gaze, her arms wrapped around his neck, and the sweet affirmation that she liked him.

Hopefully, their kiss hadn't stirred her memories of Joe.

Cell phone in hand, he speed-dialed Evans.

"It's Benton. I need a favor. You've mentioned on occasion the infamous Joe List, and I was wondering if you'd tell me what you remember?"

"I still have the important artifact somewhere in my possession." Evans chuckled. "After I grade Katherine's next exam, I plan to tuck it inside, and then return it to her. I thought it would bring things full circle."

"Am I a fool for asking?"

"No, but I think she's more significant to you than you're willing to admit."

Significant. Hmm . . . an odd choice of words.

"The infamous Joe List. Now, where did I put it?" There was the click of briefcase latches and then the rustle of papers. "I'll daresay that it's not a piece she'd want just anyone viewing. When she came to my office years ago, she was concerned that the *Argonaut* might have gotten ahold of it. Ahhh, here it is." Evans cleared his throat.

"*Why I will never fall for Joe Hillis again.* I still can't believe she wrote this during my lecture. She's always been one of those bright-eyed, attentive students. The anti-Joe qualities appear to be listed in order of importance, as her first item is: *Not a Christian.* Do you want me to read it now? I could make you a copy and give it to you tomorrow."

"Go ahead and read." Quinn sat down on the edge of the overstuffed sofa cushion.

"Her next anti-Joe sentiment is: *Not brilliant enough.*" Evans chuckled. "Followed by *Too cocky, too cute. Limited vocabulary.* Hmmph . . . Which I might add is also one of your pet peeves. Are you still there, Benton?"

Quinn found his voice. "Yes."

"It's fascinating learning the mindset of a woman you're presently interested in—isn't it? Even if it was written several years ago. Katherine's next item is: *Won't go to church with me. Carries a tennis racket everywhere he goes.* And prepare yourself, Benton . . . *Doesn't understand the term "punctuality."* She set *punctuality* in quotes. And her last item on the list, which I find rather sweet, as they must have a close relationship, is: *Not like Dad.*"

"Yes." Quinn nodded. "Just taking it all in."

"Katherine's next paragraph explains how she needs someone like her father. Concerned. Caring. Focused. Brilliant. Nurturing. Good listener. Supportive of my dreams, not only his own. Call Dad tonight. She underlined the last phrase twice."

"She still mentions Joe quite a bit, Evans." Quinn stared at a watermark on the coffee table.

"Yes, and after your date this Friday, she may feel inspired to write a *Why I will never fall for Quinn Benton List,* w*hich would prove a fascinating read. I wonder if she views that you risked *your employment for the kiss* as a pro or a con?"

It was just like Evans to kid about matters of extreme importance.

"Do you want me to fax a copy to you?"

"Yes, I'll turn my fax machine on." At his desk, Quinn pushed the power button on the shoe box-sized machine. "Fax it as soon as I hang up. Thanks."

"Why is it so important to you, Benton?"

"Just do it, Evans."

The fax came through displaying Katherine's small, yet impeccable cursive. Even though it was several years old, the artifact felt like a piece of her soul.

Chapter Thirty-Five

Tuesday morning . . .

Above the drip of the coffee maker, Quinn was surprised to hear his cell phone. Who would be calling at seven thirty in the morning?

"Quinn, can you stop by this morning on your way to work?" Ethel asked. "It won't take long."

"Sure." Why did she want him to stop by? He hoped it didn't involve plumbing or power tools, as his class started at nine thirty.

"Maybe you can drive Katherine to school this morning since you'll already be here?"

"Ethel . . ." He pulled an insulated cup down from the cupboard. "I don't think that will be well received by our peers."

"I thought it might be neighborly. Nowadays, a neighbor can't even be neighborly. I'll see you when you get here."

A professor seen driving a student to class would be as well received as a professor seen kissing a student. With a heavy heart, he entered the front room, sat on the edge of the couch and bowed his head. "Gracious heavenly Father"—he sighed—"the damage has been done. Help me to handle this situation in the right way. If it means speaking with President Morrison about it, and possibly losing my job, then so be it. Help me, Lord, to handle it in a way that is pleasing to You. Give me wisdom. If I have to avoid her for the rest of the semester, I will."

He parked his car in front of the Kings' detached garage. Ethel must have been watching for him, for as soon as he closed his door, she hurried down the narrow walkway toward him. She carried what looked like old cigar boxes, one in each hand.

"One's for you." Over the top of the gate, she handed him the Lady Wayne cigar boxes. "I made them myself."

Made what herself? Had she rolled cigars?

He glanced at a yellow sticky note on top of one: *To my favorite neighbor. Love, Ethel.*

"There's one cinnamon roll in each. They're as big as the box." Her eyes sparkled. "Don't tell Katherine, but I used a cheater recipe. Rhodes dough." Ethel giggled. "She thinks I made them from scratch." Ethel zipped her lips with two fingers.

"I won't tell. Where'd you find the cigar boxes?" They weren't the typical transport for food.

"Edwin left me a lifetime supply of them in the garage. I finally found a good use for them." She smiled. "Katherine says I'm brownnosing the president of the U of I. And I told her, I'm just sending him a sweet reminder of our visit."

"What do you mean, Ethel?" Had he missed something?

"I was hoping you'd deliver one to President Morrison for me." She nodded toward the box in his right hand. "His office is just around the corner from yours. It's worth paying him a visit just to see his view."

God's answer had come quicker than he'd expected.

He'd taught two years at North Carolina State University as an adjunct professor before applying for the U of I opening. Landing a US history professor position so close to home had been a huge answer to prayer. Why hadn't he reminded himself of this thirty-some hours ago?

"Is something wrong, Quinn?" Ethel leaned her head to one side, studying him.

"Yeah." He nodded. "You know how sometimes you get an answer to prayer, and it's not the answer you were looking for?"

"That's when I know to keep praying."

"I think you also have a bit of King stubbornness, Ethel."

"It's called Pettigrew pride." She smiled. "Sometimes, I think, we're all too quick to jump to our own conclusions. Keep praying. Make sure you heard God correctly."

He was afraid he'd heard Him loud and clear. "You have a great day, Ethel." He opened the passenger-side door and nestled the boxes on the seat.

"You, too. I'll be praying for you."

As he drove west, the beautifully manicured grounds and the ancient elm trees, which lined the Hello Walk in front of the Admin Building, came into view. "I love my job with *this* university," he told God. On the southeast side of campus, he parked in his assigned space and turned off the engine. "I love this school, this town, my colleagues, my home, Ethel King . . ." He sighed deeply. "Lord, Father God, You know what's recently transpired. I lost sight of my position here. I should have waited until Katherine graduated.

"Is delivering the roll a sign from You? Do You want me to tell Morrison?" Quinn closed his eyes and waited for words of counsel, but none came. What did the Holy Spirit's silence mean? He picked up President Morrison's cigar box. On top, the yellow sticky note read: *God bless you, President Morrison. From: Ethel King.*

As he strode the sunlit walkways toward the Admin, Quinn practiced his apology speech. "Hello, President Morrison. Here's a cinnamon roll from Ethel King, and by the way, I kissed her granddaughter on Sunday. Yes, she is a graduate student here at the U of I. Yes, I'll have been with the university a year as of next month. Thank you; while it lasted, it was the best job I'll ever have."

He placed his briefcase and the cigar box on top of his desk and slowly walked the wide granite corridor toward his superior's office. He thought of David, a man after God's own heart. Though he'd written beautiful psalms and had been abundantly blessed by God, he had also stumbled on account of a beautiful woman. "Lord, help me to mend my ways. Forgive my errors. Help me to walk a straight path. Help me to live up to the integrity of this position."

He waited in a padded chair outside President Morrison's office. After a couple of minutes, he heard his right dress shoe tapping against the granite floor. He grounded his heel. Katherine's first visit to his office, she'd done her crazy finger tapping. The memory felt bittersweet.

Lord, if You don't want me to speak with him, don't let there be an opening.

Bending forward at the waist, the trim middle-aged secretary held down the speaker button. "Mike, Professor Benton has a nine-thirty class."

How did she know? Quinn glanced in her direction.

"You keep looking at your watch, and I have a class schedule." She smiled.

Another minute ticked by. If he waited five more minutes, he could leave Ethel's cigar box with Mike's secretary and be free. Free as a jailbird.

"Send him in," Mike's deep voice announced over the speaker on her desk.

Near the expansive picture windows, President Morrison stood with his profile to the room. Tall and broad-shouldered, Mike's gaze took in the northern view of campus—historic brick buildings, acres of lawns, mature elm trees, and in the distance, the rolling hills of the Palouse.

"Good morning, Quinn." Mike turned from his six-figure view to regard him.

"Good morning, Mike. Ethel King called me this morning and wanted me to deliver this to you." He set the cigar box down on top of the cherry wood desk. "There's a large cinnamon roll inside. She also made one for me."

Mike nodded, his hands clasped behind his back. "Ethel visited me here several weeks ago, and she left quite the impression. Have a seat, Quinn."

The president of the university knew he only had eight minutes before his class, yet he wanted him to sit down. "I've only known Ethel since May, and we've grown very close." Quinn rolled his shoulders back and sat up tall. "She invites me to dinner a couple of times a week."

"I see." Mike remained standing.

Lord, if you want me to tell him, you're going to have to help me.

"The demographic studies of Moscow and Latah County indicate that we have a healthy population of senior citizens here, who, like Ethel, are passionate about this university."

Quinn agreed. Ethel was passionate about the U of I. Mike had him sit down because he wanted to talk about Ethel.

"We have families who've attended our university for four generations. Since Ethel's visit, I've mulled over the idea of having senior volunteers here on campus."

"I think you're onto something pretty special."

"I agree." Mike nodded. "My mother volunteers at a hospital in Nampa. She loves it."

There were only six minutes left before his class. Mike's stoicism when he'd first walked in wasn't because he wanted to can him; it was because he'd been deep in thought. He knew nothing about the kiss.

"Ethel said her granddaughter's a graduate student here in US history."

"Uh, yes, yes, she is." Quinn's pulse picked up its pace. "I . . . have Katherine in my Civil War class."

Wide-eyed, Mike nodded.

"Sunday evening, we went for a walk and . . ." Quinn rubbed the back of his neck. "And . . ."

"Sunday evening?" Mike's head tilted and his gaze narrowed.

"Yes, Sunday evening."

"Katherine . . . King?"

"Yes, Ethel's granddaughter."

"My wife and I also went for a walk Sunday evening." Mike's chest inflated.

Mike and his wife couldn't possibly have seen him kiss Katherine on Ethel's front porch? Quinn swallowed and for a moment felt like he'd recently dined at The Green Dragon. No, that's right, Mike Morrison lived up on Indian Hills Drive, only a few houses from Cindy's. For them to have walked the curvy hill, and crossed both the railroad tracks and, the Lewiston highway, would have been very ambitious for a Sunday stroll.

"Quinn, we're pleased with your progress here." Mike slowly lowered himself into his leather chair. "You're very admired by students and your fellow peers. Your research, adept writing, and lecture skills are only going to further advance a department that we're already very proud of. Quinn . . ." Mike reached for a pen. "Is the reason for your visit today twofold?"

Twofold? Lord, are these words from You? Quinn waited for the small voice from the inner room. Twice Mike had prodded him. Despite only four minutes remaining before his class, Quinn remained seated.

"Mike . . . I hate to disappoint you, but this visit *is* twofold."

With a slow, disbelieving shake of his head, Mike stared at the desk between them.

"While I love this university, my job, this small town, my home, and neighborhood . . . I've recently made a mistake." Quinn paused, and the small voice that had been quiet all morning whispered: *Tell him.*

"That is if you could call kissing a beautiful woman that you're in love with a mistake." He smiled slightly at his epiphany. "I need to clarify that: I've only kissed Katherine King once."

"Katherine . . . King." Mike crossed his arms behind his head and leaned back in his chair.

"Yes, in three weeks she'll officially graduate from the U of I." Three weeks sounded lame. It didn't soften anything. He'd erred on the side of big time.

"Try as we may, there's no getting around the fact, Quinn, that your actions involve a serious breach of ethics and proper standards of professional behavior."

"You're right." He'd completed ten years of higher education to have it end like this. "I knew better." He pressed his lips together and nodded. It would be so hard to tell his folks.

Elbows on the arms of his chair, Mike gripped his hands and up went the index finger steeple. Was it a sign? Was President Morrison a praying man?

"Wait until the end of the semester to pursue the matter further."

"Pardon me?" Even when elated, grown men aren't supposed to cry.

"You heard me."

Quinn tipped his head back and grinned at the ceiling. "You have no idea. I feel like the weight of the world's . . ."

"It's called grace." Mike tidied some papers on top of his desk.

Grace.

Quinn stood up and shook the big man's hand. On his way to the door, he heard Mike clear his throat.

"Today's conversation does not leave this room, Benton; we frown heavily on this type of incident."

"I understand completely." Quinn paused his hand halfway to the door handle. He couldn't even tell Katherine.

"Remember . . . one letter stands between *grace* and *grave*." Mike flipped back the lid of the cigar box. "The roll's the size of the box!" He chuckled.

The bell rang as Quinn strode down the hallway to his class. "Grace," he whispered. "Grace!" Entering his classroom, he embraced his beloved US History 112 students with the widest of smiles.

Good thing he wasn't grading exams today; he would have given everyone A's.

Chapter Thirty-Six

Wednesday morning, Professor Evans's Lewis and Clark lecture was unusually boring. Katherine found herself thinking about Quinn. During his Civil War lecture, he'd completely avoided looking toward the three students on her side of the room. History told her that when your beloved avoids looking at you, it's always a bad sign. That's when she'd officially started her Quinn List. Curious about what she'd written, she unzipped her backpack and pulled out the yellow, lined piece of paper.

Why I will never fall for Quinn Benton:

1. He dates merely to eliminate.
2. He's flighty . . . about women.
3. He's picky . . . about women.

She read through number six. The list was far too short. After a moment's contemplation, she penned:

7. He dates out-of-towners, and I have become his in-between, small-town girl.

8. The man obviously doesn't like to be alone.

9. After he'd kissed me, he apologized and said, "I should never have let that happen!"

Sick to her stomach, she folded the list and returned it to her backpack. Oh, the things she could write about the man!

294 Sherri Schoenborn Murray

Evans returned a recent essay. An A brightened the back page. A paisley-print sticky note beside it read: *Stick around after class, we need to talk.*

The loopy penmanship belonged to Professor Fancy.

Katherine glanced toward the front of the classroom. Cindy and Evans often took turns speaking and interrupting one another. Cindy took a step back toward the chalkboard, out of Evans's peripheral zone, her eyes fastened on Katherine.

"Because of Benton?" Katherine mouthed, hoping Cindy could read lips. She motioned left with her pointer finger in the direction of Benton's classroom down the hall.

"It was . . ." Professor Evans paused.

Pen in hand, Katherine attempted to give Evans her undivided attention, while behind him Cindy wrote a *"Y"* on the board, and then immediately erased it.

Was Cindy trying to get her take on the situation, so Quinn knew exactly where he stood with her before Friday? Not that much interest had been expressed in Miss Harvard. But, since their kiss, he hadn't stopped by on his own initiative once. This morning didn't count.

"Miss King," Evans said.

"Yes?"

"Have you formed an opinion?"

Evans knew that she always had an opinion. She closed one eye slightly and scanned her last paragraph of notes. "Yes, what continues to fascinate me is . . ." She looked up into Evans's smug smile. "Not only did Lewis bring a remarkable skill set to this immense undertaking, but Jefferson himself personally displayed—"

"Come, come, Miss King, your answer, while clever, is completely off track. You are my most opinion-worthy student. Note that I did not say *most opinionated*. Something has distracted you, and it's not the A-plus on your exam. Tell me, class . . ." Evans glanced over his shoulder at Cindy. "What did Professor Fancy just write and erase behind me on the board?"

The 400-and 500-level Lewis and Clark summer school class was small: nine students. Two students stretched and yawned.

Looking quite proud of herself, Angel LeFave raised her hand. "She wrote a *V* and erased it."

"Did you say . . . *B*?"

"No, a *V* with a long tail."

Katherine blinked. Chuckles reverberated throughout the room. Angel was pursuing her undergraduate degree in US history while also pursuing her MRS degree. It was a wonder she'd lasted as long as she had.

"Did she appear to have Miss King's attention when she wrote the V with the long tail?" Professor Evans asked.

Katherine glanced toward the hallway. Where was Charlene Strauss, the department chair, when a class *really* needed her?

"Yes, I think so." Angel smiled in her direction.

"May I deduce, class, that a *V* with a long tail could be a *Y*. And that a "*Y*," when written quickly on a chalkboard, could suffice for an abbreviation for the word . . . *YES*?"

Mumbled yeses reverberated about the room.

Behind Evans, Cindy reconstructed the evidence on the board.

"Did anyone see Miss King prior to Miss Fancy's unusual behavior? Was there any type of nonverbal communication between them?" Evans focused only on Angel.

"Yes, there was." Angel turned to smile at her. "Katherine had just pointed at me for some reason. I was going to ask her why after class."

"Pointed at you . . . hmm . . ." Evans's voice trailed off. "Hmmm, Miss King and Miss Fancy, I'd like to speak with you both after class."

Katherine was reminded that he had his doctorate in both history and psychology.

Before the end of class, Katherine ever so carefully unstuck Cindy's sticky note, wadded it up to the size of a spitball, and scrunched it down into the front pocket of her jeans. She'd leave it there to go through the wash, at least, ten times. It was evidence that Evans would never see.

After the bell, Katherine remained seated.

"If my assumptions are correct . . ." Evans sat down at a desk in front of hers and turned to face her. "Cindy tried to warn you that Benton is leaning toward you not being invited to Friday night's get-together."

"Again?" Her hand dropped to the desk.

"Perhaps it has something to do with your grandmother's front porch."

Did Evans also know about Grandma's rhododendron bush?

"What's his reason this time?" The man continually baffled her.

"I don't know. Perhaps, you should go to his office and inquire in person."

Her heart felt like a sticky knot. "I promised myself I would never go to his office again." Katherine's fingertips tapped together. "I'm not sure I

can make it to the Friday night get-together anyway.
Joe asked me to make him dinner. He's tired of dorm
food." She wasn't lying, but she hadn't finalized Joe's
request. Until now.

"Cindy, do you think Benton is worried about
bringing Katherine home Friday night?" Evans
whispered over his shoulder. "If that's all it is, you can
drive her home."

Cindy approached them and, keeping an eye on
the half-open door, whispered, "I don't know what
he's thinking, except Katherine's the first woman he's
kissed in two years. After being dumped without a
decent apology by his fiancée, the man deserves a little
patience."

Quinn's breakup took on black-and-white
qualities.

"Did you know him then?" Katherine asked.

"No, but Evans did. The day Sylvia left, Quinn
had seen her driving a U-Haul truck around Moscow,
and he'd wondered where she was going. She'd
packed all her stuff, left town, and called a week later
to tell him they were over. It's taken him almost two
years, but he's able to laugh about it now."

Did they think Katherine was like his fiancée—
avoiding pain, avoiding conflict, not communicating?
Had he unknowingly picked two women very much
alike?

"Even when he wasn't particularly fond of you,
he respected your spunk," Evans said.

"I'm not sure that he's particularly fond of me
yet. Can you tell Benton that I'm sorry, but I won't be
there Friday night? I'm making Joe dinner."

"Good move, Katherine." Evans grinned. "You
know he'll want you there now."

"Whichever way it goes with Miss Harvard . . ." Cindy whispered, "it's going to be difficult for Quinn to discuss it in your presence." She returned to her filing.

Was it only because of the kiss that Quinn didn't want her to be there on Friday, or was there more to it?

"Come now, Katherine, where is your fighting spirit?" Evans asked.

She knew exactly where it was: she'd left it on Grandma's front porch.

"I don't understand your advice," she whispered, her voice steady. "You encouraged what happened? And then you turned around and told him we can't see each other for three weeks."

"I merely planted a seed. You added the Miracle-Gro, with your unexpected show of fragility during your phone call to Carl. It put Benton over the edge."

Was Evans trying to encourage her? Miracle-Gro?

"He thinks you're gorgeous."

Was he trying to put *her* over the edge?

"He told Harold, his neighbor, that it hit him suddenly, and that he's beginning to trip in your presence."

She recalled his trip into Grandma's rhodo-dendron and smiled.

"When did you see his neighbor?" While she savored Benton's sentiments, she met Evans's warm gaze.

"I drop by occasionally to deliver a small bag of groceries. He's on a fixed income."

For some reason, he didn't want Cindy to overhear that he and Harold were allies. They wanted Benton and her together. She'd sensed Evans's alliance, but now she knew it.

"I want him to meet Miss Palouse." Katherine gripped her hands in her lap.

"We all do, and you and I know Miss Harvard is simply a matter of getting his hair cut. He's never even spoken to her. And the nurse, Miss Kitty Princeton, he's only spoken to once."

Kitty? She'd never heard the nurse's first name before. Throughout history, a lot of beautiful women had been named Kitty. Kitty Kallen. Kitty Kelly. Kitty Pryde . . . She didn't like the sounds of *Miss Kitty Princeton*. Would Quinn's blind dating ever stop?

Chapter Thirty-Seven

Friday afternoon . . .

Ethel was in the front yard weeding her bed of annuals when she came upon an annihilated row of orange marigolds. Fritz must have dug a hole beneath the fence and rolled in them to his heart's content. Why she had a mind to go rap on the Hamiltons' front door this very minute and give them a lecture on dog control.

She was monkeying with the latch on the front gate when Quinn Benton's dark blue Volvo drove up alongside the curb. He must have spotted her. Ethel's heart warmed. He hadn't called or stopped by since Sunday. Ethel had prayed and prayed that his and Katherine's little kiss hadn't ruined everything.

He powered down his window and grinned.

"Quinn . . ." Ethel waved both of her gardening gloved hands. "I was afraid I'd never see you again."

He chuckled. "I've been meaning to call." He set an arm along the open window, looking up at her. "I'm very late in thanking you for the delicious cinnamon roll. And, I delivered Mike's. He got a chuckle out of how large it was."

"You sure know how to make my day." She patted her heart with one hand. "I have ground beef thawed. Why don't you come over tonight for tacos or would you prefer meatloaf?"

"I can't; tonight's Miss Harvard."

The kiss had ruined everything. She sensed it.

"That makes you and Katherine both. Joe's tired of dorm food and asked her to fix him a nice meal."

"Joe sounds like a typical college student, Ethel."

"That's what Katherine said, too."

He glanced at his watch. "Is Katherine here?"

He was asking about Katherine. Maybe he wanted to see her before his date with Miss Harvard. Maybe he missed her.

"No, she walked to the store to get groceries for Joe. We miss you; well . . . at least, I do."

Ж

We miss you; well . . . at least, I do. Had Ethel slipped? Did Katherine miss him, too?

As Quinn continued up Lewis Street, he reminded himself of all the reasons Katherine would never fall in love with Joe Hillis again. Wouldn't go to church with her, lack of punctuality, limited vocabulary.

Though seeing and speaking with Ethel had been of comfort, it didn't pacify his longing to speak with Katherine one last time before he drove to get his hair cut.

He had a half hour before he needed to leave Moscow. He'd start at Tidyman's; if Katherine wasn't there, he'd go to Safeway. If heaven forbid, she and Joe were back together, he wanted to know now.

Carrying a black plastic shopping basket, Quinn cruised through Tidyman's, searching each aisle for a long-legged, beautiful blonde. He'd almost swear Katherine had worn a red V-necked T-shirt to class that day. He walked the perimeter of the store— produce, meats, fresh breads—she wasn't anywhere in sight.

His insides twisted. He wanted to see her, be built back up before he left Moscow.

Maybe she liked Safeway more than Tidyman's; some people did. He drove across the Troy highway to the Moscow Mall and parked in front of Safeway. He hurried in, snagged a basket, and searched the aisles. The problem was that Ethel hadn't been specific. He didn't know what time Katherine had left. He flipped open his phone and pressed down on six.

"Hello," Ethel answered.

"Hi, it's Quinn. I was wondering what time Katherine left?"

"Twenty minutes ago."

"And she's getting groceries first before she goes to Joe's?"

"Yes, groceries first. She's walking, so she can't buy too much."

"I see." Quinn strolled to the edge of the floral section. As he said it, he glimpsed something red out of the corner of his eye. A beautiful blonde stood near the orange display in the produce department. Katherine.

"Is everything okay, Quinn?" Ethel asked.

"No, I was just wondering if you needed anything." Did she know he was looking for Katherine? Would she tell her?

"I asked Katherine to pick me up a few things, toothpicks, cotton balls, stamps . . . nothing very heavy. Thank you, Quinn. You're always so thoughtful."

"No problem, Ethel." He flipped the phone closed and stared at Katherine's profile. He meandered to the border of Floral and Produce and, pretending interest in a rounder of white lilies, leaned down to sniff them. They were more elegant than aromatic. When he stood up, Katherine had spotted him. She rolled her cart toward him. A smile teased her lips. She was no longer Annoying; she was Alluring.

It was difficult to remember back to his office and their jarring first impression of each other, yet an inner voice told him he needed to.

Maybe their kiss on Sunday had brought back memories of Joe. Maybe they'd had such great memories together that she was willing to overlook the fact that he didn't have a brain. Maybe it was all Quinn's doing.

Bananas, two rib-eye steaks, a box of Wheaties, cotton balls, an onion, a package of mushrooms, and a bag of oranges sat in her cart. She was shopping for another man. The ten-pound bag of oranges was a bit optimistic, provided she was walking.

"Hi, Katherine."

"Hi, Benton." She glanced at her wristwatch. "I'm surprised you're here. You're meeting Miss Harvard within the hour."

He nodded and continued staring. An epiphany came to him and made the knot in his chest cinch tighter. Losing out on her might be the cost of his madness.

"How's Joe?" His voice cracked.

"He's craving real food." She shrugged.

Didn't she know that men liked concrete words?

"Joe's lucky to have you."

"Thanks, Benton." She glanced at the potted lilies he'd been sniffing. Even though he was dating another woman within the hour, she looked him squarely in the eye. Though they'd kissed on Sunday, she appeared fine, not a hint of angst.

"So tonight's Miss Harvard?" Her brows lifted.

"Yes, she resides in Harvard and works and goes to church in Princeton."

"Oh, an Ivy League girl." She nodded.

"Have you ever studied how those two pocket-sized towns received their elite names?"

"No." She again met his gaze.

"Neither have I." Were Katherine's eyes always this deep, satiated blue? Or was it the floral department's lighting, her mood . . . how did she really feel about him meeting Miss Harvard? Didn't it bother her a little? They'd kissed on Sunday. Really kissed. He searched her eyes for any telltale sign.

She smiled up at him, and her slow blink made his insides feel like marshmallow crème.

"Are you and Joe back together?" The question was an involuntary reflex that couldn't be held back any longer. Was Joe why her mood was so light, given the circumstances?

"No."

"Any chance?"

Her mouth bunched together. "No."

"What does that mean?" For goodness' sake, he had a blind date tonight. He wanted to know exactly what she meant.

"Joe and I are good friends. That's all." She gripped the handle of the cart with both hands.

They were just good friends. Funny how he could still picture her on the back of Joe's motorcycle, nuzzling way too close, with her arms wrapped around him.

"The lilies are a bit solemn for a first date." She nodded toward the rounder.

He should buy them, or Katherine would think the only reason he was here was to see her. He picked up the pot hosting three lily buds. Katherine wasn't going anywhere. She was simply making a steak dinner for a good friend. He could meet Miss Harvard in peace.

"There you are, Katherine." Tan, athletic, and good looking, Joe stopped near her side. He juggled two avocados in the air and caught them with the same hand before settling them in the top basket of her cart.

"Joe." Her cheeks were raspberry Jell-O red. "Benton's buying flowers for Miss Harvard."

"Hi, Benton." One blond brow lifted. "It's weird how you always turn up where we are."

Quinn's mouth felt dry like he'd eaten potato chips for three straight days in the desert.

"His sister is cutting his hair. She also set the appointment for Benton to be there at the same time as a young woman from Harvard, Idaho." Katherine's mood-ring eyes were now the deepest blue. "I hope it goes well for you, Mr. Benton."

"Good luck, Professor, I hope she's the one." Joe chuckled.

Ж

Did he even say anything? Somehow Quinn had paid for the lilies and returned to his car. Weren't lilies for funerals? Had Katherine been kidding when she'd said they were solemn for a first date? Had it all been a setup? Something Evans cooked up? What had Joe said? *I hope she's the one.* Was it Joe's way of saying he didn't want him to end up with Katherine?

Was Evans behind all this? If so, he was brilliant. Quinn turned left into the Key Bank parking lot, shifted into park, and speed-dialed Evans's number.

He had time.

"Evans! It's Quinn." Thank God he'd picked up. "I was just at Safeway. Please tell me you're the mastermind behind what just transpired."

"I don't usually shop at Safeway. They've never carried loose-leaf tea. I asked them to carry it at one time, but the manager didn't think it would be widely received. Did you find some?"

Quinn chuckled. Evans was good. No, he was great.

"You know exactly what I mean. I was just at Safeway. Katherine. Joe. Dinner. Together." Quinn chuckled and stretched his hand back along the ceiling of the car.

"Benton, I don't know what you're talking about. Are you saying that you saw Katherine and Joe together?"

"Nice try!" He let out some pent-up steam. "I just saw Katherine and Joe together at Safeway. This is just like you to cook something up right before I leave. I know you and Cindy want the two of us together, but this time, you've gone too far."

"I'm sorry, Benton, we haven't cooked anything up. Though we would love to see the two of you together, we've decided its best that we don't get any more involved than we already are."

Quinn propped his elbows on the center of his steering wheel. "Are you saying you didn't plan Safeway or Katherine making dinner for Joe?"

"No. Where are you? Shouldn't you be driving north? Focus, Benton. Tonight is not Miss Moscow. It's Miss Harvard."

"You're right." Quinn shifted into reverse and wrapped his arm along the back of the passenger seat. "I need to go. I'll talk to you tonight."

During the half-hour drive to Princeton, Idaho, he mulled over what had just taken place. Ethel didn't know Joe was at Safeway. Was Katherine seeing Joe on the sly, while Ethel secretly hoped to match make Katherine and him? If so, Katherine was brilliant.

Heading north, Quinn drove over the crest of Moscow Mountain. The drive would be a pain during the winter months when there were three feet of snow on the ground. Why had he ever committed to meeting a woman who lived so far from Moscow? He loved Moscow—his home and neighborhood, living so close to the university, Ethel, Tidyman's, and the farmer's market, Evans and the professors' group. He noticed little of the stunning scenery, the vibrant green patchwork blocks that rolled off into the cotton-ball clouds.

Katherine's and his time together had been so great on Sunday. Their kiss had been amazing. How could she already be with Joe?

Chapter Thirty-Eight

Quinn glanced toward the peephole and wondered why Evans's front door was locked, and what was taking them so long to answer the bell.

Cindy swung open the door. Smoke haloed the entryway chandelier.

"Sorry, we're in the aftermath of a smoke alarm. The chocolate madeleines burned."

Quinn slid off his loafers and followed her into the kitchen. The fan above the stove whirled loudly. Windows were opened; charred madeleines lay in one of Cindy's floppy silicone baking pans on the counter.

"We got to talking." Cindy's flushed, round face seemed slightly off balance, as one dangling silver earring was in, and one was somewhere else. Evans cleared his throat for her attention and pointed to his own earlobe. She headed into the living room.

"The vanilla madeleines turned out heavenly." Evans leaned a hand against the granite island. "Benton, you obviously have your poker face on, and as always, I can't read you."

"He looks unhappy." Cindy returned. Head tilted to the side, she inserted the missing bauble.

"Why do you say that?" Evans asked.

"He wears it heavy like some women wear eyeliner."

"I miss Katherine, too." Evans patted his shoulder as he walked past. "We're about to relive your dud of an evening without her."

Quinn made a cup of tea and then sat down in his usual chair. His gaze took in the empty loveseat cushion where Katherine usually sat. The evening was a double letdown.

"Okay, moment of truth, did Miss Harvard live up to her Ivy League name?" Evans asked, pouring tea.

"Your hair cut looks nice," Cindy said.

"Thank you." Quinn glanced at the empty loveseat. "Usually, I go six weeks between cuts. This time, I went eight. You're correct, by the way, Evans; Miss Harvard was a dud." Leaning forward, Quinn picked up his mug.

The news didn't appear to come as a surprise to either of them.

"Go on . . ." Evans said. "You can't simply summarize like that and expect us to feel satisfied. I've grown accustomed to your slow-moving, dramatic details ending with the clincher."

"All right." Quinn rolled a kink out of his neck. "I showed up at five thirty, right on time. My sister, Renae, has a little beauty parlor room that they built onto the side of their ranch-style home. They're two blocks off the main drag in Princeton. There's a separate entrance, several washbowls, and chairs. Miss Harvard was running late, so Renae and I caught up for about fifteen minutes before her arrival."

Evans tsked-tsked.

"My sister made our meeting feel more staged than I would have preferred. When Miss Harvard first arrived, I was facing the mirror and couldn't see her, as she'd found a magazine and a chair almost directly behind me." Quinn suppressed a yawn, blinked, and glanced at his watch.

"Renae talked off and on with Miss Harvard while she cut my hair. I came to the conclusion that she had a voice that, over time, if her personality were agreeable, I could eventually come to grips with.

"When Renae spun my chair around, Miss Harvard was reading *People* magazine. I saw Brad Pitt's face before I did hers. For an icebreaker, I asked, 'Is that Brad Pitt on the cover?' And she said, 'Yes, isn't he always?' She lowered the magazine to look at me. At first, I could only see her eyes."

Cindy's gaze narrowed. "What'd you think?"

"It was a blow. From the eyes up, she looked quite a bit like Sylvia." He shook his head. "I was caught off guard. Renae hadn't warned me. Later, when Miss Harvard tossed the magazine aside, I realized it was only the eyes. Her shoulders are broader and her mind narrower. No sense of humor. I think my sister wanted me to meet this woman solely on account of her eyes."

"Go on." Evans yawned.

"Well, in the downtime that followed, I asked her a dating question that Carl had somehow finagled out of Katherine in your driveway, the night he attempted to drive her home."

"Which was?" Cindy asked.

"If you could have been a journalist or historian for any American war, which one would you have wanted to cover and why?"

"A great question!" Evans patted Cindy's nearest hand. "Remind me to ask you later this evening, love. Katherine's question gives purpose to the dud of an evening we are presently reliving."

"Wait," Cindy said. "You asked her that while she was browsing through her *People* magazine in the beauty salon?"

"Yes, I was trying to determine if I wanted Renae to ask Miss Harvard to join us afterward for tacos."

"Well?" Evans said.

"Well . . ." Quinn smiled. "Miss Harvard said, 'You must be Renae's brother, the history professor at the U of I?' And of course, I said, 'Yes.' She proceeded to cross one knee over the other and said, 'That almost sounds like a pickup line.'"

"That doesn't sound too small town to me." Evans chuckled.

"Just wait." Quinn cleared his throat. "I said, 'I thought it might make for good beauty parlor conversation.'"

"You didn't?" Evans regarded Cindy. "Remember how I said Benton's pattern is that during the course of the evening, he purposefully blows it. Here's a prime example."

"Precisely after that, my sister gave my chair a quarter turn, so I was now looking out the window with my left profile to Miss Harvard. I heard the flipping of magazine pages again, and I was bored, so I asked her the same question again. She'd obviously given it some thought." Quinn inhaled deeply. "My fellow professors and friends, Miss Harvard's response was, and I quote: "'I would like to have been a journalist in the war that Tom Cruise was in when he starred in *Top Gun*.'"

Cindy's jaw dropped. "But it wasn't a war." She scooted forward on the couch.

"No, it was simply fighter pilots training at Miramar in San Diego," Evans murmured.

"Exactly, I didn't have the heart to correct her," Quinn said.

"I'm in shock!" Evans shook his head.

"I think she's more movie learned than book learned. Sounds like she rents a lot of videos from the little convenience store where she works."

"I'm sorry, Benton," Evans said.

"Yes, my evening was a dud. I do like Katherine's question. I plan to use it the next couple of weeks."

"Benton . . ." Evans cleared his throat. "Mashburn mentioned an attractive grad student at Wazzu." He paused to include Cindy. "Mashburn is a dear elderly professor friend of mine at Wazzu, who just retired this spring. Supposedly, this young woman is not in a serious relationship, and she's getting her master's in history, of all things."

"Dennis!" Cindy's eyes widened, and she shook her head.

"Cindy's right, Evans. Even though Miss Wazzu sounds interesting, after Miss Palouse, I plan to retire from blind dating."

"Don't tell us that," Evans droned. "You simply need a week or two off."

Quinn took a sip of lukewarm tea and studied Katherine's side of the empty loveseat across the room. She would have appreciated tonight's recap. He tried not to let his mind wander to her time with Joe.

Chapter Thirty-Nine

During Sunday's church service, Katherine's gaze lingered on the cross. Christ's suffering wasn't only physical—being betrayed by His closest companions made it emotional anguish as well. Plus, He bore the weight of the world's sins. If anyone understood her emotional suffering, Christ did. God, the Father, creator of emotion.

Katherine didn't know if she could hold out for two more weeks. Whenever she was around Quinn, a vise-like grip tightened about her heart. Every little word of hope that he spoke turned the clamp one more notch—being in his presence was painful. She wanted to bring her suffering to the cross, kneel before it, and have a good sob.

How would Christ want her to handle Benton? Of course, with love. *Dating is difficult, Lord.*

Pastor Ken's sermon focused on the heat of trials and the story of the three men in the furnace. After the perfect mid-summer sermon, they sang a closing hymn. Grandma leaned toward Quinn. "Are you sure you won't come for lunch?"

"I shouldn't. I have a pile of paperwork, laundry, ironing, a lawn to mow."

"Oh my, do you want me to come over?" Grandma offered her services.

"If it's because of me, I can go to the library," Katherine said.

"That's nice of you both, but I'll manage."

Benton had been visiting practically all semester, and now, he was literally taking Evans's advice and letting one little kiss put a wedge between him and Grandma.

Why?

Ж

Katherine set two ink pens on the top of her desk. There were still a few stragglers and two minutes left on the clock before the official start of Benton's Civil War class.

"What's a simile again?" Angel asked.

A simile had nothing to do with their midterm exam. Katherine rolled her eyes.

"You know, it's when you use the word *like* or *as*," Ronnie said, flipping her long red hair over her shoulder. "Like . . . she was as dumb *as* a pizza box."

"Is anyone else hungry or is it just me?" Angel asked, looking around.

"I'm always hungry," said Mark, a graduate student in the third row.

"Oh-hhh . . ." Angel eyed Mark while Professor Benton handed out the light blue booklets for their midterm essay exam. Mark, a fellow grad student, was a tad heavyset and like Angel below average in height.

Hmm . . . maybe Mark liked canned chili?

On a separate piece of paper, Professor Benton handed out two essay questions. Katherine chose: Compare and contrast the North and the South. Due to their social, political, and economic differences, was the Civil War inevitable and why?

Her writing flowed for the first three pages and then she made the mistake of glancing toward the front of the classroom. Seated behind his desk, with an elbow on top, Quinn appeared relaxed, if not tired. Their eyes locked. Harp and string music began to play, and Katherine felt herself smile as she strolled down memory lane.

Someone kicked her in the shin.

Wide-eyed, she returned her attention to her paper. *Do not look toward the man upfront. Angel knows.*

Despite the distractions, Katherine's thoughts flowed, with plenty of analysis. Her conclusion thoroughly supported her argument that yes, the Civil War was inevitable.

"One minute remaining," Professor Benton informed the class.

Katherine glanced down at her open backpack. Her Quinn List was tucked inside the pocket of her three-ring binder. She pulled out the yellow lined paper and peeked at her laundry list type writing. Should she tuck it inside her exam? Students began to file out.

Her pulse picked up its pace. Still seated, Benton rolled a kink out of his neck. Katherine slid the Quinn List inside her light blue booklet and on her way out, slid her essay into the middle of the pile on his desk.

Halfway to Lewis and Clark, she paused in the wide corridor to glance behind her. What had she just done? If anyone else found it, there might be awful consequences. Lord, help it not to end up in the *Argonaut.*

Ж

After Katherine's research class on Tuesday, she ran into Cindy in front of the Admin. They strolled down the elm-lined walkway.

"Do you feel ready for the midterm on Friday?" Cindy asked.

"Yes. Shame on Evans and you for putting it off till then."

Cindy stopped in the middle of the sidewalk. "We wanted to give our students plenty of time to prepare."

"For some of us, you're prolonging the agony." Katherine smiled as they resumed their stroll. "How are you and Evans?"

"Good. Though we had a little spat recently."

"Oh . . . what about?"

"At Friday night's get-together, he talked about setting Quinn up with a friend of Mashburn's, a graduate student. If Quinn took time off from his blind dating, he might figure out what's going on between the two of you."

"Ohhhh." Another matchmaking friend, another blind date, and this time, a master's student in history. If Quinn accepted it, Katherine would throw in the towel. Gone were any assumptions that Evans might be matchmaking her with Quinn. It hurt, how she'd misjudged him.

"Saturday we're going antiquing in Pullman; would you like to join us?" Cindy asked.

"Sure. Who's going?"

"So far Evans, Benton, and me."

"I'm thinking of going to Potlatch today and going swimming at the Palouse River later this afternoon." Over her shoulder, Katherine regarded

Cindy. "There's a nice swimming hole that Grandma and I used to go to when I was growing up."

"That sounds heavenly, but I better not; I have a pressure washer guy coming at two." At the end of the elm-lined walkway, they said their good-byes and Cindy headed in the direction of faculty parking.

In full sun and the heat of the day, Katherine walked the straight stretch of Sweet Avenue home. How would Benton feel about her going antiquing with them? What if his time with Nurse Kitty Princeton was pleasant? It was so easy to worry too far in advance.

"Lord," she whispered, "help me with my feelings. Give me peace instead of this turmoil. He'll probably have read my Quinn List by Saturday. He'll have met Miss Princeton by then, too. Antiquing may or may not come together. No matter what happens, give my heart peace."

Though a floor fan blew in the living room, only the rev of the machine, not its comfort, reached the kitchen. With only one midterm left to take, Katherine wanted to celebrate. She took a sip of homemade iced tea and set an elbow on the table.

"Grandma, what do you think about going to Potlatch to our old swimming hole today?"

"I can't, honey; Gladys and I are meeting the girls for a senior potluck tonight at church, and then afterward we're going to Sharon's for Scrabble. You can take Granddad's truck if you want."

Grandma had never allowed any of the grandkids to drive the old Ford that was parked in the garage. "Are you sure?"

"Your granddad would approve of the idea." Grandma popped a potato chip into her mouth. "Who else is going with you?"

"Just me."

Grandma's eyes narrowed. "What about one of your girlfriends?"

"They had plans." That is, Cindy and Angel both had plans. It was late in the day to ask Ronnie or Brenda.

"I don't like the idea of your going alone." From her wide eyes, Grandma's imagination appeared to soar.

"I plan to park by the old grain silo and walk downstream to that cozy little bend where you used to take us kids. I'm almost twenty-nine—"

"Please don't give me your 'when you were my age' speech." Grandma said. "I can speak my mind, but I know you don't listen."

Had Benton told Grandma about seeing her on Joe's motorcycle? Grandma's knickers were in a knot over something.

"I know exactly when you're hiding something." Grandma monkeyed with the corner of her glasses. "Your eyes get all wide and . . . I know you've been riding around town."

"I knew he'd tell you." Benton! He'd probably told Grandma and Miss Palouse about the kiss, too. The heavy cave door to her heart slowly slid closed.

"No, you dummy. Quinn hasn't told me a thing." Grandma's head turned as Katherine rose from the table. "Gladys has called twice—two different times—to tell me that she's seen you gallivanting around town on the back of some fella's motorcycle. And I think Quinn has too, but he won't tell me. I tried to bribe the truth out of him with a batch of cinnamon rolls, but he wouldn't fall for it. I think he'd marry you for your cinnamon rolls, but he won't even answer a little question in exchange for mine."

Trying to maintain her composure, Katherine returned to the table.

"What do you mean by that?" She inhaled deeply.

Grandma eyed the Latah County Credit Union calendar above Katherine's head. "You know I don't want to get your hopes up, honey, but the cinnamon rolls you made that day were awfully special. But, the look on Quinn's face when he was enjoying them was even more special."

Katherine's heart wanted to do cartwheels. "If you want me to believe that all I have to do is make Benton cinnamon rolls to win his affection, then he's more of a simpleton than I thought."

"Maybe you can hide your heart from you, but you can't hide it from me. I have a new sticky note for you." She rose from the table and disappeared into the living room.

"Wonderful," Katherine whispered.

"When I was praying and reading the Bible this morning, you were heavy on my heart, and I knew the verse that I stumbled on was another sticky note from God . . . just for you." Grandma's voice carried from the other room.

Dear Lord, not another verse pointing out my faults. Please. Usually I have a reserve, but not today.

"I was going to wait until tomorrow and stick it to the door again." Grandma returned to the table and sat down. "But I'd rather give it to you now."

The yellow sticky note from God and Grandma read: *When you are brokenhearted, I am close to you. Psalm 34:18.* Warm tears lapped at her eyes.

"You're hurting and . . ." Grandma patted her hand, "Quinn only has two blind dates on the calendar. I pencil them in now instead of using a Sharpie."

"Maybe three. Evans is trying to set him up with a Miss Wazzu, a graduate student."

"He blind dates as often as some people mow their lawns." Grandma shook her head.

"Next Friday when he meets Miss Palouse," she swallowed and looked at Grandma, "I can't go to the professors' get-together. What if she's the one? I can't just sit there and pretend that my heart's not breaking."

"Honey—"

"I know what you're going to say and, I have, I have been praying. He hasn't even stopped by. He completely took Evans's advice."

"I'm sure Miss Palouse is not as wonderful as she's led him to believe she is." Grandma patted her hand.

"I bet she is." Stifling a sob, Katherine covered her mouth. Marci was adorable, and she wouldn't even send a picture.

"Oh, I wish I could mend your heart." Grandma pushed her chair back from the table. "Come help me figure out what I'm wearing to the potluck."

Katherine sniffled and followed her through the living room. Grandma closed her bedroom door behind them and slid open her closet. "Which one should I wear?" She held up two hangers, an apricot-colored T-shirt and a solid pink T-shirt, one in each hand.

"The pink one." It brought out the rosy color in Grandma's cheeks.

"Quinn kissed me, Grandma." It felt good to tell another soul.

Wide-eyed, her grandmother nodded.

"Afterward, he apologized and told me it should never have happened." Tears dribbled down her cheek.

"He didn't really mean that, honey." Grandma returned the apricot-colored T-shirt to her closet. "He probably meant it as a professor, not as a man."

Could she possibly be right? Katherine sniffled. "And then he missed the first step and fell into your rhododendron and rolled right into your bed of marigolds."

"Oh, poor Quinn." Grandma giggled. "Has he ever said another word?"

"No, not really, not about the kiss." Katherine inhaled deeply.

"Oh no." Grandma bit her lower lip. "I thought Fritz had been the one in my marigolds. Poor, deaf Fritz. I thought he'd dug another hole beneath the fence." She shook her head. "I'll have to apologize."

"When you do, please don't tell the Hamiltons all the details."

Grandma waved a hand. "You kissed the night you went for a walk. Didn't you?" Wide-eyed, Grandma nudged her glasses higher up the bridge of her nose.

Katherine nodded.

"I haven't said a word to anyone. Not your mother or Quinn."

Grandma had known. Katherine waited for her to continue.

"I heard a commotion at the door. I thought it might be the paperboy. But, when I looked through the peep-hole, I saw you and Quinn instead." Grandma pointed to each lens of her glasses.

Grandma had witnessed the kiss that would haunt Katherine the rest of her days.

"I wasn't spying on you."

Katherine stared at the puff painted pansies on the front of Grandma's shirt. Tim, her cousin who had lived with Grandma before her, had said something about the front porch. Due to the peephole, the front porch was not a place for privacy.

Katherine shook her head. "I don't know if I can wait for him, Grandma."

"What do you mean?"

"I can't just sit around here waiting for him. It's soooo painful."

"Just bury yourself in your books again." Grandma's gaze narrowed, like how could she of all people have forgotten the ultimate cure for a broken heart?

Chapter Forty

Katherine wore a pair of shorts and a T-shirt over her one-piece teal-green swimsuit. She packed a hat, her textbooks, and a Mason jar of homemade iced tea. As she drove her grandfather's old red-and-white Ford Ranchero out of the detached garage, Grandma stepped out the back door. Waving back and forth, she hurried down the walkway toward her. Through the open driver's side window, she handed Katherine a sticky note.

"I was wrong, honey. Don't hide your heart behind your books." Tears shone in Grandma's eyes. "Fix your eyes on Jesus. He's our Comforter, our Counselor, our great Redeemer. If anyone understands your pain, it's Him." She patted Katherine's bare forearm.

"I love you, Grandma."

Grandma blew her a kiss and waved.

On a yellow sticky note, Grandma had written: *Fix your eyes on Jesus.*

Katherine stuck the sticky note to the front of the dash and then drove north toward Potlatch, Idaho. She'd needed an escape from Moscow, and being a predictable filler for Quinn Benton.

"Lord, forgive me for my impenitent heart. Help me to be more thankful. Grant me patient endurance through the next couple of weeks. It's not easy loving

Quinn. He hasn't called. He hasn't stopped by." Tears dribbled down her cheeks as she whispered all her cares. "I know . . . I know . . . Your sacrifice exemplifies that love is not an easy burden."

With the driver's side window down, the warm summer wind rippled her loose hair and helped to ease her spirit. At the summit of Moscow Mountain, the gently rolling wheat fields of the Palouse looked like brocaded quilt blocks of deep and pale greens. Against the open blue sky, the hills were a canvas of poetry, the drive a purging of the soul.

"Lord, when he reads the list—help him to take it lightly. Help him to have peace. You know I'm disillusioned, and I often lack patience, and I'm very bad at long-suffering and run-on sentences. But You know my heart, and You know his. Your will be done."

Before the downtown area of the small logging town of Potlatch, Katherine took a right and drove down a dirt road past a grain silo. She parked where the road ended, and a knee-high green meadow began. Fifty yards downstream, their old swimming hole hadn't changed much. Tall grass bordered this windy, narrow section of the river, curving toward a sandy beach before funneling into another bend. Katherine unfolded her lawn chair and set her book bag in the sand. After kicking off her flip-flops, she waded into the cool, refreshing water and made a shallow dive.

She breaststroked toward shore and walked the last ten feet before reclining in her beach chair in the sand. From beneath a wide-brimmed hat, she embraced the joys of summer that had been long delayed.

A half hour passed, she set her textbook aside and waded into the water once more. She floated on her back, content with the world. When she lifted her head and swam toward shore, another beach chair sat on the bank next to hers. She swam closer and stood up, searching the water around her.

A head bobbed up, twenty feet away.

"Hello, girlfriend." Cindy waved. "Cute suit."

Chapter Forty-One

"I ended up paying the pressure washer guy and leaving," Cindy said as they lounged in beach chairs. Her green-and-white striped tankini was modest and brought out the emerald in her eyes.

"Did you have to call my grandma for directions?" Katherine studied her pale pink toenail polish.

"No, Quinn was in Evans's office when your grandmother called his cell phone."

"Oh, and so were you?"

"Yes, we were enjoying madeleines and tea." Cindy cleared her throat. "Quinn was surprised that you'd ventured here alone. Ethel gave me directions, and here I am. I thought we could stop at Ireland's on the way home and split one of their cinnamon rolls."

"I'd love to." Ireland's Café, located on the edge of Potlatch, was renowned for their dinner-plate-sized cinnamon rolls, served warm with a slather of butter.

"I must admit your timing's perfect." Cindy sighed and tipped her head back against the top of her beach chair. "Midterms. Students have no idea what we professors go through to deliver the best exams possible." Cindy cleared her throat again. Her mascara had left dark smudges, and her usual perky hairdo lay flat against her head.

Opening one eye, Katherine peeked at her. "That's the second time you've cleared your throat."

"I know." Cindy tilted her head, playfully. "Quinn found your list today."

A steep dirt wall lined the opposite bank. "It took him longer than I expected."

"Leaving it in the essay was *perfect*."

"That's why he was in Evans's office."

"You know how he is." Cindy slid on a pair of large sunglasses. The green, white, and red frames resembled watermelon rind. "He was adamant that we read it."

"And . . . ?"

"He doesn't think you have many valid reasons to write him off." Cindy lifted her sunglasses to study her. "But, I suppose, if there's no chemistry."

Katherine sighed. "I'm sure he'll talk to me about it."

"Yes. I'm certain he will. I need another dip."

Cindy slowly waded in while Katherine made a shallow dive and surfaced several yards from shore. Immediately refreshed, she glanced at her books on the beach chair. She should spend a little more time on Cindy's material. She swam closer toward the bank and stood up, the water waist deep. Something brushed against her leg, giving her the willies. In her strides toward shore, she stepped on something excruciatingly sharp and, fell knee first into the shallow water. A ring of red surrounded her like a large rock had been dropped into the water close by.

"Cindy!" she yelled, searching the stream's languid surface.

Several yards away, Cindy's head bobbed up.

"Cindy!"

Cindy pushed her hair back off her forehead. "What?"

"I'm hurt. There's glass in the water. Don't stand up."

Ж

"Hurt!" Cindy panicked. "Oh, Lord, where's my phone?"

"In your purse by your lawn chair."

"Oh, Lord." Cindy ran toward the trail instead of her purse and then rerouted herself. "Help me to remain calm." She found her phone in the front pocket of her purse. Hands shaking, Cindy dropped her phone on her beach towel and crouched down to pick it back up.

"9-1-1. Yes, I can do this." With jerky movements, Cindy lifted the phone to her ear. "Operator, this is Cindy Fancy. I need an ambulance. We're at the Palouse River in Potlatch, Idaho. Our cars are parked behind the grain elevator before and just south of Main Street. My friend Katherine King's badly cut her foot in the river on something. Bloods everywhere. I can't look."

"Check for glass before applying direct pressure." Cindy flipped the phone closed. "Direct pressure. Crud, I wasn't supposed to hang up. 9-1-1," she said, redialing. "Hello, this is Cindy Fancy, are you the same sweet woman I was speaking with?—Praise God!"

"Use my beach towel," Katherine offered. "Yours is too pretty."

"We have to lift it out of the water, Katherine, and check for glass. I may have to find an artery, darling, and I've never been good with blood. Sorry."

"It's okay. You're not alone." Despite her attempt at empathy, the once-tranquil setting appeared fuzzy.

"I am not alone. I am not alone," Cindy repeated as she helped Katherine lift her leg out of the water. Cindy checked for glass before wrapping Grandma's faded blue beach towel tightly around her foot. "We need to keep it elevated, above your heart."

A horrible, numbing pain shot up her leg. "Owhh! Ooohh." Katherine gritted her teeth.

"I'm not going to tell you how it looked." While she cradled Katherine's foot on her lap, Cindy picked up her phone. "I'm back."—Cindy turned to look at her. "Her lips are blue."

The creek and Cindy swam before her eyes.

"Are you cold, Katherine?"

"Yeah-huh."

"It's ninety-five degrees out, and she's cold," Cindy informed the operator. "That's good." Cindy smiled. "There's an ambulance just out of Palouse. They're on their way right now. Thank you, Operator. You have a lovely phone voice." Cindy patted Katherine's leg. "Okay, I'll put the phone down again and do that right now. Katherine, I need to check again for glass and put direct pressure on your foot. Maybe find an artery. Katherine . . . Katherine?"

Chapter Forty-Two

Behind fluttering lids, Katherine heard Benton and Evans's familiar voices. She tried to open her eyes, but everything remained a hazy gray.

"Time to get your adverbs ready, Benton."

"Adverbs?"

"Yes, adverbs describe verbs and have an L-Y ending." Evans cleared his throat. "Such as, Katherine, you were beautifully and wonderfully made."

"She knows that's not my style," Quinn said.

"Isn't it fearfully and wonderfully made?" Cindy asked.

"Yes, I believe so."

There was silence and a simple gray haze.

Katherine woke to deep pain in her elevated right foot, and an IV drip. A curtain separated half the room. Peach-and-blue striped curtains spanned the wide windows. She was no longer in her bathing suit, but in a hospital bed wearing a faded white gown with minuscule green polka dots.

A middle-aged, heavyset nurse with a clipboard shuffled between the curtain divider and Katherine's bed. She gripped Katherine's wrist, taking her pulse. "How ya feeling?"

"A little loopy." Katherine's eyelids felt as heavy as silver dollars.

"Your friends are getting a bite to eat."

"What time is it?"

"Eleven thirty p.m."

"Is it still July?"

"Yep, July seventeenth."

Squinting, Katherine read the nurse's name tag. "Pat . . . thanks, Pat. You wouldn't happen to be from Princeton?"

"No, Kitty's from Princeton." Pat smiled. "You met her a couple of hours ago."

"I don't remember."

Pat wrote something on her clipboard. "On a scale from one to ten, where's your pain?"

"Four. Four and a quarter. Five."

Pat smiled. "Dr. Ungerbach will be in shortly."

Katherine stared at the IV inserted into a vein on the top of her right hand. On a scale of one to ten, it was an annoying six. She heard squeaky sneakers on linoleum. A doctor wearing blue V-neck scrubs stepped past the room divider curtain and cleared his throat. He was a little over six feet tall, a few inches taller than Benton. With his broad face and blond hair, he was definitely of European descent; his forefathers were probably Vikings or Norman conquerors.

"Hello, Katherine, I'm Dr. Ungerbach." He smiled. "I'm not sure if you remember me."

Squinting, she shook her head.

"You're getting some color back in your face. Healthy blood flow." He marked his chart. "Is your pain still a four and a quarter, possibly a five?"

"The IV's a six," she whispered.

He smiled. "Do you know what you stepped on?"

"Something sharp."

He smiled. "The cut was very deep and wide, severing your dorsal artery. We were able to repair it in surgery."

"Oh . . . more than stitches?" Her brain felt swimmy.

"Yes, and you'll be staying with us for a couple of days."

She frowned.

"I have a midterm Friday. Ask me anything about Lewis and Clark's expedition."

He chuckled. "Your friends know you pretty well. Do you have any questions for me?"

"Will I ev . . . er walk again?"

"Yes, Heidi." He pressed two fingers firmly on her wrist, taking her pulse.

She heard the clicking of high heels and Cindy's sweet belly laugh as the three professors congregated near the foot of her bed. They quieted, probably so Dr. Hunger . . . could keep count.

Cindy had obviously gone home, changed, and put mousse in her hair. Evans looked happy. Benton was downright serious. Dr. Hunger . . . finally let go of her wrist.

"You all shouldn't be here. You have exams to . . ." Her eyelids fluttered against her cheeks. She was already wiped out, groggy. "Cindy, can you bring me a blue boo-oklet while the material is till fresh."

"We'll see, honey." She smiled.

"She's worried about exams," the doctor said, "and depleted herself. I don't recommend too much conversation. I'll give you five minutes, max."

"It was a pleasure seeing you again, Katherine." He squeezed her hand this time instead of her wrist.

"You too, Dr. . . . Hunger . . . bottom."

He hesitated for a moment, smiled, then stepped away.

"It's Ungerbach," Cindy whispered as he exited the room.

"Write it down, please." Katherine closed her eyes.

"I think he set his stopwatch, I'll go first." Evans stopped on the right side of her bed and reached across for her left hand, the one that didn't host an IV.

"Sweet Lady Katherine"—he patted her hand—"this afternoon we thought about losing you and all you mean to us, and it was a day in which we basked in the special person that you are and will always be."

"Write that down, too. I won't remember it tomorrow ver-baaa-tum."

"A lovely ten-letter word." Evans smiled.

"I'm writing, right now, Katherine," Cindy said.

Next was grim Quinn. He reached for her hand and patted it. Maybe it helped her blood flow, because, for a moment, she felt a tad better.

"It was a hard day, Katherine." He clicked his tongue on the top of his mouth and then sighed.

She closed her eyes because it took too much energy to wait for him to say whatever he was going to say while he patted her hand.

"Has anyone told Grandma?"

"Ethel was here for about an hour. I took her home. She called your parents."

Quinn transferred her hand to Cindy's. "You two go out in the hall and close the door for a second," Cindy told the men.

"You have two minutes," Evans said, exiting.

"Where's my bathing suit?" Katherine whispered.

"It was cut off in ER."

"That's horrrrible!"

"We'll talk more tomorrow when you're feeling better. But you scared me, you know; I panicked."

"You did fine."

"Your books are still at the creek. Quinn's going to get them tomorrow after class. He'll take Ethel, and she'll drive the truck home."

It was too much information; her head swam.

"And the doctor, the cute Hungarian, is keeping a tight vigil."

Chapter Forty-Three

Cindy's last comment was odd; it floated around on an air mattress in Katherine's head. She worried that she'd forget it. She should have had Cindy write it down. Except for the nurses turning the lights on and then off to monitor her IVs, she slept peacefully.

A breakfast tray was delivered. She peered at the applesauce, apple juice, dry wheat toast . . . where was the orange Jell-O? She recalled Cindy's odd comment: *The cute Hungarian doctor is keeping a tight vigil.*

Pat went off duty and was replaced by June, a sweet, elderly woman with short gray hair and glasses. She was so sweet; maybe her husband was a pastor.

"Just press the buzzer if you need anything," June said.

"Where's the buzzer?"

"It's the black button right here on the side of your bed." There were several black buttons on both sides of the bed. June stepped closer and pointed to one specific button.

"Thanks, June. Are you a Christian?"

"Yes, Katherine, are you?"

"Yes. I thought you were. You have an ethereal glow about you."

June laughed softly.

After she left, Katherine felt weepy and alone. How close had she been to death? She'd never heard the angels sing or felt an out-of-body experience. She remembered little except that for a moment she'd witnessed Cindy's panic. And if she relaxed long enough, Nurse Kitty Princeton's pale blue eyes peered at her above a blue hospital mask.

Grandma showed up at ten that morning with a vase from home stuffed with purple gladiolas that were now in bloom along the white picket fence. They were beautiful—the epitome of her grandmother's beloved summer garden. Grandma patted her hand and kissed her on the forehead.

"When did you find out?" Katherine asked.

"Not until I got home from the potluck, about ten. Quinn left a message on the recorder. I almost didn't listen to it. I almost went to bed." Grandma shook her head. "I thought you were asleep upstairs, and I was trying to be quiet. I got right back in the car. I'm so glad that I missed all the excitement and worry." She smoothed Katherine's hair away from her face. "Do you have insurance?"

"Yes, thank God! I have great coverage through the university."

Grandma smiled.

"What did Benton tell you?" Katherine relaxed into the pillow.

"Not much on the recorder, but enough to get me here. Later, he told me that you severed an artery and the bleeding was really bad, and if Cindy hadn't been at the river, the Lord might have taken you home."

"Is that how he worded it?"

"Yes."

It felt good to hear Benton talk about God.

"I told him that you'd wanted me to go with you to the river. I'm glad that Cindy went instead."

Shortly after Grandma left, squeaky sneakers resonated down the hallway. Katherine glanced at Cindy's note on the side table. *Ungerbach*, she reminded herself. *Ungerbach*.

"Good morning, Katherine." The cute doctor held up his clipboard as he read her chart. "Is your pain still a four, four and an eighth?"

"Yes." She wished she could put a decorative curtain around her catheter bag.

"I'll have the nurses up your pain medication. I don't want you above a three, three and a quarter. Are you still feeling anxious?"

"About . . . ?"

"Your midterm exam."

"No." Maybe Cindy could bring her a blue booklet. "Can you write me a note? Maybe they'll give me extra time. I have a solid excuse."

The corner of his mouth twitched. "You need to rest. You lost a lot of blood yesterday and were in surgery for over an hour and a half. I don't know how much you remember?"

"I don't remember surgery at all."

He grinned. "Prior to surgery, you were on morphine. I recall that you said you were feeling no pain, and that you were melting."

She recollected nothing. When she looked right in Dr. Ungerbach's face, he was more attractive than she remembered. "Maybe I'm repressing."

"Morphine gives you a very warm, relaxed feeling. It was a good description."

"How will I get to classes?" She looked at her elevated foot.

"It's probably best that you take a couple of weeks off and don't get around too much. Couch to bathroom, that's about it."

"You're making me feel anxious, Doc."

He smiled. "In about a week, you might manage on crutches with absolutely no weight on your right foot."

"Is Ungerbach German, Hungarian . . . ?" She held up her wrist.

"German." Glancing at his wristwatch, he took her pulse.

It wasn't the first time Cindy had been wrong.

Ж

Cindy showed up after their Lewis and Clark class with a sack lunch from Taco Time. She sat down in the chair on the right side of the bed and unwrapped a soft taco. "How are you feeling?"

"The pain's a three instead of a four. They upped my meds. Did you bring me a blue booklet?"

"Yes." Cindy set it on the side table. "Only because I knew you'd insist. It'll give you something to do, but it can't count. Journal in it, if nothing else."

Katherine leaned back in the pillows. "What happened at the river? I don't remember much."

"Neither do I; it was awful. I was so relieved when the ambulance arrived." Cindy glanced toward the door. "Quinn's meeting a student at one thirty and then coming shortly thereafter. I thought I'd get a few questions out of the way first." Cindy set her soft taco aside and stood up, watching the door. "What do you remember about last night?"

"At the river or when I was on morphine?"

"Morphine."

"Nothing." Katherine looked at the ceiling. "I'm afraid to ask."

"You were funny. You lost some inhibitions, my dear."

"Like what?"

Cindy giggled and glanced toward the door again. Fearing the worst, Katherine closed her eyes. "Let me see . . . after ER they rolled you down the hallway. The bleeding was under control, and you were chatty. You told the young Hungarian that someone had kissed you once and then fell into your grandmother's rhododendron bush."

"I didn't." Katherine's eyes flashed open.

"Was that Quinn?"

"Please tell me I didn't."

"You did. I believe that was your first comment to the young Hungarian. Dr. . . ." Cindy leaned forward, looking at her note. "Ungerbach. He said that you didn't need to explain further. I thought it honorable of him. Next you said, 'Nothing ever happened again.'"

"It sounds like you were taking notes."

"Auditory learning has always been my strength."

Katherine nodded. It made sense. "Was Benton present?"

"I don't think . . . hmm." Pursing her lips together, Cindy tried to remember.

"Thank God!" Closing her eyes, Katherine relaxed deeper into the pillow.

"Then you asked the doctor if he was from Princeton. He said no that he'd attended the University of Washington. Some of the nurses said that you were asking them if they were from Princeton."

"Does Benton know?" Maybe she should keep her eyes closed forever.

Cindy smiled and patted her hand. "He may have overheard a little. You were on a stretcher when he first saw you. Don't you remember?"

"I'm in a state of deep, dark repression."

"That's when you called him Dr. Zhivago."

"Oh no. I didn't! Please tell me you're only kidding."

"No, honey, I'm not."

"Ohhhh!" Maybe he wasn't shocked. Maybe Benton had heard it a hundred times.

"And, I'm not done yet."

Katherine inhaled deeply and tried to be brave.

"You told Quinn that whenever your grandmother's not home, you always watch the same movie. He asked what movie, but you didn't answer him." Cindy patted her hand. "You can't tell a man something like that and not expect his mind to wander."

Katherine draped a forearm over her eyes and wanted to die. She'd spilled out her deepest darkest secret that she hadn't even confessed to herself.

"What movie do you watch, Katherine?"

"Who knows, I was on drugs."

"If you don't straighten this out, the men are going to think the worst."

"It's not a bad movie. There's no nudity. It was just one of my favorites. That's all. Tell them that. And remind them that I was on drugs, and I still am." Katherine sniffled. "And that they have to be nice to me."

"Yes." Cindy giggled. "Dr. Ungerbach called it morphine-induced alter ego. If anyone is going to bring Quinn to his senses, it's going to be the young Hungarian."

Katherine peeked out from behind her forearm at Cindy.

"It's not just me talking. Evans senses it, too."

"Senses what?"

"The young doctor is smitten."

Chapter Forty-Four

The phone rang. Katherine reached over the side bar of the bed and picked it up with her left hand.

"Hello."

"Katherine, it's Dad. How are you feeling, honey?"

"Better. It's all still a blur, but better."

"That's good. We were hoping to come this Friday after I get off work, but I wasn't thinking. The reunion is this Saturday. Greg and Shirley are going to be in town, and they were planning to stay with us."

"I'm fine, Dad. I have Grandma and a great group of friends taking care of me."

"That's what Mom said too. We love you and are keeping you in prayer."

After their phone conversation, she picked up the essay booklet. The trick was to tie her class notes in with the textbook and prove she had a thorough understanding of each. Her brain felt extremely heavy as she leaned back into the pillow.

At 4:00 p.m., Brad, the young German doctor, checked in on her. "*American Scripture.* Sounds interesting." He noted the book that someone, probably Grandma, had left for her on the side table.

"It's Professor Benton's book."

"Dr. Zhivago?" He nodded.

He'd obviously overheard.

"You can tell a lot about a person's brain when they're on morphine."

"Do you mean their alter ego?"

"No, their brain. You have an active brain, and you're funny."

"I'm embarrassed by your first impression of me. I'm usually a very boring person."

"I doubt that very much." He glanced at his watch.

She felt healthy blood flow returning to her face. "How many more days do you think I'll be here?"

"When you can walk to the bathroom without passing out, you'll be released."

She looked at her bandaged foot, suspended fourteen inches off the bed.

"Is Professor Benton the Eliminator?" Dr. Ungerbach asked.

Could all her ramblings hurt Quinn's career? "He blind dates every Friday. That's probably what I was referring to. Was he present?"

"No, only Nurse Pat. You had just told me that you are a King and that I am a Vi-king."

What kind of impression of her did he have? "I, um . . . I'm so embarrassed. I almost need morphine to apologize." She closed her eyes. Maybe she should never reopen them.

"Your color is a definite improvement." He chuckled.

Ж

When she awoke from her afternoon nap, Benton was asleep in her guest chair, her blue backpack near his feet. He'd driven to Potlatch and rescued her things. The sweet man.

Nurse Pat carried in her dinner tray and rolled the side table in front of her.

Katherine's appetite had returned. She felt ready for something hearty, like Grandma's meatloaf. She uncovered the soup bowl to see shimmering beef broth. Green Jell-O, a piece of dry wheat toast, and a cup of tea rounded out the meal. It was official: they were starving her.

"It was a wine bottle." Quinn yawned and rolled a kink out of his neck. "A cheap Gallo wine. I even found the label."

"Who went with you, Grandma?"

He nodded. "I used her kitchen tongs to retrieve the glass. She drove home your grandfather's truck."

"Thank you." Katherine picked up the toast.

"Promise me you'll never do that again."

She paused from chewing to look at him. He appeared so serious that she nodded.

"Good."

That was easy.

"From now on, you'll always wear an old pair of tennis shoes when you swim in non-chlorinated water."

She nodded.

"You'll always swim with a buddy."

His stern voice inspired warm color to rise in her cheeks.

"And . . ."

It was evident he was running out of promises.

"You'll . . ."

The spoonful of Jell-O wiggled all the way to her mouth.

"Never wear a swimsuit to the emergency room again. That's why the young Hungarian-barbarian is interested in you."

Had she been in her swimsuit on a stretcher? What an embarrassing possibility. Had Benton seen her in her bathing suit? Had Miss Princeton? Had he run into Miss Kitty in the hallway?

"You know firsthand that he's also interested in me for my alter ego."

"You should already have been sent home. He's making a special exception for you. Evans said if it was anyone else . . ." Benton's chest inflated.

"Anyone else . . . what?"

"They would have only spent one night."

"Dr. Ungerbach said when I can crutch to the bathroom without passing out, I'll be released."

"Usually, Katherine, patients are wheeled out when they're passing out." Bunching his mouth, he looked like a jealous orangutan. Did he care for her? He'd driven to Potlatch and retrieved her books. He was here visiting her. Had he come to his senses?

"After my morphine-induced alter ego performance, I believe he's also interested in my mind."

Eyes large and dull, he'd obviously lost his sense of humor.

"I'm sorry I called you Zhivago. I thought it once the first day of class. It's something about your eyes, and poof, seven months later, I see you when I'm on morphine, and well you do have marvelous eyes."

Quinn cleared his throat and looked up at her IV drip bag. "I think Ungerbach's putting something in your meds to get his kicks." He sighed and patted the arms of his chair. "Would you prefer that I call you on the phone and read to you, or that I sit in this chair and read to you?"

"Tonight?" She glanced at the book. Was he actually going to spend time with her here in a public place?

"Yes. What's my curfew?"

"Ten."

"Then I'll be here at nine."

How romantically confusing.

Standing up, he patted the metal railing on the side of her bed. She waited for him to squeeze her hand, or brush her hair away from her face, or kiss her forehead, but he was hesitant about all three. She wouldn't worry too much about it—they had a date tonight.

She woke several hours later to Dr. Ungerbach standing on the left side of her bed. "Katherine, you have company, and I wanted to tell you that I'm off duty now and heading home for the evening."

"Oh, thank you. Good night." She stretched and realized that Quinn was seated in her guest chair. She smiled softly and turned her head his direction. For their date, she hadn't even brushed her hair. As he stared back, harp and string music begin to play. Though faint, the melody hadn't left her heart.

"I heard that you have a date this Friday with Kitty, one of our nurses," Dr. Ungerbach said.

"Yes, we have a mutual friend—Professor Linton."

"Visiting hours end at ten." Doctor Ungerbach squeezed her hand.

"Thank you, Doctor."

After his squeaky tennis shoes were no longer audible, Quinn cleared his throat. "Boy, he tried to put me in my place."

"You are dating Miss Princeton, and he's concerned about his patient's rest."

"Every time I've been here, he squeezes your hand." His chest puffed out as he watched the doorway.

Was Quinn jealous? He almost acted like it.

"Did you bring the book?" she asked.

"No, Ethel brought your copy by the other day. I have it right here." He patted the book on the side table.

Which book was it? Two different titles came to mind.

"I believe you stopped reading on chapter three. They're very long chapters, by the way." He flipped through the pages, clearing his throat. "Leaving the unsuspecting Heyward . . . Hmmm . . . Who's Heyward?" He scanned the page and glanced over at her. "Nothing's ringing a bell."

Katherine suppressed a giggle.

He flipped back to the cover. "Hmm . . . A*merican Scripture*." And, then he carefully slid the jacket off. His dark brows gathered. "What is this, Katherine?"

Under the starched sheet and single blanket, she curled the toes of her left foot. "*Last of the Mohicans* by James Fenimore Cooper."

"Yes, but why is it—" He shook his head.

"I switched covers a while ago when you were being an ogre about me reading your beloved book."

"Oh, I see." He nodded. "When you were reading The *Last of the Mohicans*, you were really reading *American Scripture*?"

She nodded.

"Why?"

She pulled the covers up a little higher. "You'd intrigued me, and I didn't want you to know."

"Why?" His dark brows gathered.

"Because you were being such a bully and I was busy. And I didn't want you to know I was enamored with your—"

"Enamored?"

She'd known he'd be this way. She glanced at the clock above the sink area. He could very easily argue with her for the next forty-five minutes.

"I'm sidelined, a casualty; you can't argue with me now. I've been taken out of the game for rest and rehabilitation."

"You're talking nonsense."

She stared up at him. Did the Lord know she'd needed a break from his heart-wrenching search for love?

"What's happening with the doctor and you? Something's going on." Thankfully, he kept his voice low.

She leaned her head slightly forward and wrapped her hair into a high bun before resting back into the pillow. "As soon as I'm discharged, we're driving to Fresno to meet his parents. He said that he knew the minute he set eyes on my ankle that I am the woman of his dreams."

"Is that the truth or a lie?" Quinn tucked the book under his arm and paused near the foot of her bed.

How could he possibly believe her?

Finding the correct button, she turned off the lights.

Quinn sighed deeply and finally retreated. He was dating a nurse this weekend. Why should he be so troubled by a doctor showing her attention? Maybe it had been her tone.

Learn from this: Never agree to a date with the professor you're in love with in your hospital room and, pretend to be interested in your doctor. Once you're alone in the dark, it doesn't sit well. She sniffed.

Chapter Forty-Five

In the dark, the phone rang beside Katherine's bed. It would take her longer to find the button for the light than it would to find the annoying phone.

After the third ring, she cradled the receiver to her ear. "Hello."

"Hello, Katherine, it's Quinn."

She nestled back into the pillow. "Hello, Benton." He'd probably just gotten off the phone with Nurse Princeton and Miss Palouse, and he was bored.

"I behaved like an ogre. Katherine, I'm sorry."

Like a *jealous* ogre. He'd purposefully left out that word. She waited for him to expound upon his apology, but he remained silent on the other end of the line.

"I'm sorry I teased you. We're not meeting his parents, and I fibbed about Fresno."

"Apology accepted. While I have you on the phone, I'd like to share with you an idea I've been mulling over."

"Okay." She stared deep into the darkness and didn't let her imagination do the moon boogie.

"I want . . . I want you to stop thinking about Hungerbottom and get back to who you've been thinking about for the entire semester."

She relaxed deeper into her pillow. It was so like Benton to be so utterly unromantic. "Well, Mr. I

Want…" She paused to yawn and while she was at it, it felt so good to close her eyes.

"Are you still there, Katherine?"

"Yes."

"Is he there now?" Quinn whispered.

"No." The dummy.

"Good. I do not want you accepting any dates with him."

"Dr. Ungerbach has not asked me out. He just has an extremely kind bedside manner."

"I'll make you a deal." He inhaled. "I'll stop blind dating. No Miss Palouse. No Miss Princeton. No Miss Wazzu."

"You're out of order, Benton, which clearly reveals that you need to meet Miss Palouse." Katherine wrapped the phone cord around her left elbow. "Miss Princeton chronologically should come first. And besides, I want you to meet Miss Palouse. I always have. I don't want you to question her on account of me."

"Do you have questions about Ungerbach?"

Hmm . . . She took her time. "He's attentive, but he hasn't asked me out. I try not to let my mind wander to all the what-ifs."

"I'll stop blind dating." In the dark, he sounded weak, like one more straw might break him.

"Benton, I want you to meet Miss Palouse."

"Why?"

"If we ever did become a couple, I wouldn't want you to have questions about a woman that you spoke with for months on the phone, but never met, who lives only fifteen miles away."

"Katherine."

"And besides, you're only a week away from meeting her."

"Eight days. A lot can happen in eight days."

His sweet tone made her feel like Nurse Pat was sitting on her ribcage. She tipped her head back and inhaled deeply. After all these months of talking about Miss Palouse, he couldn't change his mind now.

Chapter Forty-Six

"Dr. Ungerbach wants you to walk today, Katherine," Nurse June said as she parted the curtains. A healthy amount of sunlight streamed into the room.

Katherine looked at her elevated foot and her IV bag.

"I need to put more clothes on before I walk down the hall."

"Of course." June lowered the suspension apparatus supporting Katherine's injury and carefully moved her foot from the sling. With June's help, Katherine edged both legs over the side of the bed. She already felt sweaty.

"First time's always the hardest," June whispered.

Two blonde nurses arrived; one was younger and one middle-aged.

"I'm Lisa," the middle-aged nurse said. "We'll be your crutches today. Dr. Ungerbach said to take you on a little cruise around the room. You're to hold your injured foot behind you. June, you're in charge of steering the meds."

The nurses sat one on each side of her on the bed, and Katherine lifted her arms over their shoulders.

"Tell us when you're ready," the younger nurse said.

"We're your crutches, but you still have to do the work," Lisa said.

"Okay, on the count of two," Katherine said. "One . . . two." The pain in her foot went up to a seven as the women lugged her about the room.

They made it halfway to the door; for some reason it was wide open, and so was the back of her gown! "Who's going to shut the door, so no one sees me when we turn around?"

"Fiddlesticks!" Nurse Lisa said. "We're going to have to walk to the door."

They made it all the way to the door before Katherine passed out.

She became cognizant a few minutes later. Her arms were still around both nurses' shoulders, but they were now seated on the side of her bed, her foot beneath her.

"What happened?" she whispered.

"We walked too far," Nurse Lisa said. "Feeling better?"

"Maybe." Katherine laughed lightly and looked to her left. The young nurse's blue eyes appeared familiar. Katherine's gaze dropped to the white plastic name tag on her poodle-print smock. It read Kitty.

Chapter Forty-Seven

"Lord, You let me live." A tear slid down Katherine's cheek. "I don't think it was only so I could make a complete fool out of myself—be totally humbled—and flunk all my classes. I know You have a plan for my life and that I need to trust in Your perfect and sovereign plan for me.

"In the meantime, can You please help me to stop making a fool out of myself?" She sniffed and sank down on the bed and pulled the sheet over her head. After a couple of minutes of feeling sorry for herself, someone gently gave the sheet a tug, and she found herself staring into Professor Evans's kind green eyes. He was in his teacher attire—nice pleated slacks and a short-sleeved button-up light gray shirt.

"It's not a good sign." He glanced toward the hallway. "The sheet over your head. Worried me at first, and then I heard you crying."

She sat up and tucked the sheets beneath her armpits. "I wasn't crying. I was just sniffling."

He held up a small Ziploc bag. "I brought madeleines. Push your little buzzer and ask them for two cups of tea."

Tea and chocolate madeleines were the perfect pick-me-ups. Sugar was exactly what she needed.

"How's Cindy?"

"Buried in lesson planning. She sends her love."

"I met Miss Princeton today."

Evans's eyes had brightened above his melamine mug of tea before he lowered it to his knee. "Is that why you were crying?"

"No. I keep hearing things I said when I was on morphine."

Evans smiled. "Go on."

"And Kitty is pleasant and pretty. There's potential."

"Sounds like several of the others. How's the young Hungarian?"

She held her mug steady. Was Evans here on a mission? "He's German and very attentive." She emphasized the *very* part for Benton's sake.

"Hmmm . . . what do you think?"

Most likely Evans was on a mission.

"I'm afraid that Dr. Ungerbach's first and favorite impression of me is when I was on morphine."

"You were exceptionally funny that night." He patted the bar that ran along the side of her bed. "I'm here to clear the air regarding something I've said."

"Yes." Katherine was glad that it wasn't something she'd said.

"You've heard me mention the Wazzu grad student a time or two. The one I've been trying to line Benton up with for a blind date."

"Yes." She managed a brave smile.

"Just between you and me . . . I lied. Mashburn never told me about her. I'm the one trying to get you and Benton to meet as a blind date. The Wazzu history grad student who's never been married is you. I thought it would be amusing for you two to meet for a not-so-blind date."

"Amusing?" She glanced at her IV drip as Evans's words calmed her spirit.

"What do you think, Katherine?"

She shrugged. "Maybe in a couple of weeks, we'll see how things go."

"It's all about strategy." His brows gathered. "Tomorrow night is Miss Princeton. Next Friday is Miss Palouse. How about the following Friday? That'll give you a little bit of time with the doctor, and get you closer to the end of the semester as well."

"What do you mean by the latter?"

"If it's possible for you two to wait until the end of the semester, if would be best for Benton's career."

"Oh." She nodded. "I still don't understand why you encouraged the kiss in the first place."

"The heart hears what it wants to, Miss King." He smiled."

Maybe it was the meds, but tears filled her eyes. She swallowed a large lump in her throat. "Kleenex, Evans. I'm going to need the box." She took the flat colorless box from his outstretched hand.

"Between now and the end of the semester, do not give into Benton." Evans ordered.

Maybe it was the subdued hospital room setting, but she needed color. The rolling hills. Grandma's summer garden. Pizza. Evans's gray shirt blocked her view of the gladiolas. She just wanted to sob and let it all go.

The heart hears what it wants to. Oh, Evans. Was he trying to break her?

Chapter Forty-Eight

"Another thing that you told me about your Dr. Zhivago that I don't think you remember is . . ." Holding his clipboard, Dr. Ungerbach waited for Katherine to lift her gaze.

"I can already tell that you're making this one up." She inhaled deeply, trying to prepare herself.

"You said he's not ready for you to be the only woman in his life."

She burrowed her head deeper into the pillow. "Why did I blabber so much? How far is it from the ER to the operating room?"

He laughed. "We were waiting momentarily, and for some reason, probably morphine-induced, you confided in me."

"Does it happen a lot?"

"No, not often enough."

Their time together felt like an embarrassing, awkward date. Maybe she needed protein.

"I'm still unbiased if you'd like to talk about the Eliminator."

She pushed on the appropriate button, raising her bed to an eighty-degree position, and tucked the blankets beneath her armpits. "He blind dates every Friday."

"Every Friday?" His sandy-blond brows knit together.

"Small-town women that he talks to on the phone."

"Wow!" Brad shook his head. "How can he go out with women he's never met . . . when he's already met someone like you?"

His sentiments were beautiful, but, like the Gallo wine bottle, painfully sharp. Would she ever recover from Brad's epiphany?

"I can see your pain level is presently at a ten. I'm sorry."

Maybe her injury was God's way of taking her out of the game. Maybe God, the wise coach that He was, was benching her for a broken heart.

Ж

Dr. Ungerbach checked in on Katherine at three o'clock Friday afternoon. He looked at her chart. "You've been motivated. You've walked twice; I see, and you're studying."

Books were piled beside her on the bed. She capped her highlighter. "Do I have your permission to go home tomorrow?"

"Yes. I'll write up your departure ticket." He cleared his throat. "I have Monday off and, I was wondering how you'd feel about me driving you up to the college for your makeup exam?"

"Oh, wow." That would eliminate the need to have Grandma in her gardening hat wheel her around campus. "That's thoughtful of you."

"What time should I pick you up?" Brad's brows lifted.

Katherine blinked. "It'll be in the Administration Building; how's morning for you?"

"I'll pick you up at nine thirty. Afterward, I'll take you to my place for green tea."

"Oh." There were strings attached. "Sounds like you're a health nut?"

"Just a little." He held out his thumb and arched forefinger, about an inch apart.

"I probably won't be very good company."

"I doubt that very much." Healthy color tinged his cheeks.

How could he even look at her? She hadn't had a shower in days, and her hair—she wouldn't think about her hair.

Ж

Ethel was surprised to see Quinn's car parked near the back gate. She watched through the window above the table as he strolled to the back door. His blind date with Miss Princeton was in a few hours, and here he was. She set the pair of salt-and-pepper shakers that he'd given her on the table, and then hurried and opened the door before he had a chance to knock.

Mid-air, he still pretended to knock. "Hi, Ethel. I'm on my way home and have about an hour to kill."

"There's still some decaf left from last night. Would you care for a cup?"

"That sounds great." While Ethel set two cups of coffee in the microwave, Quinn opened the fridge and set the creamer on the table.

"You're using them." He sounded pleased to see the Currier and Ives set on the table.

Ethel nodded. "The old corks had dried up, and the salt and pepper leaked out the bottom. I can't tell you what a pain it was to find little corks in this town. But they're so worth it."

"Katherine found them. I talked her into letting me be the one to buy them for you."

"Before I forget, she gets released tomorrow morning at ten, and I was wondering if you could bring her home? I know you mentioned a while back something about your peers frowning on you driving her a—"

"I'd be happy to."

The microwave dinged.

"Good." Ethel giggled as she transferred the cups to the table. "I just remembered that I found the article I was telling you about. The reason I couldn't find it is, I had it laminated, and it was in the file cabinet and not that old album." Ethel headed to the curio cabinet for the precious article.

"It was a half-page article in *The Columbian*, let me see . . ." She looked at the date in the top right corner. "September 10, 1984." She handed Quinn the article and sat back down.

A picture of Katherine and her Grandpa Crang—Pattie's father—was positioned in the upper section of the page. They were both dressed in forestry-green volunteer shirts, as the picture had been taken at Fort Vancouver, where they'd volunteered. A ten-year-old, Katherine had her arms wrapped about her grandfather's shoulders. Stocky, with a beard and glasses, it was evident that emotion misted the elderly man's eyes. The article was entitled: "A Shared Love for History."

There was no mistaking it—as Quinn regarded the photo, tears surfaced in his eyes. Ethel rose from her chair and looked over his shoulder to view it also. "Her grandpa Crang always used to call her his *little darling*. Katherine's sparkling eyes and wide smile revealed that she was missing one of her molars. An adorable child, she was now a beautiful young woman; that is if one could ever get past her pigheaded, stubborn King pride.

The article was a summary of Katherine and her grandfather's close relationship, and their shared love for places of the past.

"I don't know if I can finish reading this." Quinn tipped his head back and inhaled deeply.

"Just read it in small chunks," Ethel said. "You're not going out with that nurse, Miss Kitty Princeton, tonight until you've read the whole thing."

Ж

As was normal for her on Friday evenings, Katherine studied. She poured herself into the Civil War. She looked forward to the final weeks of the semester, when she'd be back in class and Benton would cover the Reconstruction period. Presently, he was on his date with Miss Princeton, and in about two hours he'd discuss the outcome at Evans's. The phone rang on the table beside her. Turning, she picked it up.

"Hi, honey," Grandma said. "I spoke with Quinn earlier and asked if he'd mind picking you up tomorrow, and he said he'd be happy to."

"Thanks, Grandma."

"I put fresh sheets on the bed in the spare room for you. I don't want you climbing the stairs."

"Thank you. Have you seen him lately?" Katherine glanced toward the partially opened door. Voices of staff workers echoed down the hall.

"Yes, he stopped by here before his date with Miss Princeton."

"What do you think, Grandma?"

"I don't know. One minute he's talking about you and the doctor, and the next he's talking about the nurse. They've chatted on the phone a few times, and he said that he felt obligated to follow through with their date."

The knot in her gut at the mention of Quinn's name wasn't as noticeable. "Grandma, this week has been difficult, but some good's come out of it. Maybe I need to move on and stop waiting."

"Oh, is that what you've been doing—waiting? I thought you were recuperating and studying."

"That too."

"I think this doctor's interest in you is making you feel impatient."

"You've always told me there's a purpose to all that happens and that God has a plan. It's like the road that my heart's been taking had a dead-end sign posted and I didn't see it. I was so busy enjoying the scenery that I wasn't paying attention."

"Oh, I hate being in the middle. And you know how I don't want to give you hope unless I'm sure…" Grandma whispered.

"Yes." Katherine closed her eyes and nodded.

"I'm still not sure. But, last night when we pored over the old photo albums, Quinn took his time, Katherine, especially with a couple of photos."

"Do you remember which ones?"

"He just stared at the one of you and your dad, the day of your college graduation. In his own way, he was emotional." Grandma sighed. "Remember I took that one out in the parking lot behind the Kibbie Dome with the rolling hills behind you. You looked especially beautiful and happy that day."

Katherine leaned back in the pillow. It was one of her favorite photos, a close-up of her father and her, standing cheek to cheek. "What do you mean emotional, Grandma?"

"His eyes. There was something in Quinn's eyes… maybe tears."

Chapter Forty-Nine

When Katherine awoke, her breakfast tray table was positioned on her left, and on her right, a card sat propped by the telephone. Her name was printed in capital letters on the front of a white Hallmark envelope.

She pushed the correct black button and elevated the bed to a comfortable sitting position. She opened the envelope. Who had dropped it by early this morning or late last night? A pair of bright fuchsia flip-flops atop white sand brightened the front of the card.

How perfect. She giggled, running her finger beneath the seal.

I'll be in surgery this morning, but I wanted to let you know that I'll call and check on your progress sometime today—Brad.

His number was printed near the bottom of the card. Katherine stared blindly at the closed curtains. Dr. Ungerbach was indeed interested.

Ж

Nurse Pat helped Katherine get in the shower. She leaned on her crutch and washed her hair. It was awkward but worth it. Grandma had packed clothes for her. The Levi's skirt was perfect, only one hoop to get her feet through.

By a quarter to ten, she was seated on the edge of the bed, ready and waiting. Alone in the room, she glanced at the mirror above the sink. Her long, blonde hair, now dry, hung loosely about her shoulders. From the waist up, she looked normal, like a clean Katherine King.

Ten minutes later, Benton wandered into her room, wearing an untucked polo shirt, cargo shorts, and sandals. "Katherine . . ." He smiled. "You're looking quite well."

Nurse Pat pushed a wheelchair into the room and handed him a pair of crutches. "Katherine, these are both loaners. Dr. Ungerbach worked out a deal for you."

"Will you thank him for me?"

"Of course. Now, put your weight on your left, and I'll be here if you need me." Pat set the brake and held out her arm. Katherine swiveled and was able to smooth the back of her skirt before she sat down.

"I'll be in charge of the gladiolas," Katherine said.

Benton poured most of the water out of the vase into the sink and handed it to her. Pat pushed Katherine's wheelchair down the hallway, through the reception area, and out the double doors, all the way to Quinn's car. She was finally going home.

While Quinn drove, Katherine held the gladiolas in her lap. She wouldn't ask about his date. If he wanted to tell her, he would. If he didn't tell her, she knew that Cindy would.

He cleared his throat. "Cindy and Evans are antiquing in Pullman this morning."

"That's right. She asked me earlier if I wanted to go. At the time, it sounded fun."

"I thought so, too." He patted the wheel. "We could pick up your meds and meet up with them."

His spontaneity surprised her. "I'm not great on crutches yet."

"We have a wheelchair in the trunk."

"I don't think I should." She looked at her foot.

"I don't care if you sleep. They'll be glad to see you."

He wanted her to go; she heard it in his voice. She reflected on Brad's card. "I have a midterm on Monday."

"You were ready for it a week ago."

While Quinn patronized Olson's Drug, Katherine prayed in the car. "Lord, I'm tired of being confused. I just want black and white. Please, no more gray. Your will, Lord, Your perfect plan, not mine, amen."

Quinn handed her back her insurance card, a small bag, and a bottle of spring water. "The pharmacist said to stay ahead of the pain and take two tablets from the big bottle every four hours, and not to exceed more than eight in twenty-four hours."

She popped two pills in her mouth. Instead of taking Main toward Grandma's, Quinn stayed on Highway 98, heading west out of town toward Pullman.

"Benton, I'm not up for it." She laid her head back against the headrest and closed her eyes.

"It was because you had really great insurance that you were there as long as you were. You should have been home two days ago, but he kept you longer."

"I passed out on the way to the bathroom. He tried to send me home earlier."

"I'm sorry, I didn't know." He sighed.

"How was your date with Miss Princeton?"

"Fine. We dined in Moscow at the Chinese restaurant on Main, across the street from The Green Dragon, as you call it. They have great cashew chicken."

"Did Evans tell you that I met her?"

"Yes, he said your comments were that she's pleasant and, pretty and has potential."

"To a T. What were your comments last night?" Katherine gazed out the passenger window. Did she really want to know?

"She had some interesting things to say about your doctor."

"Oh."

"Supposedly he's a water sports fanatic. Has a race boat, water skis, jet skis . . . I've lost track . . . and evidently a large shop."

"And what did you think about Kitty?"

"She . . ." He patted the wheel. "She said Hungerbottom thinks you're *the one* because you showed up due to an accident involving water, and maybe the bathing suit had something to do with it, too. Kitty said that he plans to get in touch."

"I asked him, and he said the first time he saw me, I was in a hospital gown." She leaned back against the head support. "I was also on drugs. I've been embarrassed all week by things I've *heard* that I said. I don't remember a thing."

"You were pretty smiley when you called me Zhivago."

"I'm sorry."

"I'm not. I've heard that Omar Sharif is one of the, uh . . . most attractive men to ever walk the planet." He glanced at her. "You were not yourself. You were flirty."

"I'm sorry, Quinn. But I don't want to go antiquing. My head feels swimmy."

He nodded and, a half mile later, took a right off the Pullman-Moscow highway. At first, she thought he might just turn around, but instead, he headed east on the scenic back roads, passing the small local airport. He pulled out his cell phone, and speed dialed someone.

"Here, tell Evans for me. They're expecting us." He handed her the phone.

"How's our patient?" Evans's voice came on the line.

"Hi, Evans. It's Katherine. I'm not feeling up for it. I'm sorry."

"I told him he was too ambitious. You need your rest."

"Thank you for understanding." It was difficult telling two of her favorite people that she wasn't up for spending time together. She set Quinn's phone in the console.

"After we have dinner with Ethel, I'll take you to my place for a movie."

What happened to not seeing her until after Miss Palouse? And professor-student relationships? And . . . her head hurt. "I better not. I have a midterm Monday, and I've studied very little lately."

"As long as you're on those drugs, you're going to be too tired to study. You may have to just settle for a couple of Bs and be happy and a bit dingy on the couch watching a movie with me."

She looked at her hands. "So Miss Princeton didn't ring any bells?"

"No, I'm afraid I did most of the talking last night, and she proved to be a kind listener. I made it to Evans's house about nine thirty."

"Wow—early for a Friday."

About a mile past the small local airport, he took a left on a gravel road that ran straight north through miles of rolling green wheat fields toward blue hills in the distance. Twenty feet past a row of mailboxes, he pulled off to the side of the road and shifted into park. No buildings, farmhouses, or tractors were in sight, simply miles of wheat. He left the engine running and the air-conditioning on.

"I finally know what I want." He turned to face her, his eyes wide and somber. "I want us to spend more time together, a lot of time. I want it to be just you and me, no other people, no other distractions. No more blind dates, Katherine. And I want you to stop thinking about Ungerbach and get back to who you've been thinking about for the entire semester."

"Well, Mr. I Want, you're going to have to wait."

"Why's that?"

"Well, for one, due to my painkillers, I'm not myself. I can actually look right in your eyes and not feel . . . or even imagine I feel . . . a thing."

"Are you saying that's not usually the case?" His voice sounded like he'd lost sixty pounds.

Maybe she should not have admitted that. She monkeyed with the buttons for the door lock. Twice, a clicking sound took place. "I'm not going to cancel Monday."

"Because of your exam or Ungerbach?"

"Both."

"I know with you, one has precedence over the other."

She blinked. He was using up a lot of her mental energy.

"Look at me, Katherine."

She turned her head slightly to gaze at him. On painkillers, it was amazingly easy to look into Quinn Benton's beautiful, deep-set eyes and not feel moved. She stifled a yawn. "I'm sorry, but I'm exhausted again."

He got out of the car. At first, she thought he was going to walk around to her side, but then he walked straight ahead on the gravel road. He walked and walked, and then he kept walking to the crest of the hill, where the crisp green wheat fields rolled into the summer sky. He stood still in the center of the gravel road, a mere dot on the horizon. Maybe he was having a talk with God. A long talk.

Thank goodness, he'd left the air-conditioning on. Feeling rummy, she leaned back against the headrest and closed her eyes. She drifted into a relaxed oasis where there were no more questions.

Ж

In Grandma's gravel driveway, Quinn swung open her passenger door. "Hand me the crutches," he said. She slid them out the door to him. He propped them against the middle of the back passenger door. "You're tired, and I'm going to carry you inside."

"Benton, please don't. What if you drop me?"

He ignored her, bent down, and tucked his right arm under her knees and his left around her back. She placed her arms around his neck and blinked. He closed the car door with his hip and regarded her in the bright sunlight. The soft, emotive look in his eyes surprised her. Now that she was home, he was definitely different.

"We're all going to church tomorrow," he said, propping the gate open with his left knee. "Evans, Cindy, Grandma, you, and me."

"Evans?"

"Yes, and Cindy."

Was it the first time he'd called Grandma . . . Grandma? Speaking of Grandma, she held the back door open, so Katherine had to stop staring in his eyes. She had a date with Ungerbach on Monday.

"I made up the bed in the main floor guest room. Do you want to lie down on the couch or the bed?"

"The bed, Grandma."

"I made a dump cake for dessert to celebrate."

"It sounds awful." Katherine noted a pleasant aroma in the kitchen.

"Easiest cake I've ever made. You just dump it in a pan," Grandma said.

"It smells good." Turning sideways, Quinn carried her through the doorway into the living room and from there to Grandma's sewing room, map room, guest room.

"How's your foot feeling?" He gazed into her eyes.

"The pain's a five," she said as he set her down. The covers were already pulled back. "I'll try and sleep off the other medicine before I take any more."

He knelt down beside the bed and took her hand. "I can take you to your exam on Monday, Katherine. You'll just have to go in a little earlier. Eight fifteen. And the earliest I could bring you home would be one thirty. You could wait in my office. Read and sleep."

She looked from his eyes to the pastel quilt coverlet. "That's very sweet of you, Benton, but...

with all the trouble I've already caused you this semester, I don't think it's a good idea." *What in the world was he thinking?* "There is something you can do for me." She moistened her lips.

"Yes, anything."

"Can you look out this window?" She nodded over her right shoulder to the lace curtain-covered window. "It's Saturday. Is Hannah out there with her little lemonade stand?"

Holding back the lace in one hand, he peered toward the street. "Yes, I see her."

"There's some quarters on the windowsill, to the right of the front door. She's saving up for a puppy. Sweetest little girl in the whole wise world. And I'm a tad parched."

"Whole *wide* world, darling."

Darling? She'd always loved the sweet term of endearment. Did he know? Did Grandma tell him?

Katherine flung her forearm over her eyes and swallowed tears. Boarding her in his office for half a workday! What was he thinking?

In Quinn's absence, the phone rang. After two rings, Grandma answered it. "Hello—I'm sorry, Katherine's resting at the moment. May I take a message?—Err, wait a moment while I find a pen."

Grandma! She hadn't even asked if she'd take the call.

Quinn returned carrying two Dixie cups of lemonade. "When you call Brad back, ask when you can cut back on the meds. At the pace you're at, you'll sleep through Monday's exam." He brushed her hair away from her face, smiled at her tenderly, kissed her forehead, and squeezed her hand.

Now that she was home, he was definitely different.

Chapter Fifty

Grandma delivered a tray with a cup of hot tea and an oatmeal cookie. "Your doctor called and left his number. He said he was checking in."

"Thanks, Grandma." Katherine read through her Lewis and Clark history notes for a spell and fell asleep.

Quinn knocked on the door frame, waking her. "Hey sleepyhead, how about joining Ethel and me for dinner at the table?"

She nodded and stretched. After he disappeared into the hall, she slowly lowered her left foot to the floor before reaching for the crutches. Without a mishap, she hobbled to the door.

"In case you've forgotten, Ungerbach called," Quinn said from the kitchen. "There's a sticky note on the mirror."

"Thank you." Unfortunately, there wasn't a phone in the spare bedroom. She crutched into the kitchen. She'd call Brad after—she surveyed the table—toasted cheese sandwiches and tomato soup.

Katherine ate half her usual portion. It was amazing how much her appetite had shrunk on the hospital's Jell-O diet.

"This cake is delicious." Quinn winked at Grandma.

"I wish I'd found this recipe forty years ago. It's so easy. You just dump everything in the pan and pop it in the oven. Don't even have to stir."

Despite its name, the dump cake was surprisingly good, with cherries, crushed pineapple and pecans.

While Grandma and Quinn washed dishes, Katherine called Brad from the living room.

"Hello." Brad's voice brought back memories of the kind physician that he was.

"Hi, Brad, it's Katherine. Is this your mobile number or your home number?"

"My mobile. I'm at work, but I'm not in the middle of a surgery." He chuckled.

"Good."

"Are you calling me back to cancel Monday's get-together? Or simply calling me back?"

"Simply calling you back." She hopped one legged to a dining chair and sat down.

"I'm relieved. What time would you like me to pick you up Monday?"

"About nine thirty, if it still works for you." She looked straight ahead out the lace curtains and sensed that Grandma and Quinn were unusually quiet in the kitchen.

"Nine thirty is great. I have to work tomorrow, but I have Monday and Tuesday off. Try and keep both days open, if you can."

"I've been sleeping a lot. I'm not the greatest company."

"Your body is healing. You need to rest."

There was a long, awkward pause.

"I'll call again tomorrow, Katherine."

"Okay. Oh, um, when can I cut back on the pain medicine?"

"I'd wait a few days. You want to stay ahead of the pain. How's Quinn Benton been?"

"Attractive, I mean, attentive," she whispered.

"Is he there?"

"Yes."

After she hung up the phone, it rang again.

"Can you get that Quinn?" Grandma asked as Katherine crutched her way to the table.

"Hello," he said, answering it. "Oh, hello, Cindy. Yes, it's Quinn." Grinning, he turned his back to Katherine. "No, we're not talking marriage yet, but we're both thinking in that direction. The Nazarene church is on the corner of Third and you know the road that Les Schwab Tires is on.—Take care, we love you guys, too."

"Who's thinking marriage?" Katherine asked as he returned to the table. "You and Grandma?"

He chuckled. "Ethel, do you mind getting your gardening hat and gloves on? Your house is awfully small for the conversation your granddaughter and I are about to have."

Katherine swallowed. He had definitely come to his senses. "You seem to have forgotten last week's dilemma: grad student and faculty relationships are very frowned upon."

"I'm up and walking to my hat right now. I'm putting it on my head." Grandma puttered from the table.

Katherine was surprised she wasn't calling Pattie King first.

The back door swung open and closed.

A tad light headed, she remained seated at the table and recalled Evans's order: *Do not give in to Benton.* Using her left leg, she rose and maneuvered the crutches beneath her armpits.

"Katherine . . . I'm sorry." She hobbled past him toward the living room.

What did he mean sorry? Sorry that he dated a girl from every bordering town? Sorry for apologizing after he kissed her? Sorry that he hadn't even bought her a card?

She paused and planted the crutches' rubber soles in the green shag carpeting and looked sideways at him.

"I'm sorry I haven't always said what's on my heart. Now's a good time for me to set things straight before you and Brad go any further."

"Now's not a good time, Quinn. I'm sorry."

He winced slightly.

"I have questions, and I'm going to answer them just like you answered your questions."

"My situation was different."

"Yes, you had never met any of them before."

"Exactly!"

She hobbled toward the guest room.

"You already know there's a spark." He followed her.

"You were infatuated with the unknown."

"At least, let me tell you what I've planned to tell you." He followed her. "What I need to tell you."

She made it to the guest room and leaned the crutches against the sewing machine table before hopping to the bed. After plopping down, she straightened her skirt. The exercise made her dizzy. She propped her head against a pillow and looked at him as he leaned against the doorframe, his hands shoved into the front pockets of his cargo shorts. She blinked. Yes, he was standing still.

"I'm ready now."

"There's a lot I want to tell you, Katherine. But only because you're pale, I'll wait for a more appropriate time."

Ж

Quinn rolled her wheelchair down the aisle of the Nazarene church. The crowded parking lot to the sanctuary would have proved a long distance for her on crutches. Using her good foot, she hopped to the middle of the row and sat down beside Cindy. Quinn rolled the wheelchair to the rear of the church and folded it up before returning to sit between her and Grandma.

"You look well, Katherine," Evans said. "Good color with—"

Without asking, Quinn took her hand in his.

"A helpful, somewhat good looking man beside you."

Feeling anxious, Katherine nodded and looked toward the front.

"I know you're not ready." Quinn slid his hand out of hers.

She sighed, relieved.

The worship time was good and harnessed her thoughts toward God. When Pastor Ken strolled to the pulpit, Katherine prayed that his sermon would honor God and pierce their souls.

"Turn with me in your Bible to Galatians 1. Our aim should be to please God and not men."

Katherine closed her eyes—already the sermon pierced her soul while Quinn's hand remained within reach.

"Am I now trying to win the approval of men, or of God? Or am I trying to please men? If I were still trying to please men, I would not be a servant of Christ. – Galatians 1:10."

The throes of college had just been summarized in one verse. If she had her undergraduate years to live over, she would have written this verse in lipstick on her dorm room mirror.

"Thank you, Jesus," Grandma whispered under her breath.

Grandma could obviously relate to the verse. Each year she tried to win the judges' approval at the fair. A brown ribbon was her best finish yet.

Quinn's hand was so near, if she took it, her future would be easier. She lowered her head, but Brad's sentiments had moved her. She owed him at least Monday.

Chapter Fifty-One

Without asking Katherine's opinion, Grandma invited Quinn for lunch. Katherine sat at the table and spread butter on six slices of bread while Grandma preheated a pan on the stove for toasted cheese sandwiches. Quinn dumped a can of chicken noodle soup into a saucepan.

"Katherine, a gentle reminder that our foursome is going to the Micro tonight," Quinn said, keeping his back to her as he stirred in a can of water.

"It's the first I've heard of it, so how can it be a gentle reminder?"

"Well, *A Beautiful Mind* is playing at the Micro."

Katherine loved the Micro, a small, three-dollar theater that was housed in a yellow bungalow near Main Street.

"Quinn, the only reason I went to church today is that I had the wheelchair. There was no fear of anyone stepping on my foot."

"It might be a decade before *A Beautiful Mind* is playing at the Micro again." He glanced briefly over his shoulder at her.

"In a decade, you'll have to find sitters," Grandma said. Moving from the table to the stove, she placed three slices of bread, buttered side down, in the pan.

The two were ganging up on her. "I have a final tomorrow morning."

"Study for a couple of hours this afternoon," Quinn said.

"What happened to the good old-fashioned interrogatives?"

"What?"

"I hear a lot of declarative and imperative, and when it comes to dating, I'm quite fond of interrogative."

He nudged Grandma beside him at the stove. "I do believe our Katherine King is feeling better."

Maybe he didn't have it in him to ask her out.

He scratched the side of his neck, inhaled, and looked at her over his shoulder. "Our threesome would appreciate your company tonight, especially me."

"Another declarative, Quinn. Formally asking a woman out is a part of maturing."

He swallowed and glanced at Grandma. "We're, uh, Evans and I are hoping to double-date tonight. We thought we'd go to the Micro to see *A Beautiful Mind,* which is one of my favorite movies of all time." He sighed. "Would you go with me, Katherine?"

She raised her brows. He'd completed the challenge.

"No, thank you." If her foot were in running shape, now would have been a perfect time for flight.

"Katherine!" Grandma whispered.

"It's okay, Ethel. Do you mind if I make a call?"

"Yes, you don't need to ask." She flicked her wrist.

"Watch the soup for me, please." Exiting the kitchen, he flipped open his phone.

Over her shoulder, Grandma cast Katherine a look of disapproval. Then she mouthed, "I can't believe you."

"Hello, Evans, it's Quinn.—Yes, it was a good sermon. The reason I'm calling is I asked Katherine to double-date tonight with us at the Micro, and she said 'No, thank you.'"—There was silence before Quinn added, "I am, too."

Quinn sounded down. Katherine frowned. She couldn't eat with them at the table. It would be too uncomfortable.

"Grandma, can you have Quinn deliver lunch to my room?"

"Why?" Grandma set a hand on her hip.

"You know why." She maneuvered on crutches through the doorway into the living room, past Quinn on her way to the guest room.

"I agree. She has not been herself." Quinn was deliberately loud.

She lay on the twin bed and stared at the popcorn ceiling. His timing was poor. She had her first date with Brad tomorrow, and she shouldn't be going to a movie with Benton; she needed to focus.

She reached over and turned on the bedside lamp, and then she opened the textbook for Lewis and Clark and stared blindly at the page. Someone knocked on the door. It wasn't Grandma's rap.

"Come in."

Quinn entered empty-handed, swung a folding chair that was positioned near Grandma's sewing machine close to the bed, and sat down, facing her.

"Katherine, I was wondering . . ." He cleared his throat. "If you would go with me to the Micro tonight to see *A Beautiful Mind*?"

It was strange. Last week she would have begged and pleaded to see Quinn behave so pitifully in love, but this week, after all she'd been through, she was numb.

"No, thank you." She returned her gaze to the textbook.

"Why?"

She curled the toes on her left foot. "I . . ." Turning, she looked into his deep brown eyes. "I have to study for my test."

"You've been ready for weeks."

Turning her profile to him, she read the top paragraph of the left page.

"Katherine, would you go with me to the Micro tonight to see *A Beautiful Mind*?"

She looked directly in his somber gaze. "No, thank you."

He smiled softly. "It doesn't hurt as much the third time." He rose and returned the chair to its place near the sewing machine.

"Katherine." He paused, setting his hand on the door molding. "Would you go with me to the Micro tonight to see *A Beautiful Mind*?"

"No."

He smiled. "It doesn't hurt as much the fourth time."

The man was hopeless!

In Quinn's absence, she studied for at least five minutes before he delivered her lunch tray. He waited for her to sit up a little taller against the headboard before setting the wood tray on her lap.

"Katherine."

She almost started her response with "Yes," but caught herself. "What, Benton?"

"Tonight Evans, Cindy, and I are going to the Micro. You know the yellow historic bungalow near one of the busiest intersections in Moscow? *A Beautiful Mind* is one of my favorite films, and I haven't seen it for quite some time."

"It only came out last year."

"Yes, well, I was wondering if you'd care to join us. The Micro is an intimate little theater with seating for probably one-hundred, one-hundred and twenty people at the most, and we can get you a seat near the wall where you wouldn't worry about anyone stepping on your foot."

"No, thank you."

He swung the folding chair next to the bed again, sat down, and faced her.

"Why not?" Eyes wide and full of emotion, he studied her.

"I have a test tomorrow, and I also have my first date with Brad, and I want to be focused for both."

"Evans was right; I am a distraction for you." He smiled.

He'd always been. Was it simply meeting Brad, or was it when he'd upped her medication that her heartache became manageable?

"Quinn, are you eating in there too?" Grandma asked from the kitchen.

"No, I'll be there shortly."

When Quinn returned a half hour later to retrieve her tray, she pretended to be asleep. He reached across her for her tray and paused for a moment before he left. In the midst of pretending, she actually fell asleep and was awakened two hours later by the phone ringing in the next room.

After two rings, Grandma answered. "Hello. Yes, please, wait a minute. I'll get her for you." She appeared in the doorway. "Telephone."

"Who is it?" Katherine yawned.

"I can't keep track."

Katherine rolled her eyes and went into her new routine of carefully getting out of bed, hopping on her left foot to her crutches, and maneuvering to the phone.

"Hello."

"Hi, Katherine, it's Quinn."

Grandma was conveniently in the kitchen.

"Would you go with me to the Micro tonight to see *A Beautiful Mind*?"

"No, thank you." She hung up on him.

"Grandma, you knew it was Quinn!"

"He said to tell you that I couldn't keep track. So that's what I did."

The phone rang. Katherine picked it up. "Hello."

"Hi, Katherine, it's Quinn. Would you go with me to the Micro tonight to see *A Beautiful Mind*?"

"Quinn, I'm trying to study. Get a life." Again, she hung up on him.

"Katherine!" Grandma said from the kitchen.

"That's the seventh or eighth time he's asked me."

"Oh, dear."

The phone rang. Katherine answered it. "Hello."

"Hi, Katherine, it's Quinn. Would you go with me to the Micro tonight to see *A Beautiful Mind*?"

"A beautiful mind is not what you are depicting at the moment." She hung up on him. She pulled a chair next to the phone and waited for it to ring, but it appeared that he was taking a break. After five minutes, she returned to the guest room.

The phone didn't ring.

Not only was Quinn providing her with study time, he was also giving her a chance to call Brad and cancel. She knew the man! She recalled the sweet sentiments Brad had written in his card. For some reason, she'd opened up to him when she was on morphine, and it was probably because of his warm hazel eyes, or were they blue? Or maybe it was simply because she needed someone unbiased to talk to.

Had Quinn given up now that she'd declined him nine, or was it ten, times? She studied Lewis and Clark until she couldn't keep her eyes open. The phone rang in the other room. There was no way she could hobble on crutches and make it in four rings.

"Katherine, it's for you," Grandma said.

"Who is it?"

"Lover boy."

Which lover boy? She crutched into the living room. She had to be careful about not saying "no" too quickly and hanging up.

"Hello."

"Katherine, it's Quinn. I was hoping we'd reconcile. One of my favorite movies of all time is playing at the Micro, *A Beautiful Mind.* It's directed by Ron Howard and received four Academy Awards and a Rotten Tomatoes rating of seventy-eight percent. I was hoping you don't have plans."

"I'm sorry, I've seen it."

"Yes, well, so have I, but it's one of those films where once is not enough. And from my experience, it's even more enjoyable the second time because you're not so keyed up about his delusions."

"How many times have you seen it?"

"This will be my third. Will you go, Katherine?"

"I feel like I've mastered Lewis and Clark, and I was just thinking that I'll reread *American Scripture* for the evening."

"I'll buy you popcorn and a root beer, and we'll sit with Evans and Cindy and . . ."

"I'll think about it."

"Good." Click.

He hung up on her.

Katherine moved to the couch and rested her foot on the coffee table.

"Grandma, do you mind getting *American Scripture* for me? It's in my bag from the hospital."

"Are you going with Quinn?"

She shrugged. "I haven't decided yet."

"When a girl says, 'I'll think about it,' it always gives a fellow hope."

"I honestly am thinking about it."

"I think you've been horrible."

"The experience has probably been good for him, Grandma. I think Benton has a difficult time asking women out."

"Most men do."

"I don't think he's had to do it very much," Katherine said.

"He made up for it today!"

Chapter Fifty-Two

The back door opened and closed. In the kitchen, someone set down what sounded like a brown paper shopping bag on the table. Grandma remained seated in the recliner, working a crossword puzzle from the Moscow-Pullman newspaper.

"Who's in the kitchen, Grandma?" Katherine asked.

"Quinn. He's making bacon-and-cheese omelets for dinner."

"I thought you said he doesn't eat pork."

"Well, he did the other day. He usually doesn't eat pork chops."

Katherine shook her head and reread the start of the seventh chapter of *American Scripture*. The smell and sounds of bacon frying permeated the living room.

"I hope he doesn't burn the bacon this time." Grandma slid her pencil behind one ear. "I better put the fan on." Rising from the recliner, she went into the kitchen, opened the window above the sink, and turned the fan on above the stove.

"Don't worry, I'm not leaving the kitchen this time," Quinn said over the crackle of the bacon frying.

"I wasn't worried." The dishwasher creaked open, and Grandma added to the noises in the kitchen as she unloaded it.

Ten minutes later, Quinn entered the living room. "Dinner's almost ready."

Over the top of the hardback novel, Katherine studied him. He wore khaki shorts and a Princeton-orange polo shirt. From fifteen feet away, she detected pine cologne. Her stomach knotted. Tonight was a date.

Uneasiness coursed through her like morphine—maybe she'd gone too long without painkillers. "I'm still going tomorrow. Just because I'm going to see *A Beautiful Mind* with the professors' group does not mean I have any intentions of canceling Brad tomorrow."

Quinn gazed at her softly and smiled.

"You should have worn that polo last Friday."

"Why?"

"It's Princeton orange."

"Well, then, it's perfect for tonight."

"Why?"

"You'll figure it out." He winked.

After a delicious omelet, Katherine brushed her hair and looked in the medicine cabinet mirror. Her eyes beheld a hazy sparkle. *Boy, all of a sudden Mr. I Want knows what he wants.* She still wore the same outfit she'd worn to church, her jean skirt, a jade-green short-sleeved shirt, and a brown leather belt.

Grandma knocked on the bathroom door. "You better hurry up. Brush your teeth and put some Dentyne in your purse."

"Grandma!"

Ж

The Micro Theater was in an older bungalow home on Third Street near one of the busiest intersections in Moscow. Katherine and Quinn waited in the foyer for Cindy and Evans.

"I'll get us a large popcorn. What would you like to drink?" Quinn asked.

"Root beer's great; thanks."

With a smile, she watched him as he stood in line. Though he was comfortably dressed, Quinn looked amazingly handsome. A smile lit her lips. She was quite possibly the second love of his life. Her eyes widened at her premature thinking; that is after she took care of Brad tomorrow and Quinn took care of Miss Palouse this Friday.

The snack area was roomy, with large paisley maroon carpeting. Katherine glanced at a couple leaning against the wall—Joe Hillis talked with Anna, from the Chinese restaurant.

She smiled as Joe approached holding Anna's hand.

"Kate, what happened to you?"

"I stepped on a broken wine bottle last week while swimming in the Palouse River." She steadied her crutches.

"Bummer. Do you remember Anna?"

"Of course." Katherine smiled. "Anna, it's nice to see you again."

"Joe talks about you a lot," Anna said.

Holding two drinks and cradling a large popcorn, Quinn neared Katherine's left elbow.

"Quinn, remember Joe Hillis, and this is his girlfriend, Anna."

"The professor again?" Joe grinned, meeting Katherine's gaze. Several years ago his charm had completely entangled her, and now they were the best of friends. In hindsight, she could see God's hand in all that had taken place.

"There you two are," Evans said. "We were afraid we were running late."

"Cindy, Evans," Quinn said, waving them over. "Meet Joe Hillis and his girlfriend, Anna. Joe's one of Katherine's friends from years ago."

"Oh, uh, hello, Joe." Evans held out his hand. "I remember reading about you in the *Argonaut*, a tennis player."

Cindy also shook Joe's hand.

The professors' group sat in the back row of the intimate theater. At the end of the row near the wall, Katherine felt secure that no one would step on her foot. Quinn tucked the crutches beneath the seats. Evans and Quinn sat in the middle of the foursome. Evans set down his soda, elbowed Quinn, and then set his arm around Cindy. Quinn set down his soda and then, lifting his arm a tad, looked at Katherine.

She shook her head. Were the men up to something? The Please No Smoking sign spanned the screen. They hadn't even gotten to the previews, and Quinn was attempting to set his arm around her.

"Quinn," she whispered, "this is a public place, and you like your job."

He smiled. "I'm glad you didn't mention Hungerbottom." He popped a kernel of popcorn into his mouth.

She glanced across the aisle and down about five rows at Joe. His arm was already around Anna. For some reason, Joe glanced back at her. By the crane of his neck, he was trying to see if there was anything he could tease her about.

Katherine cuddled a little closer to Quinn. Joe grinned.

"I saw that, Katherine," Quinn said.

"Well, I was looking over there when he glanced back here, and I didn't want him to think I was looking at him. Because I wasn't. I was looking at them. They look happy together."

"I think so too, except he keeps looking at you."

Katherine sighed. "Thanks for the popcorn and root beer . . . and movie and . . . the omelet."

"Shh . . ." he whispered. "We're about to watch *A Beautiful Mind,* and that's not what you are portraying at the moment."

She'd have liked to dump her soda all over him, but resisted the temptation and sipped it instead.

"Crud!" Benton blurted out.

"Shh!" Evans said. "Previews are my favorite part."

"It's her, the loon!" Quinn stared at a dark-haired woman two rows behind Joe.

"Did she see you?" Evans asked.

"Yes, two seconds ago, she scoped out the theater."

"She's looking back here," Evans whispered. "Kiss Katherine."

Wide-eyed, Katherine stared at the back of Joe's head.

"No, Evans!" Quinn said.

"Katherine." He sighed, turning toward her. "It's the loon, the Uniontown woman who liked me, I mean *really* liked me."

"Remain calm." She stared straight ahead at the screen and questioned if this was all a part of some scheme.

Quinn let out a heavy sigh.

"Remain calm. She'll probably think we're a couple because you're seated beside me."

While the first preview played, Quinn turned to look at her. A little bit of the projector light caught the upper half of his face, and in the dimly lit room, the emotion in his eyes surprised her. Open, raw fragility. How could she have green tea with Brad tomorrow when Benton could look at her like this?

He'd never pursued a second date, never tried to hold anyone else's hand, because—she smiled—all along he'd been in love with her.

She gave in a little, with a gaze that told him: As soon as I've graduated, we are going to make out.

The next preview started, and Evans cleared his throat. "Good thing we sat in the back, Cindy, don't you think?"

Katherine stared at the screen. Quinn's shoulder bore into hers. The loon, whoever she was, glanced back at them a couple of times. Joe did too, grinning.

John Nash, the main character in the movie, was a student at Princeton University. That's why Benton wore his Princeton-orange polo. In the dark, in the last row of the theater, she smiled and relaxed against his shoulder.

Ж

"I've always feared running into her somewhere," Benton said during their drive home. "I don't need to worry ever again. Thank you, Katherine."

"I've forgotten how you met Miss Uniontown." Uniontown was a small, back-roads town, far removed from the highway, on the way to Lewiston. Tall silos dotted the rolling landscape.

"In March, Evans and I went to Uniontown for their annual Sausage Feed. It's a great event. While we waited in the food line, Evans got to telling some of the people around us that I'd recently started dating again. Casual conversation. Miss Uniontown wasn't really a date. It was more of a gastronomical extravaganza that felt like a date. Evans and I loaded our plates with sausage, mashed potatoes, and sauerkraut, and when we sat down, the loon sat down across from me. She wouldn't leave me alone. Ask Evans, he witnessed the whole ordeal."

"I believe you."

"Katherine, I want you to know, I usually don't approve of public displays of affection."

She smiled. "It's my turn to apologize. I have an outing tomorrow, and I'm sorry if I got your hopes up."

He sighed. "Please don't ever look at me that way and apologize, Katherine. It doesn't sit well."

She gazed out the window at the passing moonlit streets.

"In two weeks, Katherine." He reached across the console for her hand—"You'll no longer be my student, and I can court you wholeheartedly."

In the meantime, was he only courting her halfheartedly?

"Don't forget Miss Palouse, Quinn." Her voice sounded hollow.

"I forgot her six days ago." Had it been only six days since her accident?

Was he trying to break her? That was what tonight was all about—breaking Katherine King. She leaned her head back against the headrest and closed her eyes.

Chapter Fifty-Three

At 9:42 a.m. it was official: Brad was running late.

"Did you give him directions?" Grandma looked out the window above the kitchen sink.

"No, he never asked. I assumed he looked at my admittance papers."

"Does he drive a big cream soda colored truck?"

"I don't know."

"He's here," Grandma said, lifting her chin.

Feeling a tad uneasy, Katherine remained seated at the kitchen table.

"And he's wearing a Hawaiian shirt just like your Uncle Will's."

When it came to Hawaiian shirts, Uncle Will's philosophy was the brighter, the better. With two ballpoint pens in the front pocket of her Levi's skirt, Katherine crutched to the back door. Through the top glass, she caught a brief glimpse of bright orange and blue hues. Maybe Brad's taste in shirts was the reason he hadn't married at an earlier age. When she opened the door, she needed sunglasses.

"Good morning, Katherine. Hi, Ethel." He looked past Katherine into the kitchen, where Grandma stood drying her hands. "Has Katherine told you I won't get her home until later this afternoon?"

Grandma nodded. "My brother-in-law wears Hawaiian shirts just like yours."

"Where does he find them, do you know?"

"The Salvation Army in Spokane."

Brad chuckled. "Sounds like he gets a better deal than I do."

She needed a hoisting crane to get up into his Dodge quad cab Cummins diesel truck. Katherine leaned her crutches in the open door.

"I may have to give you a boost." He chuckled.

Using his arm for leverage, she got her left foot up to the floorboard, and he pushed her up the rest of the way. It was an awkward, humbling experience.

He slid behind the wheel. "I need a heavy-duty truck to tow my boat."

She tried to remember his hospital attire. It had been far more subdued. "How's Quinn Benton?" He glanced at her as he drove west toward campus.

Wide-eyed, Katherine stared straight ahead. "Fine. Why?" Maybe he'd heard about the Micro. Maybe someone from the hospital had also been at the theater last night.

"Has he come to his senses yet?"

"About . . . ?" Katherine stalled.

"About you, of course." Brad glanced across the cab at her.

"He's been more attentive since the hospital, yes."

"Nurse Kitty used to date one of my good friends. She told me her blind date with Quinn was a disappointment." Brad drove up to the Admin Building and parked near the registrar's office. The man knew his way around campus.

"I'll drop you off here and find parking. Wait for me. I'll walk you up."

He'd have to park somewhere a permit wasn't required. He might have quite the trek. "Thanks, Brad."

He slid the wheelchair out of the back of the truck and half lifted, half assisted her out of the cab. After she was seated, he set the chair's parking brake. "I'll meet you here."

Katherine maneuvered the wheelchair to a less conspicuous spot in the shade of a large nearby elm tree. Classes were in session, so only a handful of students milled outside. At this very moment, Benton's Civil War class was in full swing.

"Lord, I feel anxious. Help me to handle Brad right. I pray he doesn't like me too much. In Jesus's name, amen."

Several minutes later, Brad's bright Hawaiian shirt announced his return as he strode around the side of the brick building. She rolled the wheelchair into the sunlight and waved as he drew near.

"Katherine . . ." Someone chuckled.

Without turning to look peripherally, she knew it was Joe.

"For being injured, you get around, Kate." He halted a few feet away.

"Hi, Joe. How did you like the movie last night?" Placing her hand over her eyes, she saw Brad approach, about eight yards away.

"Not as much as you did. Anna and I are more *Romancing the Stone* types."

Katherine swallowed. "Joe, meet Brad, my doctor."

"Nice to meet you, Joe." Brad held out his hand.

Joe's forehead wrinkled. He shook Brad's hand, looking sideways at her.

"Brad's taking me to a makeup exam." Katherine felt healthy blood flow enter her face.

"Uh, call me, Kate. We need to catch up." Joe openly studied Brad. "Anna doesn't want me calling you anymore, so you'll have to call me."

She nodded.

Brad pushed her wheelchair toward the registrar's entrance. "Do you two keep in touch?"

"Yes, we're good friends. We both played tennis for the U of I team. He's the head coach here now."

"Did I detect a slight look of disapproval?" Brad glanced back over his shoulder.

"Maybe." Katherine left it at that.

They took the elevator to the third floor. Brad pushed her wheelchair down the hallway. Katherine gripped her hands in her lap and reminded herself that Quinn, Evans, and Cindy were all in class—there was no chance of running into them.

At the end of the hallway sat Anita Dougal, the hall secretary.

"Hi, I'm Katherine King. I missed Professor Fancy's midterm exam and—"

"I have it right here for you." Anita lifted a painted rock paperweight off her desk and handed her an essay booklet, a white sheet of exam questions, and a clipboard.

Brad steered her chair behind the secretary's desk and set the parking brake. Katherine glanced around. There was no place for him to sit, and he'd brought a glossy *Powerboat* magazine. She would have sworn there was usually a chair to the right of Anita's desk.

"It'll take me a full hour, Brad. I'm sorry; I didn't know there wouldn't be seating."

"There's the library or the Commons," Anita said.

"I'll check out the Commons. Good luck." He winked at Katherine.

"Thanks."

Learn from this: Never have your German doctor wearing a Hawaiian shirt bring you to an exam in the same hallway as the professor you're in love with. It's very, very awkward.

Ж

Out of the three essay questions, Katherine chose Question B: How accurate is the following : The Lewis and Clark expedition was an example of egalitarianism. The trials of the trail brought a diverse group of people together, turning the expedition into an idealized "American melting pot." Refute or support this interpretation. With her head bowed, Katherine began writing.

She glanced at her watch. Four minutes were left to wrap up her conclusion. Despite her minimal study over the weekend, her thoughts flowed. She quickly skimmed through the essay before turning it in to Anita. From there, she maneuvered her wheelchair out into the main hallway. She didn't have to wait long before Brad jogged up the stairs.

There was a wholesomeness about him that shone.

"The Commons is a happening place." He wheeled her chair into the elevator.

"Yes, it's definitely the hangout. Did you get something to drink?"

"Yes, a SoBe."

"You sound like a health nut."

"Not really."

He drove north of town, past Rosauer's Grocery, for a quarter of a mile before turning right into a newer development, and then left into the driveway of a traditional-style, two-story home. The yard was small; the shop that Quinn had envisioned appeared to be the attached four-car garage.

"I heard your garage is full of water sports equipment."

He chuckled. "My motto is every man has to have at least one or two boats to work on." He hopped out and swung open her door.

Apprehension kicked in. "Have you taken a patient home before?"

"No, this is a first, I promise." He waited while she swiveled herself to face him, and he again assisted her during the last three-foot drop.

"I go in through the back. The alarm's there." He unlocked the side garage door, and the warning alarm buzzed until he pressed a four-digit code. Next, he flipped on the overhead lights. A glossy yellow boat on a trailer was in the first bay, and a longer, bright red boat was parked at an angle across two bays. "This one's my pride and joy." He pointed to the Santa-red boat. "It's a twenty-seven foot Hallett with an inboard engine, in case anyone asks."

"Where do you go boating around here?" She leaned against her crutches.

"The Snake's only a half hour away." Two newer-looking jet skis filled the triangular gap between the boats.

"You have a theme."

He chuckled and led her through the mudroom to a sparsely furnished great room. The mismatched furniture looked secondhand while the new monster-screen television probably cost several thousand dollars.

He's a bachelor, she reminded herself.

"That's the most comfortable seat in the house." He nodded toward a worn, dark green upholstered couch with paisley print. She leaned the crutches against the side of the coffee table before sitting down.

Behind her, a cupboard opened and closed. "I have several flavors of green teas and decaf."

"Plain ole green tea is great."

"That's how I am. I don't care much for the flavored stuff." Turning toward the sink, he filled the mugs at the instant hot water tap.

"Do you have any buddies that you boat with?"

"I usually go with my brother who lives in Lewiston. There're a doctor and a male nurse at the hospital that have gone with me a few times. Not everyone's comfortable in a boat going eighty plus."

"Eighty miles per hour?"

"Yes." He set two mugs down on the scratched coffee table in front of her.

"The last time I went boating, I blew a head on the Hallett. So I'm down to the Old Yeller." He sat down a foot away from her and stretched his right arm along the back of the couch behind her.

The afternoon might prove more difficult than she'd foreseen. For a moment, she prayed with her eyes wide open.

"I have a younger brother who's into motorcycles, but never boats," she said.

"What about your dad's hobbies?"

"He's very much a family man . . . camping, Boy Scouts, and now a few grandchildren."

"Have you heard the acronym phrase for *boat*?"

"No." Even their conversation had a theme.

"Break out another thousand." He grinned.

"Good thing you're a doctor."

He grinned. "I always carry tools and spare parts. I have a half Craftsman rollaway under the deck of my Hallett."

"Your other boat doesn't break down as much?"

"Only because it's rarely in the water." Returning his mug to the table, he swiveled to face her.

She looked around for a coaster but didn't see one. Water spots marred the surface of the wood coffee table. She set her mug down and straightened her skirt.

"How do you feel about Zhivago?" He knit his blond brows.

Boy, he'd gotten right to the point. She shrugged. "I'm a little mad at him. I almost died. Didn't I?"

"Yes."

"I almost died, and I had a young German doctor show an interest in me, and he didn't appear to come to his senses until Saturday, and I'd accepted your offer by that time."

Brad smiled softly and looked at the four inches of worn couch cushion between them. "He came to his senses?"

"Yes." She sat up a little taller. "He pummeled me with *I wants*."

"What do you mean?" Brad's eyes narrowed.

"You know . . . 'I want to spend more time with you. I want you to stop thinking about . . .'" Maybe it was due to the glimmer of hope in Brad's eyes, but her mind went blank.

"Have you been thinking about Dr. Ungerbach?"

She gripped her hands together tight against her tummy. She shouldn't have mentioned the *I wants.*

"You're a great guy, Brad, and . . ." To protect Quinn, it was best she not say another word.

"Sounds like you were ready to be his girl."

"I was. Maybe in a few weeks when I've graduated."

"Well, if it's any consolation, Kitty said that during their date, most of their conversation revolved around you. That even his prayer at the table included you."

A wave of warm emotion engulfed her. "That's kind of you to tell me." She looked at the coffee table. "You didn't have to tell me that." Tears ebbed, and she swallowed a large lump in her throat. Quinn had prayed with one of his blind dates, and about her.

"Should I take you home now?"

Chapter Fifty-Four

Katherine picked her mug up off the coffee table and peered inside. There was only half a gulp left. Brad rose and took the mug from her. Was he going to pick up his car keys from on top of the granite island? Instead, reusing the tea bag, he refilled the mug at the hot water tap and then returned to set the mug on the coffee table in front of her.

He maneuvered into the far corner of the couch and studied her.

"I've felt numb lately. Could it be the drugs?"

"I doubt it." He shook his head. "After a near-death experience, sometimes people look at life differently."

"I don't want to just talk about me," she whispered.

"I do."

She sighed. "If you could be a doctor in any American war, what war would you want it to be?"

"I was just reminded that you are a history buff. Hmmm . . ." He placed an arm along the top of the couch. "For American wars, the Civil War's main anesthetic was chloroform, definitely not my choice. If I remember correctly, the Civil War was the first time Quinine was used to treat typhoid fever."

"It was."

He nodded. "I would have to say I'd prefer a more modern war. There would be less shock, suffering, a higher percentage of success, lives saved.

"Good question, Katherine. That's one I've never been asked on a first date before."

Like she'd foreseen, green tea was their first date.

During the drive home, he cleared his throat. "Do you have anything planned tomorrow?"

She intertwined her fingers in her lap. "I have a date next Friday with Quinn that should answer a lot of questions for me. I'd like not to clutter my head too much because of it."

"Are you saying I only have until Friday?"

Was he kidding?

He stopped first in line at a red light at the intersection of Third Street and Highway 95, and looked over at her. Though Brad appeared completely serious, she was tempted to peer over her shoulder at the Micro Theater, which sat one block west.

"You're beautiful, intelligent, and honest, Katherine. Three qualities that, from my dating experience, don't often merge."

Off in the distance, the one-way, three-lane road curved around a large grain silo. She reminded herself of his extreme sports. "And, you like challenges?"

"How about I pick you up after lunch tomorrow, and we head to Lewiston?" He glanced from the red light to her. "We'll boat in the afternoon, and there's a little diner that we can eat dinner at and still have a nice view of the boat."

It sounded funny, but she knew what he meant. "With my foot and all—"

"I won't go fast; it'll be more of a scenic boat ride."

"I don't think so, Brad. I have studies and meds; already my brain feels cluttered."

"You're giving me hope." He grinned.

She peered over her shoulder at the Micro Theater. Did Evans and Benton plan the loon? Maybe it had been pure luck that the woman glanced back at him. The loon could have been any woman off the street.

"Katherine. Earth to Katherine." Brad cleared his throat.

"I'm sorry . . . Brad." She sighed and gave into her epiphany. "They knew we were having green tea today, and they did their best to confuse me."

"The professors' group?"

Did they want what was best for her? Evans had tried to set her up with Carl. Quinn blind dated small-town women every week. And now, she'd allowed her professor to kiss her, and he hadn't even met Miss Palouse yet.

"Yes, the professors' group."

Ж

Grandma made a pot of decaf coffee and joined Katherine at the kitchen table. Setting her elbows on the Formica tabletop, Grandma gripped the mug with both hands.

"Quinn stopped by on his way home for lunch and asked if you were home yet. I told him no. He looked like a lost little boy, Katherine. I wish you could have been here to see his face."

The viselike grip only briefly squeezed her heart. "My time with Brad was enjoyable, Grandma."

Grandma adjusted her glasses. "Cindy called too. What a sweetheart. We became best friends at the hospital. She wants to have a potluck at her house next Sunday."

"That'll be fun, Grandma. What are we going to bring?"

"I think I'll make Carol's raspberry Jell-O salad again." Grandma rose from the table, opened a cupboard, and pulled down her wooden recipe box.

The phone rang. "That phone has never rung as much in its life as it has this summer." Grandma giggled. "Hello.—Yes, she's here, Quinn. I'll get her for you." She covered the receiver. "It's four thirty, which means he's finished with his office hours and is on his way home. He's probably in the car."

Using one crutch, Katherine carried her mug to the sink. She took the receiver from Grandma and hopped to a chair at the mahogany dining table in the living area and sat down.

"Hello."

"Hi, Katherine, it's Quinn. How did you feel about your exam this morning?"

"Considering everything, it flowed."

"Yes, that's what Cindy thought, too. She gave you an A. I was in her office when she read through it."

"Good. What did you give me on the last exam?"

"I haven't graded them yet."

"That's not like you, Mr. Punctual."

"Ask him if he's coming to dinner," Grandma said from the kitchen.

Katherine paused. "Did you hear that?"

"Yes. Ask her what I can bring."

"Grandma, what do you want Benton to bring?" Katherine held the receiver toward the kitchen.

"Tell him I just want him to get my little kettle barbecue going. I thought we'd have burgers. I even made a macaroni salad."

"Did you hear that, Benton?"

"Yes. Prepare me, Katherine. How did it go today?"

"It went better than I expected. He's a nice guy."

"Uh-huh. Did he ask you out for a second date?"

"Yes."

"Did you accept?"

"I'm a little undecided."

"I see." There was a slight pause. "What time does Ethel want me to start the barbecue?"

Ж

In the shade of the crabapple tree in the backyard, Grandma set up lawn chairs. Benton dumped a quarter bag of briquettes in the bottom of the barbecue. After squeezing lighter fluid on top, he lit a match.

"I'll let it heat up for a while." He sat in the remaining chair on the other side of Grandma.

"I'll go get the patties and condiments ready." Grandma pushed herself out of her lawn chair.

Alone with Benton, Katherine set her hands in her lap and tried to relax. "How was your day, Mr. Benton?"

"Good. I'm still grading midterms. Have I addressed the Quinn List with you yet?"

"No, I've been curious about your response."

"Sometime soon, I'd like you to come over to my place, and we'll go over it together, line by line."

"Why can't we read it here?"

"I'd prefer to discuss it at my place."

"Why?" She studied his somber brown eyes.

"Because."

She waited for him to elaborate further, but he didn't. "What did you think?"

"I'd prefer to discuss it at my place."

"Benton, you're a mystery."

"I am. So green tea was your first date; what's he planning for your second?" He rose to check the briquettes.

"He invited me to Lewiston to meet his brother, and maybe go boating and have dinner at some diner where we can see his boat."

"Hmmm . . . what kind of boat?"

"A bright yellow, sixteen footer something."

"Hmmm."

"So this Friday is Miss Palouse?"

He sat down, this time in the lawn chair beside her. "You know meeting her is now just a formality."

She wanted to pen his words in the journals of her heart.

"Will you be at Evans's?" he asked.

"Right now my Friday's free. Next week's Miss Wazzu. What else do you know about her?"

The sunlight that filtered through the leaves of the crabapple tree brought out amber highlights in his dark hair. "She's pursuing her MA in US history, supposedly very bright and, according to Mashburn, very attractive."

"I haven't met Mashburn."

"He's eccentric." Quinn shrugged. "A retired history professor from Wazzu. His wife is his equal in both IQ and physical appearance, which leaves Mashburn's taste in women up for grabs."

"What's Miss Wazzu's phone voice like?"

"Evans is getting her number for me. I haven't spoken to her yet."

"Are they all rolling into one yet?" She smiled.

"A little. I'm waiting to see what happens with you and Brad. After Miss Palouse, I'd like to be finished with blind dating."

He deserved some kind of medal for his honesty. She reached out and squeezed his hand. A warm sparkle replaced the somberness in his eyes.

Grandma opened the window above the sink. "Phone, Katherine," she bellowed.

"Who is it, Grandma?"

"Joe."

"Get his number, and she can call him back on my phone." Rising to his feet, Quinn strolled toward the house.

Grandma descended the steps and handed him a plate of hamburger patties and a sticky note. "Tell her it wasn't Joe, it was Brad." Grandma shook her head and waved. "I can't keep track."

Katherine closed her eyes.

Quinn chuckled. Using a spatula, he transferred the patties to the barbecue rack and, then he handed her the sticky note and his phone.

"Press *send* after you're through dialing." He sat down beside her, gripping the chair's arms.

"Brad probably heard Grandma yell out the window that it was Joe—didn't he?"

"Yes, and now you're calling him from Quinn Benton's mobile phone."

"Should I go in the house?"

He shrugged.

"Do you mind asking Grandma what she told him?" Katherine glanced toward the kitchen window.

Quinn crossed the lawn. This was the part about dating she didn't like—hurting a guy's feelings. In his absence, Katherine silently prayed. "Lord, help me to be wise and to handle both men with love. Amen." Quinn soon returned to sit in the chair beside her.

"I'm not sure if you want to hear what Ethel said."

"What'd she say?" Katherine inhaled and tried to prepare herself.

"She told him that you are sitting in the shade of the crabapple tree with me. And that it would be easier for you to call him from my mobile phone than for you to limp into the house."

"She sure knows how to paint a pretty picture."

Quinn chuckled. "She's had that talk with you, too."

Katherine dialed Brad's number and pressed *send*.

"Hello." Brad picked up immediately.

"Hi, it's Katherine calling from Quinn Benton's phone." It was almost exactly what she'd said a month ago to Carl when she'd leaned against Quinn beneath the maple tree on Lewis Street.

"Yes. Hi. I regret that I didn't invite you to just stay for dinner tonight while you were here." He paused. "Why is Quinn there?"

"Grandma invited him over for a barbecue."

"Does that happen very often?"

Leaning into her left shoulder, Quinn was undoubtedly listening. "My grandmother and Quinn are close. Quinn dines here a few times a week."

She waited for Brad to say something, but he was quiet. "Are you still there, Brad?"

"Yes, should I be?"

Oh, if she could only walk to the front of the house.

"I agree; it's an awkward situation."

"Common sense tells me not to get any more involved than I already am. I'm sorry, Katherine."

She closed her eyes. "I am, too."

The line went dead. She clicked *end* and handed it back to Quinn.

"I'm sorry, Katherine, it's because of my being here. Isn't it?"

"Most likely." Katherine sighed and looked toward the lilac bush near the corner of the house. Brad had been so attentive at the hospital, such a buoy to her spirits.

"I'm still trying to figure out what you two have in common."

"Benton!"

"Besides me, name two things that you have in common."

"We both like plain green tea, and he's a Christian."

"What do you think about his hobbies?"

"Water is a common theme. Enough, Benton, I'll have nothing new to share on Friday night if you keep pummeling me with questions."

He smiled. "After dinner, we're going to my house."

"I prefer the interrogative approach."

"Katherine . . ." Quinn cleared his throat. "After dinner dishes, will you go with me to my place?"

"No." Why his place?

"Based on last night and our personal history, you surprise me."

He was referring to the Micro. The back door creaked open, and Grandma started down the steps carrying a platter.

"I hope you two aren't arguing again." Grandma placed the large white platter that boasted rows of tomato and onion slices and lettuce leaves on the folding card table. "Katherine, what do you want on your burger?" Grandma set a bun on a sturdy paper plate.

"The works, please."

"Even onions?"

"Yes, Grandma!"

Ж

Quinn washed dishes. Katherine sat at the table and dried. Grandma put leftovers away and then pulled the pocket door closed as she exited to the living room.

Grandma!

Quinn folded the dishcloth and set it over the faucet.

"Katherine, would you please do me a very special favor?"

She finished drying the spoons and putting them away before she closed the silverware drawer and looked up at him.

"Please give me a week before you see Brad again?"

"What about Miss Wazzu?"

"I'll cancel."

"I have questions about Brad."

While Quinn winced, she questioned if she were indeed telling the truth. She was. She questioned how many miles per gallon his truck got, and if he often wore ridiculously bright Hawaiian shirts.

"I persevered through all your pocket-sized towns," she admitted during his silence.

"Was your perseverance painful?"

It had to be on account of the half tablet of painkiller medication that she could gaze into Quinn's eyes. "I tearfully prayed a lot."

"Tearfully?" He swallowed.

She nodded.

"And, now you're interested in someone else?"

"Brad said that after a life-threatening experience, people *sometimes* look at life differently and, I want you to meet Miss Palouse." Was next Friday night worth the present torture? Though she had questions about Brad, she knew she loved Quinn, and he finally desired to hear of her love for him.

"You're getting back at me. I was such a fool, Katherine. Stand up. Get your crutches. I have something to show you."

Chapter Fifty-Five

He parked in the narrow driveway that ran alongside his macadamia-nut-colored ranch-style duplex. She followed him to the brick walkway and up three steps to the front porch. He held open the screen door for her.

Whatever he had to show her was in the house.

"Take a seat on the couch. Would you like a glass of water?" He strode through the living room ahead of her.

"No, thanks." An ironing board was set up in the front room next to a hamper full of unfolded clothes. A wrinkled Yale-blue polo lay strewn over the board.

"You should wear your Wazzu-red polo next Friday." She sat down in the deep-cushioned couch. His front room had a slightly musty smell similar to his office; perhaps it was attributable to his collection of old books, which lined an open bookcase.

He pulled open a drawer in a roll-top desk. "Wazzu's red is more of a maroon, and I'm leaning strongly toward canceling Miss Wazzu."

"Where are you planning to meet?"

"Alex's is my favorite restaurant in Pullman."

The only entry into Alex's was a long, steep flight of stairs. Katherine grimaced.

"Where did I put it?" Quinn ran a hand distractedly through his hair.

If he were searching for her Quinn List, it would be a difficult hour.

"Found it!" With a wide smile, he sat down beside her, setting two papers on the coffee table in front of them. The paper nearest her was the list of all the reasons she'd never fall for Quinn Benton. She leaned toward him a bit to look at the other sheet. It was also her handwriting. The title read: *Why I will never fall for Joe Hillis again.*

Her heart stopped. Evans had provided him with ammunition.

"Evans was going to return it to you in one of your last essays, but he keeps forgetting to."

It was too much to grasp.

"I can't believe Evans shared it with you." She leaned against Quinn, gripping his arm.

"Do you see the contrast between the two?" His eyes sparkled as he held up the Quinn List. "Your first line regarding Joe was . . . *Not a Christian.* Your first line regarding me is *He dates merely to eliminate.* He chuckled. Two: *He's flighty . . . about women.* Three: *He's picky about women.* Four: *In the shade of an enormous maple tree, he was exactly what I needed him to be, a towering strength in the chaos of my social life.*" In case you didn't hear it, Katherine, that is a positive, not a negative. He cleared his throat, patting her knee. "I can't bring myself to read reason number five out loud. I'm not sorry that I kissed you, Katherine." He sighed.

"Your list is proof that you are in love with me. And you wanted to be the only woman in my life." He smiled.

"You weren't supposed to have both lists to compare and contrast."

"Evans is gifted at reading between the lines. Cindy was only so-so."

Tears rolled down her cheeks. She wiped them aside. It would be so perfect and easy to give in right now, but she already had put some hope and planning into Friday night, and besides, Quinn Benton had strung her out like Christmas lights into late July.

It was her turn.

"Katherine, I'll cancel Miss Wazzu if you tell Brad that you're in love with me."

Brad already knew. She suppressed a smile. "I have questions about him, and like you, I'd like to answer them."

"Katherine, I can't believe you said that." He searched her eyes. "You love me. Look at the way you're clinging to me. It almost broke your heart to tell me what you just did."

She sniffled.

As he cradled her face in his hands; there was so much love in his eyes.

He loved her. Really loved her.

"Are you still taking any of that pain medication?" He brushed her hair back away from her face.

"I'm down to half a tablet a day." She swallowed, was he going to finally kiss her again? Eyes wide, she bit her lower lip.

"Stop taking it. The Katherine King I know would never have this high of a pain threshold." He gathered her lists and strode across the room.

"I need to take you home now, Katherine. Get your crutches."

"Why?" He hadn't even kissed her!

Ж

Tuesday afternoon, Katherine answered the phone. It was Brad.

"I'm still in Lewiston. My brother and I are planning on boating again this evening, which means I won't return to Moscow tonight until after nine. Which will be too late to visit, won't it?"

Maybe Grandma's *persistent* comment was right. "Yes, I've been going to bed earlier than usual." She glanced back at Grandma in the kitchen.

"How has Quinn been?"

"Attentive."

"Does he have a blind date this week?"

"Yes, Miss Palouse. He's been trying to meet her for months. Hopefully, it will come together for him this Friday."

"So you're available Friday?"

"Well . . ." She curled the toes of her left foot. "It's become a tradition for me to attend the professors' group, in which we discuss Quinn's blind dates."

"How 'bout I take you to dinner Friday night, and we both attend the professors' group?"

"Brad . . ." Wouldn't that be a shocker. "I feel it's unfair to get your hopes up. I know how I feel about—"

"It's a chance I'm willing to take."

Ж

Quinn plunked Cindy's Lewis and Clark class notes on the coffee table beside Katherine's propped-up foot. "Your grandma waved me down at the gate."

He sat down on the sturdy coffee table, facing her, and regarded the seascape painting overhead. It was an old reproduction that nicely stretched the length of the couch.

"I wish you would have asked me if it was all right to bring Ungerbach to the professors' group." He shook his head. Brad would be there the same night as his recap of Claire. What was Katherine thinking?

"I'm sorry. I agree, but he was insistent. I need to be firmer with him."

"The man's insistency might get you down the aisle."

She gazed up at him, her eyes soft and full of emotion.

"Katherine, are you off your pain meds yet?"

"No." She clasped her hands together. "Brad says I'm taking such a small dose that it's like I already am."

As of late, her love for him was becoming more and more visible, like rainwater on waxy leaves, it glistened. And then she did things like inviting Brad to the professors' group.

"You know Miss Palouse is just a formality now for me." He wanted her to know, to dispel any doubts she might have of his love for her.

Wide-eyed, Katherine leaned forward and picked up the class notes. "Grandma said you left your book on the kitchen table."

She was dismissing him. After last night, it was such a blow. Exiting the room, he patted the molding to the kitchen doorway and glanced back at her. Her face was hidden behind Cindy's notes. He grabbed the book off the table, and on his way to the back gate, waved at Ethel in the yard. Weed in hand, she waved back, and then started toward him.

"You look disheveled, I mean distraught." Ethel ambled closer and using her forearm brushed her hair away from her eyes.

"Ethel . . ." He frowned, inhaled deeply and gathered composure. "Pray for me. I never thought Katherine would be a woman to play games, but she is."

Ethel nodded. "You know I hate being in the middle, Quinn. You're like family now, and your pain is like mine."

He waited for Ethel to add words of hope.

"My father, Pete Pettigrew, was an old-time boxer in the days when there'd be no limit to the rounds." She nudged her glasses higher up the bridge of her nose.

"Yes." He didn't like the direction the conversation was heading.

"He could outlast anyone. He'd always take more punches than he threw, and looked like a complete underdog until the end." Ethel swallowed. "He had incredible willpower, determination . . ."

Quinn waited for the punch line.

"Katherine's stamina for stubborn reminds me of him."

It felt more like a dose of reality than hope. Quinn glanced toward the house.

"And then on the day of her accident"—Ethel's eyes widened—"before she left the house, she was emotional for Katherine. She gave me a brief view past her King veneer into her tender heart and . . . you were there."

"What do you mean, Ethel? You're being vague."

"Stay in the ring."

A twinkle sparked in her round blue eyes.

He waved a hand toward the back door. "She just dismissed me. It's like her heart's had amnesia ever since she met Brad."

"She cried."

"Kings don't cry." He shook his head.

"The day of her accident before she drove Edwin's truck, she broke down and told me about the kiss and, she cried." Ethel shook her head. "She cried about you."

"What?" He started for the back door. Katherine cried. His heart returned to the front porch, her arms clasped about his neck, the delight in her eyes, the love.

"You can't tell her." Ethel's voice rose. "She'll never forgive me. She's a King and a Pettigrew, too…"

What was going on? Was Katherine putting up a wall till he met Claire? He'd never intended for the confusion, the heartache.

He pulled into his driveway and after turning off the engine, glanced at the book in the passenger seat. For all they knew, it could be Katherine's copy—*The Last of the Mohicans* beneath the cover. If it were, it would give him an excuse to return to the Kings' and end on a better note with Katherine before her date with Brad.

He flipped to the title page. It was indeed *American Scripture*. Bummer. A flash of yellow near the front caught his eye; a sticky note from Ethel.

When you are brokenhearted, I am close to you. Psalm 34:18. I'm praying for you, Ethel. Warm tears infused his eyes.

"Thank you, Lord, for these words of comfort, and Your timing." He let the verse sink in and soothe his soul.

Chapter Fifty-Six

The evening of Quinn's date with Miss Palouse, Katherine didn't want to recall any of the wonderful adjectives he'd used to describe Claire. Still a few came to mind—caring, nurturing, very down-to-earth, great listener, honest . . . She sounded like Mother Teresa. And for him to even pursue a blind date with her meant she was a Christian.

Katherine wiped a tear from her eye. Why had she accepted a date with Brad? She just wanted to wear her old comfy pajama pants, kick back, and watch a movie—one movie in particular.

After showering and changing into a lightweight cotton skirt and her white ruffled short-sleeved top, she crutched into the kitchen.

The front door bell rang.

"Who could that be? It's not your doctor." Grandma strode past her toward the door. "He called while you were in the shower. He said he'll be running a couple of hours late, an emergency surgery."

Katherine said a silent "Yippee" as she crutched across the living room.

"Hi, Mrs. King, is Katherine home?" It was Hannah holding a puppy.

"Hannah, you got your new puppy!" Katherine crutched closer. The puppy was adorable, glossy black with tan markings.

"We just got him today. He's only six-months-old, and his name's Bruno." The puppy stretched its neck to lick Hannah's cheek. "He's a dachshund."

"Oh, isn't he sweet." Grandma stroked his back.

"Can you tell your boyfriend thank you for me?" Hannah looked at Katherine.

"Uh . . ." She couldn't very well ask a ten-year-old *which boyfriend*? She swallowed. "Why? What did he do?"

"He put a twenty dollar bill in the fish bowl when I wasn't looking."

"Are you sure? Sure it was him?" Katherine leaned against her crutches.

"Yeah. You'd just got home from the hospital and, he said you were craving my lemonade."

Quinn Benton. Warm waves gushed at her heart.

"I saw the twenty dollar bill *after* he went back to your house. Bye." Hannah nuzzled the puppy against her cheek and then started down the porch steps.

"Congratulations, Hannah," Katherine called after her and sighed. Of all nights for Hannah to remind her of what a wonderful man Quinn was.

Not wanting to be alone, she sat at the kitchen table. Head bowed Grandma worked on a crossword puzzle, a dictionary near her elbow.

"Sharon canceled our get-together tonight. Her son's in town. It's just Pittsville. I looked forward to tonight all week, and . . ." Grandma shook her head. "What's wrong, honey? You look as depressed as . . ." She glanced at the calendar and bit her lower lip. "Tonight's Miss Palouse!"

Katherine nodded. "I don't think she canceled this time. Otherwise, we would have heard from him by now."

"After how moon doggy he's been the last few weeks, you don't have anything to worry about." Grandma patted her hand.

"I don't know. There's a bond between them. Before our kiss, she was all he could talk about. It was like the kiss changed Quinn's mind. Not me."

Grandma smiled and shook her head. "He was thinking about you before the kiss. Maybe he was trying to put a wedge between the two of you by talking about her? So he could live up to all the—" Grandma did a quotes sign midair—"rules of being a professor."

Despite Grandma's biased insight, tears collected in Katherine's eyes.

"Given how poorly you're feeling about Quinn, do you really think you should go out with your doctor tonight?"

"He knows how I feel about Quinn."

"Hmm . . ." Grandma's brows gathered. "Well, Dr. Brad also knows how *he* feels about you. It's not a good combination."

Grandma made her dilemma sound like a pizza. Was she being as dumb as a pizza box when it came to men? Maybe she just needed to tell God exactly what she wanted: I want Quinn Benton with no more games, no more small towns, and no anchovies.

"Honey, I keep waiting for the Lord to show you something, but He hasn't." Grandma closed her crossword puzzle book. "And now I feel like He's left it up to me."

"What do you mean?"

"Follow me." Grandma pushed her chair back from the table. "I have something to show you."

Why was she being so mysterious? Katherine crutched behind her through the living room.

Whatever it was that she wanted to show her was in her bedroom. Grandma closed her door behind them.

Katherine looked about the tidy room.

"Meet Miss Palouse." Grandma held a hand out to her side toward the back of the white-painted door, and, a bright full-color poster.

She'd seen Kitty the nurse and Marci the Realtor, but the woman who had plagued her heart the most was Claire. *Vote for Claire Westin or be run out of town.* Katherine stared at the poster of the attractive woman who was running both for mayor and Quinn Benton's heart.

Did he know that she was two possibly three decades older than him? Would he care?

"How long has it been here?" Katherine leaned on her crutches.

"Since the day that I got my hair cut in the town of Palouse at Fran's Beauty Parlor." Grandma suppressed a smile. "Fran, the gal who cut my hair, gave it to me."

Chapter Fifty-Seven

"How was your day, Katherine?" Brad smiled over the top of the elegant, leather-bound menu. The Best Western Inn was one of the nicest dining establishments in Moscow.

"I had a good day of studying." He'd already informed her of his day—one knee replacement, and an emergency surgery that had made their date two hours later than expected.

Because she'd already had dinner with Grandma, Katherine ordered a piece of chocolate cream pie.

"I'll have a porterhouse steak, medium rare, baked potato, and ranch dressing," Brad told the waitress.

"Did you make it to classes today?" he asked over the top of his water glass.

"Yes, Grandma took me and picked me up. I surprisingly didn't fall asleep in either of my two classes."

"One of those classes is with Benton?" One sandy blond brow lifted higher than the other.

"Yes."

"How was he?"

"Professional." At the end of class, Benton had told her it was nice to have her back.

"When you first arrived at the hospital, the professors' group told me quite a bit about you."

Setting his elbows on the table, he appeared thoughtful. "I know you're from Vancouver, and that you taught there at a secondary level for four years before returning to the U of I for your master's."

"Yes." She nodded. "What about you?"

"I grew up in Spokane. I went to U-Dub—University of Washington—for my undergraduate, before continuing on to med school. I had two relationships in college, but there were problems. I didn't want to marry until I was through with my schooling, and neither of them wanted to wait that long. So here I am, a thirty-five-year-old bachelor with an extreme passion for boating."

He was well educated, likable, young, and good looking. It shouldn't be too hard for him to find Miss Right. But she couldn't be the one to tell him that.

"Do you need to talk, Katherine, about someone in particular?"

She nodded, thankful that he'd asked. "He's come to his senses. After tonight and Miss Palouse, he wants it to be just us." There, she'd said what had delighted and tormented her night and day.

"Now, Miss Palouse is the one he's looked forward to meeting for months?" Brad set his jaw to his hand.

"Yes."

"If I remember right, he told you other things in between his other dates. He's been good about keeping your hopes up. And now that you have a serious admirer, he's threatened."

"It's been a little confusing." She agreed.

The waitress delivered Brad's order—a nicely grilled steak, and baked potato, with steamed carrots and zucchini. She also slid the slice of decadent chocolate cream pie in front of Katherine. As soon as

Brad picked up his silverware, she sank her fork down through the whipped cream and, chocolate layer, and into the flaky crust.

"I wonder what brought him to his senses more... your accident or me?"

"I haven't asked him."

"You've told me how he feels. How do you feel?" He took a bite of steak and chewed.

"If Miss Palouse isn't right for Quinn, then I would like the opportunity to answer the questions I've had about him all summer." There she'd told him the truth.

"You're a bright girl, Katherine. If he continues to blind date, that will be a huge sign to you, won't it? You won't let him continue to play games, will you?"

"Quinn's not playing games; he's sincerely confused." She gripped her hands together beneath the table. "Brad, I'm the one playing games."

His eyes narrowed. He was a good guy, a decent fellow and human being. He'd been her buoy during a difficult storm, and she owed him an apology.

"Next Friday, I can't go out with you, because I'm Quinn's date, Miss Wazzu." She waited for his reaction.

He salted and peppered his baked potato.

"Evans set it up. We're meeting at Alex's in Pullman. Quinn has no idea it's me."

Brad leaned his head to one side. "In his mind, you're the one who's supposed to be there after Miss Palouse, waiting for him in the wings. Or does he know you're waiting? Oh, but that's right, you're with me. Am I supposed to make him worry?" He sprinkled chives over his potato.

"You were such a buoy to me at the hospital."

He reached across the table, and his hand gently clasped hers. "There's a history between you and Benton that I can't probably begin to compete with, but I'd like to try. The question is, has he already won your heart?"

"Yes." She had to be firm with him. "Yes, he has."

Learn from this, Katherine told herself: Don't go out with your doctor when you're in love with your professor, even if it is for just a piece of pie.

Ж

Cindy answered Evans's door and smiled warmly at Katherine and Brad. "Dr. Ungerbach, I heard your first name is Brad. I'm Cindy. I met you briefly at the hospital that day."

Brad held out his hand and smiled. "It's nice to meet you again, Cindy." Grilled asparagus permeated the main floor. After sliding off their shoes, they followed Cindy into the kitchen, where Evans stood at the island pouring boiling water into a teapot.

"Brad, nice to see you again." Evans nodded. "Quinn will be here any minute. He called about a half hour ago as he was leaving the town of Palouse."

"I didn't catch where you're from that day at the hospital," Brad said. "Your hometown."

"Beverley, a small town in East Yorkshire, known for its impressive architecture." Evans beefed up his accent.

"Aawh." Cindy audibly swooned while she transferred madeleines from a cooling rack to a scallop-edged platter.

"How did you end up here?" Brad asked.

"I met my first wife at Cambridge. She was from the States. I moved here, went through a nasty divorce, and later met my second wife in California. I accepted the position at the University of Idaho to get away from her. I've been divorced for the last fourteen years."

Evans grinned and walked around the island to greet Katherine with a hug. "Be kind tonight," he whispered and then said a little too loud, "I'm in love with my new madeleine pan."

"Flexipan," Cindy said.

"Yes, her too."

The front door clicked open and closed.

"Hello, Benton," Evans said as Quinn entered the kitchen. Katherine couldn't see him, as Brad's broad shoulders blocked the way. "As always, you're unreadable. Everyone go ahead and get comfortable."

When Brad brushed past her to the living room, she caught a glimpse of Quinn. He wore his Vandal gold-colored polo, which she deemed appropriate, as only a month ago the rolling hills outside the town of Palouse were bathed in vibrant gold canola.

While Katherine sat on her normal side of the loveseat, Brad sat on Carl's usual side. As always, Benton claimed the wingback chair. He crossed one knee over the other and avoided their area of the room by looking at Evans and Cindy.

There was not an ethereal glow about him. He didn't appear energetic enough to have just met the second love of his life. Did he know Claire was older? She'd always pictured her as young, under sixty. Cindy slid a platter of madeleines onto the coffee table.

Evans set down a large tray hosting a black china teapot and four matching cups. "I thought we'd celebrate Benton finally meeting Miss Palouse by using my first ex-wife's Staffordshire set." He poured tea and handed Katherine an exquisite matching cup and saucer.

"Thank you."

"What did your evening involve?" Evans looked at Katherine.

"Brad and I went to dinner at the Best Western. I'd already eaten with Grandma, but I had a piece of pie."

"I was running later than expected and was in surgery until almost nine," Brad said.

Evans nodded and sat down beside Cindy on the couch. "Carl called. He knew it was too early for an update, but he has one for us. His new girlfriend, Marci—from Garfield—and he are doing fabulously, and he hopes to bring her to the group sometime in the near future. Now, Benton, it's your turn."

Quinn rolled a kink out of his neck. Katherine tried to remember if the kink was out of character for Friday nights.

"I'll call her Sandra. It will be one syllable shorter than Miss Palouse. As I knew she'd be from our phone conversations, Sandra's intelligent, perceptive, and candid."

Katherine held her teacup and saucer with both hands and waited for him to describe something besides her mind. What did he think of the woman in the poster?

"We met at seven and dined at a burger place on Main Street in downtown Palouse. It was dimly lit, with a solid oak wood bar that ran the length of the establishment with old-fashioned chrome stools. We sat in a booth. Good hometown food. The fries were hand cut and exceptionally good. After dinner, we walked for at least an hour through the downtown area. The hillside on the north borders the Main Street area and the Palouse River runs along the south side of town."

"Enough about Palouse, Benton; I drive through it monthly on my way to Spokane," Evans said. "I believe we're all familiar with the little town." Evans scanned the group.

"Spokane's my hometown," Brad said, wrapping his arm along the back of the couch. His hand ended up behind Katherine's neck.

It must be for show; he knew exactly where he stood.

Was Quinn trying to prolong their anticipation?

Evans scratched behind one ear. "You've described the hand-cut fries more than Claire, I mean Sandra."

"Yes, well, I thought Cindy and Katherine would appreciate the setting. There's one main street of businesses, and a museum, and the population's around one thousand, though we only saw a handful of people there tonight."

"Yes, Benton, but what did the female seated across the table from you look like?" Evans asked.

Quinn's chest inflated. "As she described herself, Sandra has moderate-length blonde hair with, um . . . brown eyes."

"Hmph . . ." Evans said. "Her portrait is indistinct, kind of a cross between Marilyn Monroe and the Mona Lisa."

"Before our date, I knew that Sandra has made a vested interest in Palouse; she's running for mayor this November, and tonight only confirmed for me that she should win." Quinn took a sip of tea and crossed one leg over the other. "I was ready to invest in Palouse by the time we returned to her elegantly restored farmhouse. Through her front living room windows, she has a view of the pastoral rolling hills as well as the idyllic town. I've always wanted a place with a view."

Katherine smiled slightly. She reminded herself that Benton was always longwinded about his blind dates. She wanted him to get to the point. Now that he'd finally met Miss Palouse, what did he think about this woman . . . Sandra . . . Claire?

"Sandra made decaf coffee." Quinn rolled another kink out of his neck. Had she caught a hint of a smile?

"It sounds like this was your best blind date yet." Cindy picked up a madeleine.

"Most definitely." Quinn nodded.

Katherine's heart tightened like a corset being cinched.

"Did you schedule a second?" Evans asked.

"No, not yet."

Hurry up, Benton. Everyone had been waiting months for him to finally meet her, and now he was prolonging the inevitable.

Quinn tapped his fingers lightly against the side of his teacup. "Sandra's a remarkable woman; she listens right to the heart of a person."

Evans's gaze narrowed. "And . . . ?"

Katherine's throat burned with frustration and tears. What did he think of the woman who resembled Dolly Parton in both shape and appearance?

"And . . ." Quinn's gaze moved to the bowl of walnuts and lifted to Katherine's eyes. "She's older than my mother."

The binding loosened about her heart.

Poor Quinn. Poor, poor Quinn.

Evans leaned forward and carefully set down his teacup on the coffee table before he threw his head back and howled. Katherine and Cindy laughed softly while Quinn and Brad remained stoic.

"I knew there was a reason you had not described her physically," Evans said. "Usually, you give us hints throughout. This time, nothing."

"I don't know how it happened. I was with you and Guttenheimer that day at the jazz festival." Quinn's eyes grew wide. "It was my first time meeting Guttenheimer."

"Yes!" Evans pointed at him. "You were wearing that matching derby hat and tweed jacket of yours. You looked dreadful. Weren't you recovering from the flu?"

"Yes." Quinn's jaw dropped. "He gave me Claire's phone number because he thought that I'm much older than I am."

Evans slapped his leg and laughed.

"Who's Guttenheimer?" Cindy nudged Evans.

"An old colleague of mine who drives from the Tri-Cities every year for the festival. Now, next Friday is Miss Pullman, or should we call her Miss Wazzu?"

Katherine stiffened. She couldn't bring herself to glance at Brad.

"I don't know, Evans." Quinn sighed. "I'm in need of a respite. Maybe respite care." His chuckle was not convincing.

If only she weren't with Brad tonight, Quinn could take her home, and she'd hold him in her arms and reassure him that everything was going to be okay.

Ж

"I thought the evening would be far stuffier than it was," Brad said during their drive home. "They're a fun group of people. Thank you, Katherine, for allowing me to join you."

Brad had been the perfect date. Assisting her when needed, refilling her teacup, and never displaying too much attention or ownership, which he could have easily resorted to in Quinn's presence.

"You are the perfect gentleman, Brad, thank you."

"I got a bit sleepy in there, drinking herbal tea; I'm usually in bed before ten."

"Ten?"

"Yes. I get up at 4:00 a.m."

"Why didn't you say something?" According to the clock on the dash, it was one fifteen in the morning.

"I was the one who'd invited myself, and I knew it would be a late gathering. Pray for me tomorrow. I mean today." He winked across the cab at her.

If her heart hadn't already been taken . . . Brad Ungerbach was an exceptional man. She would keep him in her prayers.

Chapter Fifty-Eight

Tuesday afternoon, Katherine called Evans's office and left a voicemail message. Approximately one hour later, the phone rang.

"Hi, Katherine, it's Evans returning your call."

"Hi, Professor, I have a few questions." Katherine pulled back the lace curtain to view Grandma in the yard.

"Shoot."

"Quinn said you're getting Miss Wazzu's number, and then he'd call her."

Evans chuckled. "When did he tell you that?"

"Last night."

"The dog! He hasn't asked me."

"He also told me that he didn't want to go, but was waiting to see what happened with Brad and me."

"He may wait until the last minute. Keep me posted, and I'll work on the phone situation. The woman has to have a Washington area code. Shoot!"

Ж

Wednesday morning, Grandma drove Katherine to the parking lot near the Administration Building. Katherine took the elevator to the second floor and hobbled to Benton's Civil War class. Her backpack was lighter than normal, hosting only a spiral notebook and a couple of pens.

On one foot, she hopped to her usual seat and, leaning forward, set the crutches on the floor. Seated on the front of his desk, Benton flipped through his notes. He wore a wrinkled Wazzu-maroon polo and brown Dockers. *Bummer!* It was the perfect polo for Friday night.

"After the Civil War, the issue of loyalty emerged in the Wade-Davis Bill of 1864." His gaze roved the class. "It required voters to take an ironclad oath, swearing that they'd never supported the Confederacy in any way. In contrast, Lincoln asked voters to simply swear to future support of the Union.

"Lincoln's second inaugural address, in March of 1865, has been quoted as surpassing his Gettysburg Address, which is often referred to as one of the most famous speeches in American history."

After three pages of note-taking, Katherine's hand cramped. She shook her wrist.

Quinn paused and glanced toward the clock. Five minutes remained.

"I have an off-the-cuff question for you." Quinn's gaze roamed the class. "If you could pick any US war to have worked in as either a journalist or a historian, which war fascinates you most and why?"

He's just asked Katherine's dating question! Slightly reworded, but it was hers!

"Mark." Professor Benton nodded to Angel's new love interest in the third row.

"World War I. Even though we didn't enter until late in the war, it was the first US war in which military air strikes were employed."

Professor Benton nodded thoughtfully. "By the way, class, there is no right or wrong answer."

Angel raised her hand.

"Yes, Miss LeFave," Professor Benton said.

"I would have wanted to be a journalist in World War I, and I would have somehow prevented Hiroshima."

"Wrong war," Mark said. "You mean World War II, and would you have also prevented Pearl Harbor?" he asked, without raising his hand.

Hmm . . . maybe he wasn't Angel material.

Angel slumped in her seat. Maybe she should write a list of all the reasons she'd never fall in love with Mark. With the first four reasons being: way too smart, insensitive, inconsiderate, and undiplomatic.

"Okay, to be fair, the question needs a qualifier," Professor Benton said. "As a journalist or historian, you do not have superpowers to stop wars."

"Aw!" Angel's shoulders sank.

"What about you, Miss King?" Quinn's gaze settled on her. "If you could be a journalist or a historian in any US war, which war would you choose and why?"

She'd always pictured being asked the question in a candle lit room, not under fluorescent lighting among her peers. She toyed with her pen. "It's a broad question, considering there have been eleven US wars, including the recent Iraqi situation. Hmm . . . There's three I'm leaning toward: the American Revolution, the Civil War, and World War II. It's a tough but brilliant question, Professor."

There was a slight twitch to the corner of his mouth. "Some scholars might choose a war based on casualties."

She nodded. "Hmm . . . American war. In World War II, over 400,000 Americans lost their lives on foreign soil." She leaned back in her chair, meeting his gaze. "But I'd have to choose the Civil War, in which over 360,000 Americans lost their lives on native soil."

"And why does the American Civil War fascinate you the most?" His pupils were a soft ebony glaze. He should have asked her this question weeks ago.

"For the Union, the American Civil War was a war to preserve the principles of our founding fathers—all men are equal, and should be free. And this class has brought to light so many other reasons. The war prevented our country from dividing into two separate nations. And as you well know, I could go on."

"What about you, Professor Benton, which war would you pick?" Angel asked.

"The same as Miss King." He cleared his throat and glanced at the clock. In ten seconds the bell would ring.

"I met your Joe Hillis last week," Angel whispered. Bending down, she retrieved Katherine's crutches. "He said the two of you used to date, and now you're good friends."

"Yes," Katherine whispered, hoisting her book bag over her shoulder. "If you'd told me that five years ago, I never would have believed it." She met Angel's curious gaze.

"Because he hurt you?"

Katherine nodded.

"And time heals."

"Yes, praise God." One step from the door, Katherine glanced Quinn's direction. He was busy with a student.

"Maybe there's still hope for Greg and me, then," Angel said as they walked together to their Lewis and Clark class.

"I still feel bad about giving you the idea of serving him chili."

"It's not your fault. There were other things about me he didn't like." Angel shrugged. "In case, you didn't know . . . Professor Benton's taken. He has a picture of his girlfriend on his desk, a beautiful brunette."

"That's good to know." Quinn's sister was beautiful. She looked forward to meeting her someday.

"Even before the last exam, I knew you liked him." Angel smiled. "I could tell the first night of *Doctor Zhivago*. You had this I'm melting kind of look in your eyes. Brenda and Ronnie were only so-so."

Ж

After her Lewis and Clark class ended, Katherine remained seated while Cindy gathered her things. "You're not going to make me wait until Friday, are you, to tell me about Monday?" Cindy said. "Evans said you talked, but he'll barely breathe a word."

Katherine recalled Evans's advice: Do not tell Cindy anything. She shares everything with Benton.

"Was Monday Brad and green tea?" Katherine asked, looking at the chalkboard.

"Yes, and you never called me. What do you think of Dr. Ungerbach?"

"He's wonderful." Katherine shrugged.

Benton stepped inside the classroom. Wide-eyed, Cindy stiffened.

Had he heard?

"Katherine!" Quinn smiled. "Good, you're still here. How are you getting home?"

He didn't appear to have heard. "Grandma's picking me up. I was hoping Cindy would take a slight detour and walk me out."

"I'd love to, but I think Quinn would like to assist you today." Cindy tidied a pile of papers.

"If that's okay." He waited for her response.

"What about your office hours?"

"I may be a few minutes late." He shrugged.

While they took the elevator to the main floor, she remembered Hannah. "I haven't told you that our little neighbor girl stopped by the night of your date with Claire. She wanted me to tell you thank you for the money. That was sweet of you, Quinn."

He chuckled. "I wasn't sure if she'd figure out it was me."

"She saw the money after you'd gone in the house. They ended up getting a little dachshund puppy. Bruno is his name."

Quinn chuckled and waited for Katherine to exit the elevator first.

"Poor Ethel."

"What do you mean?"

"Don't you know . . . dachshunds are voracious diggers?"

"Oh no. Don't tell Grandma. She'll be very upset."

He chuckled and held one of the double doors open for her. "Did you go off your medication?"

"Not yet," she said, though she hadn't taken a pill for two days.

"Where is Ethel meeting you?"

"This is where she dropped me off." They stopped at the curb. In the busy parking lot, Grandma's car was nowhere in sight.

"Katherine . . ." She felt a speech coming on. "I think it's best that I give you some time off. You have questions, and my presence is causing havoc with Ungerbach's and your . . . relationship, and after what we shared Monday, seeing and being with you is painful. I don't understand."

In the bright sunlight, she held her hand over her eyes and regarded him thoughtfully. The wonderful man had again owned up to his feelings.

"You've dated half of Latah and Whitman Counties while visiting us. But now that I have one admirer, you're not going to even visit Grandma? I'm the one who doesn't understand."

"Your tone is proof that my blind dates bothered you. I'm too much of a distraction for you. Aren't I? Is that how you feel, Katherine, deep down?"

Grandma's red Chevy Nova drove into view.

"I'm tired of the games, Quinn."

"Of course, you are. You have every right to be. But I sincerely didn't know I loved you as deeply as I do until that phone call."

Miss Palouse was behind him, and Quinn was owning up to his feelings, and eloquently at that. Grandma rolled up beside them and shifted into a lurchy park.

"What phone call?" Was he referring to their walk and her phone call to Carl, or the phone call regarding her injury?

"I promise you, Katherine, no more blind dates, just you and me . . . if you'll give up Brad."

Why didn't he answer her? Katherine opened the passenger door and slid her crutches inside before easing herself onto the bench seat.

Quinn manually rolled down her window.

"Which phone call were you referring to?" Katherine attempted to sound pleasant.

"What's for dinner, Ethel?" He leaned down and managed a charming smile in Grandma's direction.

"I have chicken thighs defrosting on the counter." She leaned across the bench seat toward them. "Why don't you bring some brown rice over about five thirty?"

"I'd like that very much; that is if it's all right with Katherine."

"Let's wait until Saturday." She held her backpack in her lap and stared straight ahead through the windshield.

"Of course, it's all right with Katherine." Grandma waved her hand.

"Is it, Katherine?"

Shadows played on his face. A swath of sunlight highlighted his eyes. Someday she'd tell their daughters how she won their father's heart, and they would clap with glee. Little girls with Zhivago eyes would be so cute. Their little girls . . .

"I'm sorry, Quinn." She shook her head.

Chapter Fifty-Nine

The man is full of contradictions. One minute he's telling me he's not going to hang around, and the next minute he's inviting himself. If it wasn't for Miss Wazzu on Friday night, I'm almost to the conclusion that he's absolutely, head-over-heels in love with me. Katherine sighed happily.

"That was not a pretty picture." Grandma leaned forward stiffly, gripping the steering wheel with both hands.

"I'm tired of being confused, Grandma, and he's so confused he's almost stuttering."

"Be kind."

"I almost need to stay on painkillers if I'm going to be around him."

Grandma smiled and came to a jerky stop before the stop sign at the intersection of Sweet Avenue and the Lewiston highway. "Because you care. Because you love him."

The afternoon had been blissfully quiet, especially during Katherine's nap.

"He's my friend too." With the oven door open, Grandma basted chicken thighs with barbecue sauce. A bowl of tossed salad sat on the table with a bottle of ranch dressing nearby.

Katherine sat down and poured two glasses of milk. A knot of guilt settled in her chest. Should she have told Benton no?

"What else is for dinner?" Katherine glanced from the salad to the oven.

"Nothing. I wanted Quinn to bring brown rice, and you wouldn't let him come over. You were rude."

"Do you blame me?"

"Yes and no."

"You're mad at him about something; and as Christians, we're supposed to turn the other cheek."

It was difficult to argue with Grandma and scripture.

"He apologized, and he felt bad . . . about the kiss," Grandma said.

The phone rang. Grandma wiped her hands on a tea towel and mumbled something under her breath. "Hello.—I'll get her for you." Grandma set down the receiver and returned to the kitchen.

"Who is it?"

Grandma shrugged. "Do you want me to ask? It's a man."

Katherine hobbled to the phone. "Hello."

"Hi, Katherine. It's Quinn."

She inhaled deeply and sighed.

"I made brown rice, and I was wondering if you're still opposed to my company?"

His sweet tone softened her. "Do you know Grandma hasn't made a starch? Just chicken and salad? Did the two of you plan this?"

"Yes. If your grandma were forty years younger, we'd be an item. And I have something special to share."

She cleared her throat. "I have a wonderful idea: you bring me a half cup of brown rice and take

Grandma and her chicken and salad to your place for the evening." What did he mean, *something special to share*?

"What I have to share will make Ethel's day."

"Can you be more specific?" She stared at the shag carpeting.

"Here . . ." Grandma reached for the phone. "Let me talk to him."

Katherine handed her the phone.

"Chicken's getting cold. I'm tired of the two of you fighting. Bring the rice, and after dinner, Katherine can go to her room and study. She can put up with you for twenty minutes."

Click. Grandma hung up on him.

Quinn set a saucepan of rice on a hot pad in the center of the table, sat down and set a manila envelope off to his right.

Did the envelope have something to do with Grandma?

"Katherine, would you say the prayer, please?" Grandma asked. She was trying to soften her, making her pray when she was supposed to be uptight.

Katherine bowed her head and sighed. "Thank You, Lord, for this meal, for the hands that prepared it, for Your many blessings. We have so much to be thankful for. In Your Son Jesus's name we pray, amen."

Quinn stared across the table at her. Did he mean to?

"How are you feeling?" he asked.

"Fine, thank you."

"Are you still numb?" His brows lifted.

The man had gall. "I'm waiting for my doctor to give me his approval before I go off completely."

"So you're mildly numb?"

She looked to her left at the calendar on the wall. "Miss Wazzu, July twenty-sixth, this Friday? Have you been conversing with her?"

He shrugged. "We're on for Friday, but I've misplaced her phone number."

She narrowed her gaze. He was lying, too.

"She's the Realtor?" Grandma asked.

"No." Quinn looked at his plate. "Miss Wazzu is the grad student. Miss Garfield, the Realtor, is now Carl's girlfriend. Remember Mr. Flagrantly Good Looking?"

Grandma's brows lifted, and her eyes nearly crossed.

"You're getting closer to home. Wazzu's only eight miles away," Grandma said. "Who set you up with this one?"

"Mashburn, an elderly professor friend of mine at Wazzu." Quinn cleared his throat. "Not a close friend, so I'm not expecting, uh . . . any chemistry like Cindy refers to it."

"What's in the envelope?" Katherine regarded him.

The phone rang.

Shoot! Katherine glanced toward the living room.

"Ethel, would you like me to get it?" Quinn asked.

"No, I'll get it." Grandma rose and tossed her napkin on her chair.

"Hello—Yes, Katherine's here. May I tell her who's calling?" Grandma covered the receiver. "Katherine, it's Brad on the phone for you."

Without looking at Quinn, Katherine hobbled from the room.

Grandma placed one of the dining table chairs by the curio cabinet and held the phone out to her. Her forlorn look indicated she no longer thought being in the middle was a humorous situation.

"Hello." Katherine sat down and leaned against the solid cabinet.

"Hi, it's Brad. I'm on break right now. If all goes well, I'll get off in about an hour. Are you up for me dropping by?"

"Quinn's here." Katherine glanced over her shoulder to her textbooks on the coffee table.

"To see you or your grandmother?"

"Both."

"Has anything changed since I last spoke with you?"

"Yes and no." Katherine toyed with the phone cord. What exactly did he mean by that?

"Good."

Katherine returned to the table, leaned the crutches against the cabinets, and sat down.

"That was Brad?" Grandma asked.

"Yes." She glanced across the table at Quinn. "To be honest, I'm not sure if he's coming over or not. He asked if I was up for him dropping by, and I mentioned you were here."

His mouth twitched. "That means he's coming. The man is as confident as Carl. Do you want me to leave, Katherine? I have essays I can grade."

"It would probably be best if you did."

"Katherine! We were going to play Scrabble," Grandma said.

"If you can both play Scrabble in here quietly, that would be fine. If he stops by, I don't want you walking through the living room constantly." She sighed. Grandma's house was too small.

"I'll go home, Ethel."

Grandma patted his hand. "And leave me all by myself, alone in the kitchen?"

"Before I go, Ethel,"—he smiled warmly—"I have something very special to share with you."

If Grandma were forty years younger, they would be a couple.

"Oh, Quinn, you know how I love good news."

"President Morrison stopped by my office today."

"Yes." Grandma patted above her heart.

"He wanted me to deliver this." Quinn handed her the manila envelope.

Grandma shook her head briefly and then pinched the metal clasp together. "It's something metal."

"Read the note first," Quinn said.

"I can't wait. I'm awful."

"She is." Katherine smiled. "She always opens the present first and then the card."

"Oh, it is! It is!" Grandma pulled out a white metal sign. Wide-eyed, her hand flew to her mouth.

Katherine hopped on her good foot behind Grandma's chair.

Outlined in green, a four-inch high turtle stood on its hind legs, wearing a straw hat with a mini-cluster of strawberries pinned to the side.

The caption read:

Senior Parking Only
Minimum age 65
Proof of age required.
Violators will be towed at owner's expense.

"It's beautiful," Katherine whispered, looking at Quinn.

While Grandma read the letter, he whispered, "Mike also delivered the name plaque for my door today."

"Congratulations. A milestone."

"Mike wants Ethel to come in and have her picture taken once the signs are installed. Two parking spaces near the Admin will be for seniors. And a few in other zones around campus."

Grandma patted Quinn's hand. "I'll have you deliver a letter back to him for me. I need to pay another parking ticket." She giggled. "I'll have Mike go to the registrars for me."

"Another one?" Katherine suppressed a laugh.

Wide-eyed, Grandma nodded. "The day I stopped to pay off the first, I couldn't find parking. I thought I'd only be a minute, and they nabbed me."

Katherine sat at the table and dried dishes while Quinn washed. Grandma put the leftover chicken and rice in Tupperware containers, and then she proceeded to set up the Scrabble game.

"Grandma, Quinn said he needed to grade essays."

"One game. I'll make a pot of decaf," Grandma said.

"I'll get the creamer." Quinn opened the fridge.

Katherine sat down on the sofa and felt too restless to study. "Lord," she whispered, "If Brad stops by, help me to handle the situation with love." Beside her textbooks sat the Bible. She eyed it for a moment before leaning over and picking it up. "Give me wisdom concerning love, Lord. Open my eyes to the situation." Knowing the verse she longed to read, Katherine turned to First Corinthians 13.

"Love is patient," she whispered. Tears stung her eyes. "I have not always been patient. Love is kind. I have not always been kind. Lord, help me to be kind. It does not envy, it does not boast, it is not proud." A sob caught in her throat. "Oh, Lord, I've been so awful, help me to be humble. You know how I hate dating. I'm just not good at it."

"Your doctor's here," Grandma said, from the kitchen.

Chapter Sixty

"He's saving her an appointment," Quinn said.

The back door squeaked open.

"Hello, Dr. Ungerbach," Grandma said in the other room. "We were just thinking you might save Katherine an appointment by looking at her foot while you're here."

"That's a great idea. Hello, Quinn, Ethel. I haven't played Scrabble in years."

Katherine lifted her foot to the coffee table. When Brad unwrapped the bandages, would her foot be stinky enough to dis-infatuate him?

"Feel free to pull up a chair," Grandma said.

"Thank you, but I was hoping to see Katherine."

"How about a cup of decaf? I just made a pot."

"That sounds great."

"Ask him if he's had dinner, Grandma," she said loudly.

"Have you had supper?"

"I had a quick bite to eat on the way here, thank you."

Carrying a mug of coffee, Brad walked into the living room. His smile was broad. If she could get past another ridiculously bright Hawaiian shirt, she'd remember that he was also sweet and sincere. Katherine shimmied into the corner of the sofa.

Brad sat down beside her. "Benton's still here," he whispered.

"Grandma set up Scrabble."

Nonetheless, Brad's eyes sparkled.

"You look more beautiful every time I see you." He swallowed like he meant it like it wasn't just a great line.

Her stomach tightened. She was past being numb and into anxious.

"That was kind of you." She reminded herself of his attention at the hospital—he'd been a lifesaver.

"Katherine, I have a *K* and a *D* and no vowels," Grandma said, loudly.

"Good luck," Katherine bellowed.

"How was your day?" she asked, looking at Brad.

Silence enveloped them like gauze.

"It's ending on a very good note." He appeared to relish the moment.

"Then you definitely don't want to look at my stinky foot."

His hearty chuckle filled Grandma's front room and probably bounced into the kitchen, causing Grandma and Quinn some anguish.

"One of your first remarks to me that I *know* you remember was, 'I am usually a boring person.' You were so wrong."

She glanced at her textbooks and bit her lower lip. "I really am. Usually." Oh, he was making her feel finger tapping nervous.

"Let's see, we'll need some fresh gauze, bandages . . ."

Breath mints. Maybe he'd had a burger with the works on the way here. "Everything's in the bathroom, straight ahead down the hall, in a basket on the counter."

He returned with the small white basket and set it on the coffee table. With his back to the kitchen doorway, Brad lifted up her foot and carefully unwound the bandage. "The stitches look good. You can start giving your foot more air time. We could leave it unwrapped for a while and bandage it up before I head home."

While he washed his hands in the bathroom, Katherine examined the stitches, the bruises. She'd have an ugly scar. At least, it was on the bottom of her foot.

"Katherine, what's a word that I can use a *K*, *R* and *U*?" Grandma asked, loudly.

Carrying the first aid basket, Brad walked through the living room and halted in the doorway to the kitchen. "Ethel, see if you can spell kurta. It's a collarless shirt in India."

"Thanks, Dr. Brad." Grandma giggled. "Quinn, I hope you didn't have plans for that *A*."

Brad returned to sit beside Katherine. "One of my buddies in college wore them all the time. Kurta." He grinned.

"I was thinking of *kudos*, but you beat me to it."

"I don't think she has a *D* anymore. Do you want to join them?" Brad leaned his head toward the kitchen. "Looks early in the game."

Maybe he was past feeling that Quinn was competition, or maybe he wanted to beat him. "I'm game."

Quinn and Grandma pulled the table away from the wall. Brad sat with his back to the window while Katherine sat in her usual chair across the table from Quinn.

Brad's first word was *bolus*.

Grandma studied the word. "I've never played Scrabble with two doctors before."

Quinn held out his hand. "Hand me the dictionary, please, Ethel."

"Are you going to challenge him?" Grandma asked.

"What do you think, Katherine, should I?" Their eyes locked.

It was a loaded question. She shrugged. *Bolus* didn't sound outlandish.

"I won't challenge you," Quinn said. "But I'd like to look it up if you don't mind."

"Go for it." Brad selected four more letters.

Quinn flipped through the dictionary, ran his gaze down the left column, and closed the book.

"What does it mean?" Grandma asked.

"Bolus—larger than an ordinary pill."

"Oh, my calcium pills are bolus!" Grandma chuckled. So did Brad.

Quinn's word was *choky*.

Brad laughed. Grandma frowned. Katherine questioned if it was a word.

After Grandma's turn, Brad finally asked, "What does it mean, Professor? Choky?"

"To choke, or suffocate."

"Haven't you heard of a choky collar?" Grandma set three tiles on the board. Her *Z* landed on a triple-letter score. "Thirty points for my *Z*; not too bad for the equestrian in the group."

"You mean *octogenarian*, Grandma."

After Katherine's word of *shim,* it was Brad's turn again. His word was *pinna*.

Quinn frowned. "I'm calling you this time."

Quinn flipped open the dictionary to *P* and scanned the pages. He slammed the book shut and rolled his eyes. "It's the part of the ear that sticks out from the side of your head."

"Yes." Brad smiled. "Katherine has a beautiful pih-nuh."

Grandma got a triple-word score with the word *tax*. Katherine played an *I* below the *X* to spell *xi*.

Brad scratched his head. "What do you think, Professor?"

"This is also the first time I've played Scrabble with Katherine."

Brad didn't call her on it before playing his next word. *Tragus*.

"Just so you know, Doc," Quinn said, "Xi is the fourteenth letter of the Greek alphabet."

"Thanks, Professor."

The two were becoming friends. Katherine's cheeks burned.

"I will not call you on *tragus,* but tell me what it means. I'm tired of losing turns."

"Ethel, are you going to call me?" Brad grinned.

"No."

"Too bad, because *tragus* is the external opening of the ear."

"I thought you were a foot doctor." Grandma studied the board.

"I'm an orthopedic surgeon, and I must say, Katherine has beautiful tragi."

Katherine's ears warmed as she stared at the table.

A half hour later, Grandma won. By the jubilant look on her face, it was obvious that she was quite pleased with her accomplishment.

"What's your secret, Ethel?" Brad asked.

"Triple-letter scores. You, highfalutin doctors, are into spelling big, long words, and you're not looking for the double-and triple-word scores." She beamed.

Brad rubbed his eyes and yawned. "I've been up since four."

"Wow!" Katherine shook her head.

Brad's right hand dropped to the table and landed perfectly on top of hers. Everyone stared at his bold accomplishment. Up close, short blond hair grew on his knuckles, and his hands were exceptionally clean as if he washed them sixteen times a day.

"Who got second?" Brad asked.

"You did, by eleven points," Grandma said. "Quinn and Katherine tied."

"We tied, Katherine." Quinn smiled across the table at her like that was reason enough to give Brad the boot.

"For last place." She lifted her brows.

Brad's fingers now entwined hers. "About Friday, I won't get off work until eight, but Friday's Friday."

Brad knew Friday was taken and important to her. Her heart twisted. "I'll be at the library," she whispered.

"After my shift, I'll pick you up from the library, and we'll rent a movie or—"

"As you know from last Friday," Quinn interrupted, "it's been a tradition for our professors' group to meet on Fridays to discuss my blind dates."

"Didn't we meet at eleven thirty?" Brad's blond brows knit together quizzically.

"It'll probably be ten this week, as my date is only in Pullman. And just so you're aware, from time to time, Katherine has discussed her dates as well."

"No, I haven't, Quinn."

"She only calls me Quinn when she's mad at me." He smiled. "There was the time with Joe."

"That was not a date. That was a Mountain Dew."

"I'm talking about Chinese."

"You know that wasn't a date either. You were there."

Brad chuckled. "This Friday, I'd prefer that our date not be part of the discussion. Katherine, I'd like you to walk me to the front door. And, Ethel, is that a pocket door?"

"Why, yes." Grandma turned to look at it.

"That's great."

Katherine agreed with him. She wanted the pocket door closed when she officially ended their one-sided courtship. Benton was right: she needed to set her foot down.

Chapter Sixty-One

After Katherine hobbled into the living room, Brad pulled the pocket door closed. She had to give him credit; not only was the man proactive, he was also observant.

"I need to rewrap your foot before I leave."

"Thanks for remembering." She sat on the couch and lifted her foot to the coffee table near the basket of gauze. "Um . . . Brad, did you forget what I told you about Friday?"

Brad sat down on the coffee table and lifted her foot to rest on his knee. He started with a square piece of gauze. "No, my thinking is: Benton will be all the more surprised when it's you."

"Aw . . . that's sweet of you." She sighed. He was such a dear soul.

"And I was hoping you'd change your mind before Friday." He grinned. "But I have a feeling you won't."

Brad wrapped the tape around her entire foot and pressed the ends smoothly into place.

"You're right. I won't change my mind."

"I understand. What would you like to do Friday?"

She giggled. He did have a sense of humor.

Brad gently set her foot down on the coffee table. "I'll wash my hands, and you can walk me to the door."

While he was in the bathroom, Katherine stared at the closed pocket door. When she walked him to the door, he was planning to kiss her. Across the room, a spider inched its way down from the ceiling and, halfway down, appeared to have second thoughts, as it scurried back up its invisible cord. Was it a sign from God, telling her to run?

"Do you have enough pain medication, or do you want me to write another prescription?" Brad asked.

"I haven't taken anything for the last forty-eight hours."

"You have a high pain threshold." He grinned.

"I never have before." How high was Brad's pain tolerance? How would he handle it if she told him his Hawaiian shirt was way too bright?

"Are you ready to walk me to the door?" Lowering his chin, he studied her.

"Is it because you want me to get more exercise?"

"No." He smiled.

Her mouth went dry.

"I'd still like you to walk me to the door."

He surprised her. She looked to the closed front door and guesstimated that it was about fifteen feet, with another three feet added for moving around the coffee table. Using her left foot, she stood up and angled the crutches against her ribcage. She followed his slow lead and stopped near the left side of the door.

He moved closer. Quinn had said that Ungerbach knew how he felt. He confirmed it as he lifted Katherine's chin and stared into her eyes.

"Brad, don't." Lowering her chin, she took his hand. "I can't go out with you on Friday because I'm in love with Quinn. I'm so sorry." She met his gaze.

"I know. I saw it tonight." He blinked. "It's been a long time since I've met someone as special as you. I know I'm rushing it, but I have no other choice. If for some reason, you and Quinn don't work out, I hope you'll let me know."

"I will, Brad . . . I promise."

After he'd left, she leaned against the front door and sighed. "Dear Lord, help him find someone special. A good Christian gal, who loves water and is maybe a little color blind. He's a sweet soul. Thank You, Lord, that it's finally over. Ease his pain."

Chapter Sixty-Two

After Brad's diesel truck revved west on Hunter Street, the pocket door slid open and then closed behind Quinn. Over the top of her Lewis and Clark textbook, Katherine's gaze followed him as he sat in the recliner and placed both hands stiffly on the arms. She lowered the textbook and capped her fluorescent pink highlighter.

"Do you know how many parts there are to the human body?" he asked.

"No." Katherine peered up at the ceiling.

"Thousands. An anatomy class would do wonders for our Scrabble game."

It was touching how he'd used the pronoun *our*.

"Grandma would probably take anatomy with you, but I'm not a serious enough player."

"So what are you doing Friday night?" Quinn pushed on the chair's arms as he reclined.

"I'm not sure. The library and then a short movie. What do you think about Brad coming to the professors' get-together?" She bit the inside of her cheeks to keep from smiling.

"I feel comfortable reviewing my evening with the three of you and Carl, but when we add another person, an outsider, it isn't the same. To be honest, last Friday was awkward."

His answer was understandable.

"Katherine . . ."

"Yes." Now that she'd officially broken up with Brad, she felt so relaxed, like she'd just taken a long, hot bubble bath.

"I don't know if you remember this because of the morphine, but when you were in the hospital, shortly after you arrived, you confided to me you watch movies when your grandmother's not home."

"It's not like you think, Quinn." His first name was becoming easier to say. She'd never really liked calling him Benton, but it had sounded more formal than calling him by his first name.

"Please expound."

"I do watch movies when I'm here alone. Occasionally. There's no nudity, or anything to be ashamed of."

"Then why do you only watch them when you're alone?"

"Everyone spends their quiet time alone a little differently, I suppose."

"Katherine . . ." He returned the recliner to an upright position and moved to sit on the coffee table, directly facing her.

"Yes." Gone was the relaxed bubble bath feeling.

"Remember that Monday you skipped class due to food poisoning, and Ethel had her hair done, the day she spoke with President Morrison?"

"Yes." What was he getting at?

"I remember thinking when I visited that you looked like you'd been crying."

"I'd had food poisoning; of course, I'd been crying."

"No, you told me you were on the mend, that you'd kept down a piece of toast."

Grandma had probably told him about the *Doctor Zhivago* party, and he was letting his imagination run wild, yet accurate.

"Katherine . . . you'd been crying when you came to the door. There were visible tears in your lashes."

He was not going to take Friday away from her. She'd made it this far, through the Quinn List, and Brad, and Miss Palouse. She was going to make it to Alex's, and he was going to be so surprised when she turned out to be his Miss Wazzu. The look on his face would more than make up for his present pain. Wouldn't it?

"Katherine . . . what movie do you watch when you're here all alone?"

She stared into his eyes and locked her secret behind the chambers of her heart.

"*Raiders of the Lost Ark.*"

"You're lying."

"Harrison Ford is very good looking." She'd watched the first half hour of it yesterday when she'd felt too groggy for textbooks.

"Admit it, you're lying." His large, woeful eyes told her he wasn't very good at long-suffering either.

"I'm lying."

He pinched the corners of his eyes and tipped his head back toward the ceiling.

"Are you going to tell me the truth?"

She shook her head. If she told him that she'd recently watched *Doctor Zhivago* several times, and for specific scenes, Quinn would know it was because of her love for him. In his elation, he might also trip on the porch steps, fall into Grandma's rhododendron bush, and snag the hem of his trousers on the picket fence.

"You look awfully smug about something." He rose from the coffee table, and with his hands on his hips, paced about the room.

"Are you going to tell me?" He crossed his arms, facing her.

She shook her head. Thank goodness she'd hidden the Zhivago movie in the bottom drawer of the curio cabinet.

Stopping in front of the TV, he pressed Eject on the VCR machine. The cartridge in hand, he strode toward her. "Admit it, Katherine, you love me."

If he glanced down, he'd see that it was *Raiders of the Lost Ark* he held in his possession.

This was Grandma's doing. She must have found the tape and snitched on her. The whole world was against her except for Evans. Evans and God were her allies.

Please, Lord . . . please, Lord . . . please, Lord, help me to make it till Friday. Friday's going to be so great.

"Katherine, would you just look at yourself." Quinn sighed. "You're praying right in front of me like your life depends on it."

Her traitorous hands were even clasped together—prayer-like.

Oh, how she just wanted to lay her heart at Quinn's feet and tell him she loved him.

"Katherine . . ." He sighed. "You don't understand; when you look at me, there is so much love in your eyes. I've made big mistakes this summer in our courtship. But it takes two, Katherine. You love me, Katherine. Please face it." He sighed and set *Raiders of the Lost Ark* on the coffee table.

"Here's proof of your love for me."

She didn't have the heart to tell him that she'd really never found Harrison Ford all that handsome. Finally, his gaze lowered to read the title of the videotape. His brows knit together, and he scanned the cartridge again before returning to the VCR. Quinn only glanced toward the kitchen once. He didn't mumble Grandma's name or even tell Katherine good-bye before he exited the front door instead of the back.

She sighed and covered her face with her hands. *Friday is going to be so great*. She sure hoped Evans was right.

Chapter Sixty-Three

Thursday afternoon when the phone rang, Katherine was on her way from the kitchen to the living room. "Hello," she said into the receiver.

"Lady Katherine, it's Evans."

"Hi . . . any news?" She glanced toward the kitchen. Grandma was seated at the kitchen table, playing Scrabble by herself with an open dictionary.

"I have secured a Washington female's phone number for Benton. A married friend of Mashburn's. The woman sounds young enough, but she's actually in her fifties." Evans chuckled. "Hopefully, Benton will follow through and call her tonight, and I'll get back to you regarding where and when the rendezvous will take place."

"He told me that he's meeting Miss Wazzu at Alex's," she whispered.

"He hasn't even spoken with her yet. The dog!" Evans paused. "How are you holding up? If I didn't know better, I'd say that he is tripping over himself about now. And nice job with Dr. Hungerbottom last night. Quinn is beside himself."

"It's been a difficult but rewarding week," Katherine whispered. "I'll tell you about it sometime."

"Good, well, do your best not to give in. No matter how charming he may be. I wish I could see the look on his face when he finds out that you are Miss Wazzu."

"Wait a minute, please," Katherine said, and slid the pocket door closed.

"Do you have company?"

"Just Grandma," Katherine whispered, "and she cares for Benton so much, I'm afraid she'd say or bake anything to put him out of his present misery."

Evans chuckled. "The same applies to Cindy."

It made sense. "A couple of times, Quinn's mentioned a particular phone call. I think it may have had something to do with my accident and his feelings for me." Katherine toyed with the phone cord.

"It was the call when you were at the creek. Claire, also known as Miss Palouse, was the 9-1-1 operator that day. I'm surprised he hasn't told you."

Katherine's shoulders felt weak.

"We were at the hospital before you were. He was a wreck."

"But he was so cool to me there." Tears clouded her eyes.

"You forget how friendly you were with Hungerbottom."

"I don't remember a thing." Poor Quinn.

"You were emotionally unveiled, Katherine, and Hungerbottom was immediately taken with you. Several times I've had to remind Benton that you were on morphine."

"I feel awful. Brad is such a sweet soul."

"Don't feel so awful that you muddle Friday's plans. It's going to be great."

Katherine nodded. "Yes, it is. It's going to be great."

Katherine stared out the window at the summer blue sky. It all made sense. Quinn's vagueness, his coldness, his aloofness. She hurt for both Quinn and Brad. When she returned the wheelchair and crutches, she'd give Brad a thank-you card. And she'd pray that he'd soon find the right, wonderful Christian woman that God intended him to be with.

Grandma slid the door open. "Who was that?"

"I'm afraid if I tell you that you'll tell Quinn."

Grandma's brows gathered. "Not Joe again?"

"No, Grandma."

"Dr. Brad?"

"No, Grandma."

"Mr. Flagrant?"

"No!"

"I don't want to know." Grandma sighed.

"It's probably best you don't. Grandma, is Quinn coming to dinner?"

Her mouth bunched. "Yes, I hope you don't mind; if you do, you can eat in your room."

"I don't mind. Who called who?"

"I called him. When you and Dr. Brad were so quiet last night out here—" Grandma pointed to the couch. "You didn't see his face, but I did. He was hurting, and it was too quiet in here."

"Well, if he asks, and not before, you can let him know that he's still the only man *I've* kissed in five years."

Grandma turned and headed back to her Scrabble game. With her back to Katherine, she slid the letter tiles into the cloth bag. "I'm done with my homework for the day," she announced.

"What do you mean?"

"Quinn wanted me to find out if Brad kissed you."

"Well, remind him that there's always tomorrow."

"Katherine!" Grandma turned to stare at her. "You gave up on your own long-suffering, and now you're enjoying his. I think you're just plain awful."

Katherine bit the insides of her cheeks. Grandma was right. She was plain awful.

Ж

Katherine didn't take a good look at Quinn until after Grandma said the blessing. Several large wrinkles marred his Dartmouth-green polo. Even the tips of his collar were curled up.

"You didn't wear that polo to class today—did you?" she asked, before taking a bite of ham-and-potato casserole.

"Evans already lectured me."

Katherine raised her brows. "Looks like you left it in the to-fold pile too long."

"I did." He sighed. "Is Brad coming over tonight?"

"I don't think so."

"Who called earlier when you pulled the pocket door closed?"

Grandma was not to be trusted. "Benton, after dinner I would love to discuss this with you."

"But not now, because . . ."

"After dishes, we'll sit on the couch, and I'll discuss this with you."

He sighed and lowered his shoulders. "I'm sorry, Katherine, I haven't felt this keyed up in years."

"Why?" Grandma reached out and patted his hand.

"Katherine knows how I feel about her, Ethel."

The phone rang.

"Do you want me to get that?" Quinn asked.

Grandma looked at Katherine.

"I'll get it." Turning in her chair, Katherine positioned her weight on her left foot before standing up. The phone rang again. She only had two more rings before it went to recorder. On crutches, she crossed the kitchen at a record pace and snagged the receiver before the fourth ring.

"Hello."

"Katherine, it's Evans."

She looked at the pocket door and decided not to pull it closed.

"Hi, Joe."

"It's Evans."

"Yes, Joe."

"I see . . . Benton's there?"

"Yes."

"I'll get to the point. He called Lori, our Miss Wazzu, this afternoon. He's meeting her at Alex's tomorrow at seven o'clock. He asked Lori to pray for a woman whom he refers to as Miss Moscow. Supposedly, she's madly in love with him, but she hasn't realized it yet. He was very concerned that our Miss Wazzu know this up front."

"The dog!" Katherine said.

Evans chuckled. "Stay strong. Tomorrow night's going to be great."

Katherine hung up the receiver and with a heavy sigh stared at the top shelf of Grandma's salt-and-pepper shakers. The collection needed dusting, just like her relationship with Benton.

"That was Joe?" Grandma asked, adjusting her glasses.

"Yes." Katherine nodded.

"Does he have a dog now?"

"I think she said, 'The dog,'" Quinn said.

"Yes." Katherine returned to her chair. "A paper... that one of his athletes needed to turn in went missing, and she found it . . . all chewed up."

Benton's brows gathered.

"Her professor will never believe it," Grandma said.

"Ethel's right. Her professor will never believe it."

Katherine sighed and prayed that tomorrow night he'd forgive her.

They ate in silence.

Quinn had told Miss Wazzu about Miss Moscow. She looked across the table at Quinn. Had he asked his other blind dates to pray for a Miss Moscow? Had he vented to all of them about her? Nurse Kitty had been so disappointed about their date because all they talked about was Katherine. Somehow it made all Quinn Benton's romantic flaws redeemable.

"Did you see that, Ethel?" Benton nodded toward Katherine.

"Yes, yes I did." Grandma nudged her glasses higher up the bridge of her nose.

"That's the look I've been telling you about."

"I saw it clear as day."

"How can your granddaughter look at me that way and date Brad Ungerbach tomorrow night?"

Oh, the things she could say about Quinn Benton!

Chapter Sixty-Four

By the light of a floor lamp, Katherine studied in the La-Z Boy while Quinn helped Grandma put the dinner dishes away. Quinn stepped into the living room and pulled the pocket door closed behind him.

"I'm back, Katherine." His deep voice echoed in the trenches of her heart.

She briefly closed her eyes before lowering her textbook. He sat on the edge of the coffee table kitty-corner to the recliner and crossed his tan arms in front of him. Even though her latest impression of him was that he was flighty, his dark good looks made her heart bounce like a brand-new tennis ball fresh out of the cylinder.

Tomorrow's going to be great, she reminded herself of Evans's comment.

Quinn's brows gathered. "If I didn't know any better, I'd say that you're behaving like the old Katherine. Your face is a lovely shade of red, and you're avoiding gazing into my eyes. You're avoiding eye contact because you have a two-hour date with Ungerbach tomorrow, who for some reason, did not kiss you last night, even though it was very quiet in here."

"That was quite a run-on sentence, Benton." She glanced at him. *Grandma!*

"I love when you call me Benton." He smiled. "I think I always have."

The man was crazy about her. Ring, phone, ring. Be strong. Tomorrow is going to be great.

"You can't gaze into my eyes because you're off your pain meds. Not like before."

She should have known he'd test her.

"Look at me, Katherine."

Maybe she shouldn't have flushed the remaining pills down the toilet.

"I have a date tomorrow night, Quinn, and it's unfair of you to tempt me like this."

He laughed loudly, sweetly, triumphantly. "*Tempt* makes me think I must be tempting. What an encouraging word, Katherine."

"I didn't mean it like that. I meant . . ." She chewed on her lower lip as Evans's voice chimed in her head: *Tomorrow's going to be great.*

"I don't know what's going on with you." His look was no longer daring and playful—it was painful and somber.

"If you didn't want to give me hope, you shouldn't have told Ethel that I'm still the only man you've kissed in years, and then added your little slicing comment about tomorrow night."

"I'm sorry—I was only kidding." She meant to glance at him but found herself staring. Emotion glazed her vision. She recalled the verse *Even the rocks will cry out.*

"What's going on, Katherine?" He smoothed her hair away from her face. Traitorous tears slid down her cheeks.

"Ever since my accident, I've been so emotional," she admitted.

"What are you trying to tell me? Are you trying to totally break it off with me?"

No, why in the world would he think that? She shook her head.

He smiled. "Remember the first time I brought you home, and I wouldn't let you tell me where you live because we were playing the quiet game?"

"Yes." She'd probably liked him even then if she were honest with herself.

"I already knew where you lived."

"Huh?"

"Cindy didn't know the house number, but she'd told me about your grandmother's white picket fence, the yellow bungalow on the corner with a weeping cherry tree.

"I had so much fun that night . . ." He gazed warmly into her eyes. "That I knew it was a bad sign from a faculty-student point of view.

"I've looked forward more to our recaps on Friday nights than to my actual blind dates. And I really shouldn't be telling you this until next Friday, when the semester ends, but . . . my heart's been breaking the rules all along."

His knees cracked as he got up and headed for the kitchen.

"Quinn . . .don't . . ." Her voice quaked like Scarlett O'Hara's. Like a fat, juicy peach too heavy for the branch. Like a woman at love's edge.

Katherine stared across the room and questioned if she should call Quinn, or drive to his place, or, heaven forbid, wait until tomorrow night to meet him at Alex's. He was hurting. The way he'd blindly opened the pocket door and brushed past Grandma on his way out with just barely a "Thank you for dinner," was so unlike him.

She couldn't live with herself if she didn't call him. She sat down in a dining chair next to the curio cabinet and dialed his number. After the third ring, he picked up.

"Hello."

"Hi, it's Katherine."

"I can't apologize. I know it's wrong of me. Horrible timing. I'm still your professor, Katherine. I need to wait until the end of the semester. And I know it's terrible timing with your date tomorrow, but I can't . . ." He sighed—"I can't apologize anymore for my feelings. Maybe I shouldn't visit anymore. Even though I love Ethel . . . and you."

Could tomorrow possibly be worth their present agony?

"Katherine . . ."

"Yes."

"Cancel tomorrow night."

"Please try to understand."

"I can't."

He hung up on her.

Chapter Sixty-Five

Friday morning, Grandma dropped her off near the back entrance to the Administration Building. "Remember I won't pick you up until after one thirty. I'm taking Gladys to her eye appointment."

"I remember. Thanks for the ride, Grandma. I love you."

Katherine took the elevator to the second floor. In Quinn's history class, she slid her crutches near the base of her chair and sat down as gracefully as possible.

With his back to the room, Quinn printed *Freedmen's Bureau* on the chalkboard. A few minutes after class started, Angel arrived and sat down. She proceeded to tear a piece of paper out of her notebook and wrote something before passing it to Katherine. She waited until Quinn wasn't looking her direction to read it.

"Your ex-boyfriend Joe's concerned that you don't have his number. He still would like you to call." At the bottom in large numbers, Angel wrote his number, followed by a large smiley face.

Uneasiness ebbed in the pit of her stomach, reminding her of the Micro. The reason Joe wanted her to call was he wanted to hear the whole story.

"In March of 1865, the Freedmen's Bureau was established to help solve everyday problems of newly freed slaves—problems such as food, healthcare, and reuniting family members."

Katherine glanced up from her note taking. Quinn's Yale-blue polo looked like he'd left it too long in the to-fold pile. The collar tips were flipped up, and large crease marks wrinkled the front. Had he gotten up late?

"The bureau was successful in implementing over one thousand schools and several black colleges. For those of you who are graduate students searching for a thesis topic, this would make a fascinating subject." Despite his disheveled appearance, his lecture was fascinating.

"I have your essays here." Quinn pointed to a pile of light blue booklets on top of his desk. "If any of you have questions regarding your grade, my office hours are from eleven thirty to one thirty."

Angel bent over and picked up Katherine's crutches off the floor and handed them to her.

"Thank you. If you see Joe, tell him I'll call him soon." Katherine flung her backpack over her shoulder and glanced toward the front.

"He and Anna have an agreement." Angel picked up her exam and started for the door. "They can't call any member of the opposite sex. That's why he's been waiting for you to call."

Katherine nodded and waved for Angel to go on ahead of her.

With his arms crossed in front of him, Quinn remained seated on the front of his desk. Katherine reached for the light blue booklet that bore her name.

"Professor Benton, do you mind putting it in my backpack for me?" She turned her back to him. Leaning forward, he unzipped the front pouch, rolled the booklet, and tucked it inside.

"I hope you're going to change before your date with Miss Wazzu."

"Evans already lectured me." He zipped the pocket closed.

"If you don't, she'll think you need a wife."

He raised his dark brows. "I do hate ironing."

"Yes, I suppose that's why you've blind dated with such passion." She planted the crutch tips a foot in front of her and started toward the door.

"Katherine . . ."

She regarded him over her shoulder and recalled Cindy's remarks: when Quinn was depressed, he didn't iron. He was depressed because of her, the sweet man.

"Evans said that Hungerbottom is welcome to join us tonight."

She nodded. "Thank you." Hopefully after tonight, they'd never have to have another professors' get-together to discuss Quinn's dates.

In Evans's and Cindy's class, she sat in her usual seat in the second row, unzipped the front of her backpack, pulled out the light blue booklet from Benton's class, and flipped to the back. Written in dark blue ink, a B-minus marred the page. Her heart sank like a canoe filled with cement. She scanned through the booklet for Quinn's comments.

Nothing. Nada. Not a word.

He always penned a comment or two. She flipped through each page of the essay.

Nothing.

The gall of the man!

Wide-eyed, Katherine stared at Cindy's PowerPoint presentation. *B-minus, my foot!*

"One of Jefferson's main goals, as you all well know by now, is the expedition was a diplomatic outreach to the Indians of the Louisiana Purchase and the Pacific Northwest." Cindy clicked to a slide of Sacagawea.

Oh, Cindy, we're not eighth graders.

Quinn had finally shown his true colors: he was nursing a wound and deliberately getting retribution. After class, she'd crutch down to Charlene Strauss's office and give her an earful. If she wasn't in, she'd head to President Morrison's office. Just like Grandma, she'd go straight to the top.

After the bell, Katherine remained seated while Cindy wound the cord to her laptop.

"Is Ethel picking you up?" Cindy glanced over at her.

"Not for an hour."

"Anything new with you and Brad?"

Evans obviously hadn't told Cindy a thing. Maybe he didn't think she could keep the secret. "I'll know more after tonight."

"About Quinn or Brad?" Maybe Cindy had always been on Quinn's side and Evans on hers. It made sense.

"Do you know what the man had the gall to do?"

Cindy glanced toward the hallway. "Quinn or Brad?"

"Benton, of course."

"No." Brows raised, Cindy waited.

"He gave me a B-minus on an essay that I . . ." Katherine tried to keep her voice steady. "On an essay that I wrote before my accident. On an essay that I know undoubtedly reflected my three-dimensional understanding of the most important battles of the war." Inhaling deeply, she squared her shoulders. "He gave me a B-minus simply because I'm answering my questions about Brad. He's getting retribution for his wounds."

"Katherine, listen to yourself. You're implying…"

"Since day one, he's been playing games with me, and this one—"

"Don't do anything rash," Cindy whispered. "You and I both know you could hurt his career. Be careful."

Katherine shimmied down in her seat. "He's the one who was rash. He gave me a B-minus!" She covered her eyes with one hand. "One B-plus, a B-minus, one solid A; I'll have to get an A-plus-plus, on the final to keep my—"

"He's not thinking clearly these days." Cindy glanced toward the open door.

"What do you mean?" Between parted fingers, Katherine peeked at her one-eyed.

"Talk to him first. You owe him that."

Chapter Sixty-Six

Katherine didn't want to pray—she wanted to stay in the exact ill-tempered mood that she was in, so when she faced Quinn Benton, she could vent in such a manner. But while she was in the elevator, a familiar inner voice reasoned with her.

"Lord, I don't want to give this to You. Right now, I just want to take matters into my own hands and tell him exactly what I think about him. He knows this is solid A material." The elevator ascended one floor. Katherine sighed. "Help me to be diplomatic. Help me to handle Quinn . . .with love."

She shouldn't have vented to God; now she might not be as effective in getting her point across. "Help me, Lord, to be sensible and sensitive and to handle this maturely. He didn't even write any comments!"

Instead of a black marker on yellow paper, *Quinn Benton, Ph.D, Professor of History* was inscribed on aged brass and secured to the front of his door. She inhaled and knocked.

"Come in."

She nudged the door open, maneuvered inside and tapped the door closed with her left crutch. Seated at his desk, Quinn acknowledged her before he glanced at the clock. "When's Ethel picking you up?"

"One thirty. She's taking her sister Gladys to the eye doctor."

"Take a seat." He motioned to his new antique student's chair—solid oak with masculine lines, it was the first time she'd seen it in his office. For a moment, she wanted to reflect on some of her and Quinn's finer memories. She sat down and set her backpack near her feet.

He swiveled his chair to face her and intertwined his fingers in front of his stomach. Up went the index finger steeple. Maybe he was praying.

"How may I help you?" His Adam's apple bobbed as he regarded her.

"You know why I'm here, Quinn."

Nodding, he pressed his lips together. "Usually, you call me Quinn when you're mad at me. Except for the other night; there was almost a lyrical quality to your voice."

She unzipped her backpack.

"You know me quite well, Professor Benton." She glanced from the light blue booklet to his eyes. "You didn't even leave a comment. One comment would have at least helped me understand why you gave me such a low score. A B-minus all alone on the page is a tad devastating."

"I'm afraid, Miss King, you don't understand the true meaning of the word . . . *devastated*." There was a down-turned, almost moist look to the corners of his eyes.

He was hurting.

"A country can be devastated by war; a person can be devastated by grief. An individual who is devastated by a B-minus is using the wrong adjective, or has a warped perception of life."

"I am highly disappointed and desire an explanation." When he was in his professor mode, there was nothing flighty about him.

"I too am highly disappointed." His dour expression matched his wrinkled polo. "After Monday, I thought for sure that you would divulge your true feelings for me."

"And I haven't—therefore I get a B-minus. Interesting grading system, Professor."

"Why haven't you?"

His voice held such a tender note that she could not lift her gaze. She kept it fixated on her bare knees.

"Did he kiss you on Wednesday?"

"No. You know he didn't." Was Quinn trying to break her before tonight?

"Why not? He intended to. All the signs were there."

"I told Brad I needed to slow things down. A lot's happened this week, and . . ."

"You were thinking of me."

"I still have questions that I intend—"

"Why? To return a wrong for a wrong? I was your professor. I still am for one more week." He leaned back in his chair. "You didn't have time for a relationship, remember? You wanted to focus on your studies? And despite everything"—he inhaled—"I looked forward to the recaps because of you."

Maybe it was the pitifully sweet way he'd said it, but a "Me too," escaped her.

"What'd you say?" The break in his whisper lifted her gaze.

She lowered it quickly to the hem of her skirt. She was so tired of Evans's game, of hurting Quinn. Tonight had become too painful. She couldn't follow through. Tonight, when he saw her seated alone at Alex's—he wouldn't appreciate it.

"I said, I looked forward to the recaps, too." She met his love filled gaze and followed it to the picture of his sister. There were now two framed pictures on top of his desk. The new photo was of Katherine—the close-up of her father and her on graduation day, taken four-plus years ago.

It was one straw too many.

Quinn just stared at the picture. Tears streamed down her cheeks as she recalled Grandma's sentiments.

"I have a call to make." Benton rolled toward his desk and, swiveled his chair, so his back was to her. He dialed a number and crossed one leg over the other. "Hello, Lisa, it's Quinn Benton. Regarding this evening, I'm sorry, I'll have to decline. The young woman that I've told you about . . . —yes, Miss Moscow. It appears she's come to her senses—Yes, thank you."

He hung up the phone and wiped his eyes. "I have another call to make, Katherine," he said with his back still to her. He again dialed ten digits.

"Hello, Claire."

Katherine remained seated. Claire was Miss Palouse.

"It's Quinn Benton. I have a Miss Moscow in my office, and it's very clear that like we thought, she's completely in love with me—Yes, I wanted to thank you for your prayers and your friendship. I'll continue to keep your situation in prayer also—Thank you, good-bye."

He hung up the phone and wiped his cheeks. "I have one more call to make, Katherine." Swiveling his chair to face his desk, his profile was now visible.

She wiped her cheeks, and sniffed as he dialed the last number. Only seven digits this time.

"Ethel, it's Quinn Benton."

Katherine stared. Grandma was taking Aunt Gladys to an eye appointment. Wasn't she?

Quinn cleared his throat. "I have a young woman in my office, a Miss Moscow, and it's very apparent that she's come to her senses—Yes." He turned to look at Katherine. "She's finally admitted that she's head-over-heels in love with me."

"Thank you, Ethel." He continued looking at her and blinked softly. "I love you, too."

Carefully taking a step toward him, Katherine held on to the side of his desk and swiveled to sit on Quinn's lap. He smiled tenderly at her as she wrapped her arms around his neck.

"Quinn, you are so full of yourself. I have not admitted anything."

He smiled. "You cried, Katherine; when you saw your picture next to my sister's, you cried. Cindy was right. Giving you a B-minus got you in here. And, Ethel was right too—seeing your picture broke you." His eyes sparkled as he inhaled deeply. "I have something difficult to tell you."

She bit her lower lip and waited.

"You can't hug me for another eight days, at least in my office." His dark eyes glistened. "Now, carefully untangle your precious arms from about my neck."

"I understand." She returned to her seat and smiled at him. Complete eye contact.

"I don't think you do, not fully. But I'll tell you sometime, soon."

"Quinn . . ." She inhaled, trying to prepare him.

"Yes."

"I am Miss Wazzu."

"No." He chuckled and motioned with one hand to the phone. "I just spoke with Miss Wazzu, and her name is Lisa."

"Lisa is Mashburn's married niece who lives in Pullman. Evans also had a hand in this."

"But . . ." He shook his head. "You never would have made it up the stairs at Alex's."

She nodded. Though there was a handrail, the carpeted stairwell was steep.

"Evans planned to help me. And I was going to wear this Vandal-gold sundress that I've been saving for a very special occasion, and when you *finally* sat down, I was going to tell you, Quinn, that . . . I love you, too."

He closed his eyes and let it all sink in. "What about Brad and . . . ?" He shook his head.

"Wednesday night, I told him I was in love with you, and he was such a gentleman."

"He is a great guy."

"Talking about great guys, there's one we ought to call."

"Evans." He nodded. "He can't believe that you made it past the lists. Monday night was his idea."

It didn't surprise her. "Put the phone on speaker, Benton. I want him to hear us both."

"Cindy's probably in his office as we speak." He lifted the receiver to his ear.

There was a double knock on Quinn's door.

"It's Evans. Tell him we're still alive."

"We're still alive," Katherine called.

The door swung open. "We're just checking in." Cindy clutched her hands beneath her chin as she entered.

"Oh, honey, look at the emotion." Evans closed the door behind them. His gaze narrowed as he studied them. "I believe we've matched made something . . . beautiful."

Eyes bright and glossy, Quinn's gaze locked on Katherine's.

As harp and string music began to play one of her favorite melodies, Katherine knew that Evans was right: *the heart hears what it wants to.*

Chapter Sixty-Seven

Saturday evening - Eight days later . . .

To celebrate the end of summer school, Ethel invited Quinn over for supper—meatloaf and mashed potatoes.

"Do you have anything special planned for tonight?" Ethel asked.

"Yes, we have plans, Grandma." Katherine giggled softly and glanced at Quinn.

"What kind of plans?"

"Quinn and I are going to go for a walk." Katherine's cheeks flushed as red as an Early Girl tomato.

"With your foot?" Katherine still wasn't supposed to put any weight on it.

"We're just going around the block." Quinn's poker face was better than Katherine's, but his eyes gave him away. They were sparkling.

"You remember what happened the last time you two went for a walk?" Would it be their first kiss since their last one?

Quinn and Katherine helped with the dishes and then with the giddy energy possessed by the young, went out the back door. From the kitchen window, Ethel pretended to scrub the sink, while she kept an eye on the two. With Quinn by her side, her granddaughter crutched her way up the little side street. They took a left on Lewis and slowly headed north. Ethel ambled across the shag carpeting to view them from the far windows. For some reason, they were closing the front picket gate behind them. What in the world? Ethel caught her breath.

Their destination was the front porch.

Should she call Joyce? Ethel glanced behind her at the phone. No, she'd better check the peephole first. Maybe they'd simply forgotten something. She tiptoed over, placed her hands against the door and peeked through the itty-bitty, flea-sized window.

She blinked as her eye focused in on the scene. Almost like they'd rehearsed, Quinn handed a roll of duct tape to Katherine and did a little bow. Her granddaughter glanced at the peephole and ripped off a three-inch chunk of the gray sticky stuff. Smiling, Katherine drew closer to the door and, lifting the tape covered Ethel's little view of their world.

They were on to her. But! Ethel scurried to the phone; she was one step ahead of them.

She dialed her close friend Joyce Wooten's number. Joyce, the good neighbor that she was, picked up after one ring.

"Hello."

"Joyce, its binocular time. Katherine's at it again on my front porch. Hurry!"

"Wait a second, I need to wipe my hands. I'm eating fried chicken." There was a thud as Joyce set down the phone. Ethel could hear her shuffling around in the background. "I'm hurrying, Ethel. I have them in hand." Joyce's voice became clearer. "I'm focusing on your gate . . . your yard . . . Wow, Ethel, you need to deadhead your rhodie."

"I know. I've had quite the summer. What else do you see?"

"Katherine's arms are around his neck. They're just about to kiss. It's the same fellow as last time, just so you know. Thank goodness she's nothing like your grandson was." Joyce laughed." Remember him?"

"How could I forget?" Night and day, Tim had kept them busy with his shenanigans on the front porch.

"Are you entering any of your baked goods in the fair this year?" Joyce asked.

"No, not unless they have a dump cake category."

"I hope they don't. It sounds horrible."

"It's wonderful. The next time I make it, I'll be sure and have you over."

"I'd like that."

"What's happening?" Ethel asked, her back to the front door. "Is she gazing up into his eyes? Do they look happy? Or are they fighting . . . again?"

"Not much. They're just kissing. I think I'll enter my dinner rolls again. You know I won a white ribbon for them back in 'ninety-three."

"If I entered anything it would be my cinnamon rolls." Ethel knew for a fact there was a cinnamon roll category at the Latah County Fair. Would she have to disclose that she was using store-bought dough?

"What's happening on my front porch, Joyce? Your commentator skills have not improved."

"Not much has changed. They're still standing very, very close to one another in front of your door, and they're still kissing."

"Well, let me know when they come up for air."

"I will." Joyce yawned. "I will."

The end.

I hope to release the next book in the *Ethel King Series* in 2017 – God willing. Let me know if you'd like to receive an email when the time comes.

You can email me at: christianromances@gmail.com

Or go to my website: wwwchristianromances.com

Don't miss the **four recipes** that are included on the following pages.

Acknowledgements and Recipes

I'd to thank the following friends and family:

To my mom, Ethel, who by the way, makes a mean Dump Cake. The resemblance ends there.

To my beautiful niece, Brittany, who is on the front cover of Sticky Notes.

To my daughter, Cori, for reading through the manuscript with me, several different times, throughout the years.

To my editors, Pam and Carolyn, for their attention to detail, and their encouragement.

To Patty Slack, my fellow writing buddy, for her honest critique; it was invaluable to me.

To Michele, my prayer buddy.

To Kris, my dear friend, who gifted me with the book *Daytripping in and Around the Palouse* by Dawn Reynolds. It was a handy little aid for revisiting my memories of the Palouse.

Recipes are on the following pages.

Ethel's Dump Cake – No Mix Cake

1 (20 oz.) can crushed pineapple in heavy syrup
1 (21 ounces) can cherry pie filling
1 (2-layer size) package yellow cake mix
1 cup chopped pecans
½ cup butter (1 stick), chilled

1. Preheat oven to 350 F. Grease or spray with a non-stick cooking spray a 9-by-13-inch baking pan.

2. Spread the pineapple with its syrup evenly in the baking pan.

3. Spoon the cherry pie filling evenly over the top.

4. Sprinkle the dry cake mix over the top of the cherries.

5. Sprinkle the chopped pecans over all.

6. Thinly slice the butter, and place evenly across the top.

7. Bake for one hour and 10 minutes (70 minutes total) or until golden brown.

8. Check after an hour as oven temps vary.

9. Serve warm with whipped cream or vanilla ice cream. *Don't wait for a special day—make today special.*

Cake variations:
Make with pineapple-strawberry, pineapple-apple, pineapple-blueberry, apple-cherry . . .

Ethel's Cheater Cinnamon Rolls

Professor Benton and President Morrison both really liked these. Make with frozen bread dough.

1 ¼ cups powdered sugar
½ cup whipping cream
1 cup coarsely chopped pecans or walnuts
2 loaves (1 pound each) frozen white bread
 dough, thawed
3 Tablespoons butter, melted
½ cup packed brown sugar
1 ¼ teaspoons ground cinnamon
¾ cup raisins, optional

1. Grease two 9-inch baking pans.

2. In a small bowl, combine powdered sugar and cream and mix well. Divide evenly between two greased 9-inch baking pans. Sprinkle with pecans and set aside.

3. On a floured surface, roll each loaf of bread dough into a 12-inch by 8-inch rectangle. Brush with melted butter.

4. Combine brown sugar and cinnamon and sprinkle over butter. Top with raisins, if desired. Roll up from the long side. Pinch seams to seal.

5. Cut each roll into 12 slices and place cut side down in prepared pans.

6. Cover and refrigerate overnight.

7. Remove from fridge. Keep covered, and let rise until doubled, about 2 hours.

8. Cover loosely with foil. Bake in a preheated 375' oven for 10 minutes.

9. Uncover and bake 8-10 minutes longer or until golden brown.

Makes 2 dozen.

Carol's Raspberry Jell-O Salad
This is a family favorite – and great for the holidays.

3 (3-ounces) packages cherry or raspberry Jell-O
1 cup boiling water
1 (20 oz.) can crushed pineapple in heavy syrup
2 ripe bananas, mashed
2 cups raspberries (at least)
1 cup sour cream

1. In a large bowl, mix the Jell-O and boiling water until dissolved.

2. Mix in crushed pineapple (don't drain it).

3. Add mashed bananas and stir.

4. Pour about half the mixture in a 9-by-13-inch baking pan. Cover with plastic wrap and set in fridge for about 30 minutes.

5. When the first layer is set, take a spatula and slather on a layer of sour cream. Make it thick enough that you don't see the red Jell-O through the cream.

6. Carefully spread your raspberries single layer over the top of the sour cream layer.

7. Pour the remaining Jell-O over the berry layer. Cover with plastic wrap and refrigerate. Let it set up, at least an hour or two before serving.

Note: Because of the final berry layer, it takes a little more Jell-O to cover the top than it does to cover the bottom of the pan. So keep this in mind when you're pouring the first layer into the pan.

Cindy's Blueberry and Peach Bundt Cake
Cindy served this cake at the antique store in Colfax.

2 ⅓ cups all-purpose flour
1 tablespoon baking powder
¾ teaspoon salt
1 ½ cups sugar
½ cup vegetable oil
3 eggs
1 cup milk
3 peaches, peeled and sliced (approx. 3 cups)
1 cup blueberries – fresh or frozen
(If berries are frozen – don't thaw.)
Icing

1. Mix the flour, baking powder, and salt, together and set aside.

2. In a large bowl, combine the remaining ingredients, except for the peaches and berries.

3. Add the dry ingredients, and then the peaches and berries.

4. Pour into a greased Bundt pan and bake for approximately 40 minutes, or until a toothpick inserted near the center comes out clean. Cool in pan for 15 minutes before removing to a wire rack to cool completely.

Icing:
4-ounces cream cheese, softened at room temp.
½ cup powdered sugar
3 to 4 tablespoons milk or cream

5. Beat cream cheese until creamy and then beat in powdered sugar. Add milk and mix well.
6. Drizzle over the top of the cooled cake.

Christian Romances
by Sherri Schoenborn Murray

• *Fried Chicken and Gravy*
• *The Piano Girl – young adult*
• *A Wife and a River*

Visit my website for new releases and recipes at:
www.christianromances.com

Thank you and God bless.

Made in United States
North Haven, CT
18 January 2024

47614251R00300